Shadows of the Realm

Dionne Lister

Cataloguing-in-Publication details are available from the National Library of Australia www.librariesaustralia.nla.gov

ISBN: 978-0-9873078-6-6

DEDICATION

For Auntie Marcia and Nonna, it just hasn't been the same without you.

ACKNOWLEDGMENTS

This journey started long ago, and I have to thank everyone who encouraged me back then. I never realised how much these things sound like a boring acceptance speech, but here goes. Debra, Auntie and Peter, thanks for reading the first dodgy copy. Thanks to all my friends who continue to encourage me, especially Michelle and Sol, and of course my awesome writer friends Amber, Justin, Dee, Craig, Jane, Trish, Damien and Susan (I hope I didn't forget anyone) – you guys are there when the writing path gets lonely, as it is bound to do when everything you do is just you and your computer. A massive thank you to Ciara Ballintyne who helped me get my passive language under control. Of course, I wouldn't have been able to do this without the patience and love of my three boys, David, Evan and Ben. Yay team.

PROLOGUE

In a lonely brick farmhouse a child named Blayke slept under cosy blankets. He dreamt of splashing in warm summer puddles. His nostrils filled with the scents of grass and earth.

He reached dirty fingers into a puddle at his feet and tried to grab a slimy frog. The touch of his fingers on the water sent the frog dashing away, chased by the black clouds racing across the surface of the water, mirroring the sky.

Thunder boomed again and again. Thick clouds marched to its beat, effortlessly smothering the sun. Blayke's fingers sank further into the darkening puddle until his fingers touched something rough and icy—too large to close his hand around. Blayke tried to let go of the object, but his hand was stuck. Adrenalin flooded his body. He tried to shake the object loose, but to no avail.

Fat pellets of water erupted from the sky soaking him in seconds. He looked up, squinting his eyes against the pouring rain. He bit his lip against the urge to cry. Every instinct told him to run. Thunder closed around him; lightning struck meters from the quickly expanding puddle. Blayke leaned back, twisting his body in a vain attempt to break free. Sweat from his exertion mixed with the rain on his face.

His palm peeled away from its anchor, leaving layers of skin behind. Blayke fell back, landing with a splash on the sodden earth. He stared at his bleeding hand; *what had happened?*

The ground vibrated beneath him, the tremors matching the slow and powerful rhythm of the thunder. The puddle boiled, bubbles of mud bursting to the surface, contaminating the balmy air with stagnant wafts. Blayke scurried away from the deepening water on hands and knees. He scrambled to rise, but the jerking earth toppled him.

He was now at the edge of the seething pool. He watched the water drain away into the ever-growing cracks forming around its edges—the unseen depths hungrily sucked the liquid, draining it as quickly as the sky could dump it there.

The earth gave a final, violent tremor. An ebony creature surged forth amid the cacophony of trembling earth and breaking sky. It towered menacingly over small boy and tall trees alike.

The giant creature's bellowing screams assaulted Blayke. He huddled on the ground, gasping for breath. His bleeding hand throbbed, and the beating rain stung the back of his neck. Blayke scrunched his eyes tight and prayed to every god he had ever heard of to make everything disappear; the rain, the thunder, and the monster. Fear of impending death made him cry.

Rain battered him, but the earth ceased shaking. The creature's commanding voice replaced the primal screams that made the downpour seem a whisper. "I have come to take you. Look at me and behold your destiny."

Blayke lifted his head against all will and instinct, compelled by immense power within the voice. A colossal black dragon stood close, too close, dwarfing the small human as an ancient oak does an ant. The creature stared at Blayke with penetrating silver orbs.

The boy's eyes, once fixed on the nightmare, could not move. So this was it, his death was here, so soon. How could that be? Tears flowed again as he realized his short life had existed just to fill the belly of this dragon, a special dragon no doubt, but still a dragon. Blayke took comfort in the warmth of tears that mixed with the rain on his face, as the giant creature reached toward him with massive claws.

It snatched Blayke, with one swift and powerful gesture, and thrust him into a mouth full of sword-sharp teeth.

Blayke woke screaming, feeling as if he were choking on his own blood. Arcon ran to Blayke's room, arms raised, ready to fell any intruder who would dare harm his boy. Relief at the absence of an attacker was short-lived as he tried to sooth his terrified nephew. Blayke sobbed in his arms as he described the nightmare in vivid detail. Arcon knew this was a prophetic dream, marked by the Dragon God no less.

The dangerous and terrifying times foretold by the First Circle were nearing, and his nephew's nightmare confirmed the worst. Arcon, one of the most powerful realmists ever to have lived, and member of The Circle, prayed they would be given more time to prepare; their lives, and all life on Talia, depended on it.

Blayke eventually fell asleep and his uncle retired quietly to his study, where a hot cup of tea and mesmerizing flames in the hearth could not dilute his fears. The evil they had banished over a thousand years ago would return; it was already on its way.

1

Bronwyn stared over the precipice, grey eyes fixed on the black stone she had nudged over the edge with her foot. A cool breeze caressed her face, the scent of early spring tingling her nose. It was a long, long way down, and the stone she had sacrificed bounced off many larger rocks falling into nothingness, out of sight. She had thought it would be so easy to follow the stone off into oblivion, but now standing here, tensed to do just that, found it was not.

As hard as she tried, she could not force her foot to take that one, final step into peace; all she could do was look down and wonder what it would be like to fall, fall, fall. She dragged all the recent anguish she had suffered to the forefront of her mind in an effort to strengthen her resolve and leaned further forward.

Would she die on the way down, wind pushing against her face, speeding through the air while buffeted by the fear of knowing her immediate fate, or would she die at the bottom as she smashed headfirst into the rocks? Would there be time to feel the pain?

This morning began the same as any other for the olive-skinned, young woman, until her Aunt Avruellen had changed everything. "Bronwyn, how would feel about seeing the world? I've decided we're leaving tonight for a long journey."

"Leaving? What? Why do we have to go, and how long is long, exactly?"

"I have a meeting of The Circle to attend, then we have somewhere else we have to go."

"Where?"

"I don't know."

"Well, when are we coming back?"

"I'm not sure."

Bronwyn felt tears forming. The first thing she thought of was her best friend. "I'm going to say goodbye to Corrille."

"I'm afraid not. You can't say goodbye to anyone. No one must know we're leaving. Now, no more questions; I've got work to do." Avruellen had turned her back on Bronwyn and left the room. Bronwyn had understood that to mean they were never coming back, and as for her aunt not knowing where they were going, that was unlikely—Avruellen had a purpose for everything she did; she wasn't one of The Circle for nothing. Bronwyn had slammed the door on her way out.

Now Bronwyn perched on the edge of safety, hating herself for not having the courage to jump off, hating her aunt for forcing her away from her friends and the only home she had ever known. The young woman sat for a while, arms folded across her chest, scowl wrinkling her forehead, until she acknowledged her aunt wouldn't leave her behind. Since she was not going to kill herself today, Bronwyn knew she must yield to the fact that she was going to do what her aunt demanded. She stood, and accepting the depressing reality, commenced the walk home, albeit with slow steps.

Bronwyn reached home and went straight to the kitchen, as she always did, to see what goodies awaited. Avruellen and her fox Flux sat at the kitchen table, a sight that had always made her smile; until today. Her aunt pointed toward a fragrant cup of tea and freshly baked biscuits. Bronwyn took her place at the table and stroked Flux's soft, furry head.

She lingered among the familiar aromas, committing all to memory. Flux nuzzled her hand as Bronwyn sipped her tea. "Do we really have to go tonight? Why not another night, maybe another week?" Her eyes pleaded with her aunt.

Avruellen spoke with a firm voice. "You know better than to ask silly questions, dear. A lot of things in life would be different if I could change them, but I can't. Now, I've told you as much as I'm going to and it's not open for discussion. Make sure your bag is packed by sundown; we're leaving immediately after dinner." She rose, her own sorrow momentarily shadowing her face. "I've a lot to do before we leave, so I'd best get started." Brisk footsteps emphasizing her point, she left the room.

The ginger biscuits tasted so good, their crunchiness so satisfying that Bronwyn, despite her inner turmoil, couldn't help but enjoy the second-to-last meal she would ever eat at this table. Bronwyn stood as she swallowed the last morsel. "Well, Flux, I suppose it's time to pack up my whole life. Do you think it's too late to change her mind?" Flux didn't answer, just led the way to the door.

Bronwyn regretted the desire to kill herself and knew she was being an ungrateful child. All the lessons her aunt had given her in the art of realmistry, the skills she had acquired over many years, were for what lay in the immediate future and not to be thrown away in an immature bout of self-pity. She anticipated her future with fear, feeling dismally unprepared. Bronwyn pushed her anxiety aside and, adopting her aunt's brisk manner, quickly bundled necessities into a woven leather bag. Contemplating what lay ahead, Bronwyn felt she could confidently say today had been the worst day of her life. If the prophecies were right, it wasn't going to improve any time soon.

2

Arcon and Blayke ploughed through deep virgin snow. They approached their cave within the white-covered mountains, leaning into a fierce northerly wind, their faces burning with the cold. Two freshly killed rabbits hung from Arcon's pack. It may have taken them all day but at least they had found food this time. The unexpected blizzard had held them captive for days, and dried rations collected in early summer had provided their only sustenance. Starved for variety, Blayke could almost smell the rabbits roasting over their fire; saliva exploding within his mouth at the thought of tender rabbit shank. He was sure not even Arcon could ruin this meal with his dubious culinary skills.

Arcon halted under an overhang. A smooth mantle of ice sheathed the section of rough stone in front of him. Removing one of his gloves, he traced a series of lines over the rock until he heard a familiar click, and the door opened slowly, silently inward. They rushed in, the rock closing behind them. Both men ran to the dwindling fire like two little boys: shoving, pushing, and jostling until both basked in an equal share of the heat.

Arcon removed his other glove and threw both on a chair to dry. He was a wide-shouldered man of medium height, lean yet strong and many years older than his companion. His ageless, albeit weathered, face had seen almost two hundred years. Arcon's clear, blue eyes held secrets he wished to forget.

Blayke, his protégé, was a descendant of a relative. A loving boy, he had been given into the older man's care at birth. Arcon had taught him a variety of survival skills including hunting and fighting, and a rudimentary knowledge of the spiritual craft of realmistry. Blayke had a lot to learn, but was as good as could be expected for his age and lack of experience.

The two had been travelling Talia for three years. Before that they had spent time on Arcon's farm, which had provided the old man a good base. Even though he had crossed Talia numerous times over the years, he needed a place to come home to which was private and removed from the disapproving eyes of the general population.

Arcon was a realmist, realmistry being the art of syphoning energy from the Second Realm through the realmist's body and manipulating those forces, usually to heal, help, or hurt. Significant power was available for those few who had spent years learning and understanding the complex characteristics of those forces. There were two types of people on Talia: those who feared what realmists could do and disliked them, and those who understood and respected them. Unfortunately the majority were members of the first group.

The past three months in the mountains had been invigorating for Arcon's dark-haired companion, but now boredom and freezing weather had set in. The mountains were devoid of ale, girls, and fun of most sorts. Blayke had enjoyed it at first—the snow had been a wonder and, because of the altitude and time spent hunting, his body had developed to a point where his own muscled physique impressed him. Now the novelty had worn off and he had been having arguments with Arcon over the most trivial things.

Night descended unwatched. The two men sat cross-legged on the floor of their windowless refuge in front of a renewed and cheery fire, each holding crisply barbecued rabbit. Blayke had noticed his uncle was eating the long-awaited rabbit mechanically, fragrant juices dripping down his chin to fall unnoticed on his lap. "What's wrong? You're too quiet."

Arcon started before meeting Blayke's eyes. "How would you feel about leaving this paradise tomorrow?"

Blayke smiled. "I'll start packing!" His smile hurriedly retreated when he saw the expression on Arcon's face—he wasn't sure what it meant, but it didn't look promising.

Arcon continued in a more sober tone. "Tonight I must communicate with The Circle. I need you to make sure no one is spying on us." The young man nodded; it was not a difficult task, and he'd done it before. He would have to use his mind to travel one of the ethereal corridors to the Second Realm, find the relevant symbol for The Circle's meeting point and monitor the outside for intruders. It was a dangerous, out-of-body experience. Knowledgeable realmists, with enormous control and practice, could leave part of their awareness within their body while the other part stretched out to the Second Realm. The essence of the inexperienced realmist wholly left the body, and only the unconscious mind kept the lungs breathing and heart beating. They were left vulnerable by the soul link that allowed them to communicate this way; they could be attacked physically—or otherwise. If a body died whilst the soul roamed, it would be doomed to an eternity of wandering the realms—unless the person had the knowledge to inhabit another body. Any attack to sever a person's link with their body was frowned upon in realmist's circles and considered evil.

The intensity in Arcon's eyes left no doubt as to the importance of what he said. "Tonight is different from the other communications you've been involved in. As you know, The Circle meets twice a year. Tonight is the most important meeting in a long time. You may hear things that surprise or worry you, but at no time should you lose concentration. Now, more than ever, will the ones we oppose be straining to hear. If they learn even the smallest part of what we are planning..." he left it hanging, not wanting to finish by saying they would all be killed.

Blayke was momentarily distracted as a terrifying image of his nightmare dragon flashed uninvited in his mind; his body responding with a shiver. "You must concentrate as you never have before. The smallest mistake is not an option. If we reach the end of the meeting without any catastrophe you will have many questions, none of which I can answer, so you will have to put them aside. Do I have your promise on these things?"

Arcon looked at and within Blayke. Blayke could feel the older man's mind probe and both knew when he answered, "Yes," that he meant it.

The meeting wasn't until midnight so Blayke lay on the floor on his bedroll, making a pretense of resting, body still, but mind racing. Arcon stood, rubbing a thick-fingered hand into the small of his weary back before crossing the cave to open the stony slab of a door. He greeted the animal waiting in the silent winter, and his tone lightened. "Well, I haven't seen you for two days. Have you had good hunting?" The white owl, perched outside the door, blinked once.

I was wondering when you would notice I was here, freezing I might add. You can be so inconsiderate sometimes! You're lucky I didn't just fly off and offer my services to someone else.

Arcon leaned down and offered the bird his sleeved arm in conciliation. "If only. My mother warned me about bonding a self-important owl for my creatura, but did I listen?" The realmist sighed tragically then smiled and carried his ungrateful companion into the temporary warmth of the cave.

3

Zimapholous Accorterroza, or Zim as he was more commonly known, glided gracefully to the dragon city of Vellonia. He disregarded the many sheep and cattle grazing far beneath, his preoccupation with the impending meeting of The Circle dominating his thoughts.

The city lay nestled in a protected valley that had sheer cliff faces on either side, soaring a thousand metres toward the sky. Imposing stone buildings stood proudly, like ancient trees, on the valley floor overlooking the river. The river divided the city down the middle and was the descendant of the mighty flows that had sculptured the valley thousands of years before.

The stone in Vellonia was mined from the farthest points of Veresia; Feldon in the north, Argonesse in the east, Pollona in the south and Tyrrol in the west. Each of the four points contained unique energies. The realmists had guided these energies into invisible constructs to form a protection for the channels linking their world of Talia with the Second Realm.

The cliff faces overlooking the valley were peppered with large openings that led into the mountains and provided living spaces for the dragon inhabitants. Large golden spires rose to impossible heights from the verdant valley floor, climbing beyond the tops of the tallest peaks enclosing the city. The spires had originally been built to protect the city from above, but in these peaceful times also provided gilded beauty.

Thousands of years before, another race had lived on Talia. They had existed with one passion: to annihilate every other intelligent being on Talia, including the dragons. The Gormons were the epitome of evil; they fed off fear, pain, and anything of flesh and blood. They were unlike dragons in appearance but were their equal, or better, in almost every other way, including flying. The only defence from above was infusing the spires with energy from the Second Realm, which reacted solely to their enemy.

The Gormons were banished from Talia with the uneasy accord of the realmists and dragons, but not before the Gormons had laid waste to what hadn't already been destroyed by the war. Human and dragon populations had been decimated; only those who had managed to hide in the depths of Vellonia had survived. The alliance between the humans and dragons had held since that time, though some humans still feared the larger creatures' might, which was, if truth be told, cultivated by the dragons. A few of the mighty creatures, who felt they were the superior race, had circulated tales of their enormous strength and power: these same dragons had also started rumours that some of them occasionally liked to eat people. Zim, however, was not one of these dragons.

Zimapholous commenced the descent into Vellonia; his scaly mouth exposed sharp teeth in a blood-chilling grin. Warm red and gold rays filtered down to the valley floor as the sun set behind him, illuminating everything in its path. The spires appeared to be on fire, capturing and magnifying the sun's rays; Zim couldn't help but think they were going to turn molten and drip to the valley floor. The buildings far beneath him reflected the reds, pinks, and yellows, altering the hues to incorporate the colour of the stone. Oranges, greens, and blues winked among the fiery light and made a haze of colour along the valley floor almost too bright to behold.

Jaz stood outside the shimmering palace and watched Zim's graceful descent as he swooped around the spires, playing in the thermals above the valley. She wondered what her second-born son had been up to during his two-year absence. Jaz had occasionally spoken with him via the Second Realm, but Zim had been reluctant to divulge too much in case their enemies were listening.

The young dragon alighted before his mother, black scales absorbing the setting sun; no pretty colours reflected off his smooth armour. Jaz, on the other hand, was silver. Her scales reflected her surroundings, making her too brilliant to gaze upon at times; she enjoyed dazzling others.

The dragons rubbed noses, whispering ancient greetings in an archaic, musical language. Dragons, as a rule, were big on ceremony; it fitted with being imposing creatures. As a race they were civility personified, full of thees, thous, pleases, sirs, thank yous. They could become quite put out if formalities were not observed. No dragon wanted to be considered a mindless beast. The aim was to appear terrifying, but in a polite and cultured way.

After Zim landed, word raced through the city that the king & queen's son had returned. By the time the prince and his mother reached the throne room, a crowd had gathered to receive them.

The dragon queen and her son halted momentarily at the entry whilst they were announced. The guard ran clawed fingers over a large harp that stood just inside the door. Loud, sweet notes cascaded around the room, hushing the throng. The guard cleared his throat and announced them. "All behold! Here before us comes Jazmonilly Accorterroza the Shining Light of our kingdom, Queen and loyal wife to King Valdorryn Accorterroza the Second. Accompanying our Shining Light is Zimapholous Accorterroza, son of King Valdorryn and his loyal wife Queen Jazmonilly. He has journeyed two years and covered much territory to be with us here today."

Zim's father sat on his throne, which resembled an ornate bench seat. The dragons' large tail and wings made sitting in a conventional chair impossible, so the palace had been furnished with bench seats. Valdorryn's throne comprised timber inlaid with gold and platinum, the legs carved in intricate shapes depicting nature's wondrous and varied creations. Dragonflies flitted above frogs and flowers, bugs great and small nestled into carved nooks, deer, birds and vines entwined around ancient trees. The closer one looked, the more creatures seemed to be hiding among the foliage.

Zim's older brother stood beside their father; only Arcese, his younger sister, was absent. Zim knew she would be in the Temple of Cremornus, God of the Second Realm, preparing for tonight's meeting of The Circle.

For all their love of ceremony the King of Dragons fidgeted in his seat, impatient to talk to his son. He was excited that Zim had returned safely and wanted to hear news of the world. King Valdorryn had injured his right wing some thirty years ago in an embarrassing incident involving drinking too many fermented gozzle-bush berries and colliding with an ill-placed tree. In consequence, he was unable to fly long distances; being too proud to walk anywhere, he was confined to his valley. He met any news of the outside world with enthusiasm.

The king spoke before the guard could expand on his introduction. "Welcome to thee my lovely wife and far-travelled son. Please enter and attend me, that mine ears might be caressed by the sweet music of your travels." The interruption had the desired effect. The guard stood with his mouth open for a minute then shut it and withdrew. Zim and his mother approached the throne.

King Valdorryn rose and offered his wife her place on the bench throne. He embraced his son in a large, scaly hug. "Thou lookst well, my son. So what news? What news?" Zim smiled.

"Well, Sir, I have seen a lot in these past years and have many a tale. First, I must say that I am hungry, for in my eager flight home I ignored the tasty sheep grazing on the plains. I have been as far as Orton Island to the north and Zamahl to the west." His father's smile disappeared at the mention of Zamahl, and an audible intake of breath came from his mother and the remaining dragons.

The king abruptly addressed those of the court who were present and now had scaly expressions of worry. "My son is tired and hungry after his long journey. I wish him to rest and join Us for dinner this evening. That is all." The room quickly emptied. No one wanted to hear of any news from Zamahl. Not a great deal was known about the western continent. Any information that managed to filter through usually contained chilling accounts of violence, evil, and depravity. The dragons feared that just going there would mean losing your soul to unspeakable wickedness. Valdorryn spoke to his son mind-to-mind. "Meet me in my chambers in one hour." The king gave Zim a parting hug and made his exit.

Zim sent a servant to fetch a meal to his room and made the familiar trek to his much-missed chambers. He'd had weeks during the homeward journey to decide how to tell his father all he had learned, but now that preparation didn't seem enough. All that the dragons, and Talia, had dreaded for centuries was approaching— and they weren't prepared. The sick feeling in the pit of his stomach was not hunger. How could they possibly prevail this time? What could they do that they hadn't before? From all accounts it had been luck at the last moment that had sent the Gormons from this world.

As he made his way to his room, Zim sent a prayer to the skies. "Oh, Mighty Drakon, what can we do?" It was more or less a rhetorical question, so Zim tripped and almost fell over when he received a booming reply.

"Zim, my son, the Gods are with you. Have faith." The response from the Dragon God reverberated throughout the city. It was the first time in a thousand years that Drakon had reminded his children he existed. Zim tried to regain his composure as he passed his parents in the hallway. They were picking themselves up off the floor. He could only offer a shrug in answer to their distressed looks as he didn't trust himself to speak.

King Valdorryn was the first to break the silence "W..., w..., was that who I think it was?" He was staring at his son, eyes open as wide as they could go. "Was he speaking to you?"

The booming voice came again. "Yes I was, Val, and I must say, your son speaks to me more than you do.

When was the last time you prayed to me, hmm?" King Valdorryn winced, shutting his eyes tight whilst his wife fainted to the floor. By the time the king opened his eyes, Zim had left. He saw the queen lying on the floor and went to assist her. He was about to ask the heavens for divine help and stopped at the last second; this was one job he preferred to do himself.

4

Bronwyn stepped into the night, breathing deeply of a sweet coolness suggesting spring was on its way and sighing it out again when she heard the door close. Avruellen stepped around from behind and held one of the girl's soft hands between both of hers. "Life moves on—sometimes we choose when and sometimes we are chosen. I'll miss this place too, but there are so many other places in this world where you'll be just as happy, if not more so." Bronwyn tried to smile, but remained unconvinced.

"I have a feeling we're not going to another nice place just yet, and frankly I'm happy here." Avruellen didn't answer. "Do I have time to say goodbye to Corrille?"

"Sorry, my love, but there's no time. Don't make me go through it all again." Bronwyn sighed even louder this time but didn't argue.

Bronwyn and her friend Corrille had done everything together since they were children and were often referred to as each other's shadows. Bronwyn wondered sadly if she would ever see her again.

The sun had gone, but a full moon lit their way; it seemed to be trying to make it as easy as possible to find their destination. Avruellen led, and Bronwyn found herself having to jog every now and then to keep up. After half an hour they turned off the dirt road, and Bronwyn guessed they were headed for Borgen Wood.

She had spent many a happy time in the woods, meandering silently through the trees to spy on the animals that lived there. Sometimes, if Bronwyn sat as still as she could, a squirrel or otter would approach her on soft paws and sniff around for a while. Bronwyn hadn't met many people in her life, but she tended to think animals were better company, with the exception of Corrille of course, especially after hearing some of her aunt's stories about past wars and many continuing injustices in the world.

They reached the edge of the trees, and Bronwyn looked up to see the moon sitting higher in the sky, dark clouds beginning to obscure its clean, white light. They entered the canopy of Borgen Wood, and the light disappeared behind them. Flux met them inside the tree line and assumed the lead from his mistress. Bronwyn, unexpectedly, could feel her excitement and anticipation building, almost stronger than her sadness at leaving the only home she had ever known. She had never attended a meeting of The Circle but had wanted to be a realmist for as long as she had known her aunt's secret. Tonight she would get a glimpse into their mystical world and she hoped she was competent to do what her aunt asked of her, especially with other realmists watching. "Where are we going?"

"You'll see, dear. Not far now." Avruellen ignored the annoyed grunt from behind.

Travelling further into the centre of the woods, the trees thickened until their path was almost too narrow to follow. Every now and then a low branch or long-fallen trunk hindered their progress. As much as she trusted her aunt's skills, Bronwyn would have been afraid of getting lost if Flux hadn't been guiding them. An hour before midnight they entered a small clearing, twenty paces across. They walked to its centre, where the remains of a campfire blackened the earth. "Sit down and rest, for we have much work to do later, and I don't want you falling asleep on me." In reality Avruellen knew there was little chance of that. She watched her niece rush to obey, sitting and quickly moving a sharp stone out of the way of where she would lie; unfortunately Avruellen did not share her excitement.

Bronwyn lay on her back next to long-dead coals and gazed skyward. The ground she lay on had been smoothed by years of passing strangers who had used this hidden place to rest for the night. No branches hung above them here: her view to the heavens was unobscured. The stars no longer shone, and the moon had disappeared completely, the clouds blending in with the dark sky; it was like looking at a boundless, black nothingness. She shut her eyes, tired after the long walk. Bronwyn could hear Avruellen pacing, moving to the north, east, south, and west points, setting candles and chanting an ancient ward to protect them while the meeting took place. Bronwyn could feel the breath of disturbed air as Avruellen passed behind her on her way to the southern point.

When Avruellen had completed that task, she sat inside the north point of her ward, next to Flux, who stayed close for her protection, just in case. "Bronwyn, please move to the true south point. I'm ready to begin." Avruellen's usually kind voice had changed to the authoritative one she used when practicing her craft. Bronwyn stood and moved to sit opposite her aunt. Bronwyn closed her eyes and meditated. She fought the excitement of knowing she was to travel to the Second Realm, each measured inhalation drawing her awareness further inward.

Deep inside her being, where the only sound was the rhythm of her slowing heart, she waited for her aunt's command. Avruellen watched the sky, waiting for a signal. Some minutes passed before the clouds dissipated to reveal a red, angry moon. She mouthed a quick and silent prayer to the gods. It had begun. "Seek the Second Realm and find The Circle." It was hard to keep the tension from her voice, but it was important not to alarm her inexperienced niece. The critical task Bronwyn had to perform would fail if she had any doubts or fears about the job ahead.

Bronwyn searched methodically and found the pinprick of light that signified her life force. From here she would find the path her essence would follow to the Second Realm, where she could harness power, or, in this case, find the circle of light to link to and create a path for communication. Her awareness searched for the nearest corridor—not easy to find, a black hole in the darkness. If she concentrated on the image of her symbol, she would be pulled toward it and into the Second Realm.

She pictured every curve, line, and angle symbolizing her unique emblem. Her awareness was subtly pulled toward the corridor and the Second Realm, a movement so gentle it was almost imperceptible. She felt her awareness transported through the corridor, which was blacker than black, cold and infinite. When she entered the Second Realm she was overcome by warmth; she felt protected. A myriad of billions of symbols was an awesome sight, each symbol a brilliant star moving like sparks from a fire, some darting and some drifting through the boundless night that was the Second Realm.

She felt renewed, and her awareness glided with a confident purpose. She searched for a spinning circle of light that had the marks of any of the other four realmists who, together with Avruellen, were The Circle. Everyone had their own, individual symbol, and some were brighter than others. She would look at one symbol only to see it disappear and another appear nearby; symbols materialized when someone was born, winking out when they died.

Realmists only shared their symbols with those they trusted implicitly, as it enabled another to contact you mind-to-mind or find where you were within the First Realm. Anyone strong enough in the magical arts, good or bad, could invade one's dreams and even consciousness with this knowledge. Only a small portion of the population was capable of accessing the Second Realm as most had never been schooled in the secrets of the realms. As such, many held a superstitious fear or disbelief of it. Nevertheless, everyone's symbol existed within the Second Realm.

Bronwyn spied a spinning circle imprinted with three of the realmists' symbols. Before she attempted to connect, she glided around to ensure it was not being spied on. The apprentice saw nothing untoward, so she moved to the circle and intoned the secret password that would enable her to link with the communication disc. When her password was accepted, her awareness was pulled into the circle. She found this uncomfortable, for at this point she was giving some control of her mind to those connected to the disc who were stronger than her. From now on she could not leave the circle until permission was granted, usually by the strongest within the link. In the distance she heard Avruellen voicing her encouragement.

Although the circle of light appeared to be spinning when viewed from the outside, within its confines all was calm and dark. Bronwyn imagined this was how it felt to float in space. Three of the realmists had entered before her. Agmunsten, who was the strongest of The Circle and was reputed to be over 500 years old, had short, white hair; a long white beard adorned his lined face. He exuded the calm and mystery of a still lake. His dark, intelligent eyes full of life, twinkled with the promise of jokes yet to be told, mischief yet to be unleashed.

Elphus was young in comparison, 184, however in addition to studying sorcery he had a second love in life. He had married young, before his commitment to realmistry and the unnaturally long life that accompanied it. He had outlived his wife of 60 years. The pain he endured after she died had never left him, so he found a new love, food. His clothes stretched tight over his enormous belly, which sagged over his legs, and Bronwyn wondered how he managed to walk. When he nodded his greeting to Bronwyn and her aunt, who had entered when Bronwyn was safely inside, his many chins jiggled, which continued for a few seconds much like the aftershock of an earthquake. Thick black eyebrows overshadowed deep-set eyes and spider veins webbed his sallow face.

Their essences in the Second Realm were invisible, but out of politeness, each realmist conjured a diaphanous image of themself, which encased their symbol and moved as a body would have, were it there. Due to her lack of experience, Bronwyn remained as a symbol.

The other realmist in attendance was Arcon, his nephew existing as a symbol next to him. Bronwyn and

Blayke both wondered who the other was. Arcon and Avruellen nodded simultaneously to their apprentices, who transferred themselves outside the perimeter of the circle, moving their awarenesses to monitor for signs of interference or eavesdropping. Bronwyn's curiosity over who the other symbol was, was just as piqued as Blayke's. The young woman noticed that Blayke's symbol was similar to hers, the difference only a matter of two lines intersecting at a different place and one extra squiggle. Bronwyn had never seen two symbols so alike, although her experience in the Second Realm was very limited. She made a note to ask Avruellen about it later. While the youngsters skimmed the perimeter, Agmunsten commenced the meeting by jovially greeting the other realmists.

Bronwyn noticed a black shadow moving swiftly toward them. Or was it? It was still quite far away. Maybe the shadow was not really headed for them. Maybe it was just a coincidence. Nevertheless, her palms in the other realm were sweating. What if it were heading for them? There was no symbol attached to the shadow, so whatever or whoever it was, was strong in the art. Powerful realmists could render their symbol invisible in the Second Realm when they were there in spirit. The shadow grew larger and more ominous each second it rushed closer, and Bronwyn could feel its dominant strength. When the shadow was close, Bronwyn darted inside the circle. "Something approaches. A black shadow with no symbol!"

The realmists' images looked at each other. "What are we going to do?" Her symbol quivered, vibrating like the fletch of an arrow that has just embedded into its destination. Outside, Blayke had reacted by challenging the shadow. From inside the circle Agmunsten raised an eyebrow in Arcon's direction at the sound of Blayke's voice raised in challenge to the invading shape. Arcon shrugged and his cheeks reddened.

"Stop! Who goes there? Name yourself now or you shall regret it." Blayke's symbol pulsed in what he hoped was a threatening manner.

"Well, invisible youngster, of whose symbol I am familiar, I have not regretted anything in many years, except maybe that I did not eat enough humans. Prepare to be ingested." Zim materialised his dragon form and ate Blayke, symbol and all. Zim entered the circle and spat the symbol at Arcon's feet. "What have you been teaching this whelp? A sheep could best him out there." The realmists laughed and welcomed the last of the Five.

"Always late, my dragon friend. Do you disrespect us still?" There was mirth to Arcon's comment. Zim sat his large body down next to his fellows.

"No disrespect intended. I was loathe to face the subject we must address tonight. Sorry to interrupt." The meeting settled down and Agmunsten continued.

"Welcome, all. It is indeed heartening to meet with those who remain of The Circle and see two new recruits—though they have a way yet to go." All smiled at the comment. "Children, please continue with your task, however, do not challenge anyone out there. Come to us immediately if you notice anything unusual." Agmunsten turned back to the realmists whilst Blayke and Bronwyn did as they were told.

Once outside Bronwyn spoke. "Who are you?"

"I'm not sure I should tell you. Who are you?"

Bronwyn wondered whether she should answer. Once she did, he would know who her symbol belonged to. Maybe she should speak to her aunt first.

"Don't worry. I guess it's not important. Are you Arcon's student?"

"Maybe, maybe not."

Bronwyn was unimpressed by his answer. "Well, I know you're capable of being eaten by a dragon so you're obviously not fully trained. I suppose that will have to do for now." Blayke was embarrassed so ignored her taunt and resumed his travels around the circle. Sensing the conversation was over, Bronwyn did the same.

Inside the circle the meeting had progressed. Arcon was recounting his travels with Blayke. "We only made it as far as Klendar." Klendar, a city located in the northern land of Inkra, was inhabited by a dark-skinned, fair-haired race who practiced a strict religion and worshipped a god named Klar. Klar was a cruel god who encouraged the destruction of all other religions. "We were disguised appropriately of course. They tolerate traders from other countries, however some still go missing due to Klar's ongoing encouragement of human sacrifice." The other realmists nodded, and their faces told of their lack of tolerance for such barbaric practices.

Arcon continued. "Klar's current chosen one is a ruthless fellow by the name of Suklar. He has utmost authority and forbids his people to leave the country unless on a mission for Klar. The normal undercurrent of fear has increased recently, but we couldn't find out why. Incidents of human sacrifice appear to have escalated, but other than that things haven't changed. Suklar has a tight reign on his people, and it's almost impossible to find anyone who'll say anything about their leader for fear of reprisals, as Suklar has spies everywhere."

32

Zim interjected. "I may be able to shed a little light on the subject, for I made a nocturnal visit into the fringes of Klendar. The village I visited has weakened religious influences due to its nearness to the border and distance from the capital. In fact, many of the villagers fear they will soon be targeted as punishment for their lack of sufficient reverence to Suklar. They reluctantly mentioned that a darker spirit may have joined with Klar. At this stage not too much has been said, but the Dreamer within the village told me of a dream he had recently where a hooded Klar rode on the back of what he described as 'a vision from far beyond the gates of hell. A winged creature with an aura of malevolence and hunger.' Klar was riding this creature through the blackness of the space between the stars but it was unclear to the dreamer who was controlling whom. That, my friends, makes me rather uneasy, to say the least." The others sat in silence, none daring to say what they feared the dream symbolised.

Agmunsten spoke. "Dawn approaches and I must call this meeting to an end, however, I will advise you of your tasks. Due to the risks we now take, the less each of us knows about what the others must do, the better." He created a silencing bubble of energy around himself and Avruellen. Everyone outside could see, but not hear them. "The Gods have taken the unusual and worrying step of instructing me directly. You and Bronwyn must travel to Vellonia, and from there, the monastery at The Isle of the Dead Souls." He proceeded to explain what they had to do whilst they were there. When Avruellen emerged from the bubble her lips were pursed; the gods rarely interfered in human affairs. She said goodbye to her friends and left the circle.

One by one they met in Agmunsten's bubble, until only he and Elphus remained. "Well, old friend, the time is here. Do you think we're up to it?" Agmunsten had a hint of a smile.

Elphus shrugged his large shoulders. "Everything we've done over the years has been to reach this point. Now we're here, I wonder if it's all been for nothing." He yearned for his wife and considered what he had endured through the long decades without her. "To be blunt, if we had to face our foes today, I think we would lose. There should be seven of us and we're only five. The strength of our enemy outweighs ours, and we know their allies are even stronger than they are. Klar's balls! How can we hope to defeat them when we don't know anything about who they are and what they're capable of?"

It was Agmunsten's turn to shrug. "Don't lose hope yet, old friend. Our resolve must remain steadfast if we're to have any chance. Trust me when I say the gods are on our side and may have a chance to intervene. Can I trust you to do what is needed?"

Elphus sighed. "Of course. I haven't endured the torture of scores of lonely years for nothing. When it's all over I plan to join my beloved. I have a feeling she's waiting for me." With nothing left to say, Elphus departed. Agmunsten remained, having one more person to consult before he could leave.

5

Bronwyn's consciousness returned as dawn light yawned through the trees. She awoke in a body that was cold; the fire had died some time ago. Bronwyn was tired—her body may have rested but her mind and inner energies had been working all night. She sat up slowly and shook her numb hands to life. There was pain in her shoulder where she had lain on a stone. Bronwyn looked around to see Flux patiently waiting for them to return. When Avruellen sat up, he padded over and rubbed against her. "You're nice and warm, Flux. Did anything happen while we were gone?" Flux answered her, mind to mind. Avruellen nodded slowly but said nothing.

Bronwyn stood, stretched out the kinks in her body and went to collect firewood. She returned with a full armload so her aunt could start the fire, then left to gather more. Two armloads later they were warming themselves whilst enjoying some porridge. "What do we do now, Aunt?"

Avruellen blew at the porridge on her spoon. "Well, it will take us about a month to get where we have to go. We'll need more substantial clothes and maybe even horses, so our first stop will be Bayerlon." Bronwyn's eyes widened; she had heard of the largest city in Veresia but had never been there.

Her aunt had never taken her more than three days' ride from their village. She was going to ride a horse! She had only ridden a handful of times. Sometimes at the village fair they would borrow some of the older horses from the Shire's coach business, for a fee of course, and the children would be led on a ride. Most people in the village didn't have the resources to keep a horse and few required their services. Two, three, or four families would join their resources and share a horse; as such they were rarely ridden for fun.

"When do we leave?" Bronwyn was suddenly eager to be on her way.

Avruellen smiled at her change of heart. "After breakfast." Avruellen anticipated the next question and answered before her niece had a chance to speak. "The walk to Bayerlon will take about nine or ten days." Bronwyn shut her half-open mouth, knowing better than to ask her aunt how she had known what she was going to ask.

They repacked their belongings and set out for what, to Bronwyn, was the unknown. Flux led them out of the forest the way they had come, skirting around the village. Bronwyn said a second silent goodbye to her previous life as they passed, however she didn't feel as sad as the last time she had bidden her home farewell. At the outskirts of the village they continued on a southeasterly course, and by midday they had covered half the distance Avruellen wished them to travel that day. Bronwyn was happy when her aunt turned off the road, stopping under a small copse of trees, where they sat and ate lunch.

They were not travelling via the main road to Veresia's capital, but on a little-used smuggler's track. It ran parallel to the main road, with the exception of intermittent meandering turnings to avoid a tree or small boulder, and was distant enough to mask their identity from any who glimpsed them from the main thoroughfare. Not many used the track, for it was rutted and unkempt, the occasional fallen tree crossing its path. Bronwyn had never seen the track before and was quite amazed at her ignorance of its existence. Using a smuggler's route instead of the king's road made the whole journey even more exciting.

After lunch they continued into the clear and cooling day. Flux sometimes scouted ahead or ran to the side, out of sight, and sometimes trotted next to his mistress. Occasionally he would look up at Avruellen, and Bronwyn knew they were talking about something she couldn't hear. Realmists were granted a unique bond with their creatura. Bronwyn wondered if she would have one of her own one day. What animal would she choose? An animal that was strong, intelligent, and of course warm and cuddly. She knew, after growing up with Flux, that wherever you went, so did your creatura. If you had to spend so much time with them you would be silly to choose one that was unpleasant or smelly. She smiled to herself as she discounted one animal after another. Finally, she knew what she wanted and felt that somehow she had known all along.

Bronwyn spent the rest of the day imagining all the fun she was going to have with her creatura and was deep in daydreams when her aunt called a halt. The sun was low on the horizon, the air cooling rapidly. Avruellen steered Bronwyn to a suitably hidden patch of ground Flux had found.

They set up their small camp under the sky. Avruellen had not been able to acquire a tent in their village, as she didn't want to draw attention to the fact they were leaving. Her weather sense told her fine weather would prevail for a few more days. She hoped that would be enough to see them reach a town large enough where they could find the tent they would surely need in the coming weeks.

It had automatically fallen to Bronwyn to collect firewood; she felt this was only fair considering her aunt's age. They fell into a companionable routine. Her aunt would start the fire and cook dinner; it was a small reminder of home. They waited almost until total darkness before starting the fire, as Avruellen didn't want anyone seeing the telltale smoke. No one was looking for them yet, however there could be villainous characters travelling the roads, taking advantage of whomever they found.

After dinner they snuggled into their blankets next to the dwindling fire. "Aunt?"

"Yes?"

"Will I have my own creatura one day?"

Her aunt smiled but her voice was serious. "It's possible. More likely than not, however, first you have to pass a test in the Second Realm."

"What? Why?"

Her aunt shook her head. "Well, you obviously aren't ready if you have to ask me that." Bronwyn scowled at her aunt's chastisement.

Bronwyn mustered up as much hostility in her voice as she could. "Goodnight then." She lay down with her back to her aunt.

Avruellen shook her head again and smiled. "Goodnight, dear. If you plan on getting a good night's sleep, I suggest you stop grinding your teeth." Avruellen couldn't resist provoking her niece sometimes. The girl had to be tough if she wanted to withstand what was ahead. Avruellen knew Bronwyn's anger would keep her awake for ages. Avruellen, on the other hand, shut her eyes and was asleep within minutes.

Bronwyn still carried her scowl at lunch the next day. The energy needed to sustain the beast was making her tired, so she finally dropped it. In order to keep to Avruellen's schedule, they ate whilst walking. "I'm sorry I got angry. I know it's an important and sacred thing to have a creatura, and dangerous if someone has a weak character."

Avruellen had hoped a night of frustration might make her niece think about why The Circle required her, or anyone for that matter, to successfully complete a task before they could bond with the animal of their choice. "Well I'm glad you worked that out. I once had a friend at The Academy, Milly, who was quite jealous when I bonded with Flux." Bronwyn listened intently, for her aunt's stories were infrequent and always interesting.

"She had only been studying the mysteries of the Second Realm for a year and was not nearly ready, and maybe never would have been. She lacked discipline you see." Avruellen raised her eyebrows at her niece. Bronwyn had relatively good discipline but was prone to daydreaming. "Anyway, she was jealous that I had Flux and kept bragging to everyone about how much greater her creatura would be."

"She doesn't sound very nice. So what happened?"

"I was getting to that. When our teacher at The Academy of the Second Realm found out what she intended, he embarrassed her by punishing her in front of everyone. Three quick cane cuts to the bottom were considered an appropriate punishment for pride and jealousy. To wield power fairly, one must learn humility.

Her punishment made her want to punish everyone in turn, so, without permission, she completed the rites of bonding a creatura."

Bronwyn was incredulous at how disobedient Milly had been. Bronwyn would never dream of disobeying her aunt in such a way.

Avruellen continued. "It was spring, and the bears were coming out of hibernation. There was a large, black, male bear who had wintered in a cave near the academy, his ferociousness known far and wide. Bears are not recognised for being co-operative and this one was even less co-operative than the average bear. He was also cranky at having been prematurely woken from his slumber by Milly, who bonded him before he could react. What she didn't realize is that the animal must agree to the bonding, as it must spend a lifetime of working hand in hand with a human, or hand in paw as the case may be. If they don't agree, it won't work properly. As I remember it, she was in the cave ordering the bear to come and eat the Professor when the bear decided she was closer and would fill his belly just as well. By the time we arrived, the bear had already gone back to sleep. You know how tired you feel after a big meal—a nap is just the thing to help you digest." Bronwyn thought Avruellen's smile a bit mean, but if Milly was so arrogant and foolish hadn't she deserved it?

"I have a question. I thought if the animal was bonded to you it would suffer if you died? But the bear went straight back to sleep. How come?"

"Interesting question. The bonding had only just taken place, so the pain may not have been very great. There haven't been any studies done on that, actually. Usually bondings last many, many years."

Bronwyn decided to drop the topic for the time being, having no desire to make the same mistake Milly had. By late afternoon, her aunt had not slowed the pace and although she hated to admit it, she was exhausted. Bronwyn's legs were aching and she had developed a sore twinge in her left buttock. "Aunt, when are we going to stop? Aren't you tired?" She was surprised at the pace Avruellen had set and was even more surprised that her old aunt could outlast her.

"Soon dear. Just a short way to go." Avruellen answered with a self-satisfied smile, not slowing the pace one bit. Bronwyn pulled a face at her aunt's back but forced her legs to keep moving.

Finally, as it was becoming too dark to see properly, they moved off the track to another spot Flux had chosen. Even though Bronwyn was desperate to sit down, she decided to collect the firewood first. She feared that once she sat down, she may never get up again. Bronwyn dropped her pack and stepped toward the nearby trees. "Stay here, Bronny. I'll get the wood tonight. You sit and rest."

"It's OK, Aunt. I'll be back in a minute."

"I said sit! I feel fine, and you look dreadfully tired. Young people don't have the stamina of us oldies." Bronwyn ignored her aunt's cheekiness, and, as she didn't have the strength to argue, chose a soft, grassy spot, dropping to the ground with a thud. How could her aunt not be tired? It seemed impossible. Maybe she had used some kind of magic.

Bronwyn closed her eyes and within a very short time was drifting off to sleep. Her foray into dreamland was cut short by her aunt's raised voice approaching the clearing. "I've been aware of you since we started. Why have you been following us? Answer me!"

Who could have been following them? Bronwyn couldn't believe they had been in danger, and she hadn't even realized. Bronwyn obviously couldn't survive without her aunt's protection; her confidence in her ability to become a realmist was diminishing. She focused her attention from where her aunt's voice emanated and was astounded to see her aunt dragging her best friend by the ear, Flux leading the way.

She jumped up and ran over to them, aches and pains forgotten. "Corrille!" She firmly embraced her friend who was still attached to her aunt. After a few moments, Avruellen reluctantly released the reddened appendage. Bronwyn let go of Corrille and spoke to her, one excited word running into the next. "What are you doing here? Have you really been following us the whole time? I'm so stupid. I didn't even realise." Corrille looked torn between being happy to see her friend and ashamed at having been caught following them.

Avruellen stepped between the girls, arms folded in front of her chest. Her voice was low and demanding. As far as Bronwyn could tell, her friend was in real trouble. "Yes, Corrille, *do* tell us what you're doing here." Avruellen managed to growl the words, causing both girls to back away. The colour drained from Corrille's face, and before she could answer, she fainted. Bronwyn rushed over to help her friend, but Avruellen came between them, giving her niece a look which forbade her to come any closer. Avruellen turned toward her prisoner. Bronwyn watched, powerless, as the realmist loomed over the unconscious girl. For the first time in her life, she was truly afraid of what her aunt would do.

6

As Blayke and Arcon made their way down the mountain, the weather improved from a gusty blizzard to just gusty and freezing; at least visibility had improved. There were times during the first two days that Blayke wondered if they would become lost and freeze to death. Arcon was very wise and claimed to know these mountains like the back of his hand, however that was little consolation to Blayke when they had not been able to see one foot in front of themselves the whole time. If they ever reached their destination, it would be due to Arcon's creatura, Phantom the white owl, as he had been flying through the canopy and correcting Arcon if he veered off course.

They were four days from the cave. By afternoon they would reach a small mining town at the base of the mountains. Blayke was looking forward to a warm dinner that he could eat without gloves on, and a comfortable bed. The snow on the ground was thinning as they neared the town, but it was still bitterly cold. Neither man had bathed whilst they were in the mountains, so they were quite fragrant. Blayke, who was usually clean-shaven, had grown a beard and was frequently scratching at it. Ice engulfed both men's facial hair, freezing fingers that reached toward their chests.

What little warmth the sun provided was fading as it slipped behind the mountains at their backs. Arcon walked faster—Blayke wasn't the only one who didn't want to spend another night in the cold. Before too long, the men could see the shadowed outline of the few stone buildings that made up the town. The almost-invisible path they were taking materialised into a rough and narrow track, which led toward the town's inn. The inn was easy to find, as it was the only two-story building. They didn't bother with names up here, so the sign hanging out front just said "Inn".

Two donkeys were tied up in the yard, and someone had thrown woolen blankets over their backs. It wasn't that miners were particularly caring, but if your donkey died, you would have to spend a lot of time and money getting another one. The alternative for the miner was to do all the back-breaking work himself. The two men wiped muddy feet on a threadbare hessian mat, fare-welled Phantom until morning and went inside.

As they entered the hazy inn Blayke's eyes watered. The time in the mountains had been full of fresh air. This place was stale and stuffy, the smoke eliciting coughs from both men. Countless miners had left the odour of their overworked, under-washed bodies; the putrid stench leeched out of the timber.

The only two customers were the donkeys' owners. Blayke sat at a table near the open fire and removed his gloves, holding his hands as close to the flames as was safe, whilst Arcon approached the innkeeper to see about beer and lodgings. The innkeeper was a short, chubby man with an outrageously wrinkled face and large, flat nose. He smiled at Arcon's request. "Sit yoursen at that thar table and I'll bring youse the beers youse are wantin."

"Thank you, good sir," Arcon replied when he worked out what the man had said. When he reached the table he was smiling.

"What's so funny?"

"I shouldn't laugh, but the innkeeper has a rather original way of speaking. Quite quaint actually." The beer arrived.

"If youse are intrested in dinner, tonight we have a hearty soup of meat, veggies, and fresh-baked bread. Elsie's thar best cook thar is, this side of the mountains." Arcon answered in the affirmative, however wasn't game to ask what kind of meat was in the soup.

Dinner arrived promptly, and Arcon licked his lips at the smell. Blayke wasted no time in shoveling down what was on his plate and asking for seconds. "This sure beats your cooking. No offence." Arcon raised an eyebrow but said nothing, as he could admit, at least to himself, that the lad had a point. Any meals he prepared were basic, usually barbecued over an open fire, no condiments added, and sometimes burnt. Oh well, he couldn't be expected to be good at everything could he?

When Blayke had polished off his second plate, the innkeeper returned to clear the table. "Told youse she's the best cook thar is."

Blayke nodded vigorously. "What do you have in the way of dessert?"

"You can't still be hungry?" Arcon was continually amazed at Blayke's ability to eat huge amounts of food and still be hungry. He was lean, and Arcon had no idea where it all went.

"What do you expect? We've practically been starving since we've been up here. I have a lot of lost meals to make up for." Blayke turned to the innkeeper, ignoring

Arcon's bemused face. "So, good sir, what do you recommend?"

The innkeeper smiled, delighted to have such an eager customer. "Jus this mornen Elsie baked a sweet bread with custd inside. Damn delicious if yer ask me."

"Sounds just fine, good innkeeper. May I have two helpings please?" Blayke looked at Arcon, daring him to say anything.

Arcon shook his head. "I'll have another glass of ale." The innkeeper gave them a small bow and rushed off.

When they had finished Arcon stood up. "I suggest we go to bed now. We have an early start tomorrow."

Blayke stood. He was tired from their long trek over the past few days. He was, however, hoping they could have spent a couple of days relaxing before continuing on whatever quest Agmunsten had set for them. Arcon hadn't volunteered any information about what they were to do; he could be particularly stubborn when it suited him. "Why can't we stay here and just rest for a couple of days?"

"Why would I want to do that? I don't want to sit around and watch you get fat. We have more important things to do."

"When do I get to find out? I think it's only fair that if I'm expected to come along and help I at least know what it is I'm getting myself into." Blayke folded his arms across his chest in a futile attempt at looking stern.

"I'll tell you some of it tomorrow when we're on the road." He leant across so his face was near Blayke's and whispered, "Too many ears around here." Blayke looked at the two miners, doubtful they could pose any threat, but obediently followed Arcon upstairs.

The room was sparsely decorated, containing two single beds which, on inspection, were clean and compared to the cave where they had spent the past few months, very comfortable. Both men fell asleep almost as soon as their heads sunk into their pillows. Tomorrow would herald the beginning of a long journey. Arcon knew what they had to do and thought it almost impossible, but they had to try. He knew the consequences if they failed. By the time the morning sun's first weak rays made a futile attempt to melt the ice covering their window, they were ready to depart.

The sun rose on the two men as they made their way down the main street of the ramshackle town. Arcon stopped and turned to Blayke. "We have a huge task ahead of us, lad, but if anyone can do it, we can." With that, Arcon slapped Blayke on the back and resumed walking. He whistled a tune as he led Blayke out of town.

They stopped for a brief lunch of fresh bread and cold bacon bought from the Inn. Blayke was wondering how long it would take for Arcon to tell him where they were headed, as his patience was disappearing by the mouthful. By the time they finished lunch, Blayke's patience had disappeared.

Arcon rose. "Come on. We'd best be getting on with it." He turned, and after a few steps realised Blayke was not following. He turned his head. "Didn't you hear me, lad? Let's go."

Blayke didn't rise. "Not until you tell me where we're going and what we have to do. I'm sick of following you all over the place for no reason. I'm tired, I'm cold, and I'm sick of not being in one place long enough to have any friends. I'm not moving until you tell me what I want to know."

Arcon sized up Blayke's resolve. "We don't have time to muck around. Can't you just trust me?"

"No."

Arcon sighed. "All right. I'll explain it as we walk. Come on."

It was an effort to keep the smile off his face, but he had finally gotten his way, a rare occurrence. "OK then. But if you don't tell me, I'll go back to that town and have a little holiday." He had to jog to reach Arcon, who was already walking away.

Arcon flourished his hand, creating an intricate symbol in the air, too fast for Blayke to see what he had done. "It's a warding against eavesdropping. Now, as you should have already gathered, what we're looking for is extremely important. If we don't find it, all we hold dear on this planet will disappear forever, and even if we do find it, there's still a chance we'll fail. So, you can see, I don't want anyone, and I mean anyone, finding out what we're doing. If I tell you what we're looking for, I'm taking a huge risk. Our enemies will stop at nothing to defeat us, and this information will help them enormously. If they know that you have useful information, your life will be in even greater danger than it already is. How would you feel about being kidnapped and tortured for the information then killed when you've outlived your usefulness?" Arcon hoped his point was getting through. Everything he said was true, and he had enough to worry about without piling anything else onto his donkey, so to speak. He would tell Blayke if he had to, for without his cooperation fighting the Gormons, finding what they were looking for would be irrelevant.

The young realmist thought through this information. Arcon's words were definitely to the point, and now Blayke wasn't so sure he still wanted to know. Was he willing to risk his life, and the lives of everyone on the planet, because his curiosity was insatiable? Unsure of his own strength of mind in defending a secret under torture, he answered. "I guess I don't have to know right now. At least I know we're looking for something. But how will I know if I find it?"

"We'll be together for the whole journey so I doubt you'll see anything I don't." Arcon was relieved he had gotten off so lightly and made an effort not to sigh.

Blayke still wanted a little more information. "Can you at least tell me where we're going?"

"Southwest for now, but I don't actually know where we'll find what we're looking for. We could end up anywhere. Firstly, I want to go and see an old friend who may be able to help point us in the right direction."

"Where does this friend live?"

"Ellesmere. It's across the border in Wyrden. At the speed we walk it should take about three weeks."

"Three weeks! I'm not walking for three weeks. Bloody hell. Can't we get horses? Why do we always have to do everything the hard way?" Blayke pouted.

Arcon thought about it. "My friend won't be there until a couple of days before I plan to arrive so there's no point getting there too early."

"No point? Of course there is. We can get there early and have a rest for a change, maybe a few warm meals, comfortable beds etcetera, etcetera."

"The walk will do you good. It's character-building you know." Arcon had that glint in his eye. "No more arguments, Blayke. I've already made up my mind. You should save your breath; you're going to need it." He had a large grin on his face. Despite the enormity of the task in front of them, it was good to be free and on the road again.

Arcon repeated the gestures of before with a small movement at the end, which negated the ward. Some spells and wards could be seen in the Second Realm. Spells had their own pattern which lit up next to the symbol of the realmist who made them. This might draw unwanted attention. Magic wasn't always the answer.

The early morning sky had been clear, however, dark, aggressive clouds were streaming rapidly toward them from the south. Their stop for lunch lasted barely long enough for them to swallow their food. Neither man wanted to be caught outside when the rain started. Arcon estimated they had until early afternoon to find shelter, so they walked even faster.

Premature night descended as the savage storm-front reached them. The only refuge was a lone barn in the distance. Arcon made a run for it, and Blayke followed. A lightning flash lit up the sky, shortly followed by its deafening crack of thunder. Rain cascaded, stabbing naked faces with shards of near-frozen water. Both men were puffing furiously when they reached the barn. They went in and closed the door. As they stood and looked around, puddles formed around their feet from their water-laden clothes.

There was just enough light to make out that they were inside a storage facility filled with sheep and cattle feed. The large bundles of straw gave off a sweet yet sour odour, their gradual decomposition warming the air.

"Whoo hooo hooo." Phantom had found a comfortable perch in the rafters.

"You got here before the rain, hey?" Arcon looked up at his companion, who was almost invisible in the fading light.

Shame you can't fly Arcon, else you'd be dry too. The laughter in the owl's mind voice held a note of superiority. Arcon shook his head.

"What did he say?" Blayke knew they had been speaking. It happened all the time, and while frustrating, he had learned to ignore it to some degree. Still, it was no fun being left out all the time.

"Nothing important, as usual. He was just pointing out an interesting fact that I'm sure we wouldn't have realised had he not used his *vast* intelligence to impart it. We, being pathetic humans, can't fly and that's why we're wet right now." Arcon's sarcasm wasn't lost on Blayke.

"He's fairly rude for an owl, isn't he?" Blayke joined in the game.

"No, I think they are generally a rude and condescending bunch." A noise so soft it was barely audible over the rain emanated from the ground next to Arcon's shoe. "Little bugger tried to poo on me. Ha. The genius missed." Arcon moved away from beneath the bird.

"Whoo, whoo, whoo." The owl's laughter reached their ears.

Blayke walked around the barn. It was clean and he could hear only intermittent dripping. There were plenty of places they could sleep, and if they left early in the morning, no one would know they had been there. They each fashioned a pile of hay to sit on. Dinner consisted of the last of the bacon, bread, and a carrot each. The only food they had left were a couple of apples. They would have to buy provisions in the next town they came across, which, with a bit of luck, would be in time for lunch tomorrow.

As they finished their early dinner, the light deserted the barn. It was too dark to see anything other than during the occasional burst of lightning, which flickered light into every corner. Both men were tired. They rearranged their bundles of straw into beds. "Good night." Arcon yawned.

"Good night." Blayke hoped he would fall asleep quickly. He wanted to escape his not-quite-satisfied belly and the discomfort of wet clothes. However, the sound of heavy rain pounding on the roof ensured it was a while before he finally fell asleep.

In the early hours of the morning the vigorous flutter of wings awakened both men. Phantom had been swooping around the barn, then flapping madly to return to the rafters. Blayke sat up. He couldn't see anything in the dark but strained his ears. Arcon's annoyed voice came through the darkness, "Go back to sleep, Phantom's probably after a mouse." Blayke lay back down and was soon asleep.

During the night, the storm continued its assault toward the north, leaving a muddy, battered landscape behind. Early-morning light snuck through small cracks between the timbers and woke the barn's occupants. Blayke stood and brushed himself down. He felt a weight in his pocket that hadn't been there before. He put his hand in, immediately jerking it out at the shock of finding something unexpected. Gingerly replacing his hand, he felt a soft, warm body. Widening the pocket open he was surprised to see a sleeping creature; a brown and white rat. That must have been what Phantom was chasing the night before. Poor thing. Blayke would leave him here after Phantom left the barn.

They each had a pack that contained a water bottle, apple, and spare socks. As they left the barn, Blayke placed the rat gently in a dark corner under the straw. The rat looked up at him as if in thanks. "See you, little buddy. A bit of advice: stay away from owls." Blayke laughed at himself for talking to a rat, then joined Arcon outside. "Where to today?"

"We should reach a village about lunch-time. We'll eat there and buy any supplies we can. Hopefully they'll be well stocked; a lot of miners would go through there on their way to the mountains."

The road before them was saturated. The surface sucked at their feet and gripped every footstep. Each breath was visible in the cold morning air. The slight breeze was enough to turn their wet clothes into suits of torture. Both men shivered, hands and feet already numbing, so they walked fast, hoping they would soon warm up.

As lunchtime neared, the air was slightly less freezing. Blayke's clothes were almost dry now, his extremities warmer. The village was another hour away. As they drew closer to the town, the distance between houses shortened, the farm holdings grew smaller and more numerous, and the traffic on the road heavier. The road had dried out somewhat, making walking easier. The landscape was relatively flat, and Blayke found it almost boring compared to the spectacular mountain peaks they had grown used to.

In the distance, Arcon spotted four mounted men galloping toward them. "Better get off the road; looks like they'll run anyone down who happened to get in their way." They hurriedly moved to the grass and kept walking.

The horses slowed as they reached the pair, one man leading the others. He was of middle years, broad-shouldered, with a battle-scarred face, his mouth lopsidedly curled in a permanent sneer. His clothes were ragged and his horse not much better. Mercenaries maybe? Whoever they were, Arcon didn't like the look of it.

"Good day, sir." He addressed Arcon.

"Good day."

"I was wondering if you could help us. We're looking for a man, about your age, and a boy about his age, with his height and hair colour. They're wanted for crimes against the king. Our instructions are to capture them at any cost—dead is just as good as alive." He gazed meaningfully at Blayke.

Arcon answered whilst looking at the inferior members of the group. "I'm afraid I can't help you."

The leader's sneer intensified. "Oh, I think you can. Would you and your boy care to come with us?" His smile was less than inviting. The other men had moved their horses to encircle them. They all had their swords out to ensure the answer would not be in doubt.

"And with whom am I speaking?" This time Arcon turned to stare at the sneering thug, holding civility by the thinnest of threads.

"Pernoc, but you can call me Sir. I would advise you to come willingly." He looked at his nearest companion. "They did say take them 'dead or alive' didn't they? Yes, I was sure that's what they said, so maybe you don't want to come willingly?" Pernoc's horse had been inching toward Arcon, and was now almost touching him.

"Hmm, and who would they be?"

"That's on a need-to-know basis, and I'm pretty sure you don't need to know. So, old man, what do you say, hey? Are we going to do this the hard way? In fact, that would probably be more fun for the boys; they have been cooped up a while."

"I really enjoy doing things the hard way, but I think I'll be disappointed today." Arcon was making small gestures with his fingers.

The man closest to Blayke jerked his beast sideways and slammed Blayke to the ground. He jumped off the horse and stood over his prey, sword raised. His companions laughed at the helpless young man on the ground. "Should have stayed home with your mamma. Roll onto your stomach, little girl, so I can tie you up." Blayke was not sure what to do, so he did nothing. "One more chance, boy. Roll over or your head's going to roll off." His sword descended toward Blayke's throat. Blayke stared at Arcon, teeth gritted, eyes pleading.

Arcon screamed, "Burn!" His finger pointed at Blayke's attacker. The stranger's clothes burst into flame. He shrieked, his sword falling harmlessly next to Blayke's head. Blayke grabbed it and jumped to his feet as the man fell. He looked around to see where the next assault was coming from, but his eyes were drawn back to the writhing man burning to death on the ground near his feet.

The other bandits were staring, mouths agape at the bonfire that only moments ago had been their comrade. "Forget the boy. Kill him!"

The leader charged at Arcon. Arcon didn't speak, just stabbed his finger at each bandit, one by one. It happened so quickly that Blayke hadn't had a chance to move during the encounter. He now stood staring at the four bodies aflame, screams no longer escaping tormented throats. The horses bolted in fright.

"Damn horses. If this gang were only part of a contingent sent to capture us, the horses will be fleeing right back to reinforcements. Quick, we'll have to get away from the road."

Blayke didn't move, except to place his hand over his mouth and nose. He had never seen such carnage, and the smell. Burning flesh had a unique, sweet, sickly odour, and the smoke made his eyes water. He doubled over and vomited.

Arcon rushed to Blayke and helped him stand upright. He gently, but firmly, took Blayke's face in his hands. The same hands that had wreaked horror a moment ago were now the loving hands of his surrogate father. "Look at me, boy. I'm sorry I had to do that, but if I hadn't, we would both be dead. Well, you would be anyway. I'm ashamed to say I was unprepared. Flame was the first thing I thought of, and I might've panicked just a little. Come on, we can't stay here a moment longer." Blayke's face barely registered what Arcon was saying. There was no time so Arcon slapped his face.

Blayke felt the sting and bent over again, this time vomiting on Arcon's shoes. When he stood straight, his eyes held a new grim understanding of life and its other side. "I've never seen someone killed. It's sickening. I don't think I could ever do something like that." Arcon looked hurt. "Not that I think you're evil or anything." Blayke winced, knowing his reply was lame and did nothing to detract from the insult he had thoughtlessly given his uncle.

Arcon understood what Blayke was going through. Arcon had killed a few people in his lifetime; it was never pleasant. What was more than a little frightening was that the killing was easier each time. This time, when Arcon jogged away from the road, Blayke followed, eager to get away from the now-blackened corpses, and unaware of the extra weight in his pocket.

Arcon hated himself at that moment, for he knew Blayke would have to kill (probably many times) and it was he, Arcon, who had led him down that path. He told himself it couldn't be helped, and for the moment all their energy needed to be saved for the long road ahead. Unfortunately logic couldn't smother the lamenting guilt and pain, which now inhabited the space left by an innocence destroyed—his or Blayke's he wasn't sure.

Breathing deeply and clenching his fists, Arcon dismissed all thought and focused on moving forward. His legs worked more quickly now, for he felt an urgency that couldn't be ignored. He had to communicate with Avruellen and warn her. Arcon hoped she was alright. If he had felt any complacency, it was well and truly gone, scoured away by his own murderous flames. The freedom he had felt as they left the mountains had been replaced by a nervousness that was new to him. They were nowhere near finding what they sought, and now their enemies were looking for them. He felt hunted and could suddenly sympathize with the rodents on which Phantom sustained himself. They needed a plan, but only one came to mind: he ran faster.

7

Bronwyn watched her aunt watching her friend. "Aunt, please don't hurt her."

"Don't be silly. I wouldn't do that." She crouched down and placed fingertips on Corrille's brow, mumbled a few words, then stood back. Corrille's eyes fluttered opened, and she slowly sat up.

Her words raced one another in their haste to leave her mouth. "I'm sorry, Miss Avruellen. I wasn't spying or anything. I ran away and thought to ask Bronny for help, but when I got to your cottage you were leaving. I didn't know what was going on, and I didn't want you to take me back home, so I thought I'd follow you." Avruellen was staring at the young runaway, one brow raised. Corrille worried at Avruellen's lack of sympathy. "I don't want to go home, and you can't make me. If I can't come with you, I'll go my own way."

Avruellen shook her head. "I won't have you out there by yourself. You don't know the first thing about travelling. Do you have any money? No? I didn't think so. How do you expect to feed yourself, and what about protection? Not everyone in this world is going to be nice to you, and some will do their best to make trouble."

"I'm sorry."

"Not as sorry as you'll be if you don't do what I say. There are rules that must be followed if you come with us; I don't tolerate disobedience. I'm not going to tell you anything about what we're doing, and if Bronwyn does, she will be severely punished. You must not talk of anything you see with anyone but us. Do you understand?" Both girls nodded vigorously, happy to be together again.

Bronwyn rushed over to hug her aunt, "Thank you, thank you, thank you. You won't regret it. I promise." Avruellen had heard it all before and had a feeling she would.

Avruellen fussed over preparing dinner, stopping every now and then to give the girls a frown whilst they became reacquainted.

"Your aunt is so serious and a bit scary."

"She's OK. She just worries a lot, and I guess she sees you as extra responsibility."

"But I'm eighteen. It's not like I'm a baby. I can look after myself."

Bronwyn admitted her friend probably could look after herself, to some degree. She wasn't as good a fighter as Bronwyn, but she was sufficient and had the presence of mind to bring her sword when she ran away; Bronwyn felt for her own weapon, a dagger, which was strapped securely to her ankle.

"Did you bring a bedroll, or a heavier coat?" Bronwyn's question prompted Corrille to rummage through her pack.

"I've got a heavier coat but I didn't think about anything else. I didn't have time."

"We'll get you one when we reach the city."

"By the city, do you mean Bayerlon?" Corrille's eyes brightened. Like Bronwyn, she had never been far from their village—and certainly never to the capital.

"Yep. Isn't it exciting? What do you think it'll be like?"

"I suppose there'll be lots of people, especially beautiful women in lovely dresses; I've heard some women have as many as ten!"

"And handsome men, of course." Both girls giggled. Avruellen made no secret that she was listening and gave them a disapproving look.

Bronwyn changed the subject. "So why did you run away? What happened?"

Corrille fidgeted and suddenly couldn't look her friend in the eye. "I've never told anyone this. You have to promise not to tell." Bronwyn nodded, but Corrille wasn't convinced. "Promise?"

"Yes, yes, I promise."

Corrille took a deep breath and spoke quickly before her nerve left her. "Father beats me. He gets drunk almost every night, and he's even burnt me with the fire iron. Don't get me wrong, he's usually a wonderful father, but once he drinks ... his eyes seem to change. It's like it's not him. He just goes crazy. Mother leaves when he gets like that, but he doesn't let me leave, so I try and stay quiet but he always finds an excuse. I just couldn't take it anymore." Corrille turned her back to her friend so she wouldn't see the tears as they spilled over her lower lids. Bronwyn knew Corrille's father, and he seemed nice enough. It was difficult to imagine he would do such a thing.

"How come you've never told me about this before? I mean, why would he do it? He seems like he really loves you."

"Lift up my top."

Bronwyn hesitantly obeyed. An audible breath rushed through her mouth. "Oh gods, these bruises are awful. Did he really do that to you? Oh, Corrille, I'm so sorry. You should have come to me sooner. Auntie would have protected you." By this time Avruellen had come to see for herself. She shook her head when she saw what the girl had suffered.

There was little talking while they ate, and Bronwyn's usually voracious appetite had diminished after hearing what her best friend had been subjected to. Each woman was lost in her own thoughts. They slept next to each other; Avruellen and Bronwyn shared their blankets with the new arrival, who snuggled between them. Although the days were lengthening toward spring, the nights were cold. As usual, they had a big day ahead of them so they said their "good nights" early.

Avruellen couldn't say why, but she didn't trust her niece's friend. She felt great sympathy for what Corrille had endured at the hands of her father, a person who should have protected her, not abused her. However, having been a victim didn't ensure you were of good character. Well, she was here now, and maybe that was for some good; didn't they say "keep your friends close, your enemies closer"? Maybe enemy was too strong a word, but friend didn't feel right either. Just to be on the safe side, Avruellen asked Flux to hunt in the morning so he could watch over them as they slept. The fox, Avruellen's life-long companion, did as he was asked. Nothing unusual happened though, and he wasted no time bolting into the woods for breakfast when Avruellen woke.

Porridge and dried fruit was breakfast for the humans, whilst Flux broke his fast with a warm rabbit. They were travelling with few possessions, so it took only minutes to clear the camp. Avruellen led the way out of the campsite while it was still early, the girls chatting behind, Flux trotting at the rear. Avruellen wasn't taking any chances where their safety was concerned. She had known Corrille was following them from the first night and had waited to see how long it would take for her to show herself. When it seemed the girl might follow them "secretly" all the way to the city, Avruellen had thought it better to get her where she could keep a closer eye. It didn't hurt for Bronwyn to have a companion; there were times when Avruellen needed to think in silence and her niece wanted to chat. Also, she thought it might distract Bronwyn from wanting a creatura.

Something else had been worrying the realmist ever since she had dragged Corrille into their immediate company. Avruellen had assumed the sense of being watched would disappear when the girl had been "discovered," but it had not. She hoped The Circle's meeting hadn't been compromised. The eerie sense of being followed had not diminished at all; in fact it felt stronger. She wondered if the enemy knew what they were up to. Even though Avruellen knew her fox was always wary, she contacted Flux and warned him to be extra watchful.

Lunch was a welcome time to rest sore feet. They found a clear, inviting stream not far from the road. Large, flat, moss-covered rocks were in abundance under the trees and they were comfortable enough to sit on. The trio took off their shoes and rubbed tired feet through the cool grass. Flux padded to the water's edge and put his nose delicately near the flow, tongue flickering in and out too fast to follow, drinking in the cold water. Their meal was another simple affair of hard cheese and fruit, after which they all bathed. It was too cold to luxuriate for long, but no one liked being whiffy. They hadn't bathed since before the meeting. The day was warm for this time of year, so everyone felt it was a good opportunity to be clean for a change.

Avruellen's pace increased after lunch, the growing sense of urgency spurring her on. She had been unable to figure out why, and that worried her all the more. The girls were practically jogging to keep up with Bronwyn's tall aunt. "Your aunt has the stamina of a person half her age."

"You have no idea." Bronwyn and her aunt kept the secret of her real age. No one knew why practicing realmistry increased longevity, but it could increase a lifespan up to tenfold. Bronwyn was looking forward to a long, long life—but it had negative aspects the young girl could not possibly imagine.

Using power from the Second Realm was not forbidden. Most people didn't believe it could be done, but the population's general ignorance and superstitions ensured prejudice against so-called realmists was ingrained. If you claimed to be a realmist, most either thought you a liar or feared you. In order to hide her true vocation, Avruellen had found when she had been somewhere for a number of years, it was wise to disappear or fake her own death. As a consequence, she had left many good friends and family in her wake. Her old heart had broken too many times to count, so if Bronwyn noticed a lack of affection it was probably true; an inevitable by-product of a person whose emotions had been sacrificed to duty. Avruellen hoped Bronwyn didn't end up as closed to love as she had.

Avruellen berated herself for harping on what couldn't be changed. She had to keep all her thoughts on the present. Were they already being targeted? The noble realmist was surprised at how she, the most powerful woman on Talia, could feel so helpless. She looked back at her charges. "How are you going back there?"

"Fine. Why the speed? You'd think we were being chased by Zebla's hounds." Zebla was an evil goddess, who myth had it, disguised herself as a white snow wolf to capture the affection of Nevus, the god of winter. When the god saw Zebla (in her wolven form) he felt such great affection, he welcomed her into his family and escorted her to his mountain-top cave. On the first night, as the god slept, Zebla assumed her true form and placed a collar of flame around his neck. The collar, a visual embodiment of her power, captured the god. The snow of a hundred years, which lasted throughout his incarceration, covered the earth and led to the starvation of many men and beasts, only melting when he managed to escape and gain control of his winter. He would not have escaped had it not been for a jealous underling, Phyrmon, who coveted Zebla's interest. Phyrmon set Nevus free when his mistress was away. When Zebla returned, she knew instantly what had happened. As far as the legend goes, poor old Phyrmon was currently passing his days as a guinea pig for Zebla's fascination with poisons. She tested each new poison she created on Phyrmon. He was constantly subjected to slow death by excruciating pain, only to be brought back again and again. The gods could be so cruel.

"Not Zebla's hounds, dear, but it's rude to be late for an appointment."

"What appointment?"

"You'll see dear, you'll see, but only if you can keep up." With that, Avruellen forged ahead. The girls looked at each other, rolling their eyes, and with no other choice, ran to catch up.

Despite Avruellen's misgivings, the next few days unfolded uneventfully. They were making good time. If nothing untoward happened, they would be in Bayerlon on the ninth day, as scheduled. Three nights before their planned arrival they came upon a homestead not far from the road. The occupants were a couple whose children had recently married and left home. Their farm produced vegetables, milk, and cheese. Avruellen decided it would be nice to sleep indoors for a change and had an eye on what appeared to be a small, vacant, timber cottage situated away from the main house. The travellers approached the inviting homestead to ask if they could spend the night (for a fee of course) in the compact domicile. The farmer and his wife agreed. Not only did they provide lodgings, they offered freshly baked bread, vegetable soup, and roast meat for dinner. Avruellen and Bronwyn declined the meat but were more than happy to accept the rest. Corrille was ecstatic to eat meat for a change. She had eaten very little before her exposure due to her own lack of foresight, but once she had become part of the little group, her repast matched the fruit, bread, and cheese, of which she was now heartily sick.

Avruellen paid the couple a few coppers. They took the food to the cottage to eat in private. The interior proved to be homey enough, albeit with a mildly musty odour. It was apparent it had been vacant and closed up for a while, but remained in good order. A small, square table, surrounded by two chairs, sat in the corner opposite the door, and two single beds crowded the other back corner, next to them a comfortable rocking chair. The beds were bare, so Avruellen made the girls drag the mattresses outside to release some of the dust. Whilst they did their job, Avruellen dusted the table and laid out the food, plates, and cutlery they had been given.

Bronwyn moved the rocking chair to the table and ate with her plate in her lap. She had never realised how comfortable furniture really was. This trip was the longest stretch she had ever gone without sleeping in a proper bed or sitting upright in a chair. Nature was beautiful, but could be terribly uncomfortable.

The warm food elicited lots of "mmms" from the girls. Fresh, soft bread with a generous spread of butter on top was a nice change from the bread they had brought, which apart from now being hard and stale, was almost gone. "Do you think the lady would sell us some food? With Corrille here, no offence, the food won't last until we get to the city."

"I'll ask her tonight. Maybe if she doesn't have enough fresh bread, you can get up early and make us some." Avruellen smiled at Bronwyn's horrified expression.

"Ah, no thanks. I suppose I could go without bread for three more days."

After dinner Corrille and Bronwyn took the plates to the homestead and washed them. The lady of the house gave them some cups and a fresh pot of tea. Avruellen smiled to see the girls enter with the fragrant brew. Avruellen had appropriated the rocking chair and was soon comfortably rocking and sipping. When they finished their tea they went to their newly made beds, which Avruellen had prepared. No one wanted to sleep on the floor, so Corrille and Bronwyn shared a bed top to tail.

A voice speaking in Avruellen's head woke her shortly after she had drifted off. She sat up. *Arcon?*

Sorry to startle you, but I had to warn you. Blayke and I were attacked this afternoon, and he was almost killed. You must be extremely careful. We had to leave more than one body behind. The enemy must know who we are, and I wouldn't be surprised if they knew about you and Bronwyn.

Oh gods, I've had a weird feeling since the meeting. I feel as if we're being watched. At first I thought it was Corrille...

Arcon interrupted. *Who's Corrille?*

Bronwyn's childhood friend, long story. Anyway, it wasn't her. The feeling won't go away and seems to be intensifying the closer we get to Bayerlon. Are you alright?

Apart from Blayke's blunt introduction to death, we're ok. Be careful. We can't lose anyone. Sorry I can't come and help, but we've got our own problems. I'd better go. Take care.

You take care too. The presence left Avruellen's mind.

Arcon had taken a great risk to warn them. If the enemy were watching his symbol in the Second Realm they may have followed him to Avruellen. He must have thought the other risk outweighed what he had just done. Things were *not* going well. How many people had Arcon killed? Avruellen had to assume they were coming for her and Bronwyn already. She just hoped they weren't close. Sleep was not going to return, so she lay awake thinking until morning.

They were packing their belongings when there was a knock at the door. Avruellen opened it to see the farmer's wife with a basket full of food. "I've prepared some breakfast. There are also a few things for your journey."

Avruellen stood aside and let the woman place the basket on the table. "Thank you. Your hospitality is without measure. If only everyone were as nice."

The woman smiled. "It's the least I could do. I have a feeling your journey may be a long and dangerous one. I only hope you and your girls get where you're going safely. Enjoy the food, and good luck."

After she left, they sat down to a hearty breakfast of pancakes with fresh butter and honey. "Mmm. This sure beats the watery porridge we've been eating." Bronwyn shoved in another mouthful. After breakfast they transferred the rest of the food from the basket to their packs. There was a fresh loaf of bread, fruit muffins, jam, biscuits, and fried potato cakes. There was some cooked bacon that Avruellen put in Corrille's bag. Along with the dried fruit, porridge, and small piece of cheese, which was still in Bronwyn's bag, they would have enough food to get them to Bayerlon.

Before they left, Avruellen warned her charges: "Without trying to scare you, I need you to be watchful. If I ask you to do anything, anything at all, I expect to be obeyed instantly. No one goes out of my sight, at any time, for anything. We do everything together from now on. Do you understand?" It was a rhetorical question; they both nodded. "Good. OK. Let's go."

Corrille narrowed her eyes, and Bronwyn could see she resented being told what to do. In a way, Bronwyn felt too old to be treated like a child, however, she knew deep down that her aunt must have a reason. In fact, she had noticed Avruellen was jumpy, always turning her head this way and that—not her usual demeanor.

After they set out, Bronwyn noticed Flux was also acting strange. One minute walking with them, the next ranging out to the side, behind or ahead, and they went for hours at a time without seeing the fox. Bronwyn worried. Whatever had upset her aunt must be important. She hoped it was something they could cope with. Her philosophy of not worrying about anything until it happened was hard to uphold in the present circumstances. She hoped it wasn't too long before she set her eyes on Bayerlon.

In the distant Third Realm, a barren wasteland where the Gormons waited and cultivated their hate, what passed for laughter shrieked forth from the creature. Its watchfulness in the Second Realm had paid off. *Stupid humans.* One fool had led him to the other. Before long he would know them all, and when it was too late for Talia, they would know him. He grated his scaly palms together, careful not to cut himself with his own claws. Two of his High Priests had already travelled the ethereal corridors to Talia. Even now they were adjusting to clumsy human bodies. Soon, soon. It would all be his, soon.

8

The sun's rays warmed the castle walls. Clear winter light played around the queen's chambers, drawing out subtle pink and orange hues within the stone.

"What do you think, Sarah?" Queen Gabrielle held up a newly embroidered vei,l and Sarah paused in her effort to arrange her mistress's hair. Pale pink and blue flowers traced a delicate path around the edges of the material.

"It's beautiful. Verity will love it."

"I hope so. Now all we have to do is find her a husband." The queen smiled. Sixteen was a little young to be married, but as her daughter would one day be queen, she had already started the search for a suitable husband. Plenty of noble (and otherwise) families had offered their sons, but so far Gabrielle was not convinced someone better couldn't be found.

"What about you? I hear Petro is back in the city."

Sarah blushed and hurriedly finished the braid she was working on. "Yes. I saw him last night, actually. He's leaving again in a few days. I doubt he'll ever ask me."

The queen's lady-in-waiting was thirty and had never been married. She was a beautiful woman, slightly built with long, blonde hair. It wasn't as if no one had ever been interested; she was just too shy. The one man she had developed an affectionate relationship with was

Petro, the travelling salesman. He went from town to town, city to city, selling cheap baubles to vain women, although it was also said his selection of fabrics were some of the finest.

There was a quiet tap, tap, tap, and Gabrielle jumped. Sarah approached the locked door. "Who's there?"

"Hermas, my lady." Sarah unlocked the door, allowing the old man to enter. Ever since the night, seventeen years ago, when Leon had attacked Gabrielle, she had always made sure her door was locked from the inside.

Hermas had been chief advisor to the king's father and then the king. Gabrielle remembered a time when he cut a noble figure: much taller than her, with thick, black hair. As far as most knew, he was now retired. He stooped to stand at an equal height as the queen, thinning, white hair gently touching his shoulders. He had served the family for most of his life, and had been given quarters in the castle after his 'retirement'. Hermas was considered part of the family and was like a grandfather to Verity. The queen loved the gentle, intelligent man and was one of the only people who knew his senility to be a well-contrived act.

The queen stood and offered him her hands. "How have you been, crazy old man?" Gabrielle was smiling.

"Have you seen my cat?"

"You don't have a cat."

"Yes I do. She can talk you know. Maybe I'll find her in the garden at sunset chasing the mice. Sorry to bother you." He bowed as he walked backward to the door. The cryptic conversation was a way of life, because anyone, including Leon, could be listening. The truth was, Hermas was not retired; he secretly worked for the queen, collecting information and keeping an eye on people she didn't trust. The ambiguous conversation told Gabrielle to be in the garden at sunset.

"What a funny old man. You really are nice to him."

"He's like a father to me. From the day I came here as a nobleman's daughter he treated me like a queen. Just because he's a little crazy, doesn't mean he doesn't deserve our respect. He achieved a lot of good in his lifetime."

"I hope you treat me that well when I've turned into a weird old spinster and can no longer serve you, My Lady."

"What are you worried about? I'm older than you. With a bit of luck you'll be the one who has to mop up my dribble." Sarah screwed up her face.

There was a loud knock at the door. Sarah rose again, "Who's there?"

"The King. I've come to see my lovely wife." Sarah opened the door and curtsied as the king entered.

"Please leave us, Sarah. I won't be needing you until mid afternoon."

"Yes, My Lady." She curtsied again, shutting the door behind her.

Gabrielle stood and met her husband's embrace. "Why must you always lock that door, my love? It offends me that you don't feel safe in our home." Gabrielle shrugged but offered no answer. She had never told her husband what his brother had done, because other than Leon's threat to kill her, which she never doubted, she knew the trust and love Edmund felt for his brother. Whilst she knew the king loved her, she wasn't willing to test his loyalties without any proof of what had happened. When she had given birth to Verity, everyone naturally thought the child was the king's, and only two people in the castle knew it might not be. She had lived with that truth day after day. Despite the possibility of who her father may be, she could not help but love her daughter, a fact which made her feel immense guilt.

The king looked at his wife, waiting for an answer to his oft-asked question. Gabrielle hoped her reply would satisfy him. "You are so trusting, my love. Not everyone loves the king and his family you know. There are always those who'll try to harm us. I wouldn't be the first queen to be targeted. It was you who told me about the kidnapping of your great grandmother, Queen Lurline."

The king acknowledged her reasons with a small nod. "Yes, well you are ever the cautious one, and I would rather see you safe and happy. If that locked door saves your life even once, it's worth my slight offence." He kissed her forehead.

"I'm *so* glad you feel that way."

"No need to get all funny with me."

"Would I do anything to upset his highness?" She looked up at him through long, dark lashes. He laughed and kissed her mouth. He slowly unwrapped her arms from his waist and stepped back to the door.

"That was a quick visit. Are you sure you won't stay longer?" Gabrielle pouted.

"Off to talk trade with an emissary from Wyrden. Apparently a hailstorm has ruined seventy percent of their fruit crop and they want some of ours. Their beef has always been quite good, however I hate to say that Veresia's population are close to being vegetarians. I just don't know if I can make my subjects eat all that beef. There's only so much I can order people to do." He winked and rubbed his hands together. In most other countries the minister for trade would conduct negotiations, but his love of economics drove the king to participate in such dealings whenever he had time.

"You bad, bad man." Gabrielle shook her head. He was usually known for his generosity, however, his competitive nature sometimes got the better of him. After he left, a spring in his step, Gabrielle re-locked the door. There were two guards standing at the doors to the reception room that led to her bed chamber. Unfortunately, Gabrielle knew the guards would not only obey her husband but Leon as well, so she left nothing to chance.

Gabrielle moved to the window. Her chambers overlooked the east gardens, numerous fields, and in the distance, the river, which flowed to the Pearl Sea. The ancient stone wall that separated the castle from the vista was as tall as ten men. There was a system of underground stone tunnels, which diverted some of the water to the city. Her husband's great, great grandfather had built a large dam under the city for use in any protracted siege to guard against the water being poisoned or cut off. The castle and city were well protected.

Winter was ending. The days had started to warm up, although nights and early mornings were bitterly cold. The queen happily noticed newly-formed buds on the Azaris tree that would explode into purple flowers when spring finally matured, and down in the garden beds small green shoots were fighting their way out of the near frozen earth. For a moment she forgot her troubles, imagining the colour and warmth spring would bring.

Unseen by the queen, the young boy stood behind a wall, in a secret corridor. He looked through a strategically placed crack in time to see the king leave after his short visit. So far there was nothing to report. The only people who had visited the queen were the crazy man and the king. Tired after standing there for the past hour, he wished he were tall enough to sit on a chair and look through the stupid crack, but he wasn't. Although he was supposed to make sure he didn't miss anything, he didn't think it would hurt to sit on the floor and rest his feet for five minutes. He sat on the ground in the dark. Nobody used torches in the secret passageway lest someone see the light shining from any number of spy holes. He wasn't a timid boy by nature, however sitting in the pitch black was not his idea of fun. At least he wasn't hungry these days. Ever since he had started spying for Prince Leon he was never hungry. And he had a comfortable bed to sleep on, even if it was in the stables.

He carried out odds and ends for the prince, things he knew Leon didn't want anyone else knowing about— especially his brother. His days and nights consisted of running secret messages to certain people the prince did not wish to be seen to be associated with, spying on others, and occasionally taking a beating simply because the prince enjoyed inflicting pain. The boy figured a few scars were a small price to pay. If the great prince had not saved him from the brothel where he had lived with his mother, he would have eventually been sold as a slave, or worse. He knew of other boys who were sold to men for their perverted pleasures. He shuddered. Anything was better than that.

His mother had been excited to receive the gold piece it cost Leon to buy him. A tear came to his eye when he thought of his mother. He hadn't seen her since the night Leon had taken him, which, by his reckoning, was about six months ago. He dragged the back of his hand across his eye to remove some offending moisture. He was too old for that nonsense: ten-year-old boys weren't supposed to cry, especially not for someone who had never loved them. The young boy knew his mother wished he had never been born; she had told him so every day. He had never received the hugs or kisses he had seen other parents bestow on their children. Not wanting to wallow, he stood up and resumed his position, eye to the crack. He hoped someone worthwhile would turn up or his afternoon was going to be very boring and Leon would have an excuse to inflict another thrashing. He stood and waited.

For a moment the boy thought his waiting had paid off. On sunset the queen emerged. She spoke to her guards. "I'm going for dinner. I will be back with my husband later." The guards nodded. *Well that's just great, nothing.* He had stood here for half the day, and there was nothing to report. His stomach grumbled. He had been told to stay there all day, and for Leon that meant until after the queen had returned and gone to bed. Remembering the oat biscuits he had pocketed from the kitchen that morning, he grinned. Although ravenous, he savoured his two biscuits, chewing every mouthful ten times.

He decided he could sit down again seeing as the queen was gone. He was just settling to the ground when he heard soft footsteps. He jumped up, hoping he hadn't been caught sitting on the job. "Ah, there you are. I've decided you can have the night off. Follow me." The boy did as he was told—and hoped the only thing waiting for him would be dinner.

***

Gabrielle wandered around the garden, pretending to admire the trees that were sprouting new growth. She headed toward a large maple and stood where she could enjoy the sunset. Hermas silently appeared at her shoulder. "Good evening, my queen." He executed a small bow.

"Good eve to you, good sir. Did you find your cat?"

"Yes. In fact she was hiding in this tree, but I think you've scared her away again."

"I'm sure she'll be back. Why don't you enjoy the sunset with me." Hermas took a quick look around and lowered his voice.

"My nephew is up to something. One of his hounds was sniffing around at King Suklar's court. It seems some arrangements are being made."

The queen's voice was even quieter. "What arrangements?"

"I'm not sure. But one of the hounds at the meeting was a priest of You Know Who."

Goose bumps crowded the queen's arms and she shivered. She fought the urge to grimace and managed a smile before speaking louder. "What a lovely sunset. I'm so glad I had someone to share it with. Do let me know if your cat doesn't come back. I'm sure we can get you another." Hermas bowed again and when he raised his head Gabrielle was walking away.

Her curiosity was piqued. They had code names for everyone. The person they referred to as Hermas's nephew was Leon; hounds was just another word for his lackeys; and the priest of You Know Who was one of the priests who spread the depraved word of the god, Klar. King Suklar of Inkra, who worshiped Klar, was an unknown quantity at this stage. His kingdom kept its own council and distance from all other countries; one never knew who had their alliance—if indeed anyone could. The cruel way King Suklar treated his subjects was also widely known. The queen had a lot to think about as she made her way to the dining hall.

The king rose as she approached the table. "Hello, my love, did you have a nice afternoon?" The queen wanted to relay the new information to her husband but couldn't risk anyone hearing. She would have to keep quiet on the subject for now. "Yes, thank you. How were the negotiations?"

"Quite successful is how you would rate them. Wouldn't you agree, Perculus?" The king turned to his advisor, selected for him by his brother. Edmund loved and trusted Leon as a brother, however, he wondered how he could have chosen this idiot as his advisor. Perculus was arrogant, egotistical, and too busy listening to the sound of his own voice to notice what was really going on. His constant fawning in pursuit of favouritism disgusted Edmund. The king preferred no-nonsense people who were intelligent enough to have their own ideas and bold enough to suggest them.

"Ah, yes, my king. Although, I must pronounce, any negotiation you are involved in is successful; for us of course." He looked quite proud of his ability to flatter the king. The king looked at Gabrielle and blew out a loud breath. She shook her head and gave a small smile. The whole routine would be laughable if Gabrielle didn't have her suspicions. She knew the real Leon and what he was capable of. What was his purpose in employing Perculus as King's Aide? She realized her husband could see his advisor's shortcomings, but did he distrust him enough to keep his secrets to himself?

Verity came around and kissed her mother and father on the cheek. "Where have you been, darling? The food was almost here before you."

"Sorry, Mother. Lisbeth and I were studying Ungar's Myths and Prophecies, and we lost track of time. My stomach started grumbling and I realised dinner would be ready." Verity had a large appetite for a girl, but as she was tall and loved exercising outdoors, she was healthy and always drew admiring glances.

The food arrived, but Leon was nowhere to be seen. Gabrielle wondered if his absence had anything to do with whatever dirty plan he was concocting. She saw her husband looking around the room until the arrival of his meal grabbed his attention. When they were at Bayerlon Castle the king insisted everyone eat dinner together, as he wanted to maintain a close family. "I find a good negotiation always works up an appetite. I wonder if this beef is from Wyrden? I hear it's tasty and tender, yet rather affordable." He laughed.

Gabrielle looked over at Perculus who was shovelling the food in as fast as he could swallow. He chewed open-mouthed because of a chronic health problem that prevented him from breathing through his nose. He was a tall man, slightly shorter than the king, however his frame was portly. The man was greedy with food and money, his fat belly a testament to his lifestyle. A napkin crudely placed under his double chin was quickly soiled by the negligently handled, part masticated food. The queen stopped watching lest she lose her appetite.

"So, where is the lovely Sarah?" The king also required a distraction from his advisor.

"She's probably making the most of her time with Petro. Apparently he leaves again in a few days."

"Ah, young love. I remember when we were young. The things we used to get up to." Gabrielle giggled at her husband and Verity rolled her eyes.

"Too much information, Dad."

"How do you think you got here?"

"Seriously. I don't want to know, thanks." Gabrielle, for the millionth time since her daughter had been born, silently prayed Edmund was her father.

Gabrielle and Edmund had been attracted to each other from the beginning, which was unexpected since their marriage had been arranged. As the years had passed, they had become best friends and were secure in their trust of one another. Gabrielle's decision to keep quiet about what had happened with Leon continued to rob her of sleep. If her husband ever found out, it would break his heart, and if he ever doubted Verity was his daughter, he would never, ever forgive Gabrielle or Leon.

Leon entered the dining hall as Gabrielle was finishing her meal. He bowed to his brother and quickly sat in the space left for him next to Perculus. When one of the young serving girls placed Leon's plate in front of him, his thankful smile was lewd. The girl rushed back to the kitchens in fright. "I'll catch up with her later."

"Must you frighten the staff, brother? The poor girl is only thirteen and not ready for your suggestive advances. In fact, I would appreciate it if you could treat them with some respect. They work hard for us you know." Edmund had noticed a change in his brother a few months ago, and now his trust in his brother was lessening by the day.

"You do pay them, albeit not much. I would think it part of their job to satisfy the king's brother: whatever his wish." Gabrielle sneered in disgust but kept silent.

She was careful not to provoke Leon. Her dream was to slice her knife across his depraved throat.

The king, to Gabrielle's surprise, gave his brother a menacing look. "Do not speak so in front of Verity or the Queen."

Leon kept a neutral face, hiding his anger at being chastised. "Alright, just to make you happy, I'll behave." Leon turned to Perculus. "Why is it that no one can take a joke around here?"

Edmund wasn't too sure about his brother's ability to behave where women were concerned. Leon was a very handsome man. Edmund could see the way women looked at him, and what girl didn't want to marry a prince? He doubted Leon would behave as he had just promised.

Sensing a possible conflict, Gabrielle motioned to Verity and they excused themselves to retire to the queen's chambers.

"So, Prince, what kept you from joining us at the beginning of dinner?" Edmund used the term as a way of reminding his brother, not only of his responsibilities, but also his place within the family. Edmund may not have seen all Leon's weaknesses but he was aware of his brother's yearning to be king rather than prince.

Leon's face became a careful mask, "I was making last-minute arrangements for a trip I must undertake." He turned to Perculus. "Please explain to my dear brother what will be happening." The king ignored the slight and turned to Perculus.

"Ah, well." He cleared his throat and ran a podgy finger across the inside of his collar. "This morning we received a request from Inkra. King Suklar wishes to meet with Prince Leon to ascertain if he is a suitable match for his first-born daughter."

Edmund kept the shock from his face. Inkra was not a friend of Veresia; they would have been at war had Suklar thought he was capable of winning. "Why was I not informed of this?" The king loomed over his advisor. Perculus shrank back toward Leon. Perculus's lank brown hair stuck to his head with nervous sweat.

Leon spoke. "We only received the request this morning, and, as you were busy with other things, I thought it best not to bother you. In fact I thought it would be a nice surprise—since you're always pushing me to find a wife. So, toward that end, I am diligently making arrangements. I hope to depart the day after tomorrow." Leon smiled a seemingly genuine smile.

"Dammit, brother. We don't know much about these people. Do I want someone from Inkra in my castle, able to spy on us for Suklar? I'm sure I don't have to remind you that last time we sent a member of this family to Inkra they were killed. Have you thought this through? Obviously not much, since you only received the request this morning."

"Look, that murder was three hundred years ago. I'm sure all that nastiness is in the past. My plan is to go there and meet the family. If they aren't worshipers of Klar, I can't see the problem."

"Not worshippers of Klar?" Edmund's voice rose a notch. "Are you an idiot? Of course they are. It's their national bloody religion." The king's patience was stretched to the limit. What the hell was Leon up to? Even he realised it was not any Veresian man's dream to marry into an Inkran family, let alone the royal one. Edmund wondered how any of the Inkran royal family actually remained, as they were constantly killing each other to improve their position within the royal hierarchy.

Leon adopted a pleading tone that was at odds with the sneer on his face. "Look, it could be a good alliance. We know their mines are heavy with gold, and the waters off their coast produce bountiful fish. You said yourself that we know little about them, so I see this as a good opportunity for me to find out more for you without you actually endangering yourself."

"That's what we have spies for. I don't particularly like the idea of you being in danger, despite your shortcomings. What sort of protection are you planning on taking?"

"My well-trained honour guard, who, incidentally, are better than most of the soldiers in our army. I'm also taking my realmist, who can ensure we're not attacked by any other means." Leon folded his arms across his chest, quite pleased with himself.

"Well, since you've obviously made up your mind to undertake this dubious trip, I must insist that Pernus and his soldiers accompany you." He held up his hand to halt his brother's complaints. "If they don't go, you don't go."

Edmund stood and looked down at Leon. "This conversation is over. Make sure you say goodbye before you leave." He left the two men. Perculus was almost under the table in his effort to avoid getting caught between the royal brothers. Leon's clenched fists were white and he was using all his self-control to keep them from slamming violently onto the table. He silently vowed that one day his brother would pay for treating him in such a demeaning fashion. He would never show anger or embarrassment in front of anyone. He took a few calming breaths.

Leon was his usual, cold self when he spoke. "Hmm. Perculus, this is not quite what I had in mind, but I'm already seeing how I can remedy the situation. My brother will be quite unhappy when he hears the bad news." Perculus managed a half smile. "Make sure you look after things while I'm gone. Or else." He didn't have to finish the threat; Perculus knew Leon better than most. His threats were *never* empty. Perculus rubbed his dry, duplicitous hands together.

"Always, master, always."

Leon rose from his half-eaten dinner and walked away before Perculus could say any more. Unable to ignore the aroma of roast beef, the king's advisor turned back to the table and swapped his empty plate with his master's and proceeded to eat a second dinner.

Two mornings later, Boy, perched high in a tall pine tree, watched the frenzied activities of the people in the main courtyard. Horses were led out to stand in a line. Behind them came four horses harnessed to a gilded carriage, which Leon would use if the weather turned unpleasant. A few donkeys brought up the rear, carrying supplies. A small armed contingent was arranging itself into neat rows outside the main gates of the castle. Leon's personal bodyguard waited for their leader, whilst the king's men, led by Pernus, moved a short way down the road.

The king had given Pernus instructions that had surprised the veteran soldier. He had served King Edmund since he was a teenager and was a little older than his king. He knew him well, finding him to be a good king who always listened to the advice of those around him. Times had been peaceful whilst he had served the Laraulens, whom he knew to be a close family. Therefore, the instructions the king had given him concerning this trip were surprising. The king had a new distrust of his brother. Whilst he would not divulge why, Pernus assumed he had a good reason and would act accordingly. Pernus was not used to acting as a spy for his king, but he supposed it was time to broaden his horizons.

Boy watched the preparations with a mixture of sadness at missing out on an adventure, but also relief that he had his own job to do by staying at the castle. Leon had handed him over to the care of Verity, the king's daughter. She had been quite surprised at acquiring a new lackey, but had promised to take good care of him and teach him some courtly manners. Apparently, Perculus would give Boy instructions when the time was near. So far, doing what he was told had ensured he always had a full belly and somewhere warm to sleep. He intended to continue to please his master.

He could see the prince bidding farewell to the king and queen. Leon mounted whilst trumpets blasted a fanfare that was barely audible from Boy's perch. The prince sat tall in the saddle, his chest puffed out, as he walked his horse out of the main gate and down the road, past the first and largest houses in the city, gathering his retinue as he went. Some people lined the road to bid their prince goodbye, however the news had not spread far. Once the city learned one of their royal family was departing to meet his potential wife there would be joyous uproar; nothing much had happened lately, good or bad. Opinion might turn to anger when they realised the intended bride resided in the mysterious lands of a distrusted neighbour.

Boy waved an unseen goodbye and silently thanked the gods that Leon and his beatings were disappearing in the distance. Boy started his descent. His first order of the day would be to go to the river and find some frogs to play with. Leon never allowed him time to play and since Verity was his mistress for the time being, and did not require his services until after lunch, he happily jogged away from the castle walls. The young boy didn't realise it, but he was smiling his first genuine smile since being acquired by the great Prince Leon.

9

The moon hung high in the sky, its narrow crescent emaciated after its recent fullness. Avruellen sighed and let the tension melt out of her shoulders as she sat and stared into the flames. They were less than a day's walk to Bayerlon, their journey from the farmhouse uneventful. It seemed as if she had been holding her breath for the past few days. Nothing had befallen them, despite her sense of impending danger and Arcon's warning. And her misgivings about Corrille seemed unfounded—the girl had behaved and even done her share of the chores. The girls joined Avruellen next to the fire after finishing the washing up.

"How much further do we have to walk tomorrow?" Bronwyn asked.

"Until about mid-morning, if I remember correctly. It's been a while since I've been there."

"You've never been there as far as I can remember."

"That's what I was saying. It's been a while."

"What's it like? How big is it? Are there many people?"

"Bigger than you can possibly imagine and many more people than you've ever seen. In fact, because of the number of people, I find it too crowded for my liking, and it's very smelly with pollution."

"What's pollution?"

Avruellen bobbed her face forward, eyebrows inching towards her hairline. Then she remembered she had never taken her niece anywhere too far from nature. "Pollution is all the mess and rubbish that builds up around big cities. With all those people going to the toilet and throwing away food scraps, not to mention all the industry, such as tanners, it makes it a less-than-pristine place." The two girls wrinkled their noses, now unsure of how impressive the city would be.

"Don't worry. There's still a lot to see. Lots of shops with many wonderful things, dress makers, jewellers, confectioners."

"That's sweets isn't it?" Bronwyn perked up at the possibilities.

"Yes."

"Well I suppose a little smell is a small price to pay for all the other stuff." Both girls were smiling again.

"We won't have too much time to wander around I'm afraid. There are things I have to do. Sorry to remind you again, but when we're there it is very important that you listen to everything I say. You must pay close attention to each other, too, because it will be very easy to get separated and lost in the crowds. I don't have to tell you that if I have to look for either of you, when I find you, you'll wish you were never born." Both girls nodded impatiently.

Corrille quietly wished they could leave her friend's aunt and go to the city by themselves. The woman never stopped telling them what to do and had a bad habit of expecting to be obeyed. How Bronwyn had put up with it her entire life was a mystery. As much as Corrille wanted to rebel, she had to admit to being frightened of the old woman, who was a lot stronger than she looked.

It was probably safer for her to go along with what Avruellen wanted. For now, at least.

The girls tossed and turned through the night. Bronwyn dreamed of ladies in beautiful dresses, red, violet, gold, and turquoise. They strutted around the city, attracting the attention of all passers-by, their dainty shoes covered in the pollution her aunt had spoken of—golden shoes sullied by stinking dirt. A gentle mist shrouded everything; nothing was as clear as it should be, and she strained her eyes trying to see. In the dream, she was walking through city streets, not dirt as her village street had been, but cobbled with stones.

She walked ever upward through the main thoroughfare, where houses were little more than crooked pieces of timber barely held together. Poor people spilled out onto the street to talk, their ratty children played in the grimy soil with even rattier dogs and cats that should have been starving, but were not, due to the ample supply of mice and rats. She wasted no time, her muffled steps increasing their speed. She trotted past modest, but tidy, houses, some built with stone. She resisted the urge to sprint to the castle she knew would be at the top of the hill.

Even here the mist embraced all. Her journey led her past elegant homes, some of which were two story, now three, attached together, row upon row, ornate façades peeking through the fog, marble stairs beckoning her as she passed. There were few people now. Bronwyn brushed past a pretty, young woman in a pale blue dress, her eyes blank, feet walking a determined path in the opposite direction. The higher she climbed, the thicker the mist. The houses became freestanding, of neatly-cut timber, bricks and large slabs of stone. Soon she reached the castle's outer walls. She looked up and saw ... nothing.

Dense fog embraced the castle like a jealous lover. The mass looked solid and unmovable, rendering the castle invisible. Although she couldn't see it, she knew the castle was there. Bronwyn was drawn to the structure despite the fear that germinated in her belly. She heard a woman sobbing, each sob muffled by the muddy gloom. Bronwyn could hear the anguish in the woman's voice. "I miss you. Where are you? Can you hear me?" Her voice was broken, devastated. Bronwyn took a step forward, her legs moving slowly as if pushing through thick porridge. She wanted to speak to the woman, to tell her not to cry, that she was here and would help. Her lips parted but her voice would not emerge. The woman continued weeping.

Bronwyn was almost there and thought she could feel the warmth of the sorrowful lady reaching out to her through the damp air. She tried to take another step, but the resistance was too much. She couldn't move.

"Turn around." The voice behind her seemed familiar. "Come on, Bronny. Come here."

She turned and saw a tall, thin woman. Her shoulder-length black hair was shot through with dramatic lines of white. The face was old, yet not. Few wrinkles lined her face. A niggling thought told her she knew this woman, but she couldn't remember, no matter how hard she tried.

"Come on, dear. We have to get back to the markets. We haven't much time."

Bronwyn's feet moved of their own accord, toward the stranger who was not a stranger. The closer she came to the woman, the easier her legs moved. The haze in her mind cleared gradually, as they made their way down through the city to the markets. Halfway down, in front of the modest terraces, Bronwyn realised who the stranger was.

"Aunt?"

"Yes, dear. Who did you think it was?" She embraced Bronwyn. "It's almost time to wake up now. When you wake you won't remember any of this."

"Why not?"

"Because I said."

"Oh."

They continued down the cobbled streets and reached the market. Avruellen embraced her niece and bade her farewell.

Avruellen woke shortly before Bronwyn. In order to make sure her niece forgot the dream, she had to tamper with her memory, which she didn't like to do. The dream was not a normal dream, but a Realm dream. (Realm dreams were real, although to what extent nobody knew). It appeared Bronwyn had been pulled into someone else's dream; Avruellen was afraid she knew whose. Avruellen wasn't ready to answer the questions Bronwyn was sure to have, so she did the safest thing and hid the memory from her. She would have to be more careful from now on, warding their sleep every night. The further they travelled, the more tiring it became. She realised she would have to take her niece aside (away from Corrille) and teach her how to ward her own dreams. Avruellen should have taught Bronwyn before, but hadn't seen the need. Oh well, the first moment they had alone would have to do.

Bronwyn woke to a clear, crisp day. She could hear birds chirping their good mornings before she opened her eyes. Her head was fuzzy, as if she hadn't slept, and she felt confused. Slowly she sat up and peered around the camp through grainy eyes. After satisfying herself as to her whereabouts, she disentangled her body from the blankets. "You're finally up." Corrille took a closer look at her friend. "You don't look so good. Are you OK?" She led her friend to the campfire and breakfast.

"Mmm, I've got a bit of a headache. I don't think I slept very well, although I can't remember waking up in the night." Corrille sat her down on a log, and Avruellen handed her a cup of tea.

"I've put some herbs in there that should get rid of your headache. It shouldn't taste too bad."

"I've heard that before. How did you know I'd have a headache?"

"You woke me a few times last night with all your tossing and turning. I knew you'd be tired—and this remedy also happens to be good for clearing a foggy head."

Bronwyn placed the cup to her lips, screwing up her face. Amazingly it didn't smell too bad, and when she sipped the brew she relaxed. "This is actually not too bad."

"If we made cures taste good everyone would drink them just for fun, and we can't have that."

After breakfast, of which Bronwyn ate little, they packed up. By the time they started off, Bronwyn's headache was gone. They resumed their positions, Avruellen leading, Corrille and Bronwyn behind her, and Flux at the rear. Traffic had been building gradually over the past two days. This close to the city was busy, and the group had taken to walking by the side of the road so as not to have to jump on and off for the horses, carts, and carriages. Avruellen was tense but could sense the girls' rising excitement.

The nearer they walked, the more they could see, although at this stage it was mostly the towering wall surrounding Bayerlon. A faint outline of the structures within hinted at the city's magnificence. The buildings gradually rose above the walls as they hugged the hill that led to the castle, which overlooked all. They were close enough for Bronwyn to make out archers standing at equally spaced posts around the top of the wall. Toward the centre of the city, two golden spires gloriously interrupted the predominately grey backdrop of many buildings. Here and there, narrow trails of smoke rose up against the blue sky. Tendrils of city odours tickled her nose, although it wasn't as bad as her aunt had made out.

"Auntie, how long do those men have to stand up there?"

When the realmist looked at the city, she was reminded of the secrets she still kept from her niece, secrets that would break Bronwyn's heart but also, she hoped, bring her joy. These long-held secrets would have to be divulged one day; she was thankful that day was certainly not today, and Avruellen was relieved Bronwyn's question was easy to answer. "Which men? Oh, you mean the archers? They stand up there from dawn until dusk, when they are replaced by men who stand there from dusk to midnight, then different men stand there from midnight to dawn. Rather boring job I imagine, although I'm glad to see Edmund has been keeping up the security. We've had peace for so long, I doubt any of his army have actually been in a real war. It's easy in times like these to get complacent."

"Do you know the king?"

"Don't be silly, dear. How would I know the king? I just don't like titles. A bit pompous don't you think? Oh, don't pull faces; you would have thought I had just blasphemed. The king, whilst he is royalty, is nevertheless, only human." Avruellen turned away from the girls and kept going. She had to remind herself to be more careful. She still felt the less Corrille knew, the better.

There were things Avruellen should be teaching her niece about what could and couldn't be done in the Second Realm, but they couldn't take any chances that her friend would find out. The problem now was their enemy almost certainly knew The Circle was a great part of Talia's defence. This put them in even more danger. Avruellen had no doubt there would be large amounts of gold circulating for the capture, or worse, of anyone who claimed to practice realmistry.

They were close now and could see a large crowd jostling at the gates. The guards were yelling at everyone, trying to make a space through the centre of the mayhem. Avruellen stopped. "Girls, I think this is close enough. There seems to be some sort of commotion. We'll wait here for it to pass." She bent down to talk to Flux, mind to mind. *Go and have a look, but when you've finished I'm afraid you'll have to stay out here. If anything would stand out in the city, it's a fox. We could all use a night in a proper bed for a change, and I'm meeting with Hermas tonight. I'll speak to you in the morning.* Flux nuzzled her cheek and trotted off.

"What was your aunt doing?"

"Just saying goodbye to Flux. I suppose foxes and cities don't really go together too well."

"How does he understand what she wants when she doesn't even speak to him?"

Bronwyn wasn't about to divulge the nature of a creatura. "Ah, yes, well, he's well trained. Didn't you see her hand gestures?"

"No."

"Well, you just have to know what you're looking for. Anyway, who cares about some silly fox; we're about to go into Bayerlon." Both girls grinned and had to force themselves not to start running toward the gates.

Flux found himself a spot a few feet from the gates, under a dark blue carriage whose occupants were waiting for entrance into Bayerlon. The carriage had been forced off the road by the guards and was sitting to one side of the gates. Flux crouched low and could see the entrance to the city through the large spokes of the wheel.

One of the guards shouted for everyone's attention. "All make way for Prince Leon. All make way for the prince to pass." Flux relayed the information to Avruellen. With the crowd waving, cheering and straining to see the prince, no one noticed the small red fox sneak from under the carriage and head for the distant trees.

A bugle sounded, drawing the girls' attention toward the city. Soldiers on well-groomed horses were passing through the gates three abreast. They sat tall and proud in their saddles, surveying the crowd, protecting their prince. At the head of the second group of soldiers was a fair-haired man who waved and smiled at the people. Prince Leon wore a bright-red coat, gold fabric adorning the shoulders, gold buttons shining in the sun. He rode a large, white, imperious beast that pranced whilst walking. As he drew closer, Bronwyn could see the jewels on his sword handle glinting in the sun. She couldn't help but be impressed, as she had never seen anyone that grand before.

"Aunt, who is that?"

"That, my dear, is Prince Leon, third in line to the throne. He's quite impressive in that outfit, although the sword handle looks somewhat impractical. If you ran out of money on the road, it would come in handy. I'm sure it would buy a decent feed." They all laughed.

"He's single, isn't he?" Corrille enquired

"Trust you to think of that. As if he would marry a nobody like one of us. He has to marry a beautiful princess from another place." Bronwyn's answer did nothing to displace Corrille's dreamy expression.

The prince took his time lapping up everyone's adoration. He eventually passed not far from their group. He smiled at the two attractive young girls and the lady whose face was turned to the ground as she curtsied. "Did you see that, Bron? He smiled at me."

"Yeah, and he smiled at everyone else too."

Corrille frowned at her friend and hit her on the arm.

"Where are your manners, girls? You should curtsey for a member of the royal family." Bronwyn and her friend reddened at their mistake.

By the time the rest of his party passed, the air was filled with dust. Avruellen turned to the girls. "OK, we'd best get going. It could take a while for that line to pass through. Hold each other's hands; I don't want us to get separated." Avruellen grabbed her niece's hand and led the way into Bayerlon.

10

The large crowd jostled Bronwyn through the gates. She gripped her companions' hands as though her life depended on it. Unused to the proximity of so many people at once, not to mention the abundance of body odour, her excitement turned to fear, and she felt queasy. She was trying to move with the crowd, but people behind her were in more of a hurry and were pushing, shoving, and treading on the back of her feet. At one point she tripped and was only held up by Avruellen. If she had fallen, the crowd would have trampled her like a forgotten napkin after a feast. Once through the gates, Avruellen pulled them abruptly to the left. They had to push through people to find a small space of relative calm.

They reluctantly released hands once they had gathered their breath. Bronwyn and Corrille looked around, trying to see everything at once. The smells were indeed strong, but there were some nice ones mixed in with the others Bronwyn had been warned about. If she turned her head to the left, sewerage assaulted her nose, to the right she smelled freshly baked bread and biscuits. People were everywhere; some rushing into the city, some bravely squeezing their way out against the flow. A long queue had built from the delay caused by the prince's departure, and now everyone was trying to make up for lost time.

It took Avruellen only moments to get her bearings. She hadn't been to Bayerlon for many years. She had lived here long ago for more time than she cared to remember. She would start by finding a room for the night. They were at the bottom end of town, literally and socially. Any visitor to the city was greeted by basic accommodation, which progressively improved the further up the hill one walked. Generally, proximity to the castle dictated how affluent one was: the closer you were, the better; the further down the hill the less affluent, the more effluent.

A gravity-fed waste system serviced the city. Many houses were equipped with underground pipes, which travelled further than the city's walls. The poorer houses, on the other hand, let things travel as they would, down the road. Many an unwary person had suffered a bucketful of stinking slop dumped on their shoes by an impoverished inhabitant who didn't particularly care. Avruellen kept to the middle of the road as they wandered up the gradual incline.

As they walked, hand in hand, Bronwyn and her friend saw more of the great city. There were indeed women in beautiful dresses, although at this end of town they were outnumbered by woman who wore little better than tattered cloth. Grimy children clad in rags ran around on bare feet.

"Aren't they cold? Where are their shoes?"

"They've never had any. Don't worry, I'm sure they're used to it."

"That sounds awfully mean, Auntie. Doesn't it bother you that they're so poor?"

"You were always the sensitive one. Yes, it does bother me, but I've seen much worse. The king can't look after everyone. There are just too many people.

There used to be a time when each poor family was given a loaf of bread, eggs, and oats every week, but it's been such a long time since I was here last, I have no idea if that still happens. I promise you, if we are ever in a position to help these people, we will. You must understand though, that whilst some of them are truly unfortunate, some just don't care and wouldn't do a day's honest work whether you paid them or not."

"Well, I guess if they don't want to work they shouldn't get anything. But why should their children suffer?"

"I don't know. Can we stop talking about this? I have enough trouble worrying about the three of us, let alone the rest of the city."

"Come on, Bron, just enjoy the experience. Look, there aren't any more poor people up here." Corrille pointed at neatly dressed men and women.

The houses around them had changed from those of a shantytown to more respectable dwellings. Bronwyn wanted to say that just because they couldn't see any poor people, didn't mean they didn't exist. She managed to keep her mouth shut and tried to appreciate the growing beauty of the city as they left the poorer districts behind.

About halfway to the castle Avruellen turned right, into a narrow, cobbled street. She stopped in front of a three-level, grey-blue stone terrace house. They walked up four stairs to the tiled veranda. The sign out the front announced "Evelyn's Comfortable Inn." They entered directly into the serving room.

Avruellen seated the girls at a table near the fire and approached a highly polished slab of timber that doubled as the bar. The girl behind the counter was dipping tankards into a newly-opened cask of wine. "Be with you in a minute." She rushed away with the drinks but promptly returned. "What can I do for you?"

"Does Evelyn still own this place?"

"Yes, but she's out at the moment. I'm in charge when she's not here. My name's Bethwyn."

"Hello Bethwyn, I'm Avruellen. I would like a room for the night for me and my two girls." Avruellen nodded toward their table.

"Shouldn't be a problem. I think we've got three left. Do you want one with or without a view?"

"Does one cost more than the other?"

"No."

"I'll take the view then." Avruellen paid a deposit to reserve one room.

Bethwyn led them to the top floor. Their room had an expansive view over the city and out to fields beyond, where small white and grey dots grazed. They could see a shadow of the Semmern ranges in the distance. The room was large. The white-painted timber floors, pale blue walls, and four neatly made single beds, lent the room a homey feel. A washbasin stood in one corner and a small table draped with a blue cloth in the other. Although the room was clean and well presented, Avruellen pulled back the sheets to check for bedbugs. She nodded and replaced the covers. "We'll leave our things here. Our hands will be full enough when we come back from the markets."

The markets were near the bottom of town. The location was for the convenience of farmers and traders due to their position near the main gates. The richer citizens of Bayerlon could attend smaller markets toward the middle of the city, where the produce was more expensive. The tight-fisted, rich households sent a servant to the larger markets to get the day's groceries.

Because of the steep return journey up the hill, fully laden with goods, this duty usually fell to the most junior staff.

On the way down, Avruellen walked slowly so the girls could have a look around. "If, by any chance, we're separated at the markets, go straight back to the inn. It's easy to find; just follow this main road. It runs straight through the city. When you get to Middle Street, turn right and you'll eventually see 'Evelyn's'." Bronwyn noticed the main street was planted on either side with large hedges. The city was emerging from winter. The sleepy trees had been trimmed and were ready to awaken and sprout new shoots. Bronwyn imagined the boulevard would look spectacular in summer. The houses were mostly terrace style at this end of the city and there was limited space for gardens. Now and then, a couple of terraces were missing from the row, and in their place sat tranquil breathing spaces—well-tended parks and gardens—which Bronwyn found almost irresistible.

Bronwyn's nose was becoming accustomed to the city odours, however, as they neared the markets, she could smell rotting food among other things. "Is it safe to buy food here? It smells awful."

"The goods for sale will be fresh; don't worry. There's no market on a Sunday, which is the day the old food is cleared away. The farmers take most of it back home to feed the pigs and gardens."

"I'm glad I'm not a pig then, Auntie."

Avruellen laughed. The girls followed Avruellen around the markets as she bought things they would need for the days ahead. Bronwyn would have asked where they were going, but she didn't know much of the world, and was sure Avruellen would tell them soon anyway. The girls quickly found their arms laden with purchases. When they couldn't carry any more, Avruellen led the girls back to the Inn. "We'll buy the food tomorrow, on our way out of town. There's no use carrying it up and back again." The girls were enthusiastic in their agreement.

By the time they had packed the things away in larger bags, everyone was hungry. Afternoon shadows slanted across Middle Street as they ate lunch. Afterward, they made a trip up the hill to a seamstress and cobbler. Bronwyn and Corrille had fun trying things on. One of the shirts Bronwyn tried had voluminous sleeves and gaudy patterns that made her look like a court jester. They had never seen a shop with so many different styles of clothes. They each bought travel clothes that consisted of pants, shirts, new boots, and waterproof coats. Bronwyn was surprised at how good her Aunt looked in the outfit; she had never seen her in pants before. Bronwyn had only ever had one pair of trousers, which she wore when participating in sword lessons, but they were worn out, so she had left them at home.

The city streets were more shadow than light by the time they finished. When they reached the Inn, Avruellen requested baths for the two girls. "Why aren't you having one, Miss Avruellen?" Corrille liked to question everything; it was her small way of rebelling.

"I have to go and buy some horses. I'll have my bath when I return. I expect you two to stay here and wait for me. Do not, under any circumstances, leave this inn. Am I understood?" She arched an eyebrow.

"What if it catches fire?"

"Well, Corrille, I obviously expect you to use your common sense. If you leave here and it is not a life and death situation, there will be one when I find you." Avruellen stared hard at the girl. Corrille didn't answer. "Bronwyn, I'm leaving you in charge while I'm gone. Don't disappoint me."

Avruellen returned well after dark. She smiled to discover she had been obeyed. The girls had bathed, eaten, and were preparing for bed. They were yawning and Bronwyn's eyes were half closed. Avruellen answered a few of their questions about the horses, then went to take a bath. They would all wear their new pants tomorrow—their dresses being extremely dirty and requiring so many repairs that Avruellen instructed the innkeeper to burn them.

After dinner, Avruellen went upstairs to check on the girls. They were asleep. She returned downstairs and asked Bethwyn to make sure her charges stayed put. Avruellen left to meet with Hermas. The street lamps had been lit and the night was clear. Avruellen was attired against the cold in her new, soft coat, but she found the smell of treated leather, reminding her of the original, living animal that had died for her warmth, offensive. She knew the animal would have been killed for the meat, not the leather, however that was small comfort. In any case, it kept her warm. She instinctively knew the streets and alleyways of this large city, so found her way easily in the dimly lit environment.

It was too dangerous for them to meet at the castle, so Avruellen made her way to a large house in the rich quarter. She went to the rear servants' entrance. The owner was a deeply religious man who practiced as a medical physician. He was well known for his dislike of realmists. They hoped it would be the last place anyone would think of to place spies. Agmunsten had tutored the good doctor in the secrets of the Realms. Some of his miraculous medical cures could only be attributed to magic, however, the doctor was the only one to know that. The Circle needed eyes and ears throughout the world, and it was wise to have people whom everyone would least suspect.

Avruellen found the back door ajar and entered quietly, passing through a large storeroom and into the warm kitchen. Two candles brightened the gloom and cast soothing yellow light around the room, illuminating the head cook, who was baking for the next morning. She puffed as she vigorously kneaded the dough on a well-worn wooden table. She didn't say anything to Avruellen; the staff were trained to keep to themselves. As far as anyone knew, Avruellen was here to collect medicine for her sick husband.

Hermas was known to the house staff as the doctor's faithful, sometime assistant, who would stay up late for emergencies such as this, so the doctor didn't have to. No one at the castle missed the queen's *senile* friend on the three nights a week he came here. Everyone just expected that crazy old Hermas had gone to bed early. When there was nothing to do, he and the doctor played cards and reminisced about times when Edmund's father was king. These social engagements were always warded. If an enemy had managed to gain employment in the house, Hermas's deception would have been discovered and his host would have been under suspicion as having links with The Circle.

Avruellen left the kitchen by the door to the dining hall. Her old friend, Hermas, held a solitary candle, which he placed on the table. He held out his arms. Avruellen embraced him with all her strength. "Careful, you'll squeeze my dinner out."

She let go and stood back to look at him. It had been eighteen years since they had seen each other. Avruellen took in the white hair and stooped posture. Her smile faded. "You're looking older."

"You haven't changed. Don't look so sad, I'm OK. My hair's not really as white as it looks. I bleach it. I have to cultivate a certain image you know."

Her smile returned. "How is everyone?"

"They're all good. Gabrielle's daughter has grown into a lovely young lady. She takes after her mother." Hermas knew Avruellen missed them, and wasn't surprised to see her eyes glistening.

"I saw that cretin, Leon, leave the city today. What was that about?"

"He claims to have had an invitation to meet King Suklar to ascertain the suitability of a match between himself and the princess."

Avruellen shook her head.

"Yes. I know. The interesting thing is that Edmund is starting to have doubts about his beloved brother. I try to drop the occasional hint, but his eyes are usually closed to anything negative being suggested about Leon. Anyway, he's sent Pernus to keep an eye on things. You should have seen Leon try to hide his anger at that announcement."

Avruellen allowed herself a small laugh at Leon's displeasure. She had known him as an infant and teenager. He hid his character well, but Avruellen knew the true Leon. She saw his jealousy, dishonesty, and sadism. Avruellen had been the one to beat his backside to a pulp when she had found him stabbing a squirrel with iron skewers he had fashioned himself. The only thing she could do for the squirrel was kill it quickly to put it out of its misery. When she'd done that, Leon had complained she had robbed him of the pleasure. She shuddered at the memory.

"How's your young protégé? Will she be up to the task?"

"Bronwyn's well. She's grown into a strong-willed young woman. We've had more than a few arguments."

"Sounds like someone else I know."

"Now who in the world would that be?" The friendly banter was just like old times.

"Does she know about her parents?"

"Not yet. Agmunsten thought we should wait. It would upset her too much, and she might abandon what we're doing. We can't afford anything to get in the way now. This is our only chance."

"But she'll have to be told eventually. You know what the prophesies say: We all have to go to the battle with full knowledge of ourselves and our heritage."

"There's still time, Hermas. We have a couple of things to do before we're ready for that. I noticed Edmund still guards his capital as his father taught him."

"Yes. I made sure I drummed that into him as he was growing up. After his father died, he followed everything I suggested—and still does. We'll be as prepared as we can be, when the day comes."

They took a moment to look at each other. Hermas handed the realmist a very small piece of quartz. Inside the clear stone was a fossilised drop of blood. The quartz had one jagged end. Hermas held the other half in trust. Avruellen knew the significance of the stone and placed it inside the gold locket at her throat.

They faced each other. Hermas held Avruellen's soft hands in his. "I hope we meet again soon. Keep Bronwyn safe." He hugged his life-long friend.

"Oh, I almost forgot. We've got one of Bronwyn's friends with us. Her name's Corrille. She was running away from home when she caught up with us. She doesn't know what we're doing, and I plan to keep it that way. I'm not sure she can be trusted. Can you do some digging around and see what you can find out?"

"You can always count on me. I'll let you know." They kissed each other's cheeks. After Avruellen left, Hermas extinguished the candle and made his way back to the castle.

Avruellen had one last errand to run before she returned. She took a trip to an armourer renowned for exquisite work. She knew she would find the craftsman and his apprentices hard at work—being the best armourer in Bayerlon ensured he was always busy. Working well into the night was the only way he could keep up with the constant orders. It was about time Bronwyn had a quality sword. They had left her old, battered one at the cottage. It wouldn't hurt for them all to have their own daggers either.

The next morning the girls jumped out of bed early and ate a freshly prepared breakfast. Bronwyn felt refreshed and clean for the first time since leaving her home. Whilst they waited for Avruellen to settle the bill, Corrille questioned her friend. "Did you know your aunt went somewhere last night? She got back late."

"She said she had to meet with someone. Remember? I think it was an old friend or relative or something. She used to live here you know."

"Yeah. I was just curious. Do you trust her to keep us safe? I mean, we don't even know where we're going. She could be taking us to our deaths for all we know."

"Don't be so dramatic. Of course I trust her, and besides, you don't have to be here. It was your choice." Bronwyn felt bad as soon as she said it.

"Some choice. Do you want me to beat you so you can see what it feels like?"

"No. I'm sorry. Look, all I can tell you is that my aunt will do everything in her power to keep us safe. It's not like we're starving, and she just bought us some really nice clothes." Corrille nodded, but Bronwyn could tell she was still suspicious of Avruellen. She could sense the two of them didn't trust, or even like, each other and naively wished everyone could just be friends. Bronwyn loved both of them and wasn't about to take sides. They would both have to learn to get along.

The first stop in the morning was to pick up Bronwyn's surprise. Avruellen took the girls to the shop she had visited the previous night. "Why are we here, Auntie?"

"I have a surprise, just something I ordered last night." They went in and were greeted by Fingus, the proprietor. "Good morning, ladies."

"Good morning, Fingus. Are they ready?"

"Yes, Miss Avruellen. I stayed up all night to make sure they were what you wanted."

"Thank you, Fingus, you're a real gem." The blacksmith smiled. Not only had he made the customer happy, he had received a good amount of money to do so.

He disappeared out the back to collect the items. When he brought them in and laid them on the counter, the girls gasped. "Wow, they're beautiful." Bronwyn was studying the various handles. They were all ornately finished.

Fingus addressed Bronwyn. "Pick up the sword and see how it feels."

"Are you sure?"

He nodded. Bronwyn gripped the hilt and lifted it off the counter. She took a few steps into the middle of the room and assumed her fighting stance. The sword felt good. It was lighter than the one she was used to, and the grip was perfect.

Avruellen watched her niece, pleased to see she was impressed. "So, you like it?"

"Yes, it's beautiful."

"It's for you." Bronwyn stopped mid-parry.

"Are you joking?"

"No, it's really for you. I think you've earned it. Unfortunately, you might need it in the not-too-distant future. I expect you to take good care of it."

"I will, Auntie. Thank you, thank you, thank you!" Her smile was broad, however Corrille looked on with a touch of jealousy.

"Now, Bronwyn, put that away. I have something else." Fingus handed Bronwyn the scabbard. Avruellen indicated both girls should take a dagger. They were also exquisitely worked and this time Corrille smiled as well. "Thank you, Miss Avruellen. It's beautiful. No one has ever given me anything this wonderful before. It must be worth a fortune."

"Almost. I'm glad you like it." Avruellen picked up her own dagger, which she had to admit was frivolous but impressive, compared to the one she had brought with her. Amidst the ornate silverwork was a large ruby. She hadn't had a beautiful weapon for years and thought it was about time she treated herself. Three happy women departed Fingus's premises that morning.

As they made their way to the markets for the last time, Bronwyn wondered how she was going to carry such a heavy pack, then remembered they were going to ride horses. She loved horses but hadn't ridden much. Most animals she came across liked her, or so she surmised. She felt an affinity for animals that led her to feel more comfortable with them than with some humans. Seeing the poverty in a big city only reinforced the fact that man was selfish and more beastly than the so-called beasts of the animal kingdom.

By the time Avruellen bought all the food they would need, the stitching on their packs was straining with the pressure. The last stop within the city was the horse sale yards. The horses Avruellen had purchased were in the stables at the back of the property. Bronwyn jumped up and down when she saw the animals saddled and waiting, although she wrinkled her nose at the smell of the enclosed area. Avruellen approached a black horse whose coat was not unlike the colour of her hair. She indicated Bronwyn's was the dark brown and Corrille's the reddish brown.

Bronwyn grinned, rushed to the magnificent animal and stroked his nose. "I think I'll call you Prince. I've always wanted my own prince."

"Very funny, Bronny. I think I'll call my horse 'Horse'."

"Oh, Corrille, that's not very imaginative."

"I like it, and I think it's better than 'Prince.' That sounds childish." Bronwyn rolled her eyes and made every effort to hold her tongue; her aunt would have no hesitation in punishing them if they got into another argument.

Avruellen showed them how to attach their packs to their saddles. They led the horses outside, and Avruellen mounted. The stable-hand had to assist the girls. Bronwyn was very comfortable in her new clothes and couldn't imagine trying to ride whilst wearing a dress. She felt very high off the ground. "What happens if I fall off?"

"You'll hurt yourself. Just try to stay on. If you want the horse to stop, lean back in the saddle and pull the reins toward you. If you want to go faster give him a little kick in the ribs."

"I don't want to hurt him."

"You won't. If you want to change direction, gently tug the rein on the same side as you want to turn, and kick with the opposite foot. If we have to gallop, hold on tight with your legs. When we're walking, hold the reins loosely. The horses should follow each other."

Satisfied they had the basics, Avruellen made her way toward the city gates. As they rode through, Bronwyn turned and waved goodbye to Bayerlon. She had spent such a short time there, but the city felt as if it could be home. She remembered back to when Avruellen told her she would find another home one day, and now felt it could be the truth. She still missed the cottage, and her other friends in the village, but appreciated how moving on could also be fun.

She wondered where her parents had lived. She had always assumed they had all lived in, or near, the village in which she had grown up. The more she thought about it though, the more she realised no one had ever spoken about her parents, or professed to have known them. That was strange if they had lived nearby. Maybe they were from somewhere else, maybe even from Bayerlon. Bronwyn halted her line of thinking. It was crowding her head with questions and she wanted to enjoy the day, not feel sad.

After exiting the city, Avruellen guided her horse to the south. "We'll take it slow today. Your bottoms will be very sore for the next few days, and I don't want to have to listen to too much whingeing."

"We won't whinge. We're not babies you know." Corrille sat straight-backed in her saddle. Avruellen smiled but gave no response.

"Where are we headed, Auntie?"

"Pollona. It will probably take nine or ten days, depending on the countryside and the weather."

"Isn't that dragon country?" Bronwyn was scared; she'd heard some nasty stories about dragons and their insatiable appetite for humans.

"It's on the border. Don't worry. You two are too skinny to satisfy a dragon; they prefer fatter people." Avruellen managed to keep a straight face. "Since you girls are so grown up and tough, I think we can pick up the pace a bit." She knew she would regret it later, as she hadn't been in the saddle for a long time, but nudged her horse into a trot anyway. At least the girls would be too busy concentrating to complain.

Avruellen sent her mind voice to Flux. He joined them not far from the city. Avruellen gave him the news from her meeting with Hermas and reminded him they both had to be on the lookout for danger. Avruellen had felt safer in the city. If someone were looking for their symbols, they would know roughly where they were, but surrounded closely by all the other symbols, their exact location within the city would be almost impossible to estimate. The feeling of being watched had abated whilst they had been inside Bayerlon's walls. Now, however, they were riding into sparsely inhabited countryside. She felt like a very obvious target—and there was nothing she could do about it.

Avruellen had to fight the urge to turn the horse around and gallop back into the relative safety of the city. She stayed her course; there was no choice.

11

Zim strode along one of the lower hallways of Vellonia. His claws clicked on the tiles. There was a lot to prepare before everyone arrived—including making sure the city's defences were secure. He reached the room known as the heart of Vellonia. Zim used Second Realm power to open the door, forming intricate strings of the energy into a key that would open the lock also made with the same flows. He was one of only three dragons who knew how to create this key; Symbothial and his mother were the only other dragons permitted to know.

The door opened, and Zim felt heat wash over him, a crimson glow reflecting in his eyes. The room was not large by dragon standards and would have felt crowded if ten of them had decided to visit at the same time. The earth floor pulsed with Talia's lifeblood, and Zim felt the hum of natural power as it vibrated up through his feet.

Zim shut the door, walked toward the centre of the room and stood between two pillars—one obsidian, one blood-red. The pillars were as thick as a dragon's belly and cold to touch, until one started to draw power through them. These were portals that linked the earth power from Talia to energy from the Second Realm. The two energies couldn't mix until a realmist placed their hands on the pillars and became the link by inviting both flows into their body. Neither the realmists, nor the dragons, had worked out what the combined power could do, aside from charging the spires that protected Vellonia from Gormon attacks from the skies. The potential for drawing too much power and causing a disaster, or killing yourself, was too high for anyone to want to experiment.

Zim wasn't here to draw any power, just to check whether their defences were properly sustained. It was his cousin, Symbothial's, job to check that the spires were always active, but Zim hadn't seen him around much lately. He had decided to come and check for himself rather than remind his cousin of his duty.

He placed his hands on the obsidian pillar, which was the link to the Second Realm, and sent his awareness inside the stone to find the narrow rivers of power that travelled through it. He found the central river, and followed it to every stream that flowed off it. Each small stream powered one spire. He was annoyed to find that two of the rivulets were dry; the energy had been blocked at the river.

The power contained inconsistent particles—some were big, some were small, some moved fast, and some slow. Sometimes more delicate uses of the power could be affected by these differences, and in this case, some of the larger particles were clogging up the entry to the streams. Zim diverted some power from the river to move the larger particles and dissolve the blockages. When he was finished, all the spires were operational, but he was unhappy. He had trusted Symbothial to do his job. Zim went to look for his cousin.

Instead of asking other dragons where Symbothial was, he scried for his symbol in the Second Realm. This was a method of last resort, because finding someone by locating their symbol was akin to spying. Zim didn't have the time or patience to chase him all over Vellonia today. He closed his eyes and sifted through the bright signs in the Second Realm.

Zim approached his grey cousin, who was sitting on a bench seat under a milky-barked tree. The branches were peppered with green buds, nature's first whisper of spring. "Greetings, cousin," Zim said, and sat next to Symbothial.

"Greetings, cousin." Symbothial inclined his head. Neither dragon spoke for a moment, and Zim felt that his cousin was deliberately trying to annoy him.

"So, Symbothial, I was checking the spires today and found that two were inactive."

Symbothial narrowed his eyes. "And what are you saying?"

"What do you think I should say? I am simply stating a fact. The other fact I wish to state is that it's your job to make sure we are protected. All the time."

"I checked them two days ago and they were fine, *cousin*."

Zim could see his cousin's resentment and didn't wish to make it worse. "I'm sure you did, Symbothial, but the flow was blocked. It was a simple matter to fix. I think we should check them every day, just to be sure. Can you do that for me, please?"

Symbothial nodded but didn't bid farewell when Zim walked away. Zim wondered if it were time to entrust the job to someone else, but couldn't think longer on the matter. He was to meet with his parents and was already late. His mother didn't like tardiness. He started to jog.

12

A week had passed since the attack. Blayke had recovered from the shock, but nightmares still invaded his sleep. He had come to the realisation that if they were to survive to defend Talia, he would have to take other men's lives. Arcon had discussed ways of drawing power from the Second Realm to either kill or distract. Blayke made sure he knew how to kill, but was more curious about ways to distract and slow their enemy. If he could avoid taking another man's life, he would. Arcon tried to explain that they would end up with scores of people after them if he left them alive, but Blayke didn't want to listen. Deep down Blayke knew, but wasn't ready to admit to what he must become.

Blayke's other discovery since "that day" (as he now thought of it), was that he had picked up a travelling companion. The brown and white rat he had saved in the barn had hidden himself in Blayke's pocket after the attack. When Blayke discovered his uninvited passenger, he wasn't sure if he should try to leave him behind. He had brought up the subject with Arcon, who was curious to meet the small animal. Blayke handed him to Arcon, who was able to converse with him. It seemed this rat was destined for greater things. Arcon suggested Blayke take care of the creature and make sure Phantom didn't make a meal of him.

So it was, as they walked, Blayke carried the rat he had come to call Fang. He thought it was funny, and Fang seemed to like the name too. Fang slept in Blayke's pocket or sat on his shoulder, beady orbs observing their surroundings as the miles passed. Blayke found it comforting to have another pair of eyes to watch for danger, even if they were small.

The days were growing warmer, however the nights remained chill. They were walking through relatively flat grazing country, which spread out toward the north from the base of the Varsian Mountain ranges. Black and white sheep, together with eons-old granite boulders, dotted the landscape. If Blayke looked back, he could see the blue and white smudge of mountains against the horizon. It was funny to think that less than two weeks ago they had been fighting through waist-high snow and icy winds. Blayke raised his face to the sun, relishing the penetrating warmth.

A question, which had intermittently occupied Blayke's mind since the meeting of The Circle, surfaced. "I was wondering about something. At the meeting there were two people you'd never mentioned before; Avruellen and her apprentice. Who are they?"

Arcon chose his words carefully. "Avruellen has been with The Circle for as long as I have. She is a very skilled realmist and has saved my skin quite a few times. I have never met her apprentice, but I believe she is a young girl, about the same age as you. Very promising from what Avruellen says, but like you, she has a long way to go."

"What's their mission?"

"I wouldn't know lad. Even if I did, do you really think I'd tell you?" Arcon's left eyebrow was raised as he looked at his protégé. Blayke shrugged.

Late afternoon found them choosing a campsite at a small stand of trees barely within sight of the road. As Arcon and Blayke prepared dinner, Fang scrimmaged around for seeds. He was careful not to stray too far from the humans' feet as Phantom was around, somewhere. He knew the owl had been told to leave him alone, however one did not need to be a genius to know not to trust a natural enemy. Blayke usually gave him a small tidbit from dinner, so he knew he would never go hungry. He sensed Blayke's kind nature and was looking forward to the day when he could actually talk to him. The master, who went by the name of Arcon, had explained that Blayke had not yet worked out how to communicate with animals. In the meantime, the rat communicated to Blayke through the Master.

The two realmists sat down to dinner. Fang climbed into Blayke's warm pocket and nibbled on a large crumb. "When will I learn how to communicate with Fang?"

Arcon had been waiting for this question since the rodent had joined their expedition. "Whenever you want to." Arcon looked intently into Blayke's eyes and saw his excitement and fear.

"What will I have to do? It can't be easy, can it?"

"Good, you're thinking like a realmist. No, it won't be easy. Most things worth having are hard won. The more valuable the thing, the more risk and hard work to obtain it. So, lad, when do you want to start?"

Blayke didn't trust himself to speak. Fang's furry little face peered up at him from his pocket, and Blayke sensed his eagerness. It dawned on him that he could learn some interesting things from the little animal. Fang could go where he couldn't, listen to things he wouldn't be able to, and, he hoped, relay information.

The possibilities seemed endless. They could spy on people, scare women, or even plant poison in people's food, if they had to. Blayke grinned, "How about now?"

"Alright. But I will give you both this warning." Arcon looked at both his companions, the smaller of which had climbed out of Blayke's pocket and was now sitting on his knee. "You must both understand that what you are about to undertake is dangerous. I can't tell you what you will encounter, but the consequences of failure are as real as in this world. If you manage to survive, you will have a lifelong bond that neither of you can break. Fang, you will have an unnaturally long life for a rat, or a human for that matter, and there may be times you want it to end. You cannot kill yourself—the Second Realm will not allow it—and if either of you dies for any other reason, it will result in months, even years of mental and emotional anguish for the other. Are you ready for this burden?" Arcon looked expectantly at them and knew, as they did, they had no choice. The Three Realms (if that was how many there really were) commanded this for their very survival. They both nodded gravely at Arcon. He insisted on their verbal affirmation, which for Fang was a loud squeak.

They placed their plates on the ground. Arcon asked Blayke to lie on his back, hands by his sides. Fang was instructed to sit on Blayke's chest. The rat was shaking, but Blayke didn't notice as he was almost in a trance, breathing slowly and deeply, picturing the starry Second Realm. Fang shut his eyes. Arcon sent him an image of the Second Realm and showed him the path. The rat followed.

Arcon stood over two still bodies, eyes open, mind in tune with their journey. Phantom had materialised and watched unblinking from a nearby branch. He knew the gravity of what his companions would experience, having done it himself scores of years earlier. He hooted softly in protest, knowing that once this was done, there would be one less rat in the world he could eat.

Blayke journeyed through the dark, still tunnel—the only access to the Second Realm. He followed Arcon's lead and didn't notice the subtle turning from the usual path. When they emerged, it was not into the expected starry universe, but to an inky blackness. Blayke was scared and uncertain; the place they had come to was unfamiliar. He lost sight of Arcon, who was already on his return journey to Talia. His unease increased until he felt the presence of Fang next to him. In this space they were not the bright symbols Blayke knew in the Second Realm, but were invisible, nothing. He could only sense the rat, not see him. He could also feel Fang's fear, albeit mixed with his natural rodent curiosity.

Light started to seep from the horizon, slowly creeping through the darkness toward them, encompassing all in its path. The swollen river of light gathered speed as it approached. They felt overwhelming dread as it washed closer. They didn't know what to expect when it reached them and felt awe at what they could see in its wake. Rolling green hills stretched out behind the wave, azure sky above. The clarity of light was amazing—the most pure light imaginable. Blayke expected to be burnt when it reached them. Soon they were enveloped in the swell of light. The brilliance swirled around, above, beneath them, blinding the human and rodent.

No sooner than breaking over them, the wave washed past, leaving two vulnerable figures swaying, trying to regain their balance. Blayke felt different, and it took him a few moments to realise why. A heightened sense of smell overwhelmed him, and his viewpoint had changed. The hills in the distance had become mountains; the grass he had crushed beneath his feet moments ago was now chest high. He sat back on his haunches and looked down at himself. He looked incredulously at the dark brown fur that covered his body. He touched it with his small paw. His beady hazel eyes widened as this new reality dawned on him. He slowly shook his little pointed head. He remembered Fang and turned to meet his friend eye to eye. Fang's whiskers twitched in a cunning smile and Blayke understood every high-pitched squeak when he spoke. "Welcome to my world, Blayke."

13

The small village of Aspurle clung doggedly to the terraced cliff, which overlooked Blaggard's Bay. This was the most southwesterly port of Talia. A normally quiet locale where the men were fishermen, the women hard-working wives who mended the men's nets and pickled their catches. Nothing much happened, save the occasional wild storm claiming a boat or two. The nearest village was one week's sail to the north. The children lived an untamed existence, with sun-bleached hair, tanned skin and usually spent their days swimming in the bay or exploring the dangerous cliff faces and caves.

Irving was a happy, likable boy. He was exploring one of the caves a half-day's walk from home with Jeddy, another ten-year-old from Aspurle. The boys had grown up together and were practically brothers. The sea was too rough to swim today, so they had decided to continue an ongoing exploration of their surroundings. They had discovered the mouth of this cave some two months earlier, but until now, had not had a chance to map its tunnels and crawl spaces.

They entered the cave mouth with the anticipation that always preceded any new expedition. Each day brought the possibility of some important and long-awaited discovery. In the dry cave mouth, the sounds of the tumultuous ocean breaking on the rocks far below, and howling wind whipping up the seas, became a distant roar.

Irving assumed the lead, seeing as how he had discovered the cave. He strode confidently, leading Jeddy across the wide entrance cavern toward a tunnel, which veered off to the left. The first cavern was as tall as a full-grown man and half again. The tunnel leading from the entry, into which the boys now walked, was barely tall enough for them to stand upright. Indeed, in some sections, they were forced to stoop like old, arthritic men. The candles Irving had brought flickered uncertainly, throwing menacing shadows on the walls and low ceiling. The boys hummed a happy tune as they walked; the self-made music lessening their fear of the unknown.

The tunnel ran past various caverns that loomed either side, dark spaces impossible to see into, reminding Irving of the gap-toothed grin on his grandmother's face when he found her dead, face up, in her bed. He had loved his grandmother but had never been able to erase the image of a year ago. His mother had sent him to fetch Grammy for breakfast, but she had not been in any state to eat it. He shivered at the memory.

As they shuffled carefully, the tunnel sloped almost unnoticeably downward. Irving felt a growing need to walk faster. The passage had widened and the boys were again comfortably upright. "I'm going to go faster. Keep up 'cause I won't wait."

"K." Jeddy didn't need to be told to walk faster. He was growing more uncomfortable by the second, and there was no way he wanted to be left by himself. Their candles flickered more erratically with their increased speed, and whilst Jeddy feared they would be extinguished, his companion seemed not to notice, or care.

After travelling for what Irving estimated was about half an hour, a grotto opened up to the right of the tunnel. Irving motioned for his companion to stop. Neither boy wanted to speak and draw attention to themselves. The boys would be the last to admit they were scared, especially when they knew it unlikely that anyone else would be in there with them. Instead of looking at a black expanse, the boys could see inside this cavern. A small shaft of light cut through a crack in the rocks far above. Irving thrust his candle inside the space to get a better look. It seemed dry and boring, just like the rest of the cave had been so far. He tentatively stepped in, the candlelight barely touching the ceiling.

The shaft of light caught his eye. He followed the line of light toward a sparkling rock, which sat directly in front of where he had entered the cave. Instead of the light falling on the rock, it appeared to be coming from the rock and heading to the ceiling. This anomaly interested Irving. He was not going anywhere until he had investigated.

Jeddy stayed at the mouth of the grotto, clenching his sweaty hands together, quietly watching his friend. "I think we should go. It feels wrong."

"Don't be silly. You're just a scared little baby. If you want to go back, be my guest, but you won't be able to share any treasure I find. Look at the beautiful light, it's coming from the rock over there." Irving turned back to the shaft of light.

Jeddy looked, but the light didn't look beautiful to him. The light was a sickly yellow, which oozed against gravity toward the rocky surface above.

He denied his fear. "I'm not scared! OK, I'll stay. It still feels wrong, though." Jeddy let his voice trail off into the silence.

Irving had already forgotten his friend. His transfixed eyes followed the pallid luminosity to its origin behind the rock. The urge to reach the light had taken hold of him. He hurriedly climbed over the rock, scraping his knees and dripping hot wax on his hand, all of which went unfelt.

Jeddy could still see his friend from the waist up. He had stopped and was looking down at his feet. "I've found something." He bent down and Jeddy lost sight of him.

Irving knelt on the hard, rock floor, mouth agape and whispered, "Wow." He hesitated before gently picking up the object and cradling it in his thin arms.

Jeddy suddenly felt cold and hugged his arms around himself. "Irving? Are you OK? What is it?"

Irving stood and turned to look at his friend. "Look what I found. Isn't it the most beautiful thing you've ever seen?" Irving, in his rapture, didn't see the look on his friend's face for what it was. Absolute terror.

The young boy was holding the skull of a long-dead creature, one that almost no one on Talia would recognise today. The large skull was at least two metres long. It was from an infant of a long-disappeared species. The diseased glow leached from two diamond shaped eye sockets and a wide, sharp-toothed maw that Jeddy noticed had not one, but two rows of teeth. It reminded him of the sharks his father sometimes caught. Dry, leathery skin flaked off bone as Irving softly caressed the repulsive specimen. Sharp barbs cut deep into his hands, drawing blood.

As Jeddy watched, horribly paralysed by the sight, the oozing light redirected itself and surrounded Irving. The light dribbled over the young, innocent boy, crawling into every orifice, pervading his body. Eventually the light ceased its slithering invasion, now encasing the boy. The skull disintegrated into dust, and Irving stood transformed.

Jeddy screamed. Time moved slowly; it felt like an eternity in which he was paralysed in the presence of pure evil. He stopped screaming and ran.

Irving's newly yellow eye sockets emanated a palpable malevolence. Irving, as his mother and friends had known him, was no longer there. What used to be Irving looked around the now dark cave. It could see in the dark and didn't need light; in fact, light rendered it almost blind. It grinned, smelling the fear from the retreating human child. It was happy to know a feed was imminent. The alien creature ordered its newly acquired, short, human legs to move, and ran after Jeddy.

Jeddy was running as fast as he could without light. The candle clenched in his fist had gone out. He was breathing hard, his nostrils burning with damp, musty cave air. He had no idea where the creature— for he didn't consider it to be his friend anymore—was. That thought made him retreat faster. All too soon the passage narrowed. Where he should have bent down, he instead slammed his head on the rough surface. The boy slumped to the floor in a moment of stupefaction. Unfortunately for him, he was only momentarily unconscious.

Jeddy opened his eyes and in the darkness saw nothing. He opened his eyes wider in a futile attempt to see. He couldn't hear anything over his own ragged breathing. Suddenly, overpoweringly, a putrid odour slithered into his nostrils. He scrambled on all fours in an attempt to get away from the evil he knew was coming. He could hear the creature's footsteps alter from a staccato run to a slow walk. It was only steps away. Jeddy scraped hands and knees in a desperate retreat, but the tears streaming down his face were those of fear, not pain.

Jeddy knew that whatever controlled his friend was pure malevolence. He knew he was going to die. Jeddy tried not to cry, but he was only a boy. Sallow, yellow luminescence washed over him from behind, until it was lighting the way in front of him. He couldn't crawl fast enough. Jeddy sprang to his feet. As he did so, the creature tackled him from behind. When they slammed to the floor, sharp pain shot up Jeddy's arm. He looked at it. Broken bone protruded into the tainted light, midway from wrist to elbow. Nevertheless he continued to struggle, but the small, possessed body on top of him had an unnatural strength. He couldn't break free.

The creature from the Third Realm turned Jeddy over and stared hungrily into his terrified eyes, happily licking the tears from the boy's face. Bile bubbled up to Jeddy's mouth and putrid air invaded his lungs.

He looked despairingly into yellow eyes, hoping against reality that Irving was in there somewhere. The alien's cold orbs stared back. They held no sympathy, no warmth, only cruel death. The parasite that had been his best friend ripped off Jeddy's shirt. Whilst pinning him down with one unbelievably strong arm, it sniffed his torso. Jeddy felt warm saliva drip onto his skin. He wriggled in one last attempt to escape his fate. The young boy watched in dread as the creature opened its mouth and tore a large chunk out of his stomach. He vomited as pain consumed his body. He said a last goodbye to his mother and father and begged the gods to protect his soul.

The raspy laughter, which left Irving's body through bloody lips, had clawed its way up from The Third Realm. It was the last sound Jeddy heard, apart from his own screams, as he was eaten alive.

The creature fed, then waited. It was the first of the colony; the others would be here soon. His mind linked to the others, and he felt their joy at his hunt. He curled his newly acquired human body into a ball and slept. Tonight he would loose himself on the world, what an honour to be the first. He would have his pick of the humans, and knew he would be the catalyst for the fear of millions, once rumours spread. He rasped another laugh. When he slept, he dreamed of the bloody atrocities he would enjoy.

***

What The Circle had feared and anticipated had begun. Agmunsten sensed a new evil on Talia and wept, for he knew what it signified. He said a prayer for whoever had died to facilitate the arrival of the Gormons. He prayed for Talia too; he knew their preparations were incomplete and they needed more time. Agmunsten wondered how the most powerful realmist on earth could feel as helpless as the smallest mouse. He shook his head and grabbed a bottle of his best brandy. Peaceful oblivion couldn't come soon enough.

14

Muted, midday light intruded through Agmunsten's eyelids. He gingerly opened his eyes, managing only a tight squint. Light found its way through his eyelashes and the small slits he had created, which was enough to accentuate his alcohol-induced headache. He had drunk himself into unconsciousness and found he was still slumped in his chair. He remembered the reason for his inebriation and was tempted to reach for another bottle.

The aches and pains in his stiff back were relatively minor to the queasy feeling rumbling around what was left of his stomach. He would have shaken his head at his youth-like stupidity, but was wary of making any sudden movements.

Focusing his will inward, pushing through the headache, he mentally called his apprentice. Within minutes a young boy appeared carrying a tray. Mouth-watering aromas of fresh-baked bread, greasy bacon, and fried eggs filled Agmunsten's nose, and even though he felt queasy, his stomach managed a grumble.

Arie was only twelve but had seen enough of the world to know his master had drunk too much, yet again. He shivered in the chill, a result of the fire having died hours ago. "It's cold in here, although I wouldn't want to light the fire again."

"Why would that be, lad?" Agmunsten mumbled through a mouthful of bacon.

"The fumes coming out of your body might cause an explosion." He laughed at the scowl he received in reply. Instead of tending the fire, Arie opened the large, arched window next to an ornately carved timber bed, unoccupied the previous night, the white covers unwrinkled. A steady, cool breeze streamed into the room, pushing out the boozy odour.

"Arie, prepare our belongings. We're going on a trip." His apprentice nodded and left the room to gather what they would need. Agmunsten felt better with every oily bite. He finished his breakfast, or was it lunch, and went to the bath house to clean up.

By late afternoon, the master and his young apprentice were eating an early, hot dinner. Agmunsten felt restless and didn't want to spend another night at the Realmist Academy for Superior Learning. He helped run the Academy, however there were times, such as now, he left it to others. From time to time he had other pressing matters to deal with, as only the most experienced of all the realmists could have. This threat to their world, and indeed ultimately to other worlds, was definitely what he would classify as a pressing matter—or maybe depressing. He smiled in spite of himself. He felt it was always important to maintain a sense of humour, not that others always appreciated what he found amusing.

The weak winter sun was retreating for another night to the west. The two Academy members mounted their horses. Agmunsten knew the intelligence of animals and treated them with respect, but wouldn't go so far as to stop eating them. He had bonded an animal when he was young, a rather obscure one. He had never told anyone about his creatura and knew the other realmists thought it odd that he didn't have one.

An uneasy peace had blanketed Talia over the past thousand years, and since Agmunsten was busy with people all the time, he had no desire to share his life with a constant creatura companion. It was because of this that Agmunsten had not had contact with his creatura for at least 200 years. He knew the animal was alive somewhere—he had a general feeling due to the mind bond, but he never intruded. It seemed to suit both of them. He knew if he ever needed him he would be there, so in the meantime, he let the animal enjoy as normal a life as possible.

Agmunsten's slight enthusiasm at going into the world again was heightened by Arie's obvious excitement. The boy had lived his first ten years in a local fishing village two days' ride from the Academy. He had spent his next two years learning anything and everything the Academy had to teach him. Agmunsten had been quick to notice the boy's genius and aptitude for delving—the word realmists used to describe their form of acting with power drawn from the Second Realm. The boy also made a good assistant. He always did what he was told, if he thought it was the best way to do it, but also had the initiative to know when he had worked out a better way. Surprisingly, Agmunsten had learned a few things too, but there had inevitably been more than a few arguments—that sometimes became an amusing game.

Agmunsten enjoyed looking at the world through the boy's eyes. After too many years on the planet, not many things were exciting anymore. The old man had been to too many places too many times and had seen multiple lifetimes of triumphs and tragedies to be surprised or inspired by much. That was the downside of living a protracted life. Watching Arie's pleasure and exhilaration as he discovered his way through life helped Agmunsten remember what it was like to feel that way.

A few of the students and teachers came to wave them off and wish them luck, although no one knew what for. Agmunsten had kept the bad news to himself, lest he start a full-blown panic among the Academy's population and eventually into the surrounding countryside. His first port of call was to Bayerlon, and King Edmund. The news he carried was too sensitive to send a messenger. He had warned Hermas by mind message that he was coming. It was a rare occurrence, but some realmists had discovered how to eavesdrop on mind communications, especially those over long distances. Being aware of this, Agmunsten had kept his message brief.

As they exited the huge iron gates, the noises in the courtyard faded. The horses' hooves rang out loudly on the cobbled road. Agmunsten smiled; it was good to smell fresh air and to have an open road ahead. Soon, billions of stars would shimmer above and a near-full moon would light their path. Agmunsten knew this was the calm before the proverbial storm, and he would enjoy every peaceful minute. He looked over at Arie and saw a hint of a smile and knew that if nothing else, their first night on the road would be a good one.

The duo slept in the open, under the gaze of uncaring stars, rolled up in blankets in front of a lively fire. They rose early the next morning, in time to bid some of their starry companions goodbye. Arie was a competent horseman and let his eyes wander over the surrounding vista as they rode. Acre after acre of farmland led away from the Academy. Sheep and cattle grazed, the occasional chicken crossed their path, and every once in a while a farmer, tending his fields, would wave. Arie smiled at the animals, deftly avoided the wandering chickens, and waved enthusiastically at every farmer. Agmunsten observed and enjoyed.

Their journey to Bayerlon took one week. They slept by the roadside. If they had veered off into every town along the way to slumber in comfortable beds, they would have added at least a couple of days to their trip. Right now, time was of the essence. Agmunsten had been trying to avoid thinking about what was happening on the other side of the world, but now that Bayerlon loomed ahead, it became impossible. He readied himself. His words to the king would have to be chosen carefully so as to impart the urgency of the matter without revealing the horror of it. The king was not a rash man, but who really knew what he would do when faced with the possibility of the bloody annihilation of his country and all the people in it?

"Bayerlon is magnificent. Wow, look. It's huge." Arie stared at the impressive castle. "Are we really going to see the king?"

"Yes."

"Is he nice?"

"Is he nice? Well, if you're a friend he's nice, but he can be a ruthless man, which is a necessary trait in a king." Arie wrinkled his brow. "Don't worry, lad, he'll be nice to us. We've known each other since before he was your age." Agmunsten chuckled. "In fact, he used to be scared of me."

"Why would he be scared of you? You're just an old man." Agmunsten gave Arie the mouth-open, offended expression the boy was looking for. Arie laughed.

They entered the city gates and Agmunsten took hold of Arie's reins. "I would hate to lose you in this crowd." Arie sighed at the suggestion he couldn't take care of himself.

"Can we have a look around? There's so much to see." Arie was trying to look everywhere at once.

"Not today. We have more urgent things to take care of." The young apprentice didn't try to hide his disappointment and scowled at Agmunsten's back on the walk up to the castle.

Even though he couldn't get off his horse to explore, there were still many things to see. By the time they reached the castle walls, in front of which stood a full compliment of stiff-backed guards in regal blue attire, Arie had forgotten his scowl. He dismounted when Agmunsten did, and stood staring up at the imposing uniformed men.

Agmunsten approached the captain. "I'm here to see King Edmund."

"Name?"

"Agmunsten, Master Realmist and Principal of the Realmist Academy for Superior Learning. I am here on an urgent matter and wish to be presented to His Highness, posthaste."

"Just a moment, sir." The Captain spoke a few words to an errand boy at the guardhouse, who dashed off to confirm the king was indeed waiting upon such a person.

Agmunsten tried to maintain his calm exterior but was annoyed at being treated like a common salesperson. How dare they question his identity? He felt enormous frustration at his lack of authority, at times, in the world outside the Academy. It was moments like this he had to remind himself that it was the realmists themselves who had tried to cultivate a non-threatening attitude. They didn't want the general population fearing what they were capable of and attacking them. They had so successfully created an image that what they did was little more than making a few healing potions and tricks of the eye using sleight of hand, that some people not only didn't fear them, but had no respect for them whatsoever. "But it seemed like such a good idea at the time." Agmunsten's shoulders drooped.

"What seemed like a good idea?"

"Nothing, Arie, just talking to myself."

"So what else is new?"

Agmunsten's shoulders fell a little further.

Soon the errand boy returned, and the captain led them through to large oak doors, which gave entry to the vast foyer of Bayerlon's castle. Once inside they were handed over to the steward. The balding man with a superior attitude said nothing as he led them through one ornately decorated corridor after another. Every once in a while he would look behind and down his nose at them, making sure they were not touching anything.

Arie wondered at the unashamed display of wealth in the hand-woven rugs covering the stone floors, to the tapestry wall-hangings exhibited in gilded frames. Ornately carved tables and plinths lined the walls, each displaying a priceless vase or statue. Arie couldn't believe this many treasures existed in the whole world, let alone in one building. At his mother's house their only wealth was contained in the two fishing boats his father owned and one rug, which took pride of place on the floor in the living room. The rug was faded and worn, having been handed down through his mother's family for three generations.

He thought about the Academy, with its spare white-washed walls and stark classrooms. The room he shared with two other boys had sea-grass matting on the floor and thin sheets on the beds. He had to admit the blankets were warm and of good quality, having been made from local wool, which was some of the best in all of Talia. He realised he didn't actually miss the Academy. He had thought he would. He still missed his home, although he'd had plenty of opportunity to return and see his family.

The silent servant halted in front of a well-guarded set of heavy, timber doors. The stone frame was ornately carved, but the timber was plain, polished as smooth as river stone. The guards consulted with baldy, who grasped an iron handle and led them through one of the doors. He motioned them to stand just inside the door and wait.

The immaculately dressed servant strode to the middle of the room and announced their arrival. "King Edmund, I present to you Agmunsten and his servant boy." Arie was even more enraged than Agmunsten had been at his insulting treatment at the castle gates.

He whispered up at his master. "I'm not your servant. How dare he!"

"This is the first of many insults you'll have to endure, so get used to it. Didn't I mention the life of a realmist wasn't an easy one?"

Arie took a deep breath and wondered if he had made the right decision to be a realmist. He supposed it wasn't too late to change his mind.

"Chin up, boy. What we're doing is vital to the whole world. Just because this lackey doesn't understand that, doesn't mean what we're doing is any less significant."

Arie nodded, feeling a little better.

They approached the king. As the steward walked past, Arie couldn't help but speak. "Thank you for being such a good little servant. You can go now."

The man opened his mouth and eyes in giant, comical O's, skin heating to red. He raised his hand in retaliation. Agmunsten stood in between the two. "I wouldn't do that if I were you. I could turn you into a pile of horse dung if I so chose."

Agmunsten conjured up a manure odour through the Second Realm from a farm just outside the Academy. He smirked as the anger in the steward's eyes turned to fear.

The realmist turned and looked down at Arie. "That was uncalled for. I'm very disappointed."

Arie's cheeks blossomed into a nice shade of pink.

The king watched the exchange without smiling and waited until his servant left. "You are an old bugger. Can't say he didn't have that coming, pretentious old git. I'll have to have a word with him about insulting my guests." The king rose from his high-backed, gilt-armed chair and stepped down the two stairs to warmly embrace Agmunsten. Arie's chest swelled with pride at the honour they were being given. He was amazed at the king's familiarity with his mentor, as he hadn't quite believed Agmunsten's claim that he knew King Edmund.

"And who is this strapping young fellow?"

"It gives me a reasonable amount of pleasure to introduce you to my partner in this journey, Arie."

Arie bowed. "It is an honour to meet you, Your Highness."

"Likewise. Any partner of Agmunsten is welcome in my castle. I think we'll retire somewhere more private. I fear the news you have for me is not of the good variety." The king dismissed those in the room and left instructions that he was not to be disturbed for the afternoon. He took his guests to the reception area in his private chambers.

Arie was again wide-eyed at the riches surrounding him. He wandered the room, looking intently at plinths which held carved crystal vases with freshly cut flowers, artworks in gilded frames, smooth marble statuettes and small, hand-blown glass figurines of sailing ships, naked women and horses. Arie carefully keep his distance lest he break something. King Edmund and Agmunsten each took a glass of mulled wine and sat in a plush leather sofa, surrounded by blue, white, and gold cushions, all bearing the royal insignia of the Laraulen family—a snow-covered oak against a blue sky.

"Edmund, I have very sensitive news, which I don't wish to impart in front of anybody." He indicated Arie.

The king rose and opened the door, "Fetch Boy immediately." The king left the door open for the moment and approached Arie. "I've sent for someone to show you around the castle. Does that sound like fun?"

Arie swapped his serious face for a huge grin. "Definitely, Your Highness. This place is huge. It could take all day to explore."

"Probably longer. Anyway, the person I've sent for seems to know this place better than me, so you should be busy all afternoon."

Arie grinned.

It wasn't long before Boy arrived. The lads were introduced. Boy, of course, would tell Leon when he got back. This was interesting news; two strangers meeting privately with the king.

"Hi, I'm Arie." He held out his hand. Boy took it and shook.

"Hi. I'm Boy. Lets go. There's heaps to show you."

"Great." The boys walked as fast as they could without running and didn't realise their rudeness at leaving the king's presence without so much as a bow.

The king smiled at their youthful disregard for authority. His smile disappeared, however, when he sat and listened to what Agmunsten had to say.

Agmunsten skirted around the subject but gave Edmund enough information to convey a sense of urgency about what actions they had to take. "I'm sorry I can't tell you everything; it might compromise our situation. I need you to come with me to Vellonia. We have to consult with as many heads of state as we can."

"Vellonia. Hmm." Edmund lifted a forefinger to his nose. "What about Brenland? How long will it take to get King Fernis to Vellonia?"

"I sent a message to Elphus. He's going to bring him. The only problem is that it would not be comfortable for either of them to travel in a conventional way." Agmunsten was alluding to the fact that both men were grossly overweight. "When we get to Vellonia we'll speak to Zim. I hope he'll be persuaded to fly them in." Edmund looked skeptical.

Dragons were uppity creatures, full of a superior attitude. One of the most insulting things one could ask a dragon would be to ride on their back. Their response would be that they were not flying horses.

If you were foolish enough to push the point, they would consider making a meal of you to show you how superior they really were. Until now, no one had ever been known to show such a ridiculous level of idiocy.

"I suppose you want to leave tonight?"

"Very perceptive, my king. You may find Hermas has quietly organised everything you'll need. I don't particularly want it known that you're leaving the city with us."

Edmund nodded. "I'm going to say goodbye to my family. I suppose Hermas knows where I'm to meet you."

"I've always said you were a brilliant man. See you tonight. If you don't mind, I'm going to help myself to your larder."

"Be my guest."

Agmunsten bowed before he left.

Edmund sat down to consider the news more carefully. He had not been told the full story, which Agmunsten readily admitted. This only made him worry more. A knot formed in his belly. Whatever was going on, he hoped his brother was not involved. Leon had been less and less of a brother over the past few months. The king had suspicions about his only sibling he was not ready to voice, yet. If his suspicions were true, he feared he would have no choice but to have Leon executed. How he could order that was a question he did not want to contemplate. Maybe the gods would be kind and spare him the decision. Wanting to stop thinking about the possibilities, he went to find his beautiful wife. She could always cheer him up, and he needed to say goodbye.

When Agmunsten finally tracked the boys down, he found them sitting in a tree in the queen's garden, eating warm meat pies. They were laughing, faces covered in food and dirt. Arie climbed down when he was spotted.

"Where in Zebla's name have you been crawling? You're one big cobweb."

Arie shrugged and spoke through a mouthful of food. "Boy took me through secret tunnels and stuff. It was so much fun."

"Sorry to break up the party, but it's time to go." Agmunsten looked into the tree. "Thanks for entertaining Arie."

Boy assumed an expression of indifference. "It was nuthin. I had fun. See ya."

He waved to his new friend who was departing his life as suddenly as he had come into it.

Agmunsten took his dirty protégé to the castle's bathing room. When he was clean, they mounted their horses and left Bayerlon. Arie looked back wistfully at the city and all the things he didn't get to see or taste. Agmunsten could read his mind, "Don't worry, lad, we'll be back soon enough."

"When?"

"I don't know. Just soon."

"That's not a very good answer you know."

"I know. Look, I guarantee you will see things on this trip that you couldn't have imagined. I haven't told you where we're going, have I?"

"No." Arie sat taller in his seat, suddenly interested.

"Vellonia, city of the dragons."

The only reply Agmunsten got was a rushed intake of breath and a "Wow." He said no more and let the boy mull over the information for a while.

The sun was low in the sky. Agmunsten led them to a large copse of trees about an hour's ride from Bayerlon. With the light almost gone, no one would be able to see them amongst the thick foliage. King Edmund would meet them after he dined with his family. They were not telling anyone of the king's departure. Edmund would feign sickness at the table. They hoped that by the time anyone realised he was gone, two or three days would have passed; enough for the trail to have gone cold. The only ones who were to know the truth were Gabrielle and Hermas. They didn't want people asking questions—any king paying a visit to Vellonia was not there for a picnic.

Agmunsten and Arie sat within the protection of the trees—Agmunsten trying not to think of how much damage the Gormon might have done by now. They knew so little about their enemy. The last time they had come to earth was long before he was alive, and few records of that time existed. The population had been too busy crawling out of the ashes of devastation to bother writing things down. Agmunsten wondered how many there were. Could there already be scores, even hundreds? His face drained of colour and he felt nauseous.

Arie, on the other hand, was lost in a pleasurable little world, remembering his day with a new friend. Boy had been shy at first and a little pretentious, because he knew the magnificent castle inside and out. Soon enough the façade had dropped, and the boys were running through secret passageways and exploring rooms filled with ancient treasures. There was lots of laughing and play; something neither boy had had much time to do in their short lives. Arie had spent the past two years studying and serving Agmunsten, whilst Boy had spent his whole life snatching playtime in between being abused by every adult who was supposed to protect him. Both boys had enjoyed each other's company and felt that each had made a new friend.

A cracking twig and rustling leaves broke the stillness. Agmunsten jumped to his feet, hands raised, just in case. He lowered his hands when he saw the king leading his horse. This time there was no bowing, just an embrace between the men. The king tussled Arie's hair and without a word they made their way to the opposite side of the clearing.

As they rode, Arie noticed the king was not wearing any special clothes—at least the heavy coat was not special. He didn't know what was underneath. The king had donned a brimless, woollen hat, which had long flaps to cover his ears. He looked like a common worker; even his horse was nothing special—a plain, brown mare. She was smaller than what you would expect a man of his size to ride, and half her left ear was missing, the only reminder of a previous fight.

The story they would use, if necessary, was that Agmunsten, his son and grandson, had previously run a small inn. One day the son of a wealthy merchant had found himself in a fight within the inn, resulting in his untimely death. The merchant, in his grief and anger, had burned down the establishment and threatened the lives of the now innless innkeepers.

Dawn came and went. The horses walked on. At lunch they veered off the road to rest and eat. Arie had been nodding off in his saddle and was very happy to slide off and lie in the grass. Edmund tended the horses whilst Agmunsten prepared a cold lunch of cheese, already cooked bacon, and bread, all from Bayerlon's well-stocked kitchens.

"Why didn't we stop in the next town, master?" Arie always had to know everything.

"This close to Bayerlon someone might recognise our travelling companion. From now on call me grandfather, and call him," he nodded toward Edmund, who was returning from the horses, "father."

"OK Grandfather." Arie smiled. He liked calling Agmunsten 'grandfather'; that's what their relationship felt like. He was quite surprised to be calling the King of Veresia 'father'. Imagine what Boy would say if he knew, and his friends at the Academy.

"Don't tell anyone about this, Arie. The less people know, the better." The boy's face fell. He wondered how

Agmunsten knew what he was thinking. He was getting to do something very exciting and wasn't allowed to tell anyone.

He pushed out his bottom lip. "OK, *Grandfather*". Arie lay on the grass and pretended to go to sleep.

Agmunsten and Edmund sat close together and spoke quietly , out of Arie's hearing. They agreed to sleep for a short while, for they had a long ride ahead and needed their wits. Agmunsten travelled the ether and found Elphus. "We're on our way. What's your situation?"

"We left yesterday, so we're still a long way behind you."

"You're going to ride?"

"We're in a very slow, bumpy carriage. At this rate we may not get to Vellonia until the whole thing is over. It would be good to hitch a ride, if you know what I mean. Anyway, have you heard anything about the situation in Blaggard's Bay?"

"Nothing has filtered through yet, which could be a good or bad thing, depending on how much has already happened. If you're asking me how much time we have before the situation becomes irretrievable, I fear I have no answer. We may have already lost."

"Chin up. We have to stay positive. I can't believe we don't have a chance. Maybe you could consult with some god or other."

"Oh yes, I'll just snap my fingers. I'm sure one of them will answer."

"It's worth a try."

"In all my years on this planet they have only ever contacted me once. Why would they interfere now?"

"I don't know. Anyway I'm going to stay positive, even if you're not. If you hear anything let me know. Bye."

Elphus cut off the connection in disappointment at his colleague's negativity. Agmunsten felt ashamed. He was not usually like this, however couldn't shake the feeling that it was already too late. He kept his eyes shut and called out to the gods. He felt justified in his attitude when he received no reply.

They rose in the late afternoon, mounted and continued. Edmund and Arie sensed Agmunsten's mood and left him alone, speaking to each other instead. Edmund told Arie about his family, and Arie spoke about both of his families; the real family and the Academy family.

"I always wondered what our money funded. I've only visited the Academy twice. I'm glad to know you're actually learning something. I was never sure if my friend over here was just taking my money and living the good life." A smiling Edmund looked over at the realmist but saw no reaction to his friendly jibe. Agmunsten was sliding into a black mood and it was anyone's guess when he would return. It was going to be a long afternoon.

15

Blayke the rat and Fang stood eye to eye. *You're not a very good looking rat; you make a better human.* Fang's whiskers twitched in mirth.

Gee, thanks. I think I liked you better when I couldn't understand you. What do we do now? They both looked around at their new world. It was a fine day—birds chirped, butterflies flew past. Blayke shrank back as the butterfly flew past—it was as big as he was.

Fang smiled as he watched Blayke's reactions. *Don't be a coward. It's only a butterfly.*

Blayke couldn't help but squeak in laughter at his predicament. Placing forepaws on the ground, he took a two steps forward to test his new way of walking. His legs seemed to know what to do. He could feel his tail dragging on the ground behind him; a strange sensation. He stopped and stood on hind legs, sniffing the air for signs of other animals. He was already feeling more comfortable in his rodent skin and found that natural instincts were taking over. Blayke turned to Fang. *Do you like being a rat?*

I don't know how to be anything else. I guess I'm happy with it. Do you like being a human?

Yes, but I might enjoy being a rat. This is meant to be a test, but I have no idea what's supposed to happen.

Maybe we should have a look around. Follow me. Fang moved towards a small rise, which would give them a better vantage point, although they would be more exposed.

It was a long walk to the top of the small grassy hill. If he had been in human form it would have been a matter of a few steps, but in rodent form it was lots and lots of very small steps. By the time they reached the top, Blayke was puffing. *It's hard work being this small. How do you cope?*

I don't know any other way. Usually I don't need to go very far. We tend to have nests near a ready source of food. I've scared my share of cooks. Blayke, I wonder if you could explain something to me. How can a creature as small as me frighten you large humans? You'd think we were made of a lethal poison the way some of your females scream and carry on. Blayke was not sure, but he sensed the rat was offended at people's reactions to him. He supposed if women reacted to him the same way, he would be offended too.

Can't help you there, Fang. I was never scared of rats or mice, and who can say why other people are.

From the top of the rise they could see a fair distance, however Blayke's new eyes were not long sighted. Only a few metres ahead the landscape became a blur to him. He knew there were hills beyond the one they were standing on; he had seen them before his transformation. *Can you see very far?*

Fang shook his head. *That's what our noses are for. Sniff the air, see what's there.* Fang followed his own instructions and shut his eyes, turning his nose this way and that.

Blayke was about to shut his eyes when the day darkened. He looked up at the sky, but it was obscured by a large, dark shadow. *Um, Fang. I think you'd better open your eyes. What's that?* Blayke pointed up at the sky with his nose.

Fang gazed up. *Run!*

Fang shot off down the hill. Blayke wasted no time in following, running as fast as his tiny legs would move. Blayke wanted to ask what was happening, but had no breath to form the words. Fang pushed into his mind. *It's a hawk who wants lunch.*

Blayke almost stopped at the loud words that suddenly invaded his mind. He could feel the aura of where Fang had been and sent his own thought to follow the path back to Fang's mind. *I refuse to be anyone's lunch. Run faster.*

Somehow Fang ran faster, and they reached relative safety amongst the large roots of a tree. They huddled in a small space under an overhanging part of the root. The shadow swooped past the tree. The rats were breathing hard. Blayke was surprised to feel fear-induced adrenalin pump through his body. In human form a hawk would have scared him no more than a flower.

That was bloody close. We could've been killed.

Fang nodded. *Everyday things you don't think twice about are great obstacles to us. A bird you might have admired as a human is a serious danger. That wasn't a game. If he had grabbed you, it would have been the end.* Fang's beady eyes bored into Blayke's.

Blayke nodded. *You don't have to convince me. So what do we do now? Do they usually hang around and wait for a second chance, or will he go and look for some other poor animal?*

He'll soar around and keep an eye on our hiding spot. Eventually he'll go away.

They waited amongst the roots. Fang jumped from root to root to the edge of the canopy. He dashed out and looked around.

Look out! Blayke screamed into Fangs mind as the bird dove toward his friend. Fang sprinted to their overhanging root. Just before he reached it, he felt the wind from the bird's attempt.

It must be slim pickings around here. I wish he would go away.

Blayke could only nod in agreement. Nose twitching, he nervously cleaned his face. He had felt real terror at seeing his friend nearly snatched to his death.

I think we should just wait here for a while.

OK, Blayke.

No sooner had they regained their breath than they heard a rasping noise. It sounded like something being dragged over the grass and dirt. Blayke was puzzled, but Fang recognised the noise. *Get ready to run again; we have a snake coming.*

Oh no, not again. Why do we have to be so low on the bloody food chain?

Fang was desperately looking for a place to run that would not be in the path of the snake or the hawk, but he couldn't see one. His next instinct was to crawl in the smallest hole he could find, but again, there were none.

Blayke, however, was thinking like a human. *I have an idea. Let the snake see us and then follow me.*

Are you crazy? We're not humans; we're rats and we'll be eaten.

Just trust me.

No.

This is no time for an argument. You just have to trust me. If we don't do anything we're dead anyway.

Fang thought for a moment and gave in. *Whatever. Well, it was nice knowing you.*

Blayke ignored the comment and started squeaking to attract the snake's attention. The scaly head was nearing from their left. The snake's body see-sawed gracefully over the ground. When it was within striking distance, Blayke ran for open ground, away from the protection of the tree. The snake was amused that the two rodents, who were soon going to be lunch, bothered to run. It was inevitable that they would be eaten and the chase just whetted the snake's appetite.

Blayke felt the sun on his back but did not look up. His senses told him the hawk was still circling and had seen them. He risked a look behind to see he was closely followed by his friend, and the snake. The hawk dived, hurtling toward the ground. The snake was within biting distance.

Fang regretted listening to Blayke. What a typically arrogant human to think he knew how to survive as a rat. Oh well, one of them would feed the bird, the other the snake. The snake let out a hiss to terrify its prey; Fang could almost feel its acidic breath.

The hawk loomed directly above. Blayke veered off to the left, Fang followed. The snake was slower to change direction. The hawk had no trouble changing direction and was seconds from grabbing one of them. In an instant, the snake had come to the hawk's hungry attention. The reptile realised all too late what was about to happen. He felt talons poke into his underbelly as he was lifted off the ground. He could see the rats had stopped running and were watching his ascent into oblivion. He hissed at their rapidly fading, upturned heads.

Fang diverted his eyes from the rising duo and thanked his friend. *Are you kidding? Did you see that? Your human idea actually saved us. I didn't think we'd make it. In fact I hated you for a minute there.*

Well, you'll just have to learn to trust me.

It's almost unheard of for a rat to trust a human. You lot are always setting traps for us, putting out poison, or even trying to squash us with one of your gardening implements. I never thought it possible to trust one of you.

Yes, but now, I'm one of you.

Fang deliberated. *I suppose you are. Welcome, brother. I am honoured to call you friend.*

I am also honoured, brother. Say, do you know where a rat could get a nice piece of cheese around here? They laughed.

Their merriment was short-lived. A booming rush of sound was galloping towards them. They hugged the ground trying to get as low as possible. The gods only knew what was happening now. Blayke didn't have the energy to watch, so squeezed his eyes shut and prayed.

The tumultuous passage of light reverberated around Blayke as it swept past, carrying their new world with it. Sound ceased. Blayke felt his awareness being sucked away from his recently acquired body. His consciousness was without anchor, and he could see again. He felt like a single leaf on a raging river, carried helplessly through a narrow gorge as he was pushed through the dark tunnel. Any sense he had of Fang vanished. He slowed, then stopped. A great weight bore down on him. He opened eyes, which were again a part of his human body. His searching gaze met a familiar face peering out of the dark.

"Welcome home. Glad to see you survived." Arcon patted Blayke's shoulder as if to reassure himself his nephew was ok.

Blayke sat up, feeling slightly dizzy. He grinned to see Fang sitting alive and well on his leg. A familiar voice spoke in his head. *It's good to be back. Hey, how come I don't get a safer, bigger body? Life can be so unfair.*

I can hear you! It took a moment for Blayke to process the new information. *Are you OK?*

Despite the fact you tried your best to get us eaten, yes, I'm fine. Fang turned to Arcon. *I assume our issue was trust.*

Arcon nodded. "Trust and empathy. You need to be able to trust Blayke implicitly and he needs to be able to understand life from your point of view. I don't know what happened to the two of you, but the fact you've survived the bonding means you were successful. Congratulations, to both of you."

Blayke couldn't help but feel proud. He finally felt like a real realmist. Arcon slid into his bedroll. "It's just after midnight. We'll all have a snooze and get going at dawn." The young man nodded. He was exhausted. He felt as if his human body had run all those steps. Reaching down to find his tail was no longer there made him feel sad—he had enjoyed being a rat. With one hand on Fang, who was in his pocket, and the other under his head, he faded into a dreamless slumber.

Arcon was true to his word and had them up and ready before the sun had separated from the horizon. He had received a mind message from Agmunsten cautioning them to hurry. He changed his previous plan and asked Arcon to skip Ellesmere and go directly to Vellonia, the valley of the dragons. Arcon worried at the added urgency and change of plan.

A day earlier he had felt ... something. He couldn't have said what, but it was oppressive. Shortly after, Agmunsten had come through with orders, but no information. He figured he should be used to it by now. Although there was no one Arcon trusted more, he knew the Head Realmist derived a certain amount of pleasure being the only one who knew something important. Childish certainly, and one of his few faults; the others tended to allow him the small satisfaction.

By mid morning Blayke was bored. Fang had fallen asleep and Arcon was unusually quiet. "How long until we get there?"

"Actually we crossed the border early this morning. Welcome to Wyrden."

"Why didn't you tell me? I've never been to Wyrden. This is a momentous occasion."

"Gee, it doesn't take much for you to have a momentous occasion. By the end of this expedition you'll have a plethora of momentous occasions to remember, not all of them good."

"If we've just crossed the border we'll be in Ellesmere soon, won't we?"

"Change of plan. After Wyrden we're headed straight for Vellonia."

"Oh. Any reason you can tell me?"

"Believe me when I say that this time I've been left out of the loop too."

"Well, it's about time." Blayke was happy Arcon was getting a bit of his own medicine.

"Enjoy tonight, because after that we'll have to hurry."

Blayke sighed; he was tired from their constant travelling. "At least tonight we'll sleep in real beds and have a *real* dinner." Blayke couldn't help but have a jibe at Arcon's basic cooking ability. The times they had eaten at inns were some of the best food he had ever had. Arcon tended to boil everything until there was no flavour, just a grey blob of vegetable matter, with the exception of freshly killed meat, which he barbecued over an open fire. Unfortunately, they hadn't had time to hunt so their diet had consisted of dried meat rations and that grey stuff.

"If you don't watch your tongue I might send you to bed without dinner." The edges of Arcon's blue eyes crinkled as he grinned.

"Promise?" Blayke smiled.

Phantom swooped out of the sky and alighted on Arcon's shoulder. *The trees up ahead are hiding four men. Can't tell if they're common thieves or specifically looking for us.*

"Fly in and have a look." Phantom flew off. Arcon sat on the road and stretched out his leg in pretense of curing a cramp. Blayke bent down to assist. "Are you OK? Is it a cramp?"

"Men hiding up ahead. Phantom's going to have a look. Pretend to help me. A massage would be nice."

"Can't be bothered. I think I'll just look concerned." Blayke sat next to his uncle and waited for the supposed cramp to improve.

Arcon received a picture from his creatura. Phantom had a vantage point from a tree between the bandits and the realmist. He had a side-on view. The men were standing in anticipation, gazing in Arcon's direction. They were a ragged-looking lot, but their swords were clean and sharp. Phantom sent Arcon a question. *Is that enough, or do you want me to wait until they say something?*

Wait.

155

The one with the greasiest hair spoke first, although he had the good sense to whisper. Unfortunately for him, owls had exceptional hearing. "What are they doing, why have they stopped?"

The leader of the small band answered. "How the hell should I know, you stupid louse. I can't read minds can I? Looks like the old man has a cramp or something."

"How long will we have to wait? That man only paid us enough for the afternoon. Buggered if I'm going to stay here all night."

The leader took an openhanded swipe, whacking his accomplice upside the head. "Bloody well shut your trap. We'll wait as long as we bloody well have to. The wait won't seem so long if we don't have to listen to your drivel, so keep it shut." The others nodded.

Arcon had heard enough. *Wait there, Phantom. I don't want you attracting their attention. Join us when it's over.* The realmist took a few moments formulating a plan.

Arcon rose, speaking to Blayke. "They're waiting for us because they were paid to. I'm assuming they want to kill us."

The look on the younger man's face was a mix of wanting to be brave but being scared instead.

"Don't worry, lad. I have a plan. Since they know where we are, it won't hurt to use the Second Realm." Arcon shut his eyes and mumbled under his breath.

"OK, follow me." He stepped off the road and into the long grass. They were headed for the bandits in the trees.

"What are you doing? We can't fight them in there." Blayke kept his voice even.

"We're not going to fight them."

"What, are we committing suicide?"

"Don't be stupid, lad. I don't want anyone seeing what it is I'm going to do to them."

When they entered the trees they were twenty metres from the enemy. The leader had seen them coming and stood waiting. "It's our lucky day, boys. They're coming to us."

"Lucky coincidence, or do they know we're here?" Doubt coloured one bandit's voice. The leader shrugged. Arcon halted two body lengths from the group. There were some limits to what they could do through the Second Realm. Not everything was known about the other universe. If one wasn't directly targeting a single entity, the spell was not likely to work, unless the whole area designated for the spell had been physically stepped out by the realmist. By stepping out the area, they were imparting their own aura's energy, thus containing the spell. Without limiting what he was about to do, he could not be certain how far the affliction would spread. A handful of realmists had been killed, caught up in their own spells, before the rest had learned this rule.

Arcon spoke to the leader. "Good day to you."

"Good day to you, old man. How's the cramp. I noticed you were having some trouble over there." The leader was happy to have a chat; he would kill them soon enough. Arcon slowly circled the group, causing the leader to turn his head to keep an eye on him. "What are you doing?"

"I'm just admiring what a strapping group of men you have. I wouldn't want to come up against you in a physical contest."

"Well, I'm not sure this is a very good day for you then. My boys and I have been rather bored and were looking for some way to exercise our sword arms. Boys, I think I've had enough of the chat, let's finish this so we can go home."

By the time they had all drawn swords, Arcon had stepped out his circle and returned to Blayke. "Now watch, boy, and learn."

Arcon stated a single word. "Commence."

The leader took the instruction personally and stepped toward them. Blayke involuntarily stepped back, however the bandit's second step sunk into the ground to his knee.

The bandit toppled forward to the ground, and when he placed his hands on the grass, they too started to sink. His companions had not moved and so were sinking at a slower rate. The ground around them had turned to quicksand.

"What the hell is happening?" The leader's commanding voice had disappeared, in its place was a shrill squawk. "Morth didn't warn me about this! Help us, old man. For the god's sakes, HELP US!"

He was thrashing about, trying to free himself, his screams scratching his throat. It had not occurred to him that Arcon had created the quagmire.

Blayke gritted his teeth and watched, feeling some pity, despite the fact that these men would have killed them, no questions asked. He wondered if he would ever get used to the recently acquired knowledge that man could be an evil, supremely selfish creature at heart. What had he ever done to these people that they would kill him for what he assumed was probably not a huge amount of money. What gave them the right to decide he deserved to die?

The quicksand muffled the leader's screams. His companions filled in the silence with their own pleas as they sank further into the quagmire.

"OK, Blayke, let's go. The conclusion is inevitable." Blayke's eyes were cold, something Arcon had never seen before. Fang, who was perched on Blayke's shoulder, gave Arcon a sympathetic look.

"I want to see this through."

Arcon didn't argue. He placed his hand on Blayke's shoulder and waited. The bandits eventually gurgled their last breaths as the quicksand closed over their heads. "What happens now? Does the ground stay soft?"

"The effect only lasts for an hour. I could have made it last longer but I don't want innocent people or animals getting trapped."

"I'd like to wait and make sure."

"OK." They sat for a while. Arcon was saddened by the look in the boy's eyes. He had almost accomplished the task of ferreting out all the innocence and naivety from Blayke's kind spirit. He felt tortured by what he was doing. No one should have to learn the lessons he was teaching. Unfortunately their world needed them to be this way.

The hour passed and Arcon led his small group into the town of Springdale, shadowed above by Phantom. Wyrdon was a wealthy and peaceful country. The road leading into Springdale was cobbled and well-maintained. Farmers driving horse-drawn carts laden with produce, travellers clothed in the dust of their journey, and the occasional carriage that coiffured women peeped out of, shared the road in and out of Wyrdon. Trade was safe and prosperous, especially here, near the border with Veresia. They were not challenged at the city gates, even though four guards stood alert. Arcon had no doubt the men were trained to remember each and every unfamiliar face that passed through.

Arcon didn't want to waste time, however he wanted to track down the man whom the leader of the bandits had referred to as Morth. He wanted to know who wanted them dead. It would be easy to believe the great threat they were trying to stop was behind it, but he wanted to be sure. If someone completely different were sabotaging them, they were in for more trouble than they had foreseen. The Gormons could only be defeated if the whole of Talia were united. As it was, there were two countries that were constantly, and quietly, plotting against Veresia and its allies, Brenland and Wyrden.

Inkra was situated to the north of Veresia, bordering both it and Brenland. Communications between nations were strained at best, due to the different religions and styles of government. Sometimes five years would pass with no communication at all. Occasionally skirmishes broke out at the border, but it was never too serious.

Zamahl was a small continent situated to the west of the great continent that contained Veresia. Zamahl was as large as Veresia and Brenland put together. Because of its location across the ocean, even less was known about it. Arcon assumed the new threat, if not the Gormons, would be from Zamahl or Inkra. Only time would tell, and that was something they had little of.

Arcon was travelling toward the middle of town to the Goat's Head Inn. He had stayed there in the past and had always found the place satisfactory. It was a regular haunt of merchants, farmers from surrounding districts, and local shop owners. After the business of the day had been completed, people celebrated the deals they had made over an ale, or in some cases, continued an argument.

Blayke was happy enough when Arcon halted outside the neat three-level building. Freshly painted weatherboards greeted them, and a sign showing the white head of a goat on a bright blue background hung above the door. "Keep Fang hidden please. This inn has a good reputation for being clean and serving disease-free meals. I don't think they'd appreciate a plague-carrying customer."

"He doesn't have the plague. How can you say that?" Blayke glared at his uncle.

Fang piped up in their minds. *I don't have any diseases, thank you. I'm probably cleaner than you, Master.* It was Arcon's turn to be offended, although he had to admit he was exuding a pungent odour, which came of having bathed way too infrequently.

"We don't need to draw any unnecessary attention to ourselves." His voice projected a sternness he didn't employ often, so they quietly followed him inside.

Arcon pointed for them to sit at one of the tables. They were soon approached by a young and beautiful serving lass. Her long, blonde hair was tied back in a loose tail; two strikingly blue eyes peered out of a slender, heart-shaped face. She was slim with ample roundness in all the appropriate places. Blayke stared. When she reached the table, she addressed Arcon. "What will it be, sir?"

"Two ales please. We would also like a room for the night, if you have one free."

"Certainly, sir. I'll inform Mistress Eugene." Blayke was rewarded with a smile and wink before she departed to fetch the beer.

"Too skinny for my liking. Too much trouble for your liking, I would have to say."

"Do you have to ruin all my fun? Anyway, you can't stop me from looking, and if she chooses to speak to me, I'll have to answer."

"Just don't get too attached—we're only passing through, and I don't have the energy to deal with any dramas. I'd also bet she has a vigilant father who's chased off better than you."

Blayke looked down at his travel-worn clothes and didn't need to raise his arm to smell himself. He realised he must look close to a vagabond. Imagine if she saw he had a rat in his pocket. He laughed. "Hmm, maybe I'll come back when I've had a bath."

Arcon nodded, then shook his head; he approved of the bath part, but that was it.

She had a wide smile for the younger man when she placed the tankards on the slab of a table. He plucked up the courage to smile back. "Has anyone ever told you what white teeth you have?"

She giggled in reply and left to serve another table.

"Oh, lad, that was pathetic. After seeing you in action I don't think I've too much to worry about." He laughed as Blayke's face turned a sunburnt shade of red. "Have some of the ale, it might cool your head a bit." Fang was quietly squeaking his laughter inside Blayke's pocket.

Arcon ordered a hearty lunch of freshly roasted beef, bread, and mashed potatoes. It was a meal they all savoured in silence and Blayke's eyes stayed on his food for most of it. He suddenly felt like staying at another inn. He imagined her telling everyone what he'd said, making him the laughing stock of the Goat's Head Inn for days. Blayke was relieved when they finished lunch and Mistress Eugene showed them to their first-floor room. It looked towards the stables at the rear, and a muted odour of manure and straw permeated the room. It was newly swept, had clean sheets on the beds, and fresh water in the basin. Both men availed themselves of the water, and because Blayke washed last, he felt like he was removing grime and replacing it with more dirt. He hated washing after Arcon.

Arcon sat on his bed to think about where to start. Where would those bandits have originated from within the town? They must have been from around here because they had had knowledge of the lay of the land. He remembered the tone of their voices, the way they spoke; they had looked to be strong men, well-fed. They must have been manual labourers of some kind. The leader had displayed too much confidence to have been a lackey, so he had probably been in a position where he had told people what to do. It would have been good to question them, but now any evidence of their identities was gone.

Arcon finally worked out how they might find out their identities, but it would take a while, and by then Morth would either have disappeared or tried another mode of attack. "We're going out for dinner tonight, separately. There are two inns popular with the farriers and labourers of the town."

Blayke sat up and leaned forward, glad for the subject to be well and truly changed from the embarrassment of lunch. "These inns are places I would go if I wanted to hire ruffians for a quiet job. If we can subtly ask around, we can find out who, amongst the regulars, is not there. We may even get an angry wife coming around to cease her husband's drinking activities when he doesn't come home at the usual hour. One of them is bound to be married."

"What if Morth is around? Will he try to kill us again?"

"Probably, but not in full view of everyone. Be careful when you leave to come back here. Make sure you're not being followed. Fang can watch your back. Leave him to make his own way into the inn."

"OK. This could be fun. Hey, Fang, does that sound good to you?"

Fang nodded. "I'd like to find this Morth person too. I've grown attached to you, and I'd be upset if anything unfortunate happened."

Arcon took Blayke around the town to familiarise him with both locations. If he needed to make a quick getaway, he would need to know the best avenues for escape. It wouldn't do for Blayke to run to the wrong part of town and be killed by a cutthroat looking for a few coins. They wandered the streets, Fang and Blayke memorising where the twists and turns led. Arcon showed them the inns and a good escape route.

He showed them the seedy end of town, which was slightly less seedy during daylight hours. As the afternoon wore on, the desperate, addicted, and pathetic were crawling out to commence their depraved activities. The smell alone was enough for Blayke to recognise the area by the pungent odours of stale urine, vomit, and garbage searing themselves into his nostrils. "How do you put up with the smell, Fang?"

"What do you mean?"

"Well, don't rats hang out in the garbage and sewers?"

"Only the unfortunate ones. I hate garbage. If I were starving I would have to consider scrummaging a meal from a rubbish heap, but generally rats, the upper class ones anyway, make their homes in clean, warm kitchens. It's a misconception that we're all dirty. I'm quite clean and take offence at the suggestion that I'm dirty."

"Point taken. Don't get your whiskers in a knot. So, the ones that hang out in the garbage are on the same level as the people that hang out in the same kind of places, like here."

"Yep."

Blayke looked at the people as they walked past. It was sad that society not only turned a blind eye, but also accepted that to survive, men, women, and children had to prostitute, steal, and murder. A meal or addictive substance came at a higher price than it was worth.

Arcon marched them out of the area a lot quicker than they had walked in. Eventually the air smelled cleaner, and they were able to breathe without gagging. They reached the markets. Stallholders were packing up in the dimming light. Arcon made his way to The Arms and sent Blayke to The Anvil, but not before he handed the young man a dagger. "I'm hoping you remember how to use one of these enough not to hurt yourself. Hopefully you won't need it, but you never know." Arcon made sure Blayke had learned how to use swords, daggers, and even a bow and arrow, however he wanted him to hone his skill as a realmist, so he frowned on carrying conventional weapons. Arcon feared Blayke might be taken by surprise and wasn't confident he could focus his will quickly enough to fell someone with power. The dagger was a precaution.

Arcon watched Blayke and Fang go towards The Anvil, then he turned toward The Arms. He suddenly walked with a hunched back and limp. It was always good to be underestimated. He sent a thought to Phantom, who was just waking up. He had found a comfortable rafter in the barn at the Goat's Head Inn. Arcon told Phantom what was happening and asked him to keep an eye on The Anvil, just in case Blayke got himself into trouble.

The Arms was three blocks from The Anvil. Arcon hobbled up the three steps. He wondered why Inns had any steps at all, considering the patrons were usually intoxicated by the time they left, and would find it hard to negotiate any uneven ground. More drunken men had received injuries from falling down the stairs than getting into a fight whilst on the premises.

The Anvil was like any inn in any town. By this time, early evening, the noise was a loud buzz interspersed with laughter. A fire crackled in the hearth, and mouth-watering aromas filtered through from the kitchen. There were no empty tables, so he chose a large table at which two tough but weary looking men were seated. His approach was slow and disabled, duly noted by the men hunched over their ales. Finally, he stood at the end of the table, and the men pretended he wasn't there.

Arcon cleared his throat, his voice feeble. "Is there room for an old labourer?"

One of the men grunted, the other lifted his eyes to meet the old man's. "Please sit. Don't mind Tormill. He's a sour sort of fellow at the best of times, and you happen to have got us on a particularly bad day." He offered Arcon a seat.

"Thank you. My old bones can't stand for long these days." He proffered a newly gnarled hand. Arcon had used energy from the Second Realm to change his appearance, and his bones were aching as a result. Vergit was a persona Arcon had adopted in the past to gain information, so his resurrection felt like meeting an old friend. "I'm Vergit. Pleased to meet you."

"Hi, Vergit. I'm Salden."

"Pleased to meet you, Salden. Don't know if I can say the same about your friend though." Tormill was staring at Arcon with an unfriendly gaze. "Would it lighten the mood if I were to purchase a round of ale?"

Tormill's glower eased.

The ale arrived, and Arcon ordered the special for dinner, which turned out to be pork, cabbage, and potatoes. His companions remained quiet, so he nibbled at the food he normally would be wolfing down. It was frustrating pretending to be old. He considered himself lucky; he was older than everyone in the town, however, when realmists aged it was only on the outside, and slowly. Power from the Second Realm kept their bodies healthy and fit—maybe not as fit as a young man such as Blayke, but fit enough. Arcon ordered another round, knowing it would loosen their tongues.

Arcon finished his dinner and spoke into the silence. "So, Salden, not meaning to pry, but what has made your day particularly bad?" If nothing else, people liked to whinge and grumble. Maybe this was all they would need to open up.

"Well, we've been working on a bugger of a job at one of the merchant's joints; a bloody big house. Anyway, he's paying a bonus if we do the job well and within a certain time as his daughter's getting married soon. We've been working our arses off every bloody day for the last bloody month. We've been on schedule up until this morning. Mind you, that doesn't make Farcus, that's the merchant, any happier. Every bloody thing we do is not quite right. We've had to redo some things three times over. Anyway, we all shut our mouths and keep working 'cause the bonus is gonna be good. I've got my missus whinging at me every day for coming home after the dinner's cold, and Tormill here has been turfed out for the same reason."

"Silly cow doesn't appreciate how hard I work."

Salden leaned across the table and patted his mate's back in sympathy.

"Anyway, this morning half our crew doesn't turn up. The schedule's blown to buggery, and who knows if they'll be back tomorrow. All our hard work may have been for bloody nothing. If I could get my hands on Claxon and his men, I'd kill the lot of 'em."

Tormill grunted in agreement and slammed his now-empty tankard on the table. Salden raised an eyebrow at Arcon. Arcon reordered. He was slowly getting somewhere. He wondered how Blayke was doing.

In The Arms, the warm, orange glow from the fire coloured Blayke's face. He stood holding a tankard of ale, listening to his companion's stories about his recent experiences abroad. He had left Fang just outside to find his own way in. He thought he would find out whatever he could himself, and Fang would be able to eavesdrop on other people's conversations.

He found himself chatting companionably to a middle-aged man who had a luxuriously curly mane of golden hair, and a kindly face. The fellow was a travelling merchant who supplied various markets in Veresia and Wyrden. He was clothed in a spotless shirt, newly pressed jacket, and very expensive looking, shiny shoes. Blayke figured it must take a lot of time and money to look that good. He would have described the man as cultured and handsome, although he rarely had an opinion on the merits of another man's looks.

While Blayke listened, he gazed around the room, looking for any suspicious people and wondering if he should just ask around for a fellow called Morth.

Commonsense prevailed, and he decided not to be that obvious. If Morth were still looking for them, he would inevitably hear about a stranger asking after him.

"Aaron. Aaron, can you hear me?" Blayke's head whipped toward the merchant. He had forgotten to answer to the false name he'd supplied on their introduction.

"Oh, yes. Sorry. What were you saying?"

"I was just asking where you were from. I've been rambling on all night, and I realised I don't know anything about you at all."

Blayke remembered a piece of advice Arcon had once given him. If you were going to lie or make up a story, keep it simple. The less you made up, the easier it would be to remember the whole lie. "Bayerlon." He had been there a few times with Arcon and knew the city relatively well. The place was so big that no one who lived there could possibly know everyone else.

"What brings you to these parts, if you don't mind me asking."

"It's rather embarrassing, actually. I'd rather not talk about it."

"What could be so embarrassing?" The merchant rubbed manicured fingers over his small, pointy beard. His eyes lit up. "You wouldn't be running from a lady, would you? Or better still, maybe some young lass's father."

"Nothing like that. My father sent me. My sister ran away with a much older man." He willed his cheeks to go red as he stared at the floor. He looked up again. "I shouldn't even be talking about it. My father thinks it will ruin the good name of the family and I've broken a promise to him by telling you."

The merchant gave an understanding nod. "Don't worry, your secret's safe with me."

"Thank you." The sigh Blayke gave was more in relief that the man had so readily believed his story. He was feeling proud of himself.

"Look, if you're serious about fixing your little, shall we say, problem, I think I can help." The merchant leaned his pointy-bearded face conspiratorially into Blayke's so that Blayke could feel the man's breath on his nose. "I might know someone who can help. This person can find things one may have, shall we say, lost."

Blayke was not so proud now. What had he done? Now the man wanted to help him find his imaginary sister. "I don't know. I assume your friend requires money for his services, and my father didn't give me all that much. I'm afraid I'll have to track her down myself."

"I'm sure if you went home with your sister in tow, your father would be happy to pay any amount to have her home safely." The merchant took the tankard out of Blayke's hand and placed it on the mantle above the fire, his smile encouraging. "I insist. It will make your life so much easier, and I'm sure my friend won't require an unreasonable amount of money."

He gently placed his fingers around Blayke's upper arm and proceeded to pull him toward the door. It occurred to Blayke that everything happens for a reason and maybe the man he was taking him to would know, or even be, Morth.

"OK. Maybe you have a good idea. Where are we going?"

"Not far, just a couple of blocks away. It won't take long, and if you decide not to employ his services we can come back here and grab another drink." He genuinely seemed like he wanted to help. It was nice to think there were still good people in the world. The merchant followed Blayke outside, and once in the street he led the way, chatting amiably about women he had bedded. Blayke would have found the conversation more interesting if he could have forgotten what he was trying to achieve. As they walked further from the inn, the streets became more and more shadowy, and there were fewer and fewer people. Blayke felt for the dagger in his belt. The cool touch of the handle made him feel safer, and the merchant's idle chatter was calming.

Within two blocks the gentleman led Blayke down a dark, narrow alleyway, clearly the dodgiest lane they had traversed all night. Blayke was wondering if all people who could 'find' people operated from dark alleyways; it would have been a nice surprise if he had been led to a brightly lit mansion. At the end of the alley the merchant stopped and turned to Blayke. "Have you ever been fishing?"

He was caught off guard by the change in subject. "Fishing?"

"You know about bait, don't you? A small fish, used to catch a bigger one."

Blayke was figuring through what the merchant had said. He heard footsteps behind him and turned. Through the gloom he saw a plump woman whose grin was wicked and cunning. He looked into her eyes; dark eyes full of malicious glee, eyes that were looking at the man behind him with familiarity. He understood his predicament in the second it took to feel the pain in the back of his head before he blacked out.

The old woman stepped over Blayke's body and pulled a large ring of keys from her pocket. She opened the door and stood aside so the man could drag Blayke's body in. "About time, son."

"As I always say, mother, if you want a job done, you have to do it yourself."

"Yes, Morth, I know, I know. Just get him in here so I can shut the door."

Fang watched the gate close. Arcon was not going to like this. Apparently they had found Morth, just not the way they had planned. Fang looked up to the sky, but Phantom was nowhere to be seen; he was already racing to get Arcon.

16

Leon sat atop his regal, white stallion. He ignored the flakes of snow that drifted through the silence to land on his nose and lips. He had called a halt outside the walls of the northern capital of Klendar. Whilst winter had commenced it's departure in Bayerlon, icicles still adorned the trees and houses of northern Inkra.

Leon, as usual, wanted to make a grand entrance into the city. He had shed his heavier coat, wishing to display his gold-adorned, red one. He now willed himself not to shiver as he sat exposed, waiting for an honour guard to meet and lead them into the city.

It was almost laughable to Leon that they had to wait at all, and he was on the verge of taking it as an insult. As soon as they had crossed the border between Veresia and Inkra, guards had trailed them to the city, sometimes even leading the way when Leon's retinue was heading off track. The Inkrans had not spoken to any of their party, keeping a wide berth. As soon as they had sighted Klendar in the distance, the guards had ridden ahead. Leon surmised their disappearance into the city had been to inform King Suklar of their arrival. A welcoming party should have materialised by now.

Leon reflected on their week-long journey through the hitherto unvisited land. As soon as they had crossed the border, the difference had been noticeable. The road was pitted and potholed, slowing travel. Brown weeds and overgrown shrubs grew as unkempt adornments, spiking out of the snow and marking either side of the roadway. The sun remained hidden behind heavy, dark clouds, although small patches of blue occasionally managed to peek through the oppressive curtain.

Snow started falling within two days of entering Inkra, and by the time they neared the city, the horses were labouring through chest-high drifts. Some of the soldiers smiled at the white beauty, which hid the sombre surroundings. Leon only noticed the biting cold and increased difficulty travelling, not to mention the snow blindness, which had affected many of them. Some of the men had brought gossamer thin scarves to place over their eyes. These enterprising soldiers sat around the fires at night, trading pieces of scarf for food and money. The thoughtful wives who had spent days slaving over their creations would have been mortified to know they were now reduced to small, scrappy eye coverings.

Every Inkran they saw, and those weren't many, were clothed in the same grey woollen coats, shawls, and head coverings—it was almost a uniform. The houses were all the same, single-story stone huts, with the exception of one larger, two-level house in each town. Everything was neat and ordered, but dirty and morose. Each day further into the countryside saw tensions mounting amongst the troops: whilst they trusted their prince, there were those who felt they were being led into a trap. They were far into enemy territory where nothing could save them if Suklar decided their time on this earth was at an end. Leon's arrogance gave him courage. No one would dare hurt him, the great Prince Leon. He never entertained the thought that everyone else did not necessarily share his perception of his own greatness.

The men's forebodings weren't helped by the fact that two of the men had gone missing. They had been travelling along with them one minute; the next they had disappeared. Leon had refused to risk any more men by looking for them. In Leon's opinion, if his soldiers had not listened to him about the dangers of this place, they deserved whatever had befallen them. The life of a soldier was to obey his superiors; those who didn't, suffered the consequences one way or another. The fact that no search was carried out, sent a clear message to the remaining men. Leon knew no one else would wander off.

Leon flexed numb fingers within black gloves. Feeling had also fled from his feet, pain replacing the warmth. Finally, the gates started to open. The sound of stone grating across metal shrieked through the falling snow. It vibrated in Leon's teeth. He saw those closest to him squinting eyes and gritting teeth, involuntarily raising palms to cover sensitive ears.

An honour guard of grey-clad Inkrans formed on either side of the road between Leon and the entry to the city. Leon sat straighter in the saddle and ignored the urge to wiggle his fingers in the hope of generating warmth. Everyone held their breath. Would they all be paraded through the city in chains, their prince's journey a foolish miscalculation? Were they moments away from death? No one spoke. There was no announcement introducing Suklar, King and ruler of this dismal land. The only sound was the occasional clump of snow falling from where it had built up on the branches of nearby trees. Each thud caused more than a few of Leon's men to jump.

King Suklar appeared. He was borne on the shoulders of four grey-clad men, and he sat in what Leon could only have described as a heavy-set, small, ebony throne. The throne was open at the sides and front, and roofed with shiny black leather, which draped down to protect his back. The king was dressed in black with gold and silver thread around his collar. The threads chased each other around to form a symbol, which was composed of diminishing triangles, one inside the other, and so on. The throne bearers glided smoothly and expressionlessly toward Leon. As he surveyed those before him, he could see the Inkrans lacked reasonable height, and his men were typically a half to one foot taller. It was nice to have a natural advantage.

As the chair approached, Leon dismounted, feet sinking up to his knees in the freshly fallen powder. He knew he had impressed everyone already. Now he had to make a good and humble impression on King Suklar. Leon always felt that to be underestimated was an advantage, and he would pretend inferiority to gain favour. Although he had, technically, an inferior title, he felt his lineage to be superior. Veresians were the supreme race on all of Talia, and Leon was one step away from being their king—well two, but he wasn't going to let that stop him. He schooled his face into meekness, touched with a hint of awe. Any king, and particularly this one, would have been used to reverence and fear from their people. By all accounts, King Suklar was a mean and hard man, quick to take offence, quicker to take fatal action to rectify the situation. Leon wasn't stupid enough to think he was going to be a pushover.

The importance of this moment was not lost on the Veresian prince. The last person to meet with King

Suklar had been a distant uncle of Leon's, more than 300 years ago. What Leon knew about Suklar had been gleaned from spies who had never penetrated the castle, but relayed information from the outer Inkran villages. Suklar had ascended the throne after the suspicious deaths of his two older brothers. Suklar's father had been an evil tyrant and it appeared the son followed in his footsteps. Suklar had also had his two younger siblings murdered, just in case they were as ambitious as he. Leon could relate to this side of the king and admired his ability to do what was necessary to get ahead.

After proceeding at a stately pace the chair reached Leon. He bowed low. When he straightened, the king offered a barely perceptible nod. No words were exchanged. The king remained in his chair, looking down at the foreign prince as if he were watching a cockroach. Suklar's icy blue eyes gave a reception as cold as the snow Leon stood in.

Prince Leon swallowed a growl at the absence of ceremony on what should have been considered a momentous occasion, and at the obvious lack of respect he was being accorded. The Veresian soldiers held their breath as one; they had never seen royalty, in particular theirs, treated so negligently. The prince held his tongue with difficulty, lifted his head higher and returned the insulting nod. Leon told himself he enjoyed games, and this was going to be a good one. Before the end of his stay he would have the king bowing down to him.

He stood still, as the chair was turned around and the king's hand floated negligently out from behind the leather in a gesture one would use to summon a servant. Leon mounted his horse and followed, signalling his men do the same. The Veresian prince smiled to himself as he pictured how much fun he would have repaying Suklar for all his hospitality. He felt like a child on the eve of its birthday.

The city of Klendar, to Leon's surprise, was full of activity. People rushed around, heads bowed to ensure no one made eye contact. It was a wonder they didn't endlessly bump into each other. As expected, everyone was clad in grey. On closer inspection, Leon noticed coloured lines snaking the edges of everyone's collars. The colours ranged from green to yellow, red, blue, and purple. It appeared that the purple-striped people had more authority over everyone else, being the only ones who dared lift their heads as they strode along.

Dirt pathways meandered lazily through the plain, level city. No children or animals played in the streets. Every now and then two or three purple stripes harassed, and in one case beat upon, a non-purple striped citizen. Although there was much activity, the silence struck Leon as they marched toward the king's enclave. There was no chatter, laughter, or friendly banter—and there were no loud arguments. When the members of this strange society met to exchange or buy goods, they kept their voices to a whisper. Were they scared of being overheard saying the wrong thing, or did the king just dislike noise to an unreasonable extreme? Leon's men had also noticed this strange phenomenon and chose to keep quiet. Most of them were wound tight after their long journey through the unknown; the eerie lack of noise added to their tension. An impatient snort from a horse, or soldier's cough, triggered nervous starts from many of them.

Leon rode his horse into a large shadow. He turned his attention from the surrounding city and looked up to behold a monumental structure. The castle, standing a few hundred metres in front of him, was unlike its bland surroundings. The main tower, which rose from the middle of the edifice, was the origin of the exaggerated darkness on an already gloomy day. Heavy squares of pink, yellow, and grey stone climbed one atop the other, many stories high, fading into the falling snow.

The foreign prince had never seen a man-made structure so tall, nor so impressive. The castle walls were reflective and shiny—inky black stone appeared to have grown out of the ground naturally, later to be polished by the hands of man. The luminescent tower appeared as a shaft of light, a heavenly pathway toward the sky. Various-sized arched windows cut into the building at uneven heights. Obsidian walls stepped down in height from the perimeter, to lie lowest in the centre, where the bright stone stamen appeared to have burst forth.

Leon was instructed to halt at the vast doors. The lack of defence in the form of a moat or additional stone wall did not escape Leon's notice. What a foolish thing, to leave the castle unfortified.

"Excuse me, but the king is waiting. You may bring two men, as a courtesy." The young man in grey castle liveries addressed Leon as he would have addressed the commonest worker. "Follow me."

His voice carried a harsh accent, each hard consonant inflected even further, to the point of sounding stunted. Leon dismounted in annoyance but did not speak. He would not give them the pleasure of seeing they had insulted him. He would play their little game, for now.

His realmist, Fendill, and the king's captain, Pernus, accompanied Leon. The captain of his own guard, Seth, was not impressed about being left behind. Leon had explained that he resented having to take Pernus everywhere, but he preferred to have him where he could see him. Seth would never argue with his prince, so whilst he acquiesced, he also left Leon with no doubt about what he thought about the arrangements. Leon pushed his frustration aside, knowing he was clever enough to do what he needed to, right under this upstart's nose. If he didn't keep an eye on Pernus, who knew what mischief he might contrive?

In great contrast to outside, the main hallway of the obsidian castle was clothed from floor to ceiling in white marble tiles. It was an amazing display of wealth, and Leon had to admit, beauty. Every few metres there was a triangular, obsidian tile so black it looked as if it were a bottomless hole, waiting to swallow up a careless passer-by. The prince was not the only one who tensed as he passed over the first black tile.

At the end of the hallway there were two sweeping staircases, one spiralled down, the other up. The grey man went down. Leon and red-haired Fendill exchanged glances, both men trying to be reassuring, neither willing to show any fear in the face of the obvious risk they were taking. Pernus noticed the exchange. "Don't worry, I've got your backs."

"What? Oh you're still here. I'm not really all that reassured. Thanks anyway."

Pernus shrugged. The king had ordered him to keep an eye on Leon, however he was still here as additional protection, a role he took seriously. If it were up to him, he might be inclined to let Leon get himself killed, but he was loyal to King Edmund and was intent on seeing his job through to the end, if need be. The fact that the prince was unappreciative was no concern of his.

They descended two flights then continued down another corridor, which conveyed them back in the direction of the entry. This hallway was also laid with marble, this time pink, shot through with inky lines, the obsidian tiles still placed at intervals. The corridor abruptly ended in a smooth black wall. They stopped. Leon noticed his feet and hands had lost the pins and needles feeling and he was warm again, a warmth that had eluded him for many days. He could feel it coming up through his boots. Removing one glove, he felt the floor. It was warm, as if fires burned underneath, heating the tiles to a pleasant temperature. He made a mental note to find out how they had contrived that convenience. When he took over as king, he would make sure all his floors were heated; no foreign king was going to outdo him.

The grey-clad man, whose collar was adorned with purple and green stripes, turned and spoke his first clipped words since entering the castle. "Wait here. Don't move. You will be watched."

He turned to the black expanse in front of him. He spoke a few words in Inkran, a language none of the Veresians knew; Inkra was well-protected and so was its language. The door silently shimmered; its black solidity peppered with pinpricks of light, before it disappeared. The three guests couldn't help but widen their eyes at the impossibility of what they had seen. Fendill rubbed his forehead with an index finger, a sign he was furiously thinking.

They could see through to the other side of the great expanse of what appeared to be the throne room. At the far side, to which the grey man was still walking, stood a dais accessible by four tall steps. Leon imagined that the shorter stature of the Inkran king would make his ascent and descent a laughable sight. He kept his thoughts to himself.

Grey man finally reached the dais and prostrated himself in front of the massive throne. It was unclear what was happening due to the distance and the fact that the throne appeared to be crafted from the same obsidian of which the door and castle walls were made. The throne, and the king, blended into the background, which consisted of a midnight marble slab, which rose to the ceiling.

Eventually the grey-clad man stood and backed away from the throne, bowing every few paces. He continued in this manner until he reached the trio. He turned to the men and shouted in his loudest voice, the sound reverberating around the stone-clad room and causing the Veresians to jump. "You may approach. Revere and behold, King Suklar, ruler of Inkra, Highest Priest of Klar and The Ultimate Sacrifice." He lowered his voice. "You are always being watched. Do not attempt to harm Our Beloved. When you reach the dais you must prostrate yourselves as I have. Do not rise until He commands you. When He is ready to dismiss you I will be summoned to take you away. Obey and all will be well."

Leon led the way, however the grey man grabbed the sleeves of Fendill and Pernus. "You must not go further. You may watch from here."

After his first few steps Leon sensed he was alone. He turned and saw anger on his men's faces. He schooled his features into a mask of serenity whilst he mentally added this latest grievance to his list.

The grey man watched him undertake the long journey across the warm floor, until he was satisfied. When he exited the room the stone door returned, appearing as immoveable as ever. Much to their disgust, Fendill and Pernus stood transfixed, watching their prince glide unprotected, but proud, across the patterned expanse of black, white, and pink marble.

The approach was filled with tension. Leon, head held high, had a distinct lack of reverence on his face. Pernus, whose sword still hung at his side, itched to draw it in defence of his arrogant prince, and Fendill held his mind ready: ready to reach into the starry expanse of the Second Realm and strike down any who dared threaten his prince. Leon drew closer. He was close enough to see King Suklar's dusty brown face. Half-closed, hooded eyes regarded him. Leon couldn't begin to know what his adversary was thinking.

Leon stopped a foot from the base of the throne. He cast his eyes down and bowed low, however refused to prostrate himself as his predecessor had done. He was the prince of a great nation and would not demean himself for anyone. The gods knew he had endured years of playing second fiddle to his brother; he sure as hell was not going to do that for an alien king. He stayed in his position a few seconds, then rose and looked at the monarch as directly as he could. Suklar's position, high upon his dais, ensured Leon was forced to crane his neck if he wanted to look into his cold, blue eyes. Suklar was well aware of the discomfort of holding that position for a lengthy period.

After a longer than comfortable time had passed, King Suklar surprised Leon with his deep, mellow-toned voice; something unexpected from such a short man. "Welcome to our beautiful kingdom. I trust your journey was pleasant." Suklar's face remained expressionless.

"Yes, thank you. Our journey was most satisfactory." Leon smiled as sincerely as he could under the circumstances. They both knew the journey had been cold and uncomfortable at best, two of Leon's men had disappeared, and five others had lost fingers and toes to frostbite.

"Why do your men stand and watch? Why are they not here, under my observation? Are they cowards?" The king watched Leon, who was a fly trapped in the spider's web.

"I ordered them to stay there. I need no protection from a fellow royal personage. I trust you are civilised enough not to endanger the life of an important guest." The king's expression didn't change. He turned his head to the left and whispered a few words. A short, wiry man materialized out of the black. He was clad in black; a collar unadorned by stripes framed his ebony skin. A strip of loosely woven black gauze covered his eyes; the same black gauze which camouflaged Suklar's white hair. He had stood invisible in front of the inky background. On reaching the base of the dais he prostrated himself then went to do his master's bidding.

Leon watched as he crossed the floor and attempted to lead Fendill and Pernus away. The men struggled as they watched their prince. Leon signalled them to go peacefully. They reluctantly ceased struggling and were led out.

"You are here, as I understand it, to woo my daughter." Leon's next surprise was Suklar's directness.

"Yes. I have heard she is very beautiful." He decided a return of the king's directness would be to his advantage. "There is no denying the great benefit to both our nations if this union were to come to pass. We have the climate and land to grow an abundance of food, which you lack, and you have the mines, which produce many of the raw materials scarce in our country." Leon stood with his chest out, arms relaxed by his side, as he waited for an answer.

"It is true my daughter is of marrying age, however, you are only one of many possibilities. I will study you whilst you are here to see if you posses the particular qualities I expect from any man fortunate enough to marry my daughter. You and your two companions will join us for dinner tonight. You may meet Princess Tusklar and we will see if she favours pursuing the matter any further." The king rose and was immediately joined by a second black-clad man who had stood invisibly at his right shoulder. They slipped out through the charcoal expanse behind the throne.

Leon was alone for a short time. He jumped and turned at a voice, "Come with me." The same black-clad man, at least he thought, had quietly returned to lead him to his sleeping chambers. The man did not speak as he led Leon through the black and white corridors. They ascended three flights of stairs. Their passage ended in a dark stone door similar to the one guarding the throne room. This door had yet another black-clad man at either side, and opened in a similar shimmer. Leon was still in awe at the function of the door. He was led inside to an opulent set of rooms, his bed contained in the third room they entered. The silent man gestured that Leon should stay.

Leon spent his first few minutes alone pacing his apartments. He had a feeling he would get to know these rooms very well over the next few weeks, if they allowed him to stay that long. He knew he was considered handsome, and he had a way with women. Yes. He was sure he would be asked to stay.

The obsidian door was closed, however there was a second, smaller, timber door within the first reception room. He tried it. It opened. On the other side he found Pernus and Fendill. Each man sat on a single bed at either end of the room. It appeared Pernus had been stripped of his weapons.

Another obsidian door, leading to the hallway outside, stood opposite the door where Leon stood. Candles in a centrally hanging chandelier lit the windowless room. Pernus lay nonchalantly on his bed, while Fendill jumped up and surveyed his prince, almost sniffing him as a dog would. "Did they hurt you?"

"No. As you can see I'm just as healthy as when you left."

"I wouldn't have left, but that you commanded it. Was that such a wise thing to do, my Prince?"

"Quiet your distress, Fendill. I can take care of myself. They are relatively civilized, and to what purpose would they kill me, unless they wanted to start a war with my brother."

"You have a point. So, then, how did the meeting go?"

"It went as well as I could have expected. The three of us are to join them for dinner tonight where we will meet her royal highness, Princess Tusklar."

Pernus laughed. "Not much of a name. I wonder if she has tusks."

Leon frowned at the unwanted addition to their party. "I am led to believe in a direct translation, it means 'daughter of Suklar'."

Pernus nodded, his smile remained in place.

"I have received no instructions other than we join the king for dinner tonight. I assume we will be spending our time locked in here for the afternoon. I suggest we all get some rest. Do not disturb me. I will return for you when we are summoned." Leon ignored the raised eyebrow from Pernus, choosing only to notice the bow of respect from Fendill. He returned to his chambers and lay on the bed.

Leon refused to show any signs of weakness, which included impatience and fear. None of them knew what to expect, however he was not going to waste time imagining the worst scenarios. He closed his eyes and tried to visualize what his future wife would look like. It wasn't long until he fell asleep, however his dreams couldn't be controlled, and they were filled with an unseen terror. When one of the black clad men woke him, he was covered in sweat. He tried to shake off the lingering feeling of dread. It was not until he was bathed and changed that a sense of normalcy returned.

This time the grey-clad man who had initially brought them to see King Suklar, led them to dinner. They descended two flights of stairs and headed toward the rear of the castle. As they neared the dining room, they were enticed by pleasant aromas of food they had never before encountered; that was something Leon hadn't considered. Would they eat similar food to what they were used to, or would they be expected to eat some atrocity. He recalled the lack of cats and dogs on the streets of Inkra. "Pernus, tonight you will be my official taster, an honour I would not trust with anyone, but you." He slapped Pernus on the back hard enough to sting.

"Gee, thanks for the honour." Fendill gave Pernus a sympathetic look. Though Fendill loyally served his prince, he knew of Leon's shortcomings, yet held the hope that Leon would eventually show some small kindness or consideration for someone other than himself. When that happened, Fendill would feel justified in standing by him.

They were led into a large, rectangular room. Twelve heavy, crystal chandeliers hung in a line, from wall to wall, in the centre of the ceiling. They presided between two long timber tables, each inlaid table seating fifty people. The king and his daughter were seated at the head of one, Leon and his men were told to sit at the other. Leon felt another flash of temper. Had he come all this way to endure insult after insult? He breathed deeply and let his frustration out with the breath. He was seated between his two men. They, in turn, were seated next to two older, dark-haired Inkrans. Conversation within the dining hall was subdued, as it had been in the city.

Pernus attempted a conversation with his neighbour, however discovered he didn't speak his language. As he sat and listened to those around him, he realised that no one spoke Verdonese, the most common language in Talia. Pernus turned to Leon. "Do you think the princess speaks Verdonese, or just gibberish."

"The king speaks Verdonese so I'm assuming she has been educated in our language." Leon looked toward the king and his daughter. He couldn't see clearly from where he was, however, he could see she had the same fair, wavy hair as her father, which cascaded over her shoulders to her waist. She smiled at those around her and was the centre of attention. The king looked at her in disapproval, maybe at her exuberance. She was dressed modestly in a pink dress that started just below her neck and continued to the floor. Her arms were covered to the wrists. Dark brown hands protruded from the delicate, lace sleeves.

She looked up and saw Leon watching. She coyly lowered her eyes, and then looked up again through dark, thick lashes. Leon smiled. She smiled back, impressing him with her perfectly straight, white teeth. She turned to answer someone's question and didn't look at him again. The king noticed the exchange, however gave no clue as to what he thought.

The food arrived on silver platters. The royal table was served first. Each person served themselves from the main platters. The silver cutlery had handles worked with interlocking triangles, the goblets clear crystal, cut with a similar pattern. The plates were of hand-painted gold and silver, the artwork depicting small birds on delicate spring foliage.

Everyone ate without conversation, the people around them keeping their eyes on the food. It was as if it were a crime to watch someone eat. When Leon spoke, he whispered. All three men watched their surroundings, taking in all the information they could about this strange society. Leon was true to his word and made Pernus try each dish, before he would consume any. Pernus assured Leon the tastes were familiar, although more spicy than they were used to. Fragrant rice was served to mop up the exotic sauces in which the meat was cooked, and Leon enjoyed the food. It was a nice change to be taking his meal in warm, comfortable surroundings, instead of a hard camp chair, set into snow around a small, pathetic fire.

When the main course ended, the plates were removed. Clean plates were brought out, which Leon assumed would be for dessert. Before any more food was forthcoming, their escort tapped Leon on the shoulder. He bent over and whispered in Leon's ear, "King Suklar commands your presence. Whilst you are at the table do not stare at Princess Tusklar. It is against our religion. Klar punishes those who deserve it."

The warning sounded violent, delivered with the Inkran's harsh accent. Leon rolled his eyes. He was heartily sick of their ridiculous customs; it seemed their society was based on worshipping Klar, Suklar, and his daughter. If you weren't one of these three beings you must whisper and keep your head bowed. Things were going to change around here when he took charge.

Everyone stared as Leon rose and made his way to the other table. It seemed they could take notice, sometimes. He bowed when he reached the table and was rewarded with a gesture from Suklar, to sit at his designated chair opposite the princess. Suklar sat at his daughter's left and on Suklar's left side, next to Leon, sat Orphael, Suklar's realmist. That Klar would allow a realmist to interfere with his religion shocked Leon. It was as if Orphael could read Leon's mind. "We work with, not against Klar's ordinances. I am here to give information and assistance on the safety of Inkra. I am also the one who schooled Suklar in Verdonese."

Orphael was of medium build, yet still taller than those around him. His thin, straight hair hung in brown and grey strands to his shoulders. His unnaturally smooth, pale face looked sickly against his grey robe. No coloured stripes decorated his collar. More gold jewellery adorned his fingers and neck than the wealthiest madam in Bayerlon. Leon imagined his face painted with rouge and lipstick. His mouth twitched.

Despite annoyance at having to follow their archaic customs, he was polite, and refrained from staring at the princess, although he chanced a few glances. He was definitely pleased with what he saw. She was a pretty woman, not stunningly beautiful, but attractive enough. Her eyes were the same cold blue as her father's, her nose small and slightly flat and her strong chin had a rectangular finish. Her smooth skin, a shade darker than olive despite the lack of sun, stretched over high cheekbones.

The king regarded Leon in a cold and calculating way. Orphael made polite conversation, probably designed to find out as much about Leon as he could.

Above the whispers came a sweet, feminine voice. "Why do you not look at me, Prince Leon? Does my face displease you?"

Leon turned to face Princess Tusklar, then to the king. "May I speak with the beautiful princess, your highness?" Leon couldn't believe he was pandering to these upstarts, but he was here with a goal and he wasn't going to achieve it without marrying Tusklar.

"You may speak."

Leon turned to stare into her frosty blue eyes, sensing a kindred soul, something that surprised him. "On the contrary, your highness. Your face is the most stunning I have seen. Your beauty far outweighs any woman I have previously observed. I am honoured to be in the same room as you. It is almost too much that I am speaking to you. Please forgive me if I say anything foolish."

She smiled. It had a certain devious quality about it that excited Leon.

"You speak Verdonese very well. Have you studied it long?"

Suklar interrupted. "She has studied it since she was a young child. I think you have spoken long enough."

Suklar ignored his daughter's angry stare and motioned the grey man to show Leon back to his table for dessert. Leon bowed low to Tusklar. "Although I may never have the opportunity to speak with you again, I will never forget this night. Thank you, Princess."

Her face lit up at his flattery and in his defiance of her father. No one would dare insult the king, as Leon had done, by forgoing a departing bow. Suklar's face did not change, but his eyes were as hard as the basalt walls that surrounded them.

Leon strode proudly back to his table, almost expecting to be ordered to the dungeons there and then. Pernus had seen the whole exchange. He couldn't hear what was said, but, after Leon had turned his back on the table, the king had very harsh words with his daughter. At this point the whole table studied their plates as if they held the answers to all their problems. Leon returned somewhat triumphant. "I think you've opened a wasps nest with that one."

"Don't worry, Pernus, I have everything under control."

"Could you at least wipe that smirk off your face? There's no point enraging that man any more." Pernus worried for their safety. He was sure if the king took offence to Leon, they would all suffer the same fate, regardless of who had caused his displeasure.

Leon leaned down to Pernus, shoving his face close to the soldier's, noses practically touching. His face was hard and his voice a low growl. "Do not presume to tell me what to do. The fact that my brother has sent you here means nothing to me. I have killed people for less. Do not give me an excuse."

Fendill could not hear all of what was said, however he heard enough. The longer this foray continued, the more he fretted about where his alliances lay. Could he have so misjudged the prince? He chose to shrug it off for now. His priority was getting them all out of this alive, if Leon didn't make it impossible.

Pernus shook his head. Prince Leon was a bigger fool than he had thought. He hoped the king would forgive him, but he wasn't sure how long he could continue to fulfill his duties. If someone else didn't kill Leon, maybe he would. They ate their dessert in silence. If Talia needed unity to survive, things were not looking good.

Princess Tusklar retired to her rooms after her father's dismissal of the handsome prince from Veresia. She smiled to herself. He was quite a catch, and at least had some character about him. Most of the men she had been introduced to wouldn't dare risk upsetting her father, let alone insulting him in front of others. She wondered why he hadn't ordered him to death. She had already made up her mind, because the voice in her head had told her he was the one. The voice had also told her he was cruel, and she liked cruel. Together they would overthrow her father and take Inkra for themselves. She hadn't decided whether or not she would keep him alive when that was done. The voice in her head cackled and suggested she was not unlike one of those spiders that made love to its partner and then ate him alive. She liked that analogy, laughing at the thought. She craved sleep tonight; it would make the morning arrive sooner. Tomorrow would bring them one day closer to fulfilling her destiny. The voice in her head agreed and bade her goodnight; it too, was looking forward to the future, and the havoc it would wreak on the humans.

17

Avruellen and the girls had been travelling for nine days after leaving Bayerlon. As they rode up to the northern gates of Pollona, Avruellen still sensed they were being watched, but from afar. The urgency she felt on leaving Bayerlon had abated, slightly. As they travelled, they had developed a routine to setting up and dismantling their camp. Everyone had done her share of the chores, and other than the ongoing friction with Corrille, nothing monumental had occurred. Bronwyn and her friend had obeyed her and had managed not to cause too much trouble. The only argument the girls had, occurred at one of the inns along the way. There had been a group of young men enjoying an ale after work, and the most handsome of them had taken a liking to Bronwyn. Avruellen had allowed the girls to chat with the boys; she had no wish for them not to enjoy their youth, and as they were leaving in the morning, nothing much could come of it.

Corrille, unfortunately, was the jealous type who required everyone's constant attention. Avruellen assumed it was because of her low self-esteem, but whatever the reason, the outcome was the same. If she wasn't getting the bulk of attention, she became argumentative and bullied Bronwyn into the background. Bronwyn wasn't fond of confrontation, so put up with the ill treatment. Unusually, the young man could see through Corrille's tactics—men were not always that clever when it came to women. He insisted on paying attention to Bronwyn instead, which only inflamed Corrille.

When they had left the boys, and gone up to their room, Corrille verbally attacked Bronwyn, accusing her of being a selfish, egotistical cow. Bronwyn hadn't bothered to defend herself, as she felt sorry for her friend and had an idea why she was upset. Corrille, in her feisty mood, had continued insulting her until she had provoked a reaction. Both girls ended up saying things they regretted.

Avruellen could see Corrille constantly competed with her niece. It was true that Corrille had been badly abused, but that excuse would only go so far with Avruellen. There would come a point where she would have to pull the young lady into line before she caused real trouble. Since the latest incident, Avruellen had tried to keep the girls from situations where there was potential for Corrille to show her worst side. She had been successful so far, however they were entering their destination.

Pollona was a smallish city, with thousands of inhabitants. Being on the border of Veresia and Wyrden, it provided a meeting place for many. The city lay lazily on two large hills, a wide valley in between. From a distance it appeared to be two large dragons sleeping next to each other, noses facing to the north. Gates opened up to both ends of the valley and watchtowers perched on the tops of both hills. High stone walls traced the ridges at the top of either hill, like protruding spines of dragons, and houses spilled down one side of either dragon to face each other over the gap in between.

Pollonians were friendly, and Avruellen always enjoyed her time here. It was large enough to have all the comforts you could wish for and small enough that the people were not indifferent to their fellow man. Avruellen was relieved they had reached the city safely. But there were things they must do here that could jeopardise everything. She felt the locket under her shirt. The metal encasing the piece of quartz shielded it from prying energies, and protected Avruellen from its power. Avruellen had felt some peace of mind whilst she carried the object. Unfortunately, tonight she would have to pass it over to its intended recipient. None of them knew what would happen when it found its true owner. Hermas still had the other half, which would have to be given away on the night of the second full moon following this one. Avruellen hoped everyone was on target with where they had to be.

She reached the city gates first, which were unexpectedly closed. The guards stood on the roof of the guardhouse. When Avruellen stopped her horse at the base of the three-level, stone building, one of the guards yelled down to her. "Good day. I suppose you're seeking entrance to the city."

"Yes, you are quite perceptive, young man. Why are the gates closed?"

He spoke with a self-important and authoritative tone. "There've been a few sightings of a very large, dangerous animal. We're not taking any chances."

"What? You mean to tell me that a few of your highly trained guards can't protect the city from one animal? How ridiculous!"

The guard's cheeks reddened at the disdain in Avruellen's voice. "We found two of our cows one morning. We would have said they were ripped to shreds, but there was nothing left except the bloodied skulls."

"If it happened at night, why are the gates closed now?" Although Avruellen was looking up at the guards it appeared as though she was talking down to them.

"Mayor Thurgos has ordered it so. There is currently a week-long mayors' conference being conducted within the city, and the mayor wants nothing left to chance." The guard was deflated by this stage.

Avruellen shook her head. *Talk about an overreaction.* She spoke again. "So, are we going to be allowed entry, or are you going to leave us here all afternoon to be attacked by the *horrible* beast?" Avruellen had dismounted during her speech and now stood with her hands on hips.

The guard's head disappeared from the window and within a short time he exited the guardhouse with two of his fellows. They quickly opened the large gates, ushering in the trio and the few peasants who had been waiting for the opportunity. No sooner had the tail of Corrille's horse entered the city than the gates were hastily shut. The now-familiar smells surrounded them. Bronwyn regretted having her feet on the ground. She loved riding her horse, while Corrille relished being back in civilization. "How long are we staying, Miss Avruellen?"

"I'm not sure. Two, maybe three days. I have a few things to do. It depends." Avruellen was already concentrating on finding where they were going to be staying. They would be staying with another realmist for a change.

Avruellen hadn't been to Pollona for over twenty years. She normally had a good memory, but a few things had changed since then. The streets were in the same place, but some of the buildings had been rebuilt and looked different. Thankfully, some of the original landmarks remained and Avruellen soon found the house she sought. Realmist Augustine answered the door and the two women exchanged a robust hug. Avruellen spoke aloud. "You haven't changed at all, it's so good to see you."

In her mind voice she warned her friend, *Don't allude to the fact we are realmists. The young girl called Corrille shouldn't be with us, and I don't want her knowing anything that could compromise us.* Then aloud, "I would like you to meet my niece Bronwyn and her friend Corrille."

Both girls shook Augustine's hand.

"It's a pleasure to meet two beautiful young ladies. I only get older visitors nowadays, and they can be so boring." She smiled and moved her portly frame aside to allow them to enter.

"What about the horses, Auntie?"

Augustine answered. "That's already being taken care of. Frederick from next door has a small stable at the back of his house. See, here he comes now."

Frederick was a middle-aged man with a multitude of lines crowding his tanned face. His smile was as genuine and friendly as his neighbour's. "Good day to you, ladies." He tipped his hat then unloaded their bags. After he had taken the luggage to their rooms he led the horses away.

"He must be handy to have around." Avruellen winked at her friend.

"Yes, very handy." Augustine giggled like a young girl. "Come and sit in the kitchen. I'm sure you'd love a cup of tea."

"I won't argue with that."

"Auntie?"

"Yes, darling."

"I'm hungry. Would it be OK if I had something to eat?"

Avruellen shook her head. "You've got to watch this one. She'll eat you out of house and home if you let her."

"Oh don't be silly. It's my pleasure. In fact, I've been baking all morning in the hope that you girls would be hungry. I love having company." Nearing the kitchen they could, indeed, smell the delicious fruits of Augustine's morning labour.

Their hostess filled the kettle and placed it on the stove. Laid out on the table, protected from flies by a sheer fabric, were three large plates filled with an assortment of biscuits, fruit tarts, and small custard cakes. Bronwyn's mouth watered and they all heard her stomach gurgle loudly.

Augustine addressed her old friend. "Don't you feed her?"

"We had breakfast two and half hours ago."

"That's a long time you know." Bronwyn was the first to take a seat at the table. "Yum, these look good. You must have been baking for hours."

Augustine couldn't stop smiling. It really was nice to be so appreciated. Since her children had grown and left home she found it lonely. It didn't help that her children had left forty years ago and had their own lives in Bayerlon. She saw them occasionally—they knew what she was and weren't surprised that she had aged very little. The grandchildren, however, were a different story, and she knew she would have to stop visiting in the next few years. She was dreading the day she outlived her own children. Before becoming mired in sadness, she changed the direction of her thoughts.

The group sat through the early afternoon eating and chatting within Augustine's cosy kitchen. "Well, girls. Why don't we have a look around this afternoon? I'm sure Augustine could use the peace and quiet for a while." Avruellen stood and patted her full stomach. "Thanks so much for the lovely cakes. I don't think I'll be able to eat dinner."

"I will."

"Yes, Bronny, I'm sure you will." Avruellen turned to her friend. "We'll be back at dusk, I've got to get a few things."

Augustine nodded and knew that Avruellen was referring to the fresh herbs they would require for tonight. The quartz had to undergo a blessing before it was handed over. This would be a dangerous time because they knew very little about the stone, even what it would end up being used to do or how. How it would react to what they were going to do was a mystery.

Avruellen took the girls to the markets, which were in the small valley between the hills, close to the few small farms that lay drowsily on the southern side. These farmers, and those from surrounding districts, met to exchange and sell goods on the valley floor. It was convenient and meant large amounts of produce didn't have to be carted up the hills.

The girls had seen Bayerlon and enough towns now to erode the child-like excitement they initially felt at seeing a new place. Bronwyn was still interested to see everything, however, was a little more mature in her approach. "Lunch was yummy. I like your friend. She's really nice. How come she's never visited us?"

"She came once, when you were very young, but like all of us, she's probably been busy. She's got a family of her own you know, although they're all grown up and moved out now. I think she misses them."

"That's sad."

"Yes, dear, but it happens to all parents. It won't be long before you leave my side."

Avruellen tried to hide her sadness at the thought. Bronwyn stopped walking and gave her aunt a big hug. "I'll never leave you for long; I'd miss you too much."

Avruellen smiled at the sentiment, yet knew that life could be intoxicating, and Bronwyn would have many places to go and things to do. Corrille watched the exchange and fleetingly wondered what it would be like to have parents who cared that much. She shrugged off the thought and knew she would never have anyone. She resented her friend at that moment—maybe even hated her.

"Now, girls, I have to get some herbs for tonight's dinner. I'd like you to get food for the horses, please. If you go down there," she pointed to the south, "there should be some farmers with hay and grain. Ask for enough for three days. You'll have to ask them to deliver, which will be an extra charge." Avruellen gave them details of Frederick's address and some money. "You'll have some time to wander around, but I want you to meet me at the foot of the main road before the sun dips to the top of the wall."

The girls took their time walking to the animal feed tent. As usual, they were checking out all the young men. They had taken to giving them a rating out of ten. Unfortunately they both liked the same boys. If they saw an eight or nine, Corrille would lay claim, insisting she had seen him first. This particularly annoyed Bronwyn because they both knew they would never meet the boys anyway—it just seemed like an excuse for Corrille to let

Bronwyn know who was better. She did love her friend, although, the more time they spent together, the more temperamental Corrille became. Sometimes it was as if she disagreed with Bronwyn just for the sake of it. Bronwyn was confused as to why she always had to be difficult, but kept telling herself it was just the way she was, that she really was a nice girl, and had just been through a lot.

As luck had it, there were not many handsome boys around and they managed to reach the feed vendor without having any tense conversations. The farmer proved to be as friendly as everyone else had been so far. He showed them what they were purchasing, claiming it was of the highest quality. Bronwyn supposed it was, but since she didn't know much about horse feed, she had to assume he was being truthful. She paid half the money. The farmer insisted he receive the other half once the feed was delivered. Bronwyn thought this was an equitable arrangement and was proud of herself for successfully completing the transaction.

The girls spent a surprisingly amiable afternoon together and managed to meet Avruellen on time. The women slowly made their way up the winding streets to Augustine's house, which was about a quarter of the way up the hill. Augustine and Frederick waited on the front porch, sipping tea. Augustine rose, hugging Avruellen again. She was so pleased to see her old friend. They had met over sixty years ago and had been close ever since, if not in distance, then in their hearts. Avruellen thought about her circle of friends. She realised that now, most of them consisted of other realmists. She supposed she was unconsciously sick of people dying of old age, whilst she remained. There was a strange comfort in realising that Bronwyn would, unless something tragic occurred, outlive her. It brought a smile to her face knowing there was someone on this world she would leave behind.

Avruellen spent the early evening assisting her friend in the kitchen, whilst the girls took turns having a bath. Augustine had a large, luxurious tub. She filled it up and heated it through the Second Realm; it saved a lot of time and didn't require a lot of power. She had created her own corridor, snaking through the Second Realm, and transferred water from a hot spring located on the other side of Talia. If power were taken from the Second Realm it would most likely light up the realmists' symbol to a blinding brightness, therefore pinpointing to anyone floating around *here was a realmist*. If items already in existence on Talia were transferred via the Second Realm, there was no change to the symbol.

They all enjoyed a tasty, vegetarian dinner, except Corrille. Augustine was a vegetarian, but roasted a small piece of meat for Bronwyn's friend. Corrille was genuinely pleased and thanked Augustine with a hug, which surprised them all. Dessert was freshly baked apple pie and cream. Shortly after finishing the meal, Corrille was suddenly sleepy, so much so that she fell into a deep sleep at the table and had to be carried up to her room by Frederick.

Bronwyn, who was becoming less naïve, rounded on her aunt. "What did you put in her food? You haven't hurt her have you? Because if you have I'll never speak to you again."

"Calm down, child. Of course I haven't done anything to hurt her. She'll have a good, uninterrupted night's sleep is all. We have something to do she can't be aware of."

"Why didn't you at least warn me?"

"We both know that you're the last person to keep a secret. Remember the time I bought a present for Sandrine's birthday? You couldn't even keep it a secret for one day. As soon as you saw her you were so excited you blurted it out." Bronwyn remembered the day well and blushed.

Sandrine was a sweet neighbour, newly married. Her husband took ill quite young and never fully recovered, so life for them was a struggle. Avruellen bought her a beautiful dress to wear to the village spring fair. Even though Bronwyn had let the cat out of the bag, so to speak, Sandrine had still cried in joy when she tried it on.

"It ended up being OK, though."

"Yes, but this time the secret could get us all killed. Surely I don't have to keep explaining the obvious to you." It was clear Avruellen was cranky. Bronwyn realised she was worried about what they were involved in. Seeing her aunt's distress displayed a vulnerability Bronwyn had never before considered. For the first time in her life, she wondered if her aunt was capable of making everything turn out all right.

Frederick returned from putting Corrille to bed. "I'll see you ladies tomorrow. Thanks for a wonderful dinner, Tina. If you need anything just sing out."

"Thanks, Fred. We should be OK. See you tomorrow." Augustine saw him to the door and they parted with a small kiss. Avruellen smiled, pleased to see her friend happy again. Her husband had died ten years ago, and with the children gone, Avruellen knew, more than anyone, how lonely she had been.

Bronwyn washed the dishes, whilst Avruellen and Augustine prepared themselves. The rites they were to carry out were dangerous, as none of them knew how the quartz, or rather what was inside, would react. The basement would be the safest place, especially once it had been warded. The earth surrounding the basement walls provided good insulation to contain any seeping power or explosion.

Bronwyn walked down the stairs and found a room illuminated with scores of candles, forcing the shadows into the furthest corners. "Are you sure you've got enough candles?"

"This is no time for joking, Bronwyn. How many times do I...?"

Bronwyn cut off her Aunt's incipient rant. "I know, sorry. You can trust me. I won't let you down." That placated Avruellen to a degree, however she remained tense.

Augustine smiled reassuringly at Bronwyn. "Don't worry; either of you. This will all be over in a jiffy."

"What are we actually doing?"

Avruellen stood in front of her niece and looked deep into her eyes. "I am going to give you something. First we must bless it, and in doing so, commence its activation. It will be required to undergo three such blessings over time. This is a blessing we must carry out ourselves. I have no knowledge of who will be required to bless it next. Once you have this ... mineral, I guess you could call it, in your possession, you must keep it hidden, secret, and guard it with your life. Without putting too fine a point on it, you will be required to use it to save Talia when the time comes."

Bronwyn's face paled to white. She felt sick. This *mineral* could be her death—not to mention she had to use it to save Talia. What in The Third Realm was going on? She couldn't speak.

Augustine put a comforting hand on her back. "We must all do what we can and what we must. This has been your destiny from before you were created. You must believe that the gods have given you the talents to at least have a chance to do what is being asked. None of us is asked to do what is impossible, and all of us will give our lives for this, eventually." She placed a gentle and reassuring kiss on Bronwyn's forehead.

The two older realmists had set out the perimeter and warded it accordingly, ensuring anything that occurred could not go further. Avruellen lifted the quartz from around her neck. A wooden bowl, filled with the herbs she had purchased earlier, sat on the ground in the middle of the circle. Avruellen placed the amulet, chain and all, into the vessel, and Augustine gestured the others to join her. They stood surrounding the bowl. Bronwyn was nervously biting her lip, heart beating a loud staccato in her ears. The joining of hands, to complete their small circle, calmed her and slowed her heartbeat, a little. What could go wrong with these two experienced realmists here? Instead of thinking beyond her question, Bronwyn commenced her meditation sequence.

When Avruellen spoke, she had regained her composure, all thoughts of failure banished. "We stand here today to unlink a piece of the chain that binds our salvation. I order you, Bronwyn, to link with Erme, the water corridor to the Second Realm."

Bronwyn did as she was told.

"Realmist Augustine, I order you to link with Quie, the fire corridor to the Second Realm." Augustine did as she was asked.

"I now link with Zaya, the corridor to the gods, and I seek the blessing of Drakon, god of the dragons." Her voice rose and gained strength as she appealed to the god. "Do you agree to unlock this piece I present, thereby enabling the possibility of humans and dragons defeating our oldest and bitterest enemy?"

Bronwyn was only vaguely aware of the tension in the basement because she was concentrating as hard as she could on keeping her corridor open against the tumultuous current of spirit-water, which eternally flowed through its chamber and buffeted her mind.

Avruellen was relieved when the Dragon God's booming voice replied, although the relief was short-lived. "I have no desire to change the course of your future, humans. Besides it is your future, not mine. The gods have heretofore refrained from interfering in the fate of Talia. It has always been that the strong survive and the weak perish." This was not the answer they had expected.

"It was the promise of the gods that Talia would never succumb to the Gormons. The amulet was given to us as a precaution, and we have need. Would you deny us the promise you originally made?" Her desperation and anger was evident to Drakon.

"You speak true, child of Talia. However, the promise was made by *your* gods, not Me. What they promise is none of my affair." Avruellen was about to answer when Drakon spoke again. "It is my thought, however, that without the beasts of this world in existence, my children would not have food. It has also been requested by Zimapholous Accorterroza that we preserve Talia in its present form, unsullied by the Gormons. It is the promise I have made to my children, which I am upholding at the present time. I will grant you this one favour, but do not expect that I will ever have the inclination to assist you in the future. I also require a favour from the humans in time. Do I have your promise of a favour in return?"

Avruellen was taken aback. What would the Dragon God require in return? The realmist expected the price would be high. She supposed she would have regrets but decided it was wise to grant the promise. If they didn't have the amulet to help them, nobody would be there to grant favours. "I hereby promise the Dragon God his favour as our need is great. Thank you."

Without another word Drakon breathed his fire into Quie.

The fire rushed through the Second Realm and into Augustine. She swayed on her feet, but held fast. The fire engulfed the wooden bowl and its contents. At that instant they heard a loud crack. The first link, locking the amulet's abilities, was broken, but whilst the fire lingered they had to maintain their links to the Second Realm, or they may yet fail. In the moment before the fire died out, time seemed to stop. A second sickly green corridor had opened up and had followed the fire to Augustine. She was horrified as she realised that somehow the Gormons had found a way through from the Third Realm via their links with the Second. If the Gormons touched the quartz, they may snatch it away, or destroy it. Augustine tore her hands from her friends and ceased the flow through the Second Realm. The violent separation threw Bronwyn and Avruellen to the ground.

It worked. The fire had gone out and the bowl was gone. The quartz lay untouched, unchanged on the dirt floor. Augustine was battling what was seeping through the sickly green corridor, and even though the others had broken their bonds, it appeared the Gormon priest had enough power to hold open the link with Augustine. She was trapped.

Avruellen and Bronwyn lay dazed on the floor. They could do nothing but watch as the Gormon priest consumed their friend. It sucked her blood out and up the ephemeral tunnel as Augustine screamed. Crude, rasping laughter reverberated around the room. Her face caved in on itself. When the light eventually retracted, Augustine's body was like a macabre, deflated wine skin, seeping a few forgotten drops of red fluid into the dirt. The Gormon had sucked out her lifeblood and bones. The sweet, caring person they had known was gone. It had all happened in a matter of seconds. Avruellen and Bronwyn lay unmoving, staring at the carnage. Within minutes they stood gingerly, leaning on each other for support.

"Bronwyn, you must pick up the quartz. None must touch it now but you."

"Is it safe?"

"To tell you the truth, I think so, but I'm not sure."

"Oh." Bronwyn crouched over the stone on the ground. It was pretty in its own way. She studied it for a while before she had the courage to touch it. She looked inside the quartz: something lay within. Dark red, like an old scab, it was the shape of a small black-eyed bean. "What's inside the quartz?"

"A drop of blood."

"Whose?"

"Or what. None of us know."

Bronwyn took a deep breath and reached her hand to the chain, which was still as shiny and gold as before. She exhaled when nothing happened and realised her neck was sore with tension. She stood and lifted it over her head. When it settled on her chest, nothing happened. Avruellen laughed at the anticlimax; a crazy cackle of sound. She continued until she was sobbing. They had lost a friend for this. How many more of those she loved, and even those she didn't, would die before they were finished?

Avruellen hobbled over to her friend. She had never seen anything like it. Could the mess on the floor have been human? It was impossible to tell. Always the practical one, Avruellen asked Bronwyn to help dig a hole. They would have to bury the carcass in the basement, as some of the evil they had encountered may still be active on her body. There was a chance it wasn't, but they were dealing with the unknown and couldn't take the risk. They cried as they dug. When Augustine's remains were safely in the ground, Avruellen gave her their blessing and thanked her friend for her sacrifice. Only two women returned upstairs. Avruellen locked the basement through the Second Realm so that it could never be opened again. The women bathed and changed before going to bed.

Avruellen was desperately sorry they had come to seek her friend's help. She was unsettled at the reminder that she could yet bring death to other friends and to Bronwyn. As a realmist, she knew their sacrifices were for the good of the world, it just didn't feel very good right now. Avruellen would have to tell Frederick in the morning. Did he even know Augustine's secret?

She would have liked to leave Pollona now, but Corrille was dead to the world, and with the gates being guarded because of some imaginary black creature, they would look very suspicious riding out with Corrille draped unconsciously over her horse. They would just have to wait until morning.

They both had nightmares. When Bronwyn woke she thought she might have been better off having had no sleep at all. She kept reliving the moment the Gormon had extracted Augustine's life. It was horrific: she had become a twisted caricature of a human. Bronwyn knew it was going to be an effort to steer her thoughts in a different direction, but tried anyway. Corrille shared her room, and Bronwyn was pleased when her friend stirred.

They dressed and went downstairs. Unsure of what to tell Corrille, Bronwyn said nothing and figured Avruellen could come up with some excuse or other. The girls set to preparing breakfast from yesterday's ample leftovers. "Where's your aunt and her friend?"

"They probably went to see Frederick or something. I told them to let us sleep in." This satisfied Corrille, who was preparing tea.

Avruellen, in the meantime, had gone next door. She had gone early to see Frederick, but possessed no idea how to start or what to say. When he opened the door and saw her face, he knew something was wrong. He invited Avruellen in. When they were both seated, he asked her directly. "Is Augustine ... gone?" He couldn't bring himself to say the *other* word. His frame sagged when Avruellen nodded. He pulled an envelope from his pocket, his words strained against the need to cry. "She gave me this and asked me to open it if anything happened. Please read it to me. I don't think I can bear to."

Avruellen gently removed the paper from his fingers. Her voice wavered as she read. "To my dearest Fred. I asked you not to open this unless I was dead. I guess it has come to pass. Do not cry too long for me; I wouldn't have changed anything. My life has been full, and in dying last night, I have given my life, as promised so many years ago, to the realmists' cause. Yes, Love, I am a realmist. Do not be surprised, as I'm sure you've had your suspicions. Anyway, do not blame Avruellen for what has happened. I can assure you she would have put herself in my place if there had been a choice. All I can ask of you is to support Avruellen and her niece in any way you can. I must ask that you never speak of the truth of my death, or who I really was, to anyone. I'm sorry to demand this burden of you. Know that I loved you dearly and will hold you in my heart forever. Tell my children I died from the pox and my remains had to be cremated. I leave you my house and everything in it. I hope there is some comfort in this letter. Goodbye, Love." It was signed at the bottom in Augustine's precise, flowing script.

Frederick was openly crying by the end. Avruellen returned the letter to his tear-stained hand.

"I gave her a proper burial ceremony, but I've sealed the basement forever. What she says is true; she died for the most worthy cause there could ever be. She will never be forgotten, and I will make sure her bravery does not go unnoticed. We will all miss her. I will not ask anything of you, except your silence. We'll leave after lunch. You're welcome to join us for the meal." Avruellen knew her words meant little. Nothing could bring Augustine back.

"Thanks. I would rather be alone. Tell me one thing," his eyes pleaded, "was it quick?"

"Yes, very. She didn't suffer," Avruellen lied. Augustine had suffered in the moments she had battled to preserve herself, knowing what it was she was fighting and the inevitable conclusion. There was no need to burden Frederick with that information. "Goodbye, and thank you, for everything." Frederick didn't answer; he sat staring into his lap. Avruellen showed herself out.

Avruellen returned to her friend's cottage to find the girls eating breakfast. When Bronwyn saw her, she immediately poured her a cup of tea. Her aunt spoke in her mind. *Have you said anything?*

No, I thought I'd leave that to you.

Corrille spoke: "Where's Augustine?"

"I walked to the gates with her this morning. She had to leave suddenly because one of her grandchildren is quite ill in Bayerlon. She insisted we at least stay and eat lunch. She apologised about having to leave. She'd been looking forward to spending more time with us."

"I hope her grandchild is OK. She's a really nice lady."

"Yes, Corrille, she is." Avruellen tried to force down a fruit tart, for appearances. It caught in her throat and only made it to her stomach on the following swallow of tea.

"Do you need to get anything more before we leave?"

"No, Bronwyn. Augustine told me to take whatever we needed. I'll leave her some money. It's not far to Vellonia, a few days at the most."

Corrille pushed back her chair, stood and stamped her foot. "Are you mad? That's the dragon city. No one goes there. We'll be eaten alive. If you think I'm going with you, you've got another thing coming."

Avruellen cursed herself for her loose tongue. She didn't have the energy to argue with her niece's rude friend, so she spoke to Bronwyn instead. "You never mentioned that your friend was a coward. I guess we'll have to go without her."

Bronwyn saw what her aunt was doing and played along. "I know. It's a disappointment. Oh well, I suppose we can't expect everyone to be as brave as us. Don't worry, Aunt, I'm happy to go." Bronwyn looked up to see Corrille staring wide-eyed at them. "Is it OK if we leave you here? We'll have to take your horse of course, since my aunt paid for it. I'm sure Frederick could get you a job as a tavern wench or something. Maybe you'll end up marrying one of the farmers around here, having a few kids and helping on the farm. That would be a nice life." Bronwyn knew full well that her friend would not last one day living on a farm. She wanted to meet a handsome, rich young man and spend her life being spoiled and adored.

Corrille weighed up her options, deciding she would go only as far as she felt comfortable. Maybe she would run away from them just before Vellonia. "OK. I'll come, but you must promise the dragons won't hurt me."

"I promise I will protect you, however, I can't make a promise on their behalf."

"What do you mean, *on their behalf?*"

"Dragons are sensitive, thinking creatures, just as we are. They are intelligent and make their own decisions. If I tried to tell one what to do, it would probably burn me to a crisp. Be happy with my promise of protection. It's the best offer you'll get."

Bronwyn nodded. "Come on, Corrille. When we return to Bayerlon, as surely we must one day, what a grand tale we'll have to tell all the young nobles. They could not help but be impressed by a young woman who's brave and worldly enough to say she's been to Vellonia. I bet none of the other women they've met have been there."

"You're probably right. It would be rather impressive, wouldn't it?" Corrille was now happy with the arrangement as she imagined the admiration she would reap from recounting her adventures.

They spent the time until lunch resting and preparing for the next leg of their journey. Avruellen sent the girls to groom and saddle the horses whilst she packed food and precooked their dinner. Tonight would be spent under the stars. Avruellen was itching to leave. On arrival she had brought only good memories of this place. Now she would take away bad. She was desperate to discover what had gone wrong—if she couldn't work it out, it might happen again. She couldn't risk Bronwyn. If they lost her, they lost everything.

Last night had been the first time Avruellen had heard the voice of a Gormon. The memory sent uncontrollable shivers cascading down her body. It could be a sound they would have to get used to. What was to become of them? She had felt useless, standing right there within touching distance and still unable to act. The helplessness she felt whilst watching her friend die was something she never wanted to repeat. What good were their powers if they couldn't use them when it counted the most, to save a friend?

Lunch was a silent affair. Immediately after lunch they collected the horses and made their way to the gates. The guardhouse was still in the grip of phantom fear, and Avruellen had to ask them to open the gates. This was done quickly, the closing even quicker. They rode around the outskirts of Pollona and continued south. The land rolling in front of them was gently hilly and verdant. Close to the city, a patchwork of farms lay neatly, their lush square paddocks sewn together with low stone walls. By the time the cool, late afternoon air caressed their faces, the farms had thinned considerably and were eventually replaced by forest.

Flux rejoined their party at the southern end of the city where Avruellen stopped and jumped off her horse. She embraced the fox, drawing comfort from her longtime companion.

What's wrong dearest sister? Flux's concern stemmed from the fact that Avruellen was not emotionally demonstrative, and he had felt some distress through their bond the previous night.

We partly activated the quartz.

That's a good thing, isn't it?

Yes, and no. A Gormon priest somehow managed to tap into Augustine's corridor of power. It consumed her. The only thing left was her skin. It was horrible. I'll never forget it as long as I live. She buried her face in his soft fur.

I'm sorry. You know we're all destined for death, one day. It is just a matter of how and when. You will meet her again.

Avruellen nodded.

Corrille and Bronwyn had ridden a small way ahead. "What's wrong with your aunt? She seems, well, not quite herself today." Corrille was quick to sense when others were vulnerable and take advantage.

"I don't know. She seems OK to me; her usual tough self."

"Tough?"

"Yes. You are seeing her other side today—she can also be sensitive. Maybe Augustine's situation brings back memories for her. I know she must've had family somewhere, but I've never seen them, and she never speaks of them. I guess they all died and the memories are too painful."

Bronwyn was referring, in part, to her own parents, whom she couldn't remember. Even after everything that had happened, they were still on her mind. Had they known Avruellen was a realmist? Would they have approved of what Bronwyn was?

Avruellen resumed the lead, and they continued riding until dusk. There were plenty of places to set up camp with an abundance of trees. They chose a spot a few metres inside the tree line. It was slightly elevated and gradually fell away on the other side to a small stream. They resumed their routine with a minimum of fuss. It wasn't long before they were sitting around a cheerful fire, enjoying the smells of a pre-prepared dinner warming up, which gave their camp a homey feel.

Corrille was not as comfortable with travelling and sleeping outside as her companions, and Bronwyn noticed she jumped from the most benign noises. "Do you think there's any truth to that rumour about the wild beast?"

"There's usually a smidgeon of truth to any rumour, but also a lot of exaggeration. I wouldn't worry too much. Not many animals would bother eating humans, except maybe a bear." Bronwyn almost smiled as she remembered her aunt's story about Millie.

"What if there's a bear out there?"

"If there's anything out there, Flux will warn us in plenty of time."

Shortly after dinner everyone sought their beds. Avruellen had put Minx in the tea, an herb renown for its ability to relax and assist sleep. Neither woman wanted to hear the evil laughter in their dreams or watch Augustine die again and again. Flux stood guard while they slept. He was used to going days without sleep. It only happened when they travelled, besides, today he had slept from dawn until Avruellen had left the city.

He sat a few metres from the sleeping women, his ears attuned to the resonances of the forest. The scratching of small rodents ferreting around and nocturnal birds brushing the leaves as they swooped past in search of food reached the fox's ears. Occasionally there came the sound of a larger animal slowly pushing its way through the undergrowth. One sound that caught Flux's attention was the barely audible pad of four careful paws. He pointed his nose in the direction and sniffed, not believing what he sensed. If his nose was right, which it always was, he smelled an animal that did not exist in Wyrden—or even Talia any more. The animal had been extinct for years, hunted to death for its luxurious black coat.

Flux dropped low. The animal was coming in his direction. If it really was what he thought, it would be larger and far stronger than him. It was possible it was the man-eater Corrille was afraid of. He was loathe to notify Avruellen immediately, as the animal might pass without taking any notice of the sleeping humans. If Flux woke them, they would definitely make enough noise to attract the beast's attention.

Flux lay still, heart beating quickly. He waited, the scent intensifying. The creature did not change course. Flux rose into a crouch and backed quietly toward the campsite, carefully waking Avruellen. He invaded her sleep with his mind voice, tender and calming. *Avruellen, wake up quietly. Something is approaching.*

She opened her eyes, remaining still.

I think it could be the mysterious beast you heard about at Pollona. I haven't sighted it, but it smells like a Zamahlan Panther.

Avruellen sat up carefully. It would certainly explain the ravaged cow carcasses the Pollonians were worried

218

about. The Zamahlan Panther was half again as large as a normal panther and could easily have killed and devoured two large animals.

Avruellen was wondering how to handle the situation when Flux growled, a low grumble in his throat. He was looking past Avruellen. She stood up and strained her eyes through the gloom. A large, black beast, head twice as big as hers, white fangs protruding below its top lip, entered the camp. It stopped just beyond the light from the dying fire. Standing almost chest high, it was huge. Yellow-green eyes reflected the light, regarding Avruellen and Flux in equal measures. Flux growled louder.

Corrille woke to see Avruellen standing and Flux with hackles raised. She looked in the direction they stared and saw a vague outline of the huge creature. As soon as she saw its large, yellow eyes, she screamed.

Bronwyn, yanked from slumber, sat up in a sleepy confusion. It took a few seconds for her to understand the situation. She grabbed her sword and scrambled to her feet, while Corrille continued to scream—her shrill voice grating. Avruellen yelled at her to shut up, but the hysterical girl just screamed louder. No one moved.

Through the din, Bronwyn's eyes met the great cat's. She heard his voice in her mind. *So, you are the cub I must train. Can you get that girl to shut up before I kill her?* Avruellen and Flux also heard the panther and stood, mouths gaping. Bronwyn calmly turned to her friend. "Be quiet. Be quiet!" It didn't make any difference. In fear of what the beast would do, she slapped her friend across the cheek. The crack rang out, returning silence to the night. Corrille gingerly touched her red cheek, sobbing in shock.

Bronwyn turned back to the beast. *Is that better?*

Yes, thank you. Now, as I was saying.

Hang on. What do you mean you're going to train me? Train me for what?

I've been sent to bond with you. Bronwyn blinked and slowly shook her head. From what Avruellen had always said, the realmist chose whom they would bond, not the other way around. Not only that, but this animal was communicating with her in a way that should not have been possible given Bronwyn's lack of experience. This animal was not normal.

Who sent you?

Drakon. He thought you might need some help, especially after last night. If you agree to abandon your pride forever, you may join mine. If not, you will all die. So, young cub. What's it to be?

Bronwyn stared at her aunt. She was being presented with an awful choice. Never see her loved ones again, the woman who had sacrificed so much for her, and go with this mysterious creature. Or stay and be the cause of everyone's deaths. It wasn't much of a choice. She would definitely sacrifice everything she had for the safety of her family and friends. She hoped the panther was being truthful and this wasn't just a ruse to separate them. She looked at her aunt for reassurance, but all she saw was a mirror of her own confusion. Bronwyn knew she had a lot to learn about the Realms, and that without her aunt's guidance she would struggle, as she was doing now. The biggest decision of her life and it had to be made within minutes. She drew a deep breath.

Avruellen looked at her niece and back at the beast. Her shock had subsided and she considered the practicalities of the situation. If this beast took Bronwyn, they would be unable to complete the task set for them by Agmunsten. They would fail before they had barely begun. Surely Drakon would not exact his promise in this manner if he knew? Avruellen spoke to the beast, mind to mind, so not even Flux could hear. *You may not take my niece now.*

Don't speak foolishly, old woman. Drakon has ordered it. I will take her now. Do you forget your promise?

Of course not. We have an important journey to complete. When it is done, Bronwyn will be free to fulfill the promise.

The panther stood for a moment, head cocked. He seemed to be listening to something. His head straightened. *The time is now. Drakon offers no apologies or explanations. He will be obeyed.* Avruellen tried to argue but found she could not form words mentally or physically. Enraged, she realised she had been muted either by the panther or Drakon. How dare he interfere! Avruellen's distress was obvious to those around her.

Bronwyn, unappreciative of the true extent of the predicament, walked over to her aunt and hugged her tight. "I'm so sorry. If what that animal says is true, I have to go. It might be the only chance we have. I love you. Thank you for being my mum and dad. I'll miss you so much." She felt that what she said couldn't begin to tell Avruellen how much she meant to her. Tears coursed down her cheeks and dampened her aunt's shoulder. By agreeing to cut ties with Avruellen, she was giving up the possibility of ever learning who her parents were.

Bronwyn turned back to the menacing black beast and spoke calmly through her tears. *When does this bonding take place?*

Soon.

Well, just to let you know: I may have agreed to bond with you and give up my family, but I will not agree to be your puppet. I have to live, or die, by what I feel is right, or wrong, and nothing can change that. If you don't like it I'll choose to stay here and die. The panther's lips curled at the edges in a feline grin.

Say your goodbyes and come with me.

Flux growled in protest. Bronwyn kissed everyone goodbye through salty tears. Corrille was still quietly sobbing and had no idea what was happening as she couldn't hear the cat's side of the conversation. The only thing she could understand was that her friend was saying goodbye.

Within minutes, Bronwyn had fastened all her belongings to Prince. She waved a last, despondent goodbye. Avruellen, Flux, and Corrille watched as she turned her back on them and left. No one spoke. Avruellen couldn't believe what was happening. Her mind was free again, and she cursed Drakon as she crumpled to the ground. First Augustine, and now Bronwyn. The pain of the past two days was too much. Avruellen started keening and couldn't stop.

Bronwyn gritted her teeth as she forced her legs to keep moving against the pull of emotion. She left the clearing and stumbled into the unknown, her aunt's grief shadowing her reluctant footsteps into the dark.

18

As evening settled in, Arcon sat slumped on his bed at the Goat's Head Inn. Blayke had disappeared five days ago. As soon as Phantom had informed him that Blayke had been taken, he had run to the lane where Fang waited. Fang had already squeezed under the gate and inspected the yard but hadn't found a hole in the building big enough to sneak through. Fang suggested Arcon beat the door down. Arcon wasn't sure about revealing themselves; it was probably what Morth wanted. They kept an impatient eye on the terrace all night, but there had been no movement in or out. By morning, Arcon had been frantic with worry and had decided they might as well risk it. If anything happened to Blayke, they were probably all doomed anyway. The prophecy stated he was to play an integral part in defeating the Gormons.

Arcon held his arms in front of his chest, parallel with the ground, palms facing the gate. Drawing a rush of air through the Second Realm, he blew the gate, then the back door, off their hinges, timber splintering to smash against the terrace wall—right now he had no patience for subtlety. They raced inside. The house was empty, the chill indicating Blayke and his captors had probably left last night. After sifting through everything, they had to accept Blayke was gone.

Fang found a trap door in the floor in the kitchen. He followed a small dirt tunnel along its length. At the end was a second door, which opened up two blocks away.

Arcon had first tried to speak to Blayke mind to mind. Fang had already tried, but they couldn't contact him. Chances were, he was still unconscious from the blow to the head—or he was drugged. Arcon scried the Second Realm for Blayke's symbol. He found it, so knew that Blayke was still alive and in town, but he had no idea where.

As the sun set, Arcon again searched the Second Realm for Blayke's symbol. He located the signature bright light moving away from the town in a westerly direction. It had only travelled a short distance. Arcon had memorised the two symbols with his nephew's, and would never forget them. "OK, Fang, we're going. Get your stuff."

My stuff. What stuff?

"Oh sorry. I forgot. I'm so used to speaking to Blayke. Well, hop in my pocket then." The old realmist gathered his and Blayke's packs.

Arcon called out to Phantom, who alighted on the windowsill. Arcon changed his mind about walking; time for ambling was over. He had purchased two brown stallions. With Arcon's help, it took the stable-hand a few minutes to saddle the mounts. He had been prepared to leave town since finding out Blayke had been kidnapped. He knew it was inevitable that Morth would soon depart with his precious cargo.

The trio left the town, Arcon mounted and leading the other horse. He had memorised the direction from his scrying and knew where to go. He revisited the Second Realm each hour to confirm they were heading in the right direction. Morth appeared to be keeping ahead at a constant pace, indicating they, too, had horses. Arcon prodded his horse into a canter, even though visibility was limited in the darkness. He needed to catch up to them on his terms. Morth may just be trying to escape, or may be trying to lead them into a larger trap.

Arcon called Phantom. The owl landed on his heavily padded shoulder. "I don't want to ride into a trap. I need you to fly ahead and have a look. I'm worried Blayke may still be unconscious. If he is, it will make our getaway harder."

Why don't you just kill Morth and the woman he's with?

"I have a feeling it's not going to be as straightforward as that. If they overcame Blayke so easily, they are probably dangerous."

Yes, but Blayke is young and inexperienced.

"Nevertheless, I don't want to underestimate their strength."

I'll let you know as soon as I see them. Phantom shoved Arcon's shoulder down as he pushed off. He flew into the distance and was soon a small speck.

"You've been awfully quiet, little rat."

I'm just worried. I think he's OK. I'm sure I would know if he were seriously hurt. They're keeping him blocked from me somehow. How would they even know what communication Blayke's capable of? They seem to know too much.

"I don't like it either. Whoever has employed them knows what we're all about. I just don't know whether it's Gormon related."

In a way I hope it is. How many enemies can we fight at once?

Arcon was loath to answer that question, so they rode in silence, eagerly awaiting Phantom's news.

When Arcon checked the symbols in the next hour, he was happy to see they were gaining ground on the fugitives. He was hopeful they would catch them before morning. Intermittently, Phantom would relay news about the countryside they were about to cross. His information had ensured a safe trip, so far. With Phantom's help, they could cover ground more quickly than their prey. Arcon took the small comfort he could—while the others were running from them, they had no time to be doing anything unsavoury to his nephew.

It was as if the horses had slipped through another time, another place. Arcon could barely distinguish shapes as they rode past trees, hills, and rocks. Haunting bird cries punctuated the blackness of the cold, still night. The wind rushing past his numb face was created by his urgent flight to save Blayke. Arcon could feel his horse's lathered warmth through his trouser legs and knew he couldn't push him this hard indefinitely. They had to catch up to Morth soon. The situation became more precarious the longer they held Blayke.

Toward dawn Arcon had no choice but to stop and change horses. His mount trembled in near exhaustion, but the horse he had purchased for Blayke was fresher. He mounted Blayke's horse and they continued at a walk. He scanned the symbols. They were very close; maybe they would have caught them within the hour if they could have maintained their previous speed. Daylight would put Morth on a more equal footing. Arcon was frustrated to say the least. He was looking forward to paying Morth back for the stress he was subjecting him to. Morth would be lucky if he kept his life. Arcon would have planned to kill him at first sight if it weren't for the information he might provide.

The morning sun shone weak warmth on the angry realmist. Phantom flew toward his companion and could feel waves of negativity as he soared closer. He changed course and flew a semicircle to come at Arcon from behind, furiously flapping his wings for balance as he alighted on the realmist's shoulder. *You look happy this morning. Let that anger build any more and it's possible you might explode.*

"Not funny. I'm not in the mood. Why are you back here? I thought I told you to keep an eye out."

Phantom knew how upset Arcon was, but was offended nonetheless. *Well, gee, thanks Phantom for flying all bloody night. That's OK, Arcon, glad I could help.* The owl stared at the realmist with large, unblinking eyes.

"Don't look at me like that. Sorry. I know I'm being disagreeable."

That's not the word I would've used. Anyway, I'm back because they've dumped Blayke.

"What! Why didn't you send it to me? Is he alright?"

He's fine. Drugged and dead to the world … I mean, he's asleep. It seems as if Morth knows something about the Realms. It looked like he was scrying for your whereabouts. He may know your symbol.

Arcon swore. This was going to complicate things. *As soon as he knew you were going to catch them he ditched Blayke and ran, like the coward he is.*

Arcon nudged the horse into a canter. "How far away?"

About ten minutes at this pace. I'll fly ahead and make sure he's alright. The owl pushed off. Fang heard the conversation, his head and front paws hanging over the top of Arcon's pocket. Blayke and Fang had been automatically included in the mindspeak between Arcon and Phantom as soon as they had bonded. The rat stared eagerly into the distance, whiskers twitching as he tried to pick up Blayke's scent.

Fang could soon smell the unmistakable odour of the young realmist. He nervously ran his paws over his trembling whiskers. *We're almost there, I can smell him.* Arcon gently stroked Fang's back in acknowledgement. Within minutes Arcon saw Blayke's unmoving body lying face up on the rocky road, obviously discarded in a hurry, Phantom perched on his chest, moving up and down ever so slightly with each of the young man's breaths.

Arcon threw himself off the horse and rushed to his nephew, falling to his knees beside the limp body. Fang jumped out of Arcon's pocket and ran along Blayke's arm to sit on his shoulder, his usual wariness of Phantom forgotten.

Arcon stared intently at the young man's face. It was OK except for the indented purple circles under his eyes. Arcon leaned over his mouth and sniffed his breath. It had a metallic odour. Quickly fetching his pack, he dug through everything until he found what he was looking for: two different herbs, his water flask, and a mug. He placed water in the mug, cradling it in both hands. Using energy from the Second Realm, he had it boiling in seconds. Holding an equal measure of each herb in the palm of his hand, he closed his hand; when he opened it, the dried leaves had disintegrated into powder. He dropped them into the mug and let it sit for a few minutes.

Gently cradling Blayke's head in his lap, he administered the brew. It was a slow process to get the liquid down the unconscious man's throat without choking or burning him. Both creaturas looked on in concern. It was a matter of time to see if the concoction counteracted the poison Morth had given him. Arcon was delighted when Blayke's eyes fluttered open, albeit weakly.

The young realmist was relieved to see his friends looking at him instead of Morth and his evil mother. His mouth was full of the taste of what Arcon had given him. It was not pleasant, but not as bad as what Morth had shoved in his mouth when he was last awake. "Sorry, I messed up."

Arcon couldn't help but laugh. "You really are the master of understatement. Don't worry about that right now. We'll talk later. How do you feel?"

"Like I've been trampled by a herd of angry bulls. Everything aches so much that I can't distinguish one part of my body from the next. I could tell they had given me Vetchus, and I knew it wasn't fatal. I was more worried what they would do when I was unconscious."

"It's nice to know you were listening when I gave you the lessons on poisons. It's also good that it hasn't affected your memory."

"I'm so sorry, Arcon. I still can't believe I was so stupid."

"Not stupid, necessarily. I'll put this one down to youthful naivety, but I'll call the next one stupidity."

"There won't be a next one."

"Unfortunately there's always a next one. For now, I'll make up your bed and we'll stay here for the day. I'd love to get my hands on that manure-eating parasite right now, but we all need a rest."

Arcon prepared the camp, and they slept for a few hours, with the exception of Fang, who, as well as being excited at finding Blayke, had slept a while in Arcon's pocket on the way. He woke them mid-afternoon. The clear sky had clouded over. Arcon prepared food, which Blayke felt well enough to eat. Blayke managed to mount his horse by himself by the time Arcon had cleared the camp. He was slightly dizzy, but that was all. Arcon's plan was to ride a few hours in the dark, make camp and continue again in the morning. He would wait until then to ask Blayke the many questions he had.

Arcon knew they had to reach Vellonia as soon as possible, but if Morth was nearby, it would be prudent to delete him before he could cause any more trouble. Arcon scried the Second Realm for Morth's symbol. He travelled through the blackness past symbol after symbol. None were his. He travelled back and forth in disbelief. Unless Morth and his mother had died, it was impossible for their symbols to have disappeared.

Arcon opened his eyes. "Well, Blayke, I don't know how, but Morth and his mother appear to have befallen some unfortunate accident."

"What do you mean?"

"I can't find their symbols anywhere. Maybe whoever they were working for took offence at the fact they failed."

"I can't believe we'd be so lucky."

"If they were alive anywhere I'd be able to see them, unless they've been shielded." Arcon tapped the end of his nose with his index finger while he pondered the possibility of Morth being around to annoy them later.

"I bloody hope they're not being shielded. I hope they're dead. So what do we do now?"

"Get ourselves to Vellonia." Arcon nudged his horse forward and they started the last leg of their journey toward the dragon city. Arcon was eager to meet with everyone. Once they all put their experiences and information together, a pattern might emerge.

Arcon had the irritating feeling that, although he couldn't find Morth's symbol, it wasn't the last time they would be bothered by the pair. If they were still alive, and their symbols being protected, it would indicate that Morth had more power than most realmists. The alternative was worse. Whoever Morth was in league with was more powerful than Arcon cared to imagine. He promised himself he would be more careful than usual. He would not feel safe until they reached Vellonia, and that was at least a week away.

Arcon dreaded the sleepless nights he knew would be his until they reached their destination. It was at times like this he regretted his choices in life. It would have been nicer to be a blacksmith, maybe even a farmer. Phantom's voice cut into his thoughts. *But then you wouldn't know me.*

"True, my old friend. Do you ever regret the path you've taken?"

Not for all the mice in the world. I would have been bored by a normal life in the forest. I have a suspicion life would have seemed dull to you if your time were spent planting vegetables or shoeing horses. Arcon thought about it, however in this time of danger, was reluctant to agree.

He scried the Second Realm again; still no Morth. Arcon felt it was time to match wits. He would shield their symbols, which he hadn't done until now because it took a monumental amount of energy. Most of his consciousness would have to remain in the Second Realm. That meant he could not deal with everyday physical dangers.

"I'm going to shield our symbols."

Blayke inhaled sharply and explained the grave implications to Fang then turned to Arcon.

"If you do that it will take you days, even weeks to recover, even if you can hold it until we reach Vellonia."

"I'm well aware of that, thank you. Right now we don't have a choice." His voice held a strength and determination Blayke could not argue with. "Obviously the rest of you will have to keep an eye out and deal with any situations. I'll commence shielding tonight. You'll have to take turns on watch. I'm sorry to say we'll all be tired by the time we reach Vellonia, but that's as it has to be." This was a huge decision for Arcon; he was not comfortable with delegating. He liked to be in control. Leaving Blayke without supervision was almost as hard for him as the task he was about to undertake, especially in light of what had recently befallen the young man.

That night after dinner, Arcon left Phantom with last-minute instructions. When he was as satisfied as he could be that things would be taken care of, he put himself into a trance. He had never before shielded for such an extended period of time. The energy it would take might be enough to kill him, a fact he declined to impart to his companions. Blayke would have to feed Arcon, get him on and off his horse, take him to the toilet and put him to bed. This leg of their journey was going to be difficult; there was still no guarantee they would reach the dragon city alive. Arcon would have smiled, however, if he could have heard the great howl of displeasure from the Third Realm when their four symbols disappeared from view. None of them knew it, but maybe things were looking up.

19

Avruellen had finally fallen into a fitful sleep after exhausting her tears and woke with an immediate feeling of distress. She knew something dreadful had happened, and it took a few post-slumber seconds for the memory to stab her again. She quietly recalled the events of the previous night. A still-confused Corrille interrupted her thoughts.

"Miss Avruellen, are you alright?" Bronwyn's friend looked genuinely concerned.

Avruellen remembered her grief and admitted to herself it must have been quite a sight. "I'm OK, Corrille. I'm sorry you had to see that."

"Where has Bronwyn gone? Why did you let her leave with that horrible beast?" Corrille's voice accused her. "He's probably eaten her by now."

Avruellen shook her head and wondered how she would explain this without giving away their secrets. She scried the Second Realm and found Bronwyn's symbol. It seemed they had covered a goodly distance since the previous night. Avruellen wondered if they had bonded yet; probably not. They would have had to stop for a while to do that. She hoped Bronwyn survived the test; it was never easy. More than one young realmist had ended their career, and life, by making an error whilst bonding.

"I can assure you she is still alive. I know this is confusing for you, but I don't have an explanation right now."

"Are we at least going to look for her?"

"I haven't thought about it." Avruellen was telling the truth. Their task was unfinished. She had two choices: immediately continue to The Isle of the Dead Souls via Vellonia, or find Bronwyn first. There was no way for her to know if Bronwyn was definitely required at the Isle. If she was, Avruellen would be wasting her time getting there by herself. On the other hand, if Bronwyn was only to have been a spectator, Avruellen could still do whatever it was Agmunsten required.

"Corrille, I need time to think. Could you gather some more timber and I'll start breakfast." Corrille, thankfully, hastily complied with the request. Avruellen turned to Flux. *What do you think we should do?*

The fox looked at her with sympathy. *Which direction are they traveling?*

South.

That's only slightly off course. Where do you think they're headed?

The only important place directly south of here is Vellonia, although we still can't be sure that's where they'll end up.

Once again Drakon's booming voice interrupted their conversation. *Do not follow them. They have something to do for me first. You will not go to Vellonia now. If you try to follow them, I will make sure you never reach them. Am I understood?*

Avruellen suffered an uncontrollable shiver. The Dragon God was now threatening her, not to mention he was contradicting plans previously made by The Circle. As if she didn't have enough to contend with already.

His presence vanished before she had a chance to answer.

Well, Av, it looks like the decision's been made for us.

She nodded at Flux with a glum face. Everything seemed out of her control; things were definitely not going as planned.

Corrille returned, placing her armful of timber on the fire, which exuded a renewed heat. Breakfast consisted of leftovers from Augustine's kitchen washed down with strong tea. Avruellen had made peace with her decision by the completion of breakfast, resolving that she would carry out her task as best she could. She could not tell Corrille the truth, as the young woman would likely make life difficult if she knew they were not going to "save" her friend. "Corrille, I have decided we will search for Bronwyn. Flux knows her smell and can follow a trail that is days old. Don't worry. We'll find her."

Avruellen didn't like lying, but saw no other way. Corrille was immediately happy. In her eagerness to find her friend she had her horse saddled and waiting within minutes, even helping Avruellen to gather her things.

Riding out that morning, Avruellen was in better spirits than she could have hoped to be, considering. It was good to have made a decision, to have a direction, even if the decision had been made for them. In the next few days they would cross from Veresia into Wyrden then quickly into Brenland. They were travelling in a southwesterly direction, toward the seaside town of Carpus. From there they would board a boat and travel to The Isle of the Dead Souls. What would happen once they arrived was a mystery to Avruellen, and she contemplated the wisdom of taking Corrille.

If she could come up with a safe way to do it, maybe she would leave Corrille at Carpus and collect her on their return from the island. If they returned. Avruellen was a methodical person and didn't like all these ifs and maybes. She wondered how the others were doing. Having received no bad news, she assumed things were OK. Avruellen finally decided to search the Second Realm for the others; it would be comforting to know where they were. Agmunsten appeared to be more than midway between Bayerlon and Vellonia. Maybe she could ask him to keep an eye out for Bronwyn, although she didn't want to alarm him. She decided not to reveal their predicament yet and wait to see his position in a few days as opposed to Bronwyn's.

She scried for Arcon. It was a shocking thing to be looking and not seeing what she anticipated. It didn't matter how much she searched the seemingly starry blackness of the Second Realm, the symbols she expected to see were not there. It was difficult to push down the swell of panic expanding in her. There must be a good reason. Surely if something had happened to them Agmunsten would know and tell her. Should she risk contacting Agmunsten? If the Gormons were paying attention, they would find out the Head Realmist's symbol. She couldn't risk it. The out-of-control feeling was back again, and ten times worse. They had barely begun to defend Talia, and already everything was falling apart.

Avruellen took a deep breath and focused her attention on the land sprawled out in front of her. It would do no good to dwell in the negative, so she might as well ignore it, hard as it would be. She thought about Bronwyn, recalling her steadfast optimism. Her beautiful smile was always guaranteed to cheer her up. Bronwyn always considered the most positive option before the negative; a trait she had inherited from her father. For a moment she regretted not telling her niece much about her parents. The problem was, one piece of information always led to another question, and Avruellen couldn't afford to tell Bronwyn too much about her parentage; it would jeopardise their mission.

The road ahead swam in and out between low-lying hills. The recent rain had benefitted the landscape; the lush green grass was interspersed with spring flowers of red, blue, and gold. Butterflies and birds flitted around the newly blossoming trees seeking nectar and insects. In spite of herself, the realmist smiled at nature's beauty. The importance of what they were doing was reiterated to her. If the Gormons had their way, all of this would be churned into a burnt and bloody catastrophe. Avruellen drew renewed hope from the spring fragrances which filled her nose.

She turned and looked at Corrille who was riding a few lengths behind, not sure of what state her friend's aunt was in. "It's OK. I'm feeling better now." Avruellen smiled. "Come and ride with me. The journey will go faster with some conversation."

Corrille hesitated, however found her way to the side of the woman of whom she was still frightened. Not sure what the older woman wanted to talk about, she waited for her to start the conversation.

"I've been following Bronwyn's trail, and I'm thinking we'll probably catch up to her in a few days."

"How can you know?" Corrille peered sideways at Avruellen.

"When I was young, my parents taught me hunting and tracking skills. See that hoof print over there?" Avruellen pointed at an old print, left a few days ago by a horse she would never know. Hopefully a few well-placed falsities would quell the younger woman's suspicions. Her companion nodded almost imperceptibly. "There's a smaller track next to it." Corrille was turning her head to watch the spot as they rode past. "That print belongs to the panther, so they have been this way. We'll find them." Avruellen was thankful that whoever had ridden past earlier had decided to have a large dog with them, a Great Dane, if she knew her paw prints. Corrille was teetering on the brink of belief. Avruellen would not push her any more. A few subtle comments would nudge her over the edge eventually.

"I can see you're still not sure. You'll just have to trust me. I think at this stage you don't have a choice. It will be safer for all of us if we stay together." Corrille wanted to object but, unusually, saw the sense in what her friend's aunt said. She still didn't trust her and knew there was something about the whole situation that was definitely not normal. As long as she didn't know what that was, she would keep her eyes open and feign obedience, let Avruellen underestimate her. If the old woman was lying, she would find out, and then she would see what Corrille was made of.

Corrille had grown up in a tough environment and was happy lying to others. Sometimes lying was the only way to save herself from her father's drunken wrath. She had also done things that no one knew about. In fact, if anyone found out, they would be horrified; Corrille smiled in remembrance. She looked over at Avruellen who mistook the smile for friendliness and smiled back. *Foolish woman,* Corrille thought, *one day you'll regret pushing me around.* Her smile widened into a wolfish grin.

Avruellen kept smiling but shuddered at the look on Corrille's face. *That girl is more evil than I thought.*

Avruellen spoke silently to the fox trotting beside her horse. *Keep an eye on Corrille. She's planning something.*

Are you sure you're not being paranoid?

When have I ever been paranoid and wasn't right?

Never. But there's always a first time. There's something about her, but I think she's harmless.

Avruellen slowly and firmly shook her head. *I'm not asking you to share my opinion; just keep an eye on her.*

Flux nodded. *I smell a rabbit. I'll be back soon.*

And I smell a rat. Avruellen smiled at her own joke.

Very funny.

Avruellen watched Flux as he dashed off into nearby bushes.

They stopped just long enough to eat lunch because the realmist wanted to get to Carpus as soon as possible. Her plan now definitely included ditching Corrille there. If that girl discovered what she was, she would probably scream it to everyone who would listen. Avruellen didn't need any trouble from a fearful, god-fearing population. Many preachers told their congregations that realmists were acting against the orders of the gods. This, of course, was a lie, however, many religious leaders wanted to secure their place in the world and saw any competition as a threat.

Corrille assumed the brief stop was to find Bronwyn sooner. Her best friend had only been gone a short while, but she missed her terribly so was happy to eat quickly and continue. Bronwyn, in her eyes, was the one person she could trust in this world. Bronwyn was always positive and made her feel good about herself. It seemed as if every other person she had the misfortune to be associated with was there to bring her down. All the terrible things she had done in the past had been forced on her. If she had been treated with kindness instead of cruelty, the situations she often found herself in would not have occurred, therefore others were to blame for her actions, or as she thought, reactions.

She still couldn't get used to the old woman telling her what to do and comforted herself by admitting at least she wasn't being abused. Nevertheless, as soon as they found Bronwyn, Corrille planned to convince her to leave her aunt behind. Whatever her aunt was hoping to achieve was her own business, as had been made clear several times. Corrille didn't see why they had to be dragged along just so Avruellen had someone to order around.

Afternoon flowed into night with a spectacular retreat of daylight. Avruellen admired the fiery hues of sunset, which soon cooled into a vast and starry black canopy. "It's time to find a camp site."

"Why can't we ride a bit longer? I don't want to lose any more ground on Bronwyn."

"We'll injure the horses. Bronwyn and that big cat can't walk all night either. I'm sure they've stopped by now." Before Corrille could argue, Avruellen and Flux veered off the road and were headed into the trees. Not wanting to be left alone in the dark, not to mention without food, Corrille had no choice but to follow.

They stopped not far from the road, Avruellen choosing a place that wasn't a clearing but smaller spaces between trees. Avruellen directed where Corrille was to place her bedroll. She felt insulted by the order; she was old enough to find a suitable place by herself. The young woman was tired after riding all day and upset at losing Bronwyn. The tongue she should have stilled was in no mood for silence. "Stop treating me like a child. I'm so sick of you telling me what to do. If it weren't for you bringing us here, none of this would have happened." She walked over to Avruellen and looked with hatred, into her eyes. Her voice pitched lower. "If Bronwyn dies, it is because of you. If Bronwyn dies, I will have no one. If Bronwyn dies, I will make sure you pay for it, you hateful hag."

Avruellen's eyes widened, her brows rising as far as they could go. She was amazed at the girl's lack of self-control, but at least she knew unequivocally what Corrille thought of her. The older woman had too much experience to lose her temper, and was not in the least worried what the little upstart thought of her. Avruellen assumed her most authoritative expression and spoke in a calm voice.

"I'm sorry you feel that way, Corrille my dear, but you knew the rules when you joined us. I'm quite disappointed in your lack of appreciation. No one asked you to follow us. In fact, if it weren't for me, you would probably be lying half-rotted in a ditch by now. As for Bronwyn's predicament, that was out of my hands. Unfortunately, life doesn't always gift us with what we wish. Things happen, many times for no reason at all, and we must make the best of it. You may be sad that your friend has gone, but I've lost my niece and I can assure you that I will find her, with or without your assistance. If you plan to fight me at every turn, you should leave now. Your arrogance and selfishness will only make my job harder. If you wish to stay, you must apologise. I'm sure I can find it in my generous heart to forgive you and continue to watch over you. Right now I'm going to start dinner, and by the time it's cooked I expect you'll have a decision for me." Avruellen nodded once and turned her back on Corrille.

Corrille, heated with fury, stood where Avruellen had left her. How dare that woman turn things around to make it look like she was at fault? Unappreciative? Avruellen had exacted her price many times over. Corrille had been treated with distrust since the moment she officially joined their party. Avruellen had used the girls as nothing more than slave labour, setting up camp, collecting firewood and water, not to mention the days of hardship sleeping in the wilderness. Avruellen had a way of making her feel so small. How dare she speak to her that way!

As insulted as Corrille was, she knew to lose her temper again would be playing into the old woman's hands. She was not prepared to repeat that mistake so decided to walk off the anger. Not wanting to get lost, she stayed within the tree-line, but paralleled with the road. After walking briskly a while, the fire in her abated and so did her pace. She found a comfortable place to sit, at the base of a large tree whose leaves were sprouting anew after winter's nakedness. Her thoughts turned to her friend and the many fun times they had shared. Comforting thoughts caressed her tired, emotionally drained mind. Slowly she drifted into a dreamless slumber.

Avruellen had called Corrille to dinner several times. At first, the lack of response was annoying. After a while it was worrying. Avruellen sent Flux to find her. The fox's sensitive sense of smell would make his task easy. Flux followed his nose along the path she had taken. After a while he found where she had fallen asleep. Flux sent to Avruellen. *I found where she went. Unfortunately she's not here anymore.*

What do you mean? If she's not there then you have to keep following her trail.

That could be difficult. Her scent stops here. It appears as if she's vanished into thin air.

Boh! That's impossible. Wait there. I'm coming.
Just follow a parallel line to the road.

Avruellen reached Flux in fifteen minutes. She searched for any clues around the base of the trunk until she had to acknowledge that Flux was right. Flux waited patiently for her to complete the search he had already done. Avruellen was a perfectionist and found it hard to leave well enough alone once she had accepted a task.

The realmist craned her neck and looked to the higher foliage. It was impossible to see anything in the darkness between the leaves. Avruellen approached the tree and placed both palms on the rough trunk. She was going to use energy from the tree itself. The power required for what she wanted to do was only a trickle, not enough to give them up to the enemy by having to go to the Second Realm. She filled her arms and mind with the tree's effervescence. *Look skywards Flux.* The realmist craned her neck to stare high above them. She removed her hands from the trunk, turned her lined palms upward and released the harvested energy. The light illuminated everything amongst the canopy. Avruellen was careful not to broadcast too much light, lest it travel beyond the trees and attract unwanted attention.

The pair gazed around. When it was clear Corrille was not there, Avruellen placed her palms back on the trunk and returned the unused particles of power. Drawing energy from living things would not harm them, unless you took too much and left them nothing with which to sustain themselves. In this case, Avruellen had only used enough power to slow the tree's growth for a couple of days.

Avruellen thought about scrying for Corrille's symbol, but remembered she had not thought to find out what it was. The only way to find out someone's symbol was to be shown a mind image or to touch the person and follow the near invisible aura that joined the symbol to the body via the second realm. She could have kicked herself.

What to do now, Flux?

Blessing in disguise? The fox cocked his head.

Maybe. If she'd run off by herself that would be one thing. However, it appears as if she's had assistance.

"Whoever helped her is beyond my sense of smell." Flux's calm demeanor irritated Avruellen.

Does nothing ever worry you? Obviously whoever helped her is plotting against us and is more of a danger than that girl could ever be.

Not necessarily.

Avruellen blew out an exasperated breath at Flux's unfounded optimism, although, as much as this latest event was an unexpected and suspicious incident, there were some positives to come out of it. With Corrille gone, their lives on the road would be easier. Not only could Avruellen be her realmist self, the problem of what to do with the girl when they reached Carpus was solved.

They returned to the campsite where two bedrolls were laid out near the fire. "Hmm, I hope whoever took her has somewhere for her to sleep." Avruellen smiled at the thought of Corrille trying to sleep on bare, hard ground whilst shivering all the while. Flux sensed her mood and shook his pointy face.

Avruellen continued, "I know I shouldn't be amused by another's suffering, but..." The fox gave her a disapproving look, the end of his bushy tail twitching.

Avruellen ate half the dinner she had prepared whilst Flux dined on a large, warm rabbit. Avruellen would eat the rest of her vegetarian stew for breakfast in the morning. With Corrille gone, the provisions would last twice as long, even three times without Bronwyn. The realmist blew air out of her mouth in a fierce sigh. She scried for her niece, whose course appeared to be continuing toward Vellonia. The sight of her descendant's life force was comforting. At least she would be safe for a while within the walls of Vellonia.

Avruellen spoke out loud. "I wonder what Drakon wants with our Bronny. The dragons are opportunistic creatures, and I've only ever known them to help when they're going to benefit as well. If anything happens to Bronwyn, god or no god, he'll regret it." Avruellen's eyes narrowed to slits, the orange glow from the fire lending her a fierceness Flux rarely saw.

Don't worry until something happens. We have enough to deal with as it is. The fox was a practical and self-assured creature. There was usually no doubt in Flux's mind that whatever it was they needed to do to get through would be done.

"You are right, my wise creatura. What would I ever do without you?" Flux padded to her and was subsequently enveloped in a robust hug.

Avruellen changed for bed; she detested wearing dirty, horse-fragrant clothes when she slept. "Tonight we'll both get some rest." Avruellen walked a small way from their campsite and set wards. If anything breached them, physically or otherwise, they would know. For the first time, almost since they set out, they could sleep without keeping watch.

Even though the mystery of Corrille's disappearance was worrying, Avruellen fell asleep easily. As she had come to realise over many decades, problems would still be there, no worse, no better, in the morning. No amount of worrying would help them disappear. This problem would resolve itself eventually, probably at the most inopportune time, however there was nothing to be done about that.

As she slept she dreamt. She was watching a beautiful young woman with tendrils of soft, dark hair trailing across her lightly tanned face as she slept. She was wrapped in a familiar bedroll. The fire was low, its dim light fluttering softly as it strained to reach Bronwyn. The large black cat sat at her feet, surveying the surroundings. Avruellen smiled in joy. Her niece was safe. The big cat looked in the direction from which the realmist observed. "Drakon has sent you this dream. He wishes you to see that Bronwyn is safe. He is not a God without empathy. He would never ask a price you were not capable of paying." The cat looked back to the darkness surrounding the camp in a dismissal of the watcher.

When Avruellen woke, the dream lingered like sweet perfume. She rose with a smile on her face. Flux was not there. He had most likely gone to catch breakfast. Avruellen poured water from her flask into the kettle to make tea, washing her face with the remainder. She made a note to fill up all the flasks at the first stream they came across. By the time she had dressed and packed up her bed, the kettle had boiled. Flux returned whilst she was enjoying her tea.

How did you sleep?

"Very well, thank you. Almighty Drakon sent me a dream." She found it hard to keep the sarcasm from her voice. Dragons, and obviously dragon gods, had the talent of sending dreams. They could also force nightmares on a sleeper; however, whatever they sent was reality, somewhere. Knowing they could only send truth, a version of it anyway, Avruellen was satisfied that what she had seen was real.

What was the dream about?

"Bronny." Avruellen smiled as she described what she had seen. Flux grinned his foxy smile at the news, sharp teeth ever so slightly exposed.

It seems Drakon has a conscience after all. Avruellen nodded at Flux's observation.

Avruellen hummed a tune as she finished tidying their temporary lodgings. They started the day by having one last look around where Corrille had vanished. Nothing had changed since the previous night; they were unable to find any clue as to where she had gone, how, or with whom. Flux didn't like riddles. Being a fox, and therefore supposedly cunning, he felt that no one should be able to do anything that puzzled him. Flux turned the problem over and over in his mind while they continued on to Carpus. As they grew closer to their destination, the solution remained frustratingly in the distance.

They moved south from Wyrden across into Brenland. Fine days where the sun radiated welcome heat were interspersed with cloudy days that dampened Avruellen's clothes and burdened Flux's fur with an unpleasant odour. With the coast, and Carpus, only three days away, they noted a change in the land. Thick forests were thinning to large tracts of cleared farmland. This part of Brenland was relatively flat, the occasional low hill adding variety to an otherwise uniform countryside. Flux had taken to pondering Corrille's disappearance for only two hours a day.

By the time they were a day's ride from the ocean, the wind had risen to an uncomfortable, gusty cold.

Avruellen sensed a storm building far out to sea. She had spent a small period of her two hundred and four years in a seaside town on the eastern coast of Veresia. She had been quite young then, about one hundred and ten. Her incarnation was as Anna, a forty-year old spinster. After five years in the town, and numerous marriage proposals, she decided to move on. It wasn't that she had anything against men, it was just that she didn't have the will to get close to and watch another partner die. So far she had outlived two husbands and one "special" friend.

The other problem she had encountered was that she was so much older than everyone—she felt like a cradle-snatcher, even toward seventy year olds. Her appearance would have, even now, attracted men a quarter of her age. The fact that a realmist's physical appearance didn't alter significantly over time didn't help Avruellen when she thought of how old she really was, and how quickly she grew bored with people who, in comparison to her, had such little experience in life.

Flux and Avruellen were relieved when they sighted the dark, blue-grey bay and ocean in the distance. They would reach Carpus just before nightfall, and, for the first time in a while, Avruellen would sleep in a comfortable bed. Even more exciting was the hot bath she would enjoy. Flux trotted off in the opposite direction as they neared the large town. Over the years, they had found that a fox was not appreciated in any built-up area. No one believed Avruellen when she explained he was tame.

A low wall surrounded the coastal town. A cluster of houses crouched near the top of a gentle slope, which gradually fell toward the bay. At the bottom of the hill sat warehouses and two large wharves— their thick timber legs standing steadfastly out into the bay. Carpus Bay was a small inlet, just big enough for two or three large ships at a time. Two narrow cliffs enclosed it on either side. The cliffs rose steep and pointed, so much so that it was almost impossible to walk along the ridges. They ascended above the highest point of the town—an unusual formation caused by an ancient volcanic eruption. The cliffs protected the deep waters from the most ferocious storms; only southerly winds and waves funneled into the bay.

Avruellen halted her horse inside the low wall, which was little more than a boundary marking—too low to offer any protection from enemies. She gazed out to sea, and in the fading light, white foam could be seen capping the distant waves. The howling wind tore at her hair and blew dirt in her eyes. A direct southerly blew the moderate swell into the bay. One large and one small ship were anchored a short distance from the wharves. If they had tied up to the dock, the waves would have smashed them to pieces before the cargo was unloaded. It looked as if Avruellen would have to wait for calmer seas before she undertook the journey to the Isle of the Dead Souls.

She sent to Flux. *Seas are too rough. I'll wait a couple of days and see if the wind abates. In the meantime I'm going to find the most luxurious inn I can.*

But our task is urgent.

I know, but no sailor would voluntarily set out in this weather, especially if the storm is building.

I'll check back with you tomorrow.

OK, Flux. Goodnight.

Goodnight, Av.

Avruellen found the best of the four inns the town had to offer; an imposing three-level stone building with a meticulously trimmed, silver-leafed hedge that hugged the front verandah, protecting it from strong sea breezes. A robust, bright-pink, flowering plant hung in numerous pots from the verandah ceiling. She wasn't too surprised to find such a well looked after establishment because, although the town was small, many merchants came here to check on, or collect, their imported goods—and they were finicky about their accommodation.

After a hot dinner of roast vegetables and bread with butter, she bathed in a luxuriously deep tub, fragrant petals bobbing on the surface of the steaming water. Avruellen always carried sweet-smelling bath additives—just in case an opportunity such as this presented itself. She soaked until the water became too cold to be comfortable, her skin soft and prune-like.

The relaxing evening was just what Avruellen needed. As usual, she checked that the sheets were clean before she slid into them, because some people had a different idea of what that was than she did. Tonight the bed was acceptable and very comfortable. She snuggled down until the covers settled softly under her nose.

So many sad and stressful things that had happened lately. Behind closed eyes, she conjured up the image of Bronwyn sleeping peacefully, surprisingly protected by the large beast that had taken her. Avruellen held onto that happy thought as she drifted to sleep.

She dreamed again. In this dream, which felt so real, her perspective was from the corner of the living area of a weathered cottage. She had no idea where the cottage was, although she could hear a fierce wind screaming outside. As her eyes adjusted to the dim candlelight, she smelled smoke from a newly extinguished fire. For a brief moment she was comforted by its similarity to the life she had recently left.

Abruptly, through the smoke, came the sweet and metallic odour of fresh blood. How was it she could smell in a dream? Avruellen quickly understood this was not a normal dream; it was a nightmare, and it was real, somewhere.

An overturned chair lay next to a smashed dining table. A half-eaten dinner sprawled over the floor lay mashed amongst sharp pieces of broken porcelain. Amidst the ruins, in the heart of a once-welcoming home, lay the unfortunate occupant. Avruellen's dream eyes widened. A young woman, aged thirty or so, was lodged between the broken table and what could only be described as an horrific monstrosity. Her head lolled back, once-beautiful green eyes gaping at nothing. Death had not come quickly. They say the face acquires a peaceful look in death; Avruellen assumed whoever started that rumor had never seen anyone die this way.

She wanted to look away, to flee back to her body, to wake up, but she couldn't tear her eyes away from the hideous sight. A small, unblemished child's hand gripped the dead woman's pale shoulder. There shouldn't have been long, sharp talons protruding from the once innocent fingers, the spikes sunk deep into cooling flesh. The boy's arms looked thicker than they should have been whilst his torso retained its prepubescent skinniness, ribs and spine protruding through unusually translucent, pallid, green skin. Avruellen shook her head at the short, scaly tail that protruded a few inches from the base of the naked boy's spine.

The realmist gagged when she heard the slurping and crunching of human meat. The boy's face was buried in the still-warm belly, teeth exhuming entrails as he ate his way through to the spine. The victim's blood spattered the boy's skin, which had developed into an unnatural, slimy membrane, allowing blue veins to show through. Layers of old, brown and new, red blood crusted the boy's formerly-pale hair. Realisation of what this boy was becoming hit Avruellen as surely as if she had been run through with a jagged blade.

Irving's head rose from its abhorrent meal, vertebra clicking one by one with the movement. Avruellen shuddered. As Irving's green, malignant eyes met Avruellen's, she knew with an absolutely terrified certainty that she was the only person alive today who had ever seen a Gormon. It took all her effort, but she fled the horror, to return to her now-sweaty body, tangled in sheets that had lost their crispness.

Avruellen sat up, breathing heavily. She wiped her nose with the back of a shaking hand, but the sickly smell of death lingered as if to remind her of the reality they all must face. She desperately wanted another bath. Her breathing was too fast and shallow. Feeling light-headed, she forced herself to take deep breaths. *Flux? Flux, are you there?*

Yes. You're interrupting my dinner. They breed rabbits fat around here.

I'm afraid something terrible's happened. The tone of her mind voice grabbed Flux's attention; he dreaded what she would say next.

I had a dream. The emphasis on the word "dream" let Flux know it was a reality dream. *I saw a Gormon.*

She couldn't believe she was saying those words. The only words the fox feared. *Are you sure?*

I've never been more sure of anything in my life. It was in infant form. It appears as if it's possessed a young boy and is now metamorphosing into an adult Gormon.

How long will that take? Once it's an adult we'll be in real trouble.

Trust me, Flux, we're in real trouble now.

What are you going to do?

I'll have to tell Agmunsten and discuss it with him before we go any further. I'll let you know when I've spoken to him.

You know what a great risk it is to contact him.

Boh! Of course I know! But what does it matter? I have no choice. Flux let go of the mind link. He had never heard his companion so distressed. What did he expect when their worst nightmare was a reality. His appetite, unsurprisingly, was gone, however he pushed his worry to the side and set about finishing his meal. It could be his last.

20

Agmunsten slept. In his dream, he was guest of honour at a large feast and happily partaking of all his favourite foods: roast lamb, spiced roast vegetables, a rich and moist pudding filled with honeyed custard, fresh, thick cream drizzling its way from the top of the sweet mound to the plate. He looked across the dining table and locked eyes with an attractive, blonde-haired woman who must have been at least 470 years his junior. He revelled in what a good night he was having as she smiled suggestively at him. He heard a voice at his back.

Agmunsten. Agmunsten. Wake up. I have to talk to you.

Not now. I'm having a nice dream.

Wake up, damn you. This is urgent. Avruellen was practically yelling. She was in no mood for subtlety.

Agmunsten reluctantly woke up and refocused. *What is it, Av?*

Avruellen recounted her dream, instant by instant. The Head Realmist listened intently, face sad but calm when the story finished. Avruellen noticed he was neither scared nor surprised. *Did you already know about this?*

In a way I knew they were here. This is definitely a development, though. He headed off the anger he knew would be coming from his colleague. *There was no point telling you, or anyone, about what happened. It would've only started a panic, and unfortunately it wouldn't change anything. You still need to do what I've asked.*

"There's something else. Agmunsten didn't like the sound of that. *Bronwyn has left us, and her friend Corrille, horrible, ungrateful cow, has vanished. I'm afraid it's just Flux and I.* Agmunsten pondered the news.

That's unexpected. Agmunsten pinched the end of his beard between his fingers. *Why did Bronwyn leave?*

"*Interference from Drakon, I'm afraid. He sent a large, black beast to take her away. I've checked on her though, and she is safe.* Agmunsten let out the breath he hadn't realised he was holding.

This information changed things. He was sure Bronwyn's presence was necessary at The Isle of the Dead Souls, and what needed to be done had to be done soon. He wanted thinking time. *I'll reach Vellonia in two days, all going well. I'd like to discuss this with Zim. Stay put until I tell you otherwise.*

I can't get a boat anyway. The wind's blowing a gale and probably won't let up for a few days. I'll be here. Let me know as soon as you work something out.

OK. Stay safe.

I'll do my best. Bye.

Agmunsten rose from his warm bed, shivering as his bare feet touched the cold floor. He dressed and gently prized Arie awake. The boy was sharing his room, and King Edmund was in an adjoining room. Early in their travels Edmund had learned the hard way that Agmunsten was a snorer of cacophonous proportions, so whenever they weren't camping, Edmund insisted on having his own room. Arie was jealous. He found it tiring to always be getting out of bed to push Agmunsten onto his side. Usually it worked, but he was forced to make the trip between beds once or twice a night. It would be nice to have a good night's sleep for a change.

Arie reluctantly opened one eye at a time. "It's still dark. Why are you waking me up?"

"I've decided I want to get to Vellonia sooner. No more questions. I'm going to wake Edmund, and I expect you to be dressed and ready by the time I come back." Arie picked the sleep out of his eyes with tired fingers and unhappily slid out of bed.

After waking Edmund, the realmist woke the stable hand. By the time the horses were saddled, the trio were ready to leave. As usual, Agmunsten had paid for their accommodation the night before, just in case. The clip clop of hooves was the only sound in the darkness as they rode out of the yard. Arie resented the fact that everyone for miles around was sleeping comfortably in cosy beds. Edmund whispered to Agmunsten, "Why are we leaving now? What's happened?" Agmunsten had not told the king why they were going. Arie, as a young boy, was used to having his questions go unanswered, but the king? Something bad must have happened.

"I'd prefer not to talk about it. I'll tell you when we get to Vellonia." Agmunsten managed to use a superior tone even when whispering. King and boy looked at each other, eyebrows raised, disappointed the realmist chose to dismiss his king as if he really were just a member of his family. Agmunsten must have realised his lapse in cordiality and halted his horse, turning to look at Edmund and bowing his head slightly. "Forgive me. Sometimes I forget who you are, especially when you're not in your finery. If I thought it was in your best interests to know, I would tell you. Please just trust me."

Edmund nodded. "I'll always trust you, my friend. No offence taken. I'm just used to being the one in control."

Agmunsten set a quick pace. He rode as fast as he thought the horses could go without foundering. In the two days it took to reach Vellonia, Agmunsten only allowed them three hours of sleep each night. Everyone, especially the horses, was tired. It was nearing dawn on the second day since Arie had been rudely awakened. He was slouching in the saddle, eyes closed. He knew his horse was watching where he was going, so he figured why should he have to look as well? Consequently he was almost thrown to the ground when his horse stopped suddenly. Agmunsten laughed at the sight of Arie clinging desperately to his horse's neck.

They had been riding from the north, Agmunsten steering them to the eastern side of the great mountain ranges surrounding the Valley of the Dragons. Arie could only make out the dark outline of the mountains against the slightly less dark, predawn sky—a monumental expanse looming in front of them. "The only entry to the city is where the river enters into the mountains on the east side. We should reach it this afternoon."

As they rode toward their destination, the sky lightened. The stars winked out one by one, early morning light wiping them away as the sun alighted on the snow-capped mountain-tops. Arie marveled at the glowing snow, a rose-hued petal gently resting atop stark, craggy peaks. Arie admired the impressive landscape. This was a scene he never wanted to forget. The young boy was happy to feel small and insignificant against such a wonder of nature.

Agmunsten allowed them a short stop for lunch. As Arie munched on a piece of dried beef, he watched two dark shapes floating and gliding on the thermals high above the mountain tops. "Are they dragons?"

Agmunsten nodded.

"They're smaller than I thought."

"Smaller? How big did you think they'd be?"

"A lot bigger than you and I put together."

"They are, lad. They only appear so small because they're extremely far away."

"Well dah, I know that."

"I don't think you realise how high up they are. Trust me; you'll be scared enough by their size when one is standing next to you."

"Hmm, they don't look all that scary to me."

Agmunsten chose not to reply. He remembered what a shock he'd gotten the first time he'd met one. In fact, the first dragon he'd met was King Valdorryn, Zim's father. Agmunsten had been twenty-five years old and newly inducted as a realmist. His mentor at the time, a rather pleasant old man named Fernsten, had been aware of the importance of keeping up good relations between the realmists and dragons. When Fernsten died, one hundred years ago, Agmunsten had taken his place as Head Realmist.

Agmunsten had almost fainted when he had been introduced to the King of Dragons. It was not just the elephantine size of the creatures. They had a particular skill of making their eyes fierce and cold, with a subtle lifting of black lips to expose just a hint of the ivory sharpness within a mouth big enough to contain half a grown man with little effort. Agmunsten had since learned it was all for show, generally used when a dragon was meeting a person for the first time. He shared a knowledgeable smile with king Edmund; both men looked forward to Arie's reaction when he finally met one of the great creatures.

Edmund happily anticipated seeing his fellow monarch after a number of years. He had always like Valdorryn. The dragon king was relatively down-to-earth, for a dragon. He was a good-hearted creature who loved to laugh, and Edmund couldn't help but feel they should have kept in touch more often. Unfortunately they only seemed to see each other when some crisis or other surfaced; this was no exception. A familiar tension crept into his shoulders, climbing, to seize the muscles in his neck. He was afraid of what Agmunsten was going to tell them. He had not been given the full story from the start. King Edmund also knew that, although what he had concocted to fill in the blanks was rather unpleasant, the truth would be even worse. He felt a headache coming on.

The afternoon passed quickly. Arie had given up craning his neck trying to look at the impossibly high mountains. When they reached the northeastern most point of the Dragon Alps, Agmunsten turned his horse to the south. He expected to find the river entry in an hour or two. "I don't have to tell you to behave yourself with the dragons."

"No, sir. When have I ever not behaved myself?"

"Well, there was the time that Lady Eugenie Thirslyn the Second visited the Academy." Agmunsten twirled his beard end between long fingers. "And then there was the time..."

"All right, all right, you don't have to go ruining my reputation in front of 'father' do you?" Arie grinned at Edmund, who shook his head and smiled.

"If I had a son, I'm sure I would want him to be just like you." Arie puffed up at the compliment. The King of Veresia thought Arie, a nobody from a small village, was good enough to be his son, a prince no less.

"Don't go getting ahead of yourself, lad. You're my apprentice, and I can guarantee you won't be a prince any time soon."

"You always ruin my fun." Arie glared at Agmunsten's back.

"Good. It means I'm doing my job."

The trio continued in silence until Agmunsten called a halt on the banks of the Vallas River. Arie looked upstream. The river was quite wide further up, but narrowed abruptly a few metres from where they were standing. The change in width forced the water to suddenly race toward the Dragon Alps. Arie estimated they were about two hundred metres from the base of the mountains. He was surprised to see that where the river and mountains met, there was a large cave into which water sped. It rushed over rounded boulders, smoothed by thousands of years of ceaseless flow.

Arie dismounted and lay on the pebbly bank. He reached his arm over the edge, but it wasn't long enough to reach the water.

"What are you doing, lad?"

"I want to feel how cold the water is."

"Of course. I should have known. In the meantime you're dirtying your clothes. Please get up, Arie; you're getting too old to satisfy childish whims whenever they present themselves. You look silly." Arie stood up and brushed himself down.

"There you go again."

"What?"

"Spoiling my fun."

"We're not here to have fun. A dragon will be here soon to escort us into Vellonia, and I don't want him, or her, thinking I have a half-wit for an apprentice."

Arie crossed his arms in front of his narrow chest. "Next time you have somewhere to go, you can leave me behind. I don't think I like you anymore." His nose pointed in the air as he glared at Agmunsten.

"Oh for goodness sake, boy, get over it." Agmunsten shook his head. Why did children have to be so damn, well, childish? Agmunsten realised how ridiculous he sounded and laughed. "Sorry, Arie. Seems I've forgotten that we should have a little fun along the way."

"Hmm, OK then. Apology accepted." Arie was a forgiving person and Agmunsten had never known him to hold a grudge. Agmunsten didn't see himself as a particularly hard taskmaster; however, he could recall numerous occasions when he had made a student cry.

"Arie?"

"Yes, Father."

Edmund smiled; he had quite enjoyed the boy's company.

"I just wanted to prepare you for when you meet the dragons. Not only are they imposing creatures, they have a love for formality and drama. Go along with the show and try to be just as formal as they are. I promise you, they will appreciate it."

"OK." Arie thought the request was reasonable, especially since they were to be guests at Vellonia.

"How are we actually getting in? The river looks a bit dangerous."

"I'll have to let Agmunsten fill you in on that one. I've only been here twice before. Each time the dragons blindfolded me at this point."

"Why would they do that?"

Agmunsten answered, "For security reasons they like to keep everyone guessing about Vellonia's inner workings. I also suspect it's more fearsome to embark on a mysterious journey blinded. A dragon will come and greet us, we'll then be put into a flat-bottomed boat and strapped in around the waist so no one falls out. It can get rather rough."

"You mean we have to go into the cave, through that, in a boat!" Arie pointed at the jagged-edged entry through which the water rushed. Agmunsten nodded. "That's crazy. We'll be smashed on the rocks. We'll drown." Although Arie could swim, he didn't like his chances against the tumultuous waters, which bounced off numerous rocks before being swallowed up by the black-as-pitch cave mouth.

"Nothing will happen. The dragons are our friends; you have to trust them." Arie shook his head.

"Just in case, I'll say goodbye to both of you now. It's been an honour to have been included in this journey; I guess I've done a lot for my age. I've lived a full life and I got to meet the king. Not many my age can say that. I'll see you in the next Realm." Arie hugged both men and then his horse. Edmund and Agmunsten tried to hide their laughter.

"Oh, the dragons are going to love you." Edmund affectionately ruffled the youth's hair. Agmunsten stopped laughing and looked up at the sky. His companions followed his lead to see what had distracted him. A large, black shape glided in semi-circles, falling lower and lower. Arie couldn't believe the wing-span. It was wider than a house. His mouth fell open. A shadow fell over the trio, the sun eclipsed by the ebony dragon. A rush of air buffeted the humans as Zim alighted between them and the cave. Arie looked up at Zim's face, which was at least as high as The Academy's two story buildings.

Arie watched as Zim subtly inclined his enormous head. He was astounded at the beast's gentleness. Edmund and Agmunsten bowed with great respect, and Arie thought he should do the same.

"Welcome, my friends. It is an honour to accept your presence."

"I think we can cut the cow's dung. We're too old for that now. It's good to see you." To Arie's surprise, Agmunsten walked to the dragon and caressed the broad, scaly nose, which was half the size of the realmist himself. Zim almost purred with pleasure.

Arie, although in awe, walked tentatively up to the dragon. He looked into green eyes that were the size of his own head.

"Allow me to introduce my student, Arie."

"Pleased to meet you, Arie. My name is Zimapholous Accorterroza, son of the king and queen of Vellonia. Have you had a good journey?" Zim's smooth, deep voice enveloped Arie like a warm pool of water. Arie couldn't believe the dragon prince wanted to know something as mundane as how their trip had been.

"It was as good as I could have expected, Sir, except I wasn't allowed to have much fun along the way." Agmunsten raised his eyebrows in warning.

"Well, young Arie, I do hope that your stay within my beloved Vellonia will compensate." Zim handed them all blindfolds. Agmunsten knew the drill and led the others to the river's edge. Miraculously, a wide timber boat waited for them. Its polished, dark timber surface reflected the water, the sky, the rocks. Arie had never seen anything so beautifully crafted. He had to rub his eyes to make sure he wasn't imagining things when he noticed the craft was hovering just above the surface of the river, water crashing dangerously centimetres below.

Agmunsten stepped down into the vessel, which remained two steps below the level of the river bank. He couldn't count the times he had done this; always the same routine, although, thankfully, Zim had kept the formalities to a minimum this time. Agmunsten sat on the front bench seat, indicating Arie should sit in the middle of the boat, with Edmund to the rear. Leather straps floated from under each seat and fastened themselves around each waist. This surprised Arie once again. He knew there were things that could be done in this world that he had never imagined, but it was never the same as seeing something amazing occur. His elders already had their blindfolds on so the boy hurriedly tied his on tight.

The boat gently glided forward, accelerating as it went. "See you soon." Zim's voice followed them into the abrupt coolness of the cave. Arie's heart beat quickly. He wasn't sure if he was having fun or if he was scared. The vessel increased speed, air rushing past Arie's hair, musty cave odour filling his nostrils. The boat jolted, speeding up yet again. Arie's stomach was left behind and he shouted in delight. "This is fun!" His words rushed away so quickly, King Edmund had a hard time working out what the boy had said.

The straps holding them in place were tested as the boat turned sharply to the right. Arie felt the belt cutting into his side. He wasn't sure how it was possible, but the vessel continued to travel faster, always in a circular direction. Arie could feel them dropping as they speedily circled. The fear returned. The only thing keeping him from panic was the promise from Agmunsten that the dragons would never hurt them. What if the dragons had no control over this entry system? What if it was all left to chance? He wondered how many guests had actually survived to reach Vellonia.

The spiralling ended with the boat being dropped a few metres to land with a heavy splash. Arie felt like he was in an egg, which had been laid by a tree-dwelling chicken. He counted the seconds as they fell. The boat, having lost its reckless speed, glided gently toward their destination. The trio took this time to take a breath and flex each limb, ensuring no damage had been done. "I'll never get used to that. Is everyone alright?"

Edmund and Arie responded favourably to Agmunsten's question.

"Good."

"Are we almost there?"

"Probably. It's different every time. Sometimes it takes longer, sometimes not."

"Oh, strange. I wonder how it works?"

"Hmm. Seems like I have taught you something. It's important to question everything; you'll learn more that way."

In contrast with the boat ride, the end consisted of a gentle, almost indistinct, nudge against land. A deep, raspy voice came from above. "Welcome, visitors. You may remove thine blindfolds and alight from Mezza.

Arie had never considered their boat had a name. They eagerly removed their blindfolds, but Arie was disappointed to see boring black, brown, and grey rocks surrounded him. He stood carefully and quietly thanked the boat as he alighted.

The only source of light within the dark chamber emanated from a bronze lamp held by a large grey dragon.

"Symbothial Accorterroza. It's been a long time." Agmunsten gave a brief bow.

"Yes, my wise, learned friend, Agmunsten Fergus Guthwick, Strongest of the Five. You have not aged as do other humans. I find I recognise you."

Agmunsten shook his head at the mention of his full title. He had never been fond of his middle or surname for that matter and had ceased using them centuries ago.

The dragon looked at Edmund and awkwardly performed a minimal bow. "Welcome, King Edmund of our friendly neighbour, Veresia. May the crops grow plentiful and animals breed in abundance for howsoever long you rule."

"Thank you for your kind words, Symbothial Accorterroza. How is your uncle, King Valdorryn Accorterroza the Second?"

"He is well. Thank you for your interest. I will take you to him now. Please follow me."

As Arie followed Symbothial along the wide pathway, he looked him over. The large dragon—they were all large he supposed—only had inches to spare before he scraped the tunnel walls. His size was similar to Zimapholous, although his scales were grey. When Arie looked closer, the scales shimmered a pale green and pink where they were touched by torchlight. He continued to be awed by the immensity of these creatures. Arie was not scared despite knowing the dragon could kill him before he'd even realised what had happened. The boy was glad the dragons were on their side.

The path led upward, and Edmund was puffing.

"You're out of shape, my liege. Too many banquets I bet." Edmund laughed in agreement. It was good to hear Agmunsten being cheerful; he had been grumpy more often than not lately. Within minutes they popped out into a bigger tunnel. Symbothial had more headroom and Arie estimated another dragon could pass by the other quite comfortably.

Red and white tiles, laid in various geometric patterns, covered the floor. Arie studied them whilst walking. The group made a staccato procession to the throne room, continually stopped by one dragon or another who wished to greet Agmunsten: each dragon a slightly different colour, or combination of colours. One dragon, the same grey as Symbothial, and subsequently introduced as his sister, had pale blue and pink hues overlying the scales on her torso. Arie assumed they were like people, or animals: no two were exactly alike.

Finally, they reached a set of tall, wide doors. Honey-coloured timber inlaid with darker wood, mother of pearl, and amber to form an exquisite artwork. The picture portrayed a bright-scaled dragon standing serenely, wings outstretched to their limits. Hundreds of creatures crowded companionably, protected beneath the shiny canopy of its wings. A statuesque human stood beneath one wing, still only a fraction of the dragon's height, with rabbits, squirrels, ducks, and any animal imaginable, at her feet. Dragonflies, beetles, and birds were depicted, mid-flight, circling the enchanting human woman. Beneath the other wing stood a strong, young, and handsome man, sword and dagger at his hip, field mice, badgers, and fox at his feet. He smiled to his companion who smiled in return. A grape vine rose from the earth, twined many times around the dragon and reached for the sky. Bunches of juicy, green and purple fruit hung from the pregnant vine. Blueberry and raspberry bushes hid the dragon's clawed feet. A lush strawberry plant carpeted the ground in front of the woman, the ripe, fat berries so realistic that Arie's stomach grumbled.

The artwork divided in the middle as the doors swung open. Arie beheld the throne room of Vellonia. Harp notes floated around the room, soaring into the domed ceiling to mingle with birds and clouds painted there.

"All behold and welcome illustrious guests to the magnificent abode of the dragons, Sacred Vellonia. I introduce to you, our revered King Valdorryn Accorterroza and his beautiful wife Queen Jazmonilly Accorterroza and all those gathered here, three important and distinguished guests. First, I introduce King Edmund Benedict Laraulen, King of Veresia, friend and ally to Vellonia, city of the dragons. Edmund walked to the foot of the dragon king's throne and bowed low.

Agmunsten was introduced with a similar flourish, as was Arie, whose introduction was shorter than the others, due to his lack of accomplishments. Arie followed the lead of his elders and bowed as low as he could to the dragon king and queen. King Valdorryn stood and addressed the gathering, giving his own warm and tedious welcome to the travellers. Whilst Arie was overwhelmed by the impressive formalities, Agmunsten stifled a yawn. Finally, when Agmunsten was about to ask for a chair, the king dismissed most of those assembled, and motioned them to follow the royal couple, their son Zim and advisor Warrimonious, to a smaller room accessed by a nondescript doorway behind the throne.

Once away from prying eyes, Agmunsten and Edmund were enveloped in hugs by the king and queen. Arie feared his companions may be squished into oblivion, however they emerged intact from the dragons' affection. Everyone sat, and refreshments were brought. Arie found it strange to think any dragon would be a servant.

The queen addressed Arie in a melodious voice, "We are not too proud to serve each other, with none being called servant. We do what needs to be done and those who offer service do it with pride and willingness."

Arie gaped. "Can you read my mind, Your Highness?" Queen Jazmonilly smiled.

"How are Queen Gabrielle and Princess Verity?" Jazmonilly addressed Edmund. It had been many years since they had last met and there was much to catch up on. There were serious matters to discuss, however the talk remained pleasant for an hour or two whilst the travelers ate and relaxed. All knew they would have plenty of time during the night to discuss the unpleasantness Talia faced. Arie found himself growing fond of Vellonia's royalty. They were not as foreboding as he had imagined, and most of the ceremony had been left in the throne room.

King Valdorryn was black, with the exception of gold scales shimmering around his throat, trailing down to his chest. The gold shone dimly in the artificial light within the reception chamber; the position of the room within the mountain discounted the possibility of windows. Many candles burned within wall sconces; a small hole, positioned in a corner near the ceiling, provided ventilation. The humans sat on a comfortable leather couch, whilst the dragons sat on padded bench seats. Jazmonilly's silver scales were subdued in the dim light, reflecting neutral tones within the room. Arie could imagine her shining like thousands of polished jewels in the sunlight, and hoped he would be privileged enough to see it. Jazmonilly looked at the boy. Arie wasn't sure what she was thinking, but remembered she could probably read his mind. He blushed. She smiled again.

Late in the afternoon King Valdorryn stood. "I have been glad to catch up with all the good news, but now it is time for you to be shown to your accommodation. You will have time to bathe and dress for dinner. After dinner we will reluctantly partake in the unhappy discussion we have dreaded these past months." All adults nodded somberly. King Valdorryn and his queen exited to much bowing. Zim volunteered to show the humans to their rooms.

Arie looked at the floors as they traversed one hallway, ranged up two flights of stairs, wandered along another hallway and dragged themselves up two more flights to another hall. This would be where they stayed. Arie was excited to find that, for the first time in his life, he had been given his own room. His grin was wide. "Thank you, Prince Zimapholous."

"You can call me Zim. I'm glad you like it." Zim crossed the room to a large window above a human-sized table. He surveyed the view. "Come and have a look."

Arie reached the window and gazed out.

The room appeared to be three levels above the ground. Arie looked across a vast expanse of valley. Lush grass carpeted the distance between the two mountain ranges, and ancient trees sheltered pathways meandering about the valley. A wide river flowed through the landscape. "Is that the river that brought us here?"

"One and the same. It flows into the mountain where you entered and flows out to cross the valley over there." Arie followed the direction of Zim's gaze. The cavernous opening was a small, dark spot in the distance.

"But how does the water go down, then back up again?"

"How do you know the water goes down?"

"We dropped. You know, when we were in the boat. We were still in the water when we landed."

"We've diverted some for our own purposes. If you look, you will notice the river is slightly narrower here than outside."

Arie nodded. He also saw a few houses, large and small, positioned midway between mountain and river. Before he had time for any more questions Zim continued. "Agmunsten will collect you shortly and show you where to bathe. I hope you enjoy your stay here. Feel free to wander as you like. See you at dinner."

Whilst he waited for Agmunsten, Arie checked out his room. It had a white tiled floor with a blue dragon mosaic claiming the middle of the room. White sheets and a blue woollen blanket covered his bed. The smoothly polished stone walls were painted white to maximise the light within the mountain stronghold. He was excited to know he would be living inside a mountain. What backbreaking work must have been done to carve the rooms and tunnels in which the dragons lived? Arie couldn't fathom how it had been done and concluded it would have to have been realmist magic shaping the interior of Vellonia. Agmunsten, accompanied by Edmund, interrupted Arie's musings and took him to bathe.

Later, clean and clothed in washed garments, Arie sat by the window in his room and gazed out at the serene, lush valley. Animals grazed, dragons strolled somewhat cumbersomely along the pathways and flew gracefully around mountain pinnacles. Sparkling, golden spires ascended from the valley floor, shining their way beyond the top of the tallest mountain. Arie felt as if he were in a dream. The morning he'd served breakfast to a hung-over Agmunsten seemed a lifetime ago, and never could he have imagined then that he would end up in such a wondrous place as this. Arie pictured himself sitting proudly on the back of a large dragon, soaring high above Vellonia. He imagined as he looked down, the people would appear small and ant-like, as the soaring dragons had appeared from his vantage point on the ground.

Once again, Agmunsten interrupted Arie's daydreaming and gathered him for dinner. Arie noticed the floor tiles were blue and green in the hallway on his level. Agmunsten led him down one staircase to a corridor tiled in purple and orange. "What do the different colours mean?"

"What different colours?"

"The tiles on the floor. These ones are purple and orange, the ones on our level are blue and green, and the ones leading to the throne room are red and white."

"You've answered your own question."

"What?"

"Think about it."

"Oh. It's so you know what level you're on."

"Very good, lad. It's important to know these things, especially as there are very few windows around the place. If there's an emergency, the dragons need to know which direction is out. If you look closely, within the patterns are small arrows. If you follow them, you will eventually end up in safety."

"That's a good idea."

"The dragons are full of them."

In honour of their arrival, the dragon city held a banquet. The great dining hall was the biggest room Arie had ever seen. It was so large he had nothing to compare it to. The ceilings were lofty, for humans—as were most of the ceilings in Vellonia. A large row of doors opened up onto the valley floor. A mild breeze floated in, filling the room with sweet spring air. They halted at the entrance, and were once again introduced into the silence with a grand flourish. Agmunsten tapped one foot throughout the introduction, stopping short of folding his arms in annoyance. Arie could see how repeated, tedious formalities would be frustrating after a while. At the moment he could hear his tummy grumbling and wanted nothing more than to fill it with masses of delicious food.

Arie was about to start his own toe-tapping, but thankfully the introductions appeared to be over. They were led, Edmund first followed by Agmunsten and Arie at the rear, through an avenue leading directly from the entry to the king's table. Row upon row of tables and bench seats lined the room. Dragons of all colours and sizes watched with large, curious eyes. Arie noticed dragon eyes were similar to those of his cat back at the Academy. Feral was a friendly grey cat, its green irises split with black slits in sunlight. Some of the eyes regarding him were blue, some green, yellow, or purple. It was darkening outside, but lamps and candles brightened the room. In the fading light, the dragons' eyes were punctuated, not by a narrow blackness, but by rounder pupils.

Arie stood next to the table, barely able to see over the top. Small, three-tread ladders were brought to assist the humans onto their bench seats. Once seated, Arie's legs dangled in space, as did Agmunsten's. The two sat to one side of the queen with Edmund seated between King Valdorryn and Zim. The elevated seating arrangements gave the older humans a childlike appearance. Animated conversation hummed around the room. The two kings were eager to become reacquainted, not to mention King Valdorryn craved news of the outside world, as usual.

The queen addressed the young boy who sat next to her. "How do you like our beloved Vellonia, Arie?"

"It's huge. There's so much to see. I think the valley is beautiful. It makes me feel ... peaceful." The queen nodded, her small smile radiated satisfaction.

"Is this the first time you've met the dragons?"

"Yes, Queen Jazmonilly."

"And what do you think of us?"

Arie's smile lit up his eyes.

"I like you very much. Even though I knew dragons were big, I was still surprised at how big. I'm glad you're on our side." The queen nodded again. As Arie looked into her eyes he had the distinct feeling there was more behind the questions than polite chit chat. The conversation was interrupted by the arrival of dinner.

Platters were placed along the middle of the large tables, mouth-watering aromas capturing everyone's attention. King Valdorryn stood and spoke into the new silence. "In the name of Drakon, Beloved Father and Protector of the Dragons, we give profound thanks for the banquet we are to partake." The king turned to his human guests. "I am truly overjoyed at your presence. My family and I are honoured to host this feast for you tonight. Enjoy." He raised his goblet of gozzle-bush berries in a toast. Everyone imitated the king and drank heartily. Arie was disappointed to find his goblet held water.

An hour before midnight, when all that was left were crumbs on the table, the king and his guests excused themselves. Agmunsten escorted Arie to his room and gave him strict instructions to stay there until morning. The boy was disappointed he couldn't continue to explore, however when he climbed into bed he was content. His stomach availed itself of all his energy to digest the large quantity of food he'd consumed. It wasn't long before he slept.

Edmund, Agmunsten, Zim and Warrimonious joined King Valdorryn in his meeting room. Queen Jazmonilly had retired to her rooms, knowing her husband would relay anything important to her later. Warrimonious wasted no time in getting to the point. "So, Agmunsten, please enlighten us fully as to the situation we now face."

His serious tone prompted Agmunsten to answer immediately.

"They are here." Those three simple words drained the blood from every face. All breathing appeared to have ceased as each member of the meeting attempted to digest the horrific information.

Eventually Zim won the race for composure. "What can you tell us?"

Agmunsten cleared his throat. "We are aware of one Gormon at the moment. I'm not sure if any others have arrived." Agmunsten spoke through the nervous murmuring of his companions. "Avruellen had a true dream. An infant Gormon is feeding on humans. He hasn't developed his full strength yet and appears to be staying in one isolated area. We don't know where that is, however I suspect it's on the coast somewhere down south. Maybe an island."

Agmunsten knew the questions his companions would ask and headed them off. "I don't know how long until it reaches adult status, although all the information I could get my hands on from last time indicates it may be a matter of a few more weeks, maybe three months. Something I do know, is that we have a better chance of defeating it as an infant."

"Well, the choice is clear. We need to locate this abhorrent infant and slaughter it." As ever, Warrimonious was straight to the point.

Agmunsten spoke directly to the dragon prince. "I have something to ask of you, my old friend, Zimapholous."

"Your old friend hey? This should be interesting." Zim was expecting the worst.

"I, or rather, The Circle, need you to perform an important task. Will you do it?" Agmunsten knew Zim wouldn't refuse, especially as he was also a member of The Circle.

"When have I ever refused any request of The Circle? Although it might depend on what you ask. Why don't you just get to the point, *old friend*?"

Agmunsten drew a deep breath. "We need you to fly to Brenland, to King Heskin's castle. We need you to bring the king and Elphus here." Agmunsten almost shut his eyes in preparation for his colleague to burn him to a crisp.

Zim took a few deep breaths. He knew that the head of The Circle had meant no insult. In fact, there must be dire need for Agmunsten to have asked the question in spite of the reaction he would receive. "As reluctant as I am, I will not allow pride to interfere with what needs to be done. I will do it, but I may never let you forget it."

"I can live with that. Thank you, you are a credit to your race."

"Gee thanks, sorry I can't say the same about you." They shared a smile. Agmunsten had to admit, it had gone a lot better than he had imagined.

The group spent the rest of the night discussing how their objectives could be completed, however were not much closer to a solution at dawn than they had been at midnight. Their fast was broken in contemplative silence. Discussions resumed mid-morning. Only inching closer to an answer, the group conceded a few hours rest wouldn't go amiss.

Agmunsten sought Arie. He had left him alone for too long and had to question quite a few dragons before he found his charge in the upper reaches of Vellonia. Arie was with Symbothial, the dragon who had first welcomed them.

Arie was learning about the fortifications created to withstand the Gormons. He had no idea the brilliant golden spires were a powerful defence, capable of destroying the enemy. Symbothial was extremely knowledgeable; it was his job to make sure the spires remained charged. Satisfied Arie was in good hands, Agmunsten returned to his room and slept. He was woken a couple of hours later by a sharp rap on the door. He swung out of bed and shuffled to the door, grumbling as he did so. A dark blue dragon, he had not previously met, stood impatiently outside. "Sir Realmist, you are required urgently. There is an emergency. One of The Circle is dying." Agmunsten blinked to clear his grainy eyes. He'd slept in his clothes, so was ready to run.

Agmunsten had to jog to keep up with the blue dragon's large stride. What could have happened to Zim? He was in his own city, protected by more than the rocky walls. It was unlikely to be a dagger strike, the dragon's hide being too thick to penetrate with an ordinary blade. Had someone poisoned him? Agmunsten cursed himself for leaving his pack behind. This shouldn't be happening and could spell disaster for everyone, not to mention the collective grief if Zim were killed.

He rushed into one of the city's bedrooms and was greeted with an unexpected sight. His assumption that Zim had been in danger was completely wrong. A sandy haired young man sat next to a still body, deep lines of distress cutting a premature path across his youthful brow. On his knee was a rat, on his shoulder a white owl. In a split second Agmunsten realised whose face he would see when he looked at the unmoving figure. He was glad Zim was not lying there, but his heart dropped as he gazed upon one of his oldest friends. Arcon's face was pasty white, his breathing shallow, barely audible. Agmunsten swallowed his emotions and acted quickly.

He approached Arcon and undertook a brief physical examination, noting temperature and heart rate. Cupping his hands firmly, but gently, around Arcon's skull, he used realmistry, delving into his brain. Agmunsten addressed the young man, whom he now knew to be Blayke. "You shouldn't have let him do this. He's dying."

Blayke answered as he looked at Agmunsten with moist eyes. "I told him not to; we all did." His head fell forward until his chin touched his chest. Phantom hooted comforting tones; Fang said nothing.

"I want everyone out. Now!" His shouted words reverberated in the silence. Agmunsten was already ignoring the departing crowd, focusing solely on his friend and colleague. By shielding himself, and his group, for an extended period, Arcon had used most of his life force. His cells were drained, every part of his body close to collapse. It was only a matter of time before his kidneys, heart, and brain failed. The leader of The Circle replaced his hands on the patient's head. What he was about to do would take hours and drain him significantly, not to mention open them up to attack from outside—but he had no choice. To go on without one of The Circle was suicide. The realmist took a few deep, centering breaths and began. He couldn't imagine how their situation could be any worse.

21

Pernus and Fendill sat locked in their quarters. The men sat companionably at a small table, Fendill happy the soldier had thought to bring dice. Leon's realmist and Edmund's captain had been imprisoned in their rooms for what they assumed was six days, relying on the frequency of meals to estimate the passing of time. Leon had been coming and going, and Princess Tusklar had even made a couple of appearances to see Prince Leon. At these times they had shut themselves in the prince's private rooms. Pernus had dared point out the foolishness of such an arrangement, and had received a broken nose for his efforts.

The princess distressed Pernus. She had always presented as a polite and pleasant woman, but he sensed a disturbing undercurrent. He wondered if Leon's apparent escalation of violence was because of her.

It seemed the relationship between Leon and the princess was going well. It was maybe for this reason that Pernus and Fendill were waiting for their prince to return from a meeting called by the king. The soldier was on edge. Was the king happy or was he sharpening his sword? Pernus rolled the dice. Fendill laughed. "It seems you lose again. You're going to owe me a lot of money when we return."

Pernus smiled, but his reply wasn't so jolly. "If we return."

The Veresians looked at each other for a moment. Pernus was broaching a subject they had both been contemplating but had been too afraid to give voice to.

"Something's going on with her." They dared not use names, in case someone were listening. If it were obvious the princess was the subject of their conversation, they would have had dramatically shortened life spans.

"I know, Pernus. I was shocked at his reaction the other day. I would have fixed it for you, but if he noticed..."

"It's okay, it doesn't hurt too much. My soldier's instinct is yelling at me to run. Something's happening, something we couldn't have anticipated. We need a plan." Pernus was sweating. He knew Fendill was a good man, but he had been loyal to Leon in the past. Would he run straight to Leon with accusations of treason? At this point Pernus felt he had no choice but to risk it.

Fendill answered quickly, indicating he had been thinking along similar lines. He whispered, "I think," he took a deep breath, "I agree."

Pernus could see the disappointment and sadness on the man's face. Fendill spoke again, "I assume your plan is to facilitate our extraction from this place."

"As soon as possible." Pernus leaned in and lowered his voice further. "There's one thing before we leave. I need more information. King Edmund deserves to know as much as possible about what's going on here. If we escape on a hunch, I don't think our welcome will be very enthusiastic. I'm sorry to have to ask you."

"Not quite sorry enough."

"Not quite. Is there any way we can eavesdrop on a conversation between our man and her?"

"It's possible, but dangerous. They would have no idea, but the king's realmist might sense what I'm doing. I need some time to think about how I can do it.

"That's fine, I was losing anyway." Edmund's brown-haired Captain of the Guard slipped the dice into his pocket. "I'm going to take some thinking time of my own. Come and get me when you've worked it out."

Pernus rose and headed for his bed. He was a tall, strong man, with a wide chest and heavily muscled arms—an imposing figure on any battlefield. Today, though, he felt none of that strength, and was glad Fendill was there.

Fendill remained at the table, green eyes staring blankly at the wall. The problem ran around the maze of his mind but hit dead end after dead end. He was forced to retrace his steps again and again. This was the most important thing he'd had to do in his thirty-five years. He was young for a realmist of his station, Advisor to the Prince of Veresia. He knew he was a good realmist, but held no illusions about why he had been chosen for the job. It had been a struggle to remain loyal to the prince, but he told himself it was really loyalty to his king and country. He knew he had been chosen because of his youth. He was easier for Leon to intimidate than an older, more experienced realmist.

He believed Pernus when he said it was now do or die. Fendill's own instincts told him the same thing. How could this have happened? One minute he was a respected member of the court at Bayerlon, and now? Now he was virtually a prisoner awaiting execution. He had tried to hold the belief that Leon would keep him as his advisor if and when he married the princess. It could still happen, but he could see two other, unavoidable options. He knew Pernus was on borrowed time. Once

Leon had a foothold here, he would think about going against his brother. He wouldn't be surprised if Leon sent Pernus's decapitated head to Bayerlon as a gift for the king.

The other scenario was that all three of their heads were sent back to Bayerlon. Leon was not treading lightly enough for his liking. From what he could see, King Suklar was an intelligent man who did not have much patience. He was surprised Leon was still allowed contact with the princess. What they discussed in private, he shuddered to think. Were they plotting their own treason? He was not sure how the princess benefited from upsetting her father by liaising with a Veresian prince. Maybe she truly was enamoured of Leon, but who could know what a young woman was thinking, let alone one from another culture, which was practically another world.

Fendill had never bonded an animal, a decision he now regretted. If he had bonded a small animal he would have had a ready-made spy. The problem was, he didn't like animals. He saw them as dirty, smelly liabilities. He liked eating them, but that was about it.

A few hours passed. Leon returned. He had taken to entering from their room, probably an excuse to keep an eye on them. He was smirking. Fendill jumped up when the prince entered, and bowed. "You look well, my Prince. How go the negotiations?" Leon looked at his realmist, sudden distrust flicking across his face. It was gone as soon as Fendill noticed it.

"Hmm. I would have to say it's going well. My brother might get a wedding invitation sooner than he thinks. So, tell me, Fendill, my man—what have you been up to?"

Fendill ignored the innuendo. "Pernus and I played some dice earlier today; since then, nothing. I have to say, we're getting bored cooped up here like laying hens. How long must we remain so?"

"I wouldn't know. I'll ask Suklar next time I see him. I'm going to my room for a while. When the princess arrives show her straight through." Leon abruptly turned away and unlocked the door to his rooms.

Fendill revised his earlier thoughts. He was now sure his head would be joining that of his friend Pernus. Leon was either very astute or suddenly paranoid. Had the princess caused the sudden alteration in personality? Not only had Leon been shorter of temper, which Fendill had not thought possible, he was edgy, and now suspicious of his own men. They clearly did not have long to come up with a solution. He hoped Pernus was close to finalising a plan to get them out alive.

The thoughts rushing around the realmist's head ceased their frantic activity. Peaceful silence embraced his mind for an instant before a smile threw the tension from his face. He realised he had not moved since Leon had left the room. Fendill was not sure how much time had passed, but he wanted to move quickly now that he had a solution to the first part of their problem. He went to Pernus as fast as he could without running, and found the large man sleeping. Fendill stood there a moment, composing himself before he woke him. Pernus opened his eyes at the sense of another; and smiled in reaction to Fendill's excited expression.

"I know what I need to do. The princess is coming to see him soon and I have to show her into the room. When I'm in there I'll separate from my body."

"You'll do what?" Pernus's mouth hung open. "I thought you said you had a solution."

"I don't have time for your questions right now. Save it for later. Anyway, when I leave my body, there'll be nothing holding me up and I'll collapse. Leon will probably call you for help. Tell him I wasn't feeling well after lunch; that I was a bit dizzy. Make him think it was the food. You'll have to carry me to bed. Whilst my mind is floating in his room I'll be able to hear everything."

"Won't the other realmist know? Won't he be able to sense something?"

"No. I'm not utilising the Second Realm. He won't know a thing."

"How will you get back?"

"When Leon opens the door I'll come back to my own body."

"Why all the drama? Can't you just lie on the bed and travel through the door after he's closed it?"

"If I were somewhere safer I could. The doors here could be warded against such things. I can't see any wards, but they may still be there. I don't understand enough about this place to risk it—I barely understand how those shimmery doors work."

Fendill heard the door open. He turned quickly and bowed deeply at the princess. "Welcome, Princess Tusklar. Please allow me to show you to Prince Leon's rooms."

Fendill rushed to the prince's door and knocked loudly.

"Come in."

The realmist opened the door to see Leon standing in the middle of the room, back straight, head held proud. Princess Tusklar followed Fendill into the room and watched approvingly as Leon bowed. "You do me a great honour, yet again, Revered Princess Tusklar." Leon turned to Fendill. "You may leave."

Fendill's face slackened, and he dropped to the floor with a thud.

Leon stood there for a moment, arms crossed. He seemed embarrassed and not at all concerned that his advisor was lying in a heap on the floor. The princess was more alarmed than Leon. "Is he alright?"

"I'm not sure. Just a moment, princess. Pernus! Get in here, now!"

Pernus had been waiting for this invitation and rushed in. He found Leon prodding the body with his foot. "Find out if he's still alive."

Pernus squatted next to him. He lowered his face to his friend's mouth to feel for breath and felt his skin; it was still warm. The soldier stood and faced the prince. "He's still alive. He may have food poisoning; he complained of stomach cramps and dizziness after lunch. I'll take him to his bed." He didn't wait for any refusal and dragged Fendill outside.

"Close the door. I don't want to be disturbed. If he dies, you can tell me when I'm finished."

"Sorry, Princess. If he doesn't die, maybe we can kill him anyway."

"You are so funny." She approached him. "You may embrace me." He followed her orders and risked a kiss on the cheek. She purposely turned her face and kissed him passionately on the lips. Fendill would have blushed had he been in his body. He hoped this was all they were going to do; he hadn't come here to observe what Leon and the princess got up to in their private time. Fendill would be quite cranky if they didn't provide some information. He also resented the foot prod he had received. There was no doubt now about what sort of person Leon was. Fendill was hurt at the lack of concern his prince had shown when he had collapsed, but at least now he wouldn't feel any guilt about their planned escape.

After some time, to Fendill's relief, the couple unlocked lips and started talking. Tusklar remained in Leon's arms whilst they spoke. "You had something you wanted to discuss with me, Princess?"

"As I mentioned before, I would like to marry soon. I feel I have found a suitable match. I think you know him rather well." Leon smiled self-indulgently. Whilst he had hoped for success in his endeavour, he hadn't thought it would come so easily. "There is only one problem, which was foreseeable."

"Oh? What problem would that be?" Leon knew very well she knew what problem it would be. He also knew a kindred spirit when he met one, and knew her solution would be similar to his.

Her brow crinkled. "My father." She broke from his embrace and walked toward where Fendill's spirit hovered. He quickly moved out of the way. She wouldn't have known he was there, however it was hard for him to remember he was insubstantial.

She watched Leon as if sizing up what his reaction would be. The voice in her head had told her what they needed to do, and had assured her Leon would be amenable to her suggestion. The voice was not there and suddenly she felt less sure of herself. "Are you prepared to do anything to marry me?"

"Anything, Princess."

He was enjoying the game. It was even enjoyable to see she was ever-so-slightly uncomfortable with what she was about to suggest.

Tusklar sensed he was playing her. Instead of being incensed she laughed. "Your answer would be yes?"

He nodded. "Of course. I would do anything to marry you."

"I sense you would do this thing regardless of whether I were the prize." Leon wasn't sure now who was using who.

"Please, do tell me what this *thing* is."

"My father will never agree to a marriage between us. He is old-fashioned and believes only another Inkran is suitable for his daughter. I truly believe he feels no one is good enough for me and will leave me rotting as a spinster until he dies. He wants to hold the throne as long as he can. He lives for nothing else but his totalitarian power." Her eyes held fire but Leon was too mesmerised by his anticipation to take heed.

"I want that power. I will be willing to share some of it with you." She stopped speaking, waiting for some sign of his thoughts.

"I want you. I want you to have that power, and I will help you get it. Tell me what you want me to do." He had walked over to her again. He grabbed her around the waist, staring intensely into her eyes.

"I want you to kill my father. If you do this I know I can trust you, and I will marry you."

"I will kill him for you." He grabbed a fistful of the long hair tumbling down her back. He pulled it hard, exposing her throat, and she let out a small squeal of pain. "If you don't marry me, I will kill you too."

He kissed her smooth skin and she laughed. Leon released his hold on her and pushed her to the ground. He was rough with her. Fendill was disgusted to see she enjoyed it. They truly were crazy and very well suited; two monsters working together. Fendill shuddered to think what they were capable of. He fled to the other side of the room whilst Leon had his way with her. When they finished, and Tusklar opened the door to leave, he shot past her, into the comfort of his own body.

Leon followed her out, not bothering to check on the condition of his realmist. When the door shut, Fendill sat up in bed. He had been shocked by what he'd heard, but knew he should have expected it. Pernus sat on the floor, cross-legged, waiting for Fendill to return. Fendill was rather touched at the worry on the captain's face. "How are you?"

"As well as can be expected. The news is not good. I think we'd better come up with a way to escape as soon as possible. Things around here are about to get a whole lot worse." Pernus listened as Fendill repeated what he'd heard. What they had done afterwards did not surprise him in the least—actually none of it did.

They discussed different methods of escape and Pernus was amazed at Fendill's capabilities. There were times in their flight when they would need to be invisible. Whilst that wasn't actually possible without drawing power from the Second Realm, Fendill had good ideas about what he could do to aid their escape. Their biggest problem was their lack of knowledge about the layout of the castle. They both remembered the places they had been, but it was limited compared to what they needed to know. There was one other problem they faced. "Should we try and warn King Suklar about her plan?"

"Don't be so naïve, my friend. He would never believe us. To even suggest it could get us killed." Pernus admired Fendill's misplaced sense of propriety. "Besides, we can't speak to him without leaving this room. Leon would immediately smell a rat."

They discussed tactics for the remainder of the night, stopping only to eat dinner. Leon didn't return that evening and both men hoped he had not yet killed the king, as they would surely be next. They stayed up all night, ceasing their scheming only when breakfast arrived. The Inkran who brought them breakfast didn't seem any different. He was silent as usual, and didn't seem unusually tense.

When Leon arrived mid-morning, he had a slightly whimsical expression on his face. Both men rose to greet him, and Fendill spoke, "Good morning, my Prince. Are you alright?"

"Yes, Fendill. Looks like you've recovered from yesterday."

"Yes sir, thank you. I was worried when you didn't return last night. I don't trust the king. He may harm you."

"I appreciate your concern. The king has made no move to harm me, yet. I can take care of myself. I am the Ki... ah, Prince of Veresia, after all." Fendill and Pernus found it hard not to react at his slip of the tongue. Leon nodded in dismissal and walked to his door. At the last instant he turned to address the realmist. "Oh. By the way, the king has invited you and my brother's lapdog for dinner tonight in the grand hall. I will send some men to take you when it's time."

Fendill bowed, making his features as neutral as possible. This may be their only chance to escape. The captain and realmist made last-minute adjustments to their plan and waited nervously to be taken to dinner.

Leon sat contentedly in his room. The princess was enamoured of him. He was happy to admit he even enjoyed spending time with her. He didn't always see the fear in her eyes, but he knew it was there, and enjoyed it when she was as evil as he. She may try to get the better of him, but he knew she never would. He controlled the relationship and soon he would control Inkra. From there he would attack Veresia and then that would be his too. He would relish the torturing and killing of some of the citizens—in particular his brother and that slut of a queen—but he wouldn't kill everyone; he would need a workforce. If he only indulged his blood lust every once in a while it would not make too much of a dent in the population.

Late in the afternoon he dressed for dinner. He wore a white shirt, the Laraulen crest embroidered on the collar. His long, fitted coat was as black as his soul. He stood in front of the mirror and looked at himself. He cut an impressive figure. In his mind, Tusklar stood at his side, dressed in a gold-spun dress, long cape flowing down her back, crown on her head. Soon he would wear a crown, two in fact. The years his brother told him what to do, treating him as a fool, were almost at an end. King Edmund would soon be kneeling at his feet, begging him for mercy—mercy that would not be forthcoming. Leon remembered, years ago, the fear and pleading in the kitten's eyes before he had killed it. He bared his teeth as he fell further into madness.

His delusions were interrupted when two black-clad men arrived to escort him to dinner. These men had been sent by the king—they neglected to bow, summoning him with a jerk of the head. Everything would be rectified shortly; he made a mental note to kill these two as well. They would be the first to die, after King Suklar. Leon felt the coldness under his sleeve. Between elbow and wrist was the silver dagger Princess Tusklar had given him this morning. It had been anointed by one of her priests and dipped in poison that the princess had mixed herself. It was up to Leon to choose a moment to use it: the sooner the better.

Leon had been relieved to know the king's realmist was actually loyal to the princess, although when he asked why, she deftly avoided answering him by changing the subject. Leon shrugged, knowing he would find out eventually. If he didn't like her answer, she would feel pain, but he would never kill her. She was the only person who understood his needs and wants. She didn't look at him with disgust as some others had, over the years. Her eyes amplified his desire: desire to maim, kill, and watch others suffer.

His shiny shoes, polished to perfection, clicked on the buffed stone as he made his way to dinner. Suklar's men glided silently on bare feet, comfortable on the warm stone. One walked ahead, the other behind, neither bothering to look at him. Their eyes darted around, although what they feared in their own castle was beyond Leon. He found their uneasiness heightened his anticipation. They had no idea what was going to occur. The surprise Leon would deliver this evening thrilled him. On entering the dining room, the men escorted him to the king's table. The king and his daughter were not yet seated; they would come in last to make a grand entrance.

Leon sat and took time to survey the tables. He saw Pernus and Fendill sitting at the foot of the least of all tables. The men they sat with were low-ranking castle officials, as indicated by the particular colour of stripes on their collars. Tusklar had explained what each colour meant. Everyone in the kingdom wore them. One indicated marital status, the other the status in the community. At his table sat the heads of government. Each one had a gold stripe, some two, depending on whom Suklar favoured. Those with fewer gold stripes looked enviously, even murderously, at those with more.

It appeared Leon had been the penultimate to arrive. Everyone rose and bowed as the king and his daughter entered the hall. They walked regally to the table, which sat higher than the others. Leon stood and bowed deeply. In his own mind he was saying goodbye to the king, who would be dead before the night was over. Leon felt no danger. Tusklar had assured him he would not be harmed. She had won over many of her father's staff and had paid the others handsomely. None would interfere. The only two he had to worry about were those who had brought him here.

The king and his daughter sat. Suklar raised his voice. "My subjects, you may all be seated." His distinctive wave punctuated the order. He turned to Leon. "My daughter tells me you have been most attentive in attempting to win her affection. Not too attentive I hope." He ran a manicured finger over the blade of his table knife.

Leon grinned, showing hard, white teeth.

"You flatter me with the suggestion, Princess Tusklar would be so accommodating to a mere Veresian prince, such as myself. Even if she were, I am aware of the protocol all royalty must follow. I would hope the princess is not insulted by her father's suggestion of impropriety." Leon turned to the princess, who gave nothing away, her expression serene, almost bored. The king, however, slammed his balled fists on the table, causing his knife to clatter to the floor.

"I would suggest that your intention was not to insult me, for if it were, you would be put to death immediately." King Suklar sat rigid in his chair, hand poised to summon his guards. Leon came back to reality and dropped his head in submission.

"Please forgive me, Your Highness. I was merely shocked at the offence our conversation may have caused the lovely princess. I was not aware of myself for a time." He raised his eyes to the king's face. "If I deserve death for defending the Light of the Kingdom, then so be it."

He was proud of himself for that last bit. The king was satisfied, but only just. His hand moved slowly to rest, again, in his lap.

The tension dissipated when the food arrived. Spicy aromas filled the room. The king was served. Only when he commenced eating was anyone else served. Silence filled the room whilst the meal was taken. Leon sat next to the princess, who was rubbing his foot with hers. So close to her father, she was asking for trouble, but Leon understood. Knowledge of what was to occur excited them both, and Tusklar was having trouble holding onto serenity. Leon couldn't believe she enjoyed danger as much as he.

During the meal Leon almost pitied the king and hoped he was enjoying his food, seeing as it was his last meal. Leon wanted to kill him in front of everyone. He wanted everyone to know who would be ruling them, just in case they thought he would be softer than his predecessor. It would have been easier if he could have trusted his realmist and that stupid soldier of his brother's. They could have taken care of Suklar's two guards and been accidentally killed afterward. As it was, Tusklar had people ready to take them into custody at the end of the meal. Leon's attention was captured by a commotion at one of the common tables.

Pernus was trying to help Fendill, who appeared to have fainted again. Two brown-robed, minor guards rushed to the scene. Pernus was assuring everyone he would be all right. It appeared as if Edmund's soldier was requesting an escort to their room. Well, at least it would take care of them for the moment. Pernus nodded toward Leon just before he lifted Fendill over his shoulder. Leon ever-so-slightly inclined his head in recognition. He would never see those two alive again. Any regretful pangs he may have had were frozen in his cold heart.

Pernus let the guards take him to the main stairway, which would lead them to any level within the castle. They were alone. Pernus halted and placed Fendill on the ground. The guards stopped, giving him an enquiring look. Pernus knew they wouldn't be able to understand him if he spoke, so he indicated his shoulder hurt. He motioned the guards to give him a hand lifting the realmist. The guards shrugged, seeing no harm in the request. Pernus was careful not to touch his friend, however made a motion as if to help.

The moment the guardsmen touched Fendill they were trapped. Fendill gripped each one with a stone-strong hold as he funneled heat from the floor into their bodies. Fendill drew as much heat as he could, adding his own life-force to it until their blood boiled. In seconds the men collapsed, their charred veins and organs no longer able to function. Fendill stood, groggy for a moment; he had expended much energy. Pernus grabbed the men's weapons, arming himself and Fendill, who followed him up the stairs.

Their plan had not been too involved. They had no knowledge of the castle. They felt their strategy was rather pathetic, but it was the only one they could come up with that had even the remotest chance of working. They simply ran for the entry. Realistically, Pernus expected they would be killed trying to escape, but that was better than sitting in a room, waiting for it to happen. They reached the ground floor. A pair of black-clad, bare-footed guards were in their way. Surprise was on their side and it made all the difference. The guards had barely armed themselves when one already lay dead, blood seeping a slippery mess on the floor. Pernus had delivered the deathblow. He turned to dispatch the other guard, whose attention was on Fendill. Pernus slid his sword into the man's back and out of his stomach.

Fendill almost vomited as blood splattered his clothes. Breathing deeply, he blocked it out. They both needed to run; surely their escape would soon be discovered? Further down the hall their way was blocked. An obsidian door, solid and immovable by any method they were aware of, barred their escape. If they had the time to wait for someone else to open it they could just stand there, but both men knew that wasn't an option. Fendill placed his hands on the barrier. He sent his mind into what appeared to be stone. He flitted between unseen fragments, which united to form the door. The energy flickered in and out of existence. If he could send the matter somewhere else, he would have opened the door.

Pernus shifted from foot to foot, looking back the direction they had come. It would not be long until the bodies were found. He expected hordes of guards to materialise, hurtling toward them. "Can't you do it any faster?"

Fendill ignored the soldier, all his attention on the task at hand.

The trigger was so subtle he almost missed it. A fragment floated amongst the speckles that was not flickering; it was the only stable part of the door. He probed with his mind until he found a way to move it.

Upon activating the lever, the door vanished. Both men were relieved to see very large but normal doors up ahead, which didn't look so imposing after the obstacle they had just surmounted. Pernus was impressed by Fendill's achievement but thought he would save his congratulations for later.

Fendill was proud to have solved the puzzle, but his heart still pounded in fear. His discovery would mean nothing if they didn't get out of this castle and out of the city. As expected, more guards stood at the entry doors. Four men. This time the duo had been sighted. The men were armed and ready when they reached the door. Fendill was only moderately capable with a sword. He tried to think of another way he could assist. Before he could complete a reasonable thought process, two of the guards were upon him, slashing deftly. Pernus was engaged with the other two. "Back to back. Back to back!"

Somehow, in the confusion of battle, Fendill heard and obeyed. He managed to reach Pernus and do as instructed. Fendill's arm jarred as he fended off a blow intended to detach his leg. The other man came in from the side and attempted to decapitate him.

Fendill moved more quickly than he thought possible, and dropped to the ground, something he was getting a lot of practice at lately. He funneled heat from the floor up through his sword. With the reaction of heat and metal he concocted a blinding light that not only momentarily blinded the men, but caused them sharp pain. Pernus had his back to his friend and was not affected by the light, as his attackers were. As they fumbled their hands to cover painful eyes, Pernus executed them. He turned and dispatched Fendill's attackers with a skillful flurry of strokes.

Dead men littered the floor; Fendill thankful he wasn't one of them. It was unexpectedly easy to open the heavy doors, apparently the same as the doors at home. As the doors divided to show them an inviting view of freedom, an alarm sounded. High wailing echoed throughout the castle. Their escape must have been discovered. As they ran out, soldiers came from everywhere. Armed men rushed toward the castle. They both swallowed hard. It was impossible for them to fight scores of soldiers and expect to survive. Fendill and Pernus stopped, intending to say goodbye to each other as the first of the men reached them. They received no more than a passing glance, and a few shoves, as the developing mob ran into the castle. Apparently they weren't the cause of the alarm. Without asking questions they ran the opposite way.

There was no time to discuss what had just happened as Pernus led Fendill down the gradual slope to where he assumed the Veresian soldiers would have been housed. They needed horses and Pernus wanted his guard to accompany them. Although Pernus had little knowledge of this strange place, he drew on what he knew of other castles. As he expected, the soldier's quarters stood next to the stables. The place seemed deserted, most likely the alarm had stripped Suklar's soldiers from the castle's immediate vicinity. He went to the human quarters first. Pernus hesitated in the doorway. The room was empty. He carefully walked through one room to the next.

Row upon row of neatly made beds lined the walls, all empty, with none of the usual paraphernalia lying around. No packs, no spare boots, no rags to clean weapons. There was no trace of his, or Leon's, men.

Fendill followed his friend through. "Where could they be?"

"I have no idea, Fendill. I don't like the look of this. We don't have time to wonder. Let's just hope they haven't made all the horses disappear as well." They raced to the stables. A familiar smell gave hope to the men. A strong odour of dung permeated the timber construction.

Pernus almost cried with happiness when he found his beloved mare. He hurriedly entered her stall, looking her over intensely before he caressed the white diamond on her black nose. Fendill waded through dirty straw searching for his horse, but didn't find him. There were fourteen horses housed in their stalls. He knew a little about horses and chose himself a tan stallion that looked to be strong and healthy. Thankfully, the saddles were hung neatly on a board at one end of the building. Fendill and Pernus wasted no time.

The only issue Pernus could foresee was the lack of grass for the horses, due to the cold weather. Snow continued to smother everything, albeit not as deep as when they had arrived. The horses would need to eat on the long trip home, so he was hopeful there would be some food stored on the premises.

Their luck continued and they found feed housed in large sacks, stacked in an empty stall. It would be nearly impossible to carry even one, unless they held it in their arms the whole way. Pernus started to swear. Fendill held his hand up to quiet him. "Don't bloody tell me to be quiet! We have a real problem. There's no point getting out of here if the horses starve in the first week." Fendill shook his head and pointed to his ear. Pernus was still puzzled until Fendill pointed to the opposite end of the stables. Edmund's captain belatedly realised his companion had heard a noise.

Swords drawn, they crept through the filth toward a small storeroom housed at the far end, opposite where they had come in. Pernus wasn't as worried now, whoever was hiding didn't want to found by anyone. There was still a chance Fendill had only heard vermin rummaging around. The soldier placed his ear against the door, squinting his eyes as if that would assist his hearing. He shook his head at Fendill and mouthed, "Get ready."

He leaned across and yanked open the door. Two people crouched behind a pile of straw and brooms.

Pernus realised one of them did not have Inkran features. He recognised the young man as one of his newest recruits, a seventeen-year-old boy whose noble father had insisted he learn the soldiering trade with the king's best. He had been under Pernus's instruction for the past year, and showed promise. He was cooped up with what appeared to be a young Inkran girl. Pernus wanted lots of answers, fast.

"Chisholm." The lad automatically stood at attention and saluted his Captain.

"Sir."

"What is going on here? Why are you hiding in a cupboard with a young lady?" Pernus hoped he wouldn't get the obvious answer, although the other answer he'd been suspecting for some time would be a hell of a lot worse.

"I'm hiding from the Inkrans, sir."

"What about the girl?"

"She is also hiding, sir."

"Let's start with why you are hiding, Chisholm."

"Yes, sir. The night after we arrived we were herded out into the snow."

"All of you?"

"Yes, sir. They took us quite some way from our barracks. We were lined up next to each other. One of the Inkran soldiers rode down the line, slicing us across the stomachs with his sword as he went. I'm ashamed to say I practically fainted when I saw what was happening. I started falling backwards at the instant before the sword reached me. I was fortunate that Bendle fell on top of me after he was killed. I kept still and they thought I was dead. I stayed there all night, sir." The young recruit shuddered.

Pernus's face grew ashen. Rage forcefully rumbled through his body, fighting with incredulity. He berated himself for being surprised; he'd had a feeling it might have come to this. They all had. He lamely shook his head. Fendill placed a hand on his shoulder. Pernus composed himself. "Is everyone dead?"

"As far as I know, sir."

What a waste. All of his elite soldiers, all of Leon's men. So many families would never see their fathers or brothers again, and all for what? For Leon's selfish, scheming, evil self. King Edmund would be horrified. Pernus vowed to himself there and then, that if Tusklar didn't kill the traitorous prince, he would.

Pernus addressed the boy again. "What is she doing, hiding with you?" Chisholm looked at his friend, who now stood beside him, their arms touching. "She found me the next morning. Her mother had sent her to dig out some kind of herb from the snow. She saved me. She showed me where to hide and has been bringing me food; her name's Karin. We've been teaching each other our languages."

Pernus was relieved the lad was okay, but they would have to take Karin with them, probably against her will. Life was never simple. "Wait here a minute." Pernus turned his back on the youngsters and took Fendill by the arm out of their hearing.

When they returned, Pernus spoke to Chisholm. "We're on our way home. Someone has to tell King Edmund about what's happened. Saddle up two horses; Karin is coming with us." Chisholm smiled and explained it, as best he could, to Karin. She also smiled and replied in a mix of broken Veresian and Inkran. Chisholm translated to his captain. "Karin says she knows where she can get a donkey to carry food for the horses." They had obviously overheard the men's earlier conversation.

"How far away is this donkey?"

"She says it will take her about five minutes to run there."

"Tell her I'll be going too. If she attempts to compromise our situation, I won't hesitate to kill her. I can't afford to have her raise the alarm. You stay here with Fendill and prepare the horses."

"Yes, sir." Chisholm awkwardly explained the situation to Karin; he appeared to dislike Pernus' comments as much as she did. She nodded in understanding.

Fendill and the young man got to work with the horses. The realmist was mechanical in his approach to the task. His dislike of animals extended to horses. As far as he was concerned they were beasts of burden. Care need only be taken so they could do their job properly. The young soldier, on the other hand, spoke gently to the horse he had chosen. He caressed her as he worked, reassuring her the whole time.

When Fendill had finished saddling Karin's horse, he moved to the front of the barn and kept a look-out. The courtyard was eerily quiet in the snowy evening. The piercing alarm of earlier had ceased its ear-numbing squeals. If the alarms weren't to signal their escape, the only other reason he could think of was that Inkra's security had been compromised by another source. Had Suklar been attacked, or murdered, the Veresian Prince having successfully carried out his task for the princess? Leon should have been drowned at birth.

It wasn't long before Pernus returned with the girl and the promised donkey. Fendill rushed inside to collect the bags of feed. Chisholm had found two sturdy ropes, which came in handy attaching the bundles to the animal. King Edmund's captain addressed the group. "There's no use hiding ourselves. It seems something has happened in the castle. We're going to take the quickest route out of here, which is through the main street. Unless we come across any soldiers, we shouldn't have any trouble. The general population seems to be passive, but be ready to defend yourselves just in case." Pernus handed Chisholm a dagger. "Sorry lad; that's the only spare weapon I've got."

"Excuse me, sir. Does Fendill have a dagger for Karin?"

Pernus contemplated the situation. She was only a slender girl. If she attempted to attack any of them, he could kill her easily. "Fendill, give her your dagger. Get it back tonight." Fendill did as instructed.

Pernus guided them out of the stables. They mounted. The soldier felt safer seated on the filly's familiar back. Only last night he had doubted he would ever see her again. "Fendill, you ride at the rear. Let me know if someone starts chasing us, and make sure our new recruits don't wander off. Move out." Pernus coaxed his horse into a trot. He gradually nudged her to increase speed until he felt they had the balance between speed and what was safe on the slippery street.

As Pernus suspected, the populace barely looked at them. The sound of horses could mean King Suklar's soldiers, and no one wanted to be noticed by one of those. Pernus looked back at his party. He noticed Karin rode well, which surprised him. Fendill, riding at the rear, was nervously darting his head around. Pernus was also tense. His legs gripped the horse too tightly and his calloused hands squeezed the reigns until his knuckles were white.

Realisation hit Pernus and he swore at himself for his own stupidity. He yelled at everyone behind him. "I'm going to stop for a minute. Keep heading for the gates and I'll catch up."

Using his Captain's authoritative voice ensured he would not be questioned. He slowed his horse, letting the others carry on past him. He rode to what looked like a tailor's shop, ready-made items of clothing in the window. Telling his horse to stay there, he entered the shop. The man behind the counter was short, as were most Inkrans. His balding head reluctantly rose until their eyes met. There was a small amount of relief when the Inkran realised Pernus was not one of Suklar's men.

"I know you can't understand me but I need some coats, four to be exact. I don't have any money either, so I'm afraid I'm just going to have to take them. I'm terribly sorry to do this to you." Pernus made his way over to the other side of the counter, looming over the terrified shopkeeper. The man made no move to stop him as he went to a back room and pilfered four thick winter coats. "Don't suppose you've got any gloves. Oh well, never mind." He politely thanked the man as he left.

Pernus couldn't believe his luck when he realised the glove shop was only three doors down. The process was fairly similar to the last shop—no resistance. He appeared with eight sets of gloves. It was always good to have a spare set for when your other ones got too wet. He had to risk finding blankets as well. There was no point escaping this god-forsaken city if they were going to freeze to death on the first night. By the time Pernus found the blanket shop, his heart was pounding. His instincts told him he should have been riding hard for the city gates.

His relief was short-lived as he left the blanket shop, arms full. He was mounting his horse when a low, morose-sounding bell began to toll. Keepers rushed out of their shops, people out of their hovels. Everyone turned to face the castle. As one, they fell to their knees, bending at the waist to place heads and hands in the snow. Pernus wondered if this were some strange ritual executed on a regular basis, another way to punish the already downtrodden population. He rode toward the gates, slowed considerably whilst trying to hold onto his stash and avoiding prone worshippers.

He could see the gates in the not-so-far distance. Nearing his objective, he saw his companions' three horses stopped, waiting in the snow. Anger fuelled by frustration bubbled in his veins. "Those bloody fools. I told them not to wait for me. They're going to wish they were never born when I'm finished with them."

On moving closer, he noticed only Fendill was seated atop his mount. By the time he reached them it was apparent Karin had joined the meditating Inkrans on the ground. Chisholm was crouched next to her, pleading with her to get up.

Pernus swung down from his horse, hands full. "Help me here, Fendill."

Fendill dismounted and took his share of the booty from his friend. Pernus gave Chisholm his and Karin's things. "What's up with her?"

"The bell that tolled was for the king. He's dead. She mourns with her people."

"Well she'll have to finish later. Pick her up and put her in the saddle yourself if you have to."

"Yes, sir."

Chisholm put his coat and gloves on first, placing everything else on his saddle. He tried coaxing his friend one more time. She remained unresponsive. He apologized as he easily lifted her still body from the ground, but she fought him as he attempted to lift her onto her horse. Once she was in the saddle her brown eyes stared angrily at him, tears streaming down her face. The sorrow Chisholm saw there was unexpected. He could not understand how a person, so badly treated by their ruler, could be this upset when they died. He would have thought it would bring relief. He handed her the coat and gloves, ordering that she put them on. She obeyed, whilst her grief continued to wash down her brown skin.

Pernus and Fendill had remounted. "Keep an eye on her, Chisholm; make sure she's okay. Suklar's death, may he rest in peace, has bought us some time. Let's not waste it." He turned his horse, continuing toward the gate, that only a day before he and Fendill had considered insurmountable. Once out of the gates, the cobbled road turned to snow and dirt. He increased the pace as the feeling of being hunted overcame him. He prayed to the gods they would make it out alive. Edmund had to be warned. Life wouldn't be worth living if Leon got his hands on Veresia.

***

Back at the castle, Leon luxuriated with his wife-to-be in a large tub of hot water. Long-dead rose petals floated on its surface, dried the summer before and saved for such an occasion. He closed his eyes and relived the moment his dagger had sunk between Suklar's shoulder blades. There was some resistance; the feeling of the heart being ruptured had filtered through the handle so that Leon knew the moment the monarch was past the point of no return. He remembered looking at his beloved's face. Her eyes were bright with rapture. She had seen the look of complete surprise her father had exhibited when he realised he had been stabbed. She had laughed at his comical expression, his mouth in a perfect 'O'.

Leon had stood proud, drinking in her admiration. He could not hear the voice in her head cackling, adding to her joy. He did not realise she had just decided she would keep him alive, at least until the wedding. The voice had told her it should be so. Leon smeared Suklar's blood across his own forehead in an instant of pure animalism. He was caught in the moment, the warm, sticky liquid adding to his pleasure, and remnants of the blood now mixed with the water in which they bathed.

Life was good. It would soon get better. Leon recalled that Fendill and Pernus had not been there to witness his great deed. He would go to their room later and tell them what he had achieved. Then he would kill them. He would enjoy killing Pernus more than Fendill, of course. Tusklar interrupted his musing by demanding a cuddle, which led to a kiss, which led to a well-deserved passionate celebration.

The following morning, Leon confidently walked the hallways, two of Tusklar's guards as protective escorts. There would still be those loyal to King Suklar skulking around until they were weeded out. There was no reason to take any chances. Leon reached his old rooms. How far he had come in just over a week—from foreign prince to heir of Inkra's throne. He couldn't help but grin. His escort opened the doors for their new leader. Prince Leon's good mood did not last when it was clear the men weren't there.

He turned to one of the black-clad men; they all looked the same to him. "Find them. Now!"

The man ran to do as he was ordered. Leon spoke to the other one. "Find the guards who assisted them from the dining hall last night. Make it quick."

It was a good thing Suklar had trained some of his men to speak Veresian or Leon would have had to do things himself. Apparently Tusklar had needed people to practice with. Those few people were now assigned to Leon.

King Edmund's brother strode around the room in an agitated state until the guards returned. "So. Out with it. Where the hell are they?"

"Gone. The guards who were with them were found dead last night." Prince Leon understood only too well his harsh, clipped words.

"Are you daring to tell me they have escaped? Are they still in the castle at least?" Leon's face twisted in crazed disbelief. Everything was supposed to be as he wanted it. This hiccup shouldn't have been possible. The gods were on his side. His side!

The guard reluctantly informed Leon of the other dead guards found along the route to the entry. Leon's red face was in danger of exploding. As he spoke, spittle flew from his lips, hitting the unfortunate guard in the face. "I want them found, even if you have to send the whole wretched army. They've obviously escaped into the city. Do not return until they are found. If any man sent out returns without their bodies, they will be executed. Do I make myself clear?" He was screaming at the last.

The guard was mortified, even Suklar had not been this twisted. He obeyed, quickly. "I will gather my best men. We will return as soon as we find them."

Without waiting for a dismissal, the guard bowed low and dragged his companion away to gather some men. Leon headed for Tusklar's rooms. He hadn't felt this enraged for a long time. He needed to beat out his fury on someone: she would do nicely.

22

Bronwyn sat and glared at the large cat that shared her camp. It had been many days since she'd been forced to part with her aunt and friend, and she still hadn't forgiven the beast who had caused it to happen.

The cat returned Bronwyn's angry stare with a relaxed one. *You'll have to forgive me some time, young cub. We won't be able to bond with any ill feeling between us.*

"Why would I bond with you? You're horrible and mean. You obviously have no concept of love, attachment, or affection. I'm not ready now, and I don't know if I ever will be." Her arms were folded protectively. She shifted around to turn her back on the beast.

The young realmist was loath to admit it, but the time she had spent with the super-sized panther had taught her many things. There were things about Talian magic, the power generated from Talia itself instead of through the Second Realm, that she had never been shown. She wondered if any of the realmists were aware of the extent to which they could utilise the forces of nature without exposing themselves to the risks of the Second Realm. The panther was a creature of Drakon, the dragon god, so had information no mere mortal could have had.

Bronwyn didn't hear the stealthy animal as he approached her. She jumped in fright when he nudged her with his enormous, furry head. *I probably shouldn't tell you this because you've been so rude, but your aunt is okay.* Bronwyn turned to face the panther.

"What about my friend, Corrille?"

The screeching one? I'm not sure. Her symbol has disappeared. Bronwyn digested the implications for a moment. Her back tensed as she wondered if her friend was being shielded or dead.

There's no point worrying about it now. We'll eventually find out one way or another what's become of her.

"Easy for you to say." Bronwyn could feel the heat in her cheeks as she asked the next question. "Um, I've just realised I don't know your name. Do you have a name?"

The giant cat's lips turned up at the corners in a feline grin. *Yes, I have a name; nice of you to enquire.*

"So, what is it?"

Sinjenasta. It roughly translates as Servant of The Dragon God.

"Were you with Drakon before?"

In a way. It's hard to explain. I was of this Realm, but not. I am of this Realm now and have lost a lot of the powers I once had. Drakon is sacrificing me to help you. I would have lived an eternal life, but for your plight.

Bronwyn stared at the animal as the enormity of what Sinjenasta was being forced to do dawned on her. "Did you have a choice?"

Do any of us?

Bronwyn shook her head. As she felt more comfortable with her role in saving Talia, she also felt an increased sense of responsibility. If she failed, there were many whose sacrifices would have been wasted. She looked the cat in his yellow-green eyes.

"I'm sorry I've been so rude. Please forgive me? I could only see my pain. As usual I forgot about what everyone else was going through." Sinjenasta rumbled out a low purr, which brought a smile to the young woman's smooth-skinned face.

With a new attitude toward the Dragon God's panther, she understood what she had to do. "When do you want to bond?"

I thought you'd never ask. Now that you've made your decision, we can go to Drakon's sacred lake. It's within the confines of Vellonia, Valley of the Dragons.

"I know what Vellonia is."

Just making sure.

"How far away are we?"

A couple of days. We would've already been there by now, but I needed you to make the decision by yourself. You humans can be rather stubborn at times. Bronwyn couldn't help but look sheepish.

She made a move to pack. *Not so fast, cub. This is a safe place to spend the afternoon. We'll travel at night because I don't want to alert anyone to our whereabouts. Tonight I'll ask Drakon to shield you until we reach Vellonia, just in case one of your realmist friends is looking for you.*

"Why?"

Because Drakon commands it. I don't want you trying to contact any of your friends either. We have to be invisible, to everyone. The panther's wet, black nose was shoved in Bronwyn's face. She sneezed.

"I promise I won't contact anyone."

Good. Now get some rest. I hope you're not getting a cold. I'll wake you when the sun goes down.

Bronwyn's sleep was dreamless. The weight of a huge paw on her shoulder woke her. The realmist ate some of her rations and packed up her things. Sinjenasta led the way. He ran easily, comfortably loping in front of Bronwyn's trotting horse as they negotiated their way through the dark. The cat could see well, and once Prince had gotten used to the beast's smell, he was happy to follow him.

They travelled until dawn's rays signaled the start of another day. People were stirring, and Sinjenasta explained to Bronwyn that the dot high in the sky, to the west, was a dragon. Whilst she didn't quite understand why they had to be so secretive, she rushed her horse into the protection of a large copse of trees. They rested for the day and set out again that night.

Approaching Vellonia, Bronwyn saw the dark outline of the mountain ranges to the west. She had never seen mountains so high. The closer they got, the larger the outline, until it practically blocked the stars and moon out of Bronwyn's field of vision. For the past couple of hours Sinjenasta had been leading them alongside a wide river. The sound of water rushing past faster than they were travelling had a soothing effect. Bronwyn trusted the big cat, and felt safe knowing that Drakon, a god no less, was watching over them. She championed no god in particular, realmists being indebted to all gods, but she saw no problem in accepting any favouritism Drakon was willing to afford.

Bronwyn sensed they were nearing their destination. She was tired; travelling at night when she was supposed to be sleeping was difficult. She found it was easy to stay awake at first, but as the night wore on she had to force her eyes to stay open. It was tempting to close her eyes and tell herself she'd rest her eyes for only a few minutes, until she would wake in a panic, just in time to stop herself from falling inelegantly off the horse.

Sinjenasta halted at the foot of Vellonia's great ranges. Bronwyn dismounted. For some strange reason it felt like she was coming home, almost. She remembered Bayerlon had felt the same. Maybe she just liked finding new places. Drakon's panther sniffed around the riverbank near the first pile of rocks that signified Vellonia's border. He raised his head and sniffed the air, mouth open, front fangs protruding.

"Is everything okay, Sinjenasta?"

Humans have been this way in the last few days. I can smell five of them.

"Could any of them be Avruellen or Corrille?"

No. I know their scent from the night I collected you. Theirs are not among them. The brief moment of hope left Bronwyn feeling sad for her family all over again.

Sinjenasta stood silent.

"What are you doing?" Bronwyn had to wait for an answer.

Conversing with Drakon. Join me.

The realmist walked over to where the panther sat—centimetres from the edge of the river. "Now what?"

Face the river and step down.

"Are you serious? I'll fall in."

You won't, and stop questioning me. I need your implicit trust. One day one of your questions will get you killed. Bronwyn was shocked at the bluntness of the cat's words. She reluctantly did as she was told, stomach muscles clenched in anticipation of a fall into the icy water.

Bronwyn stepped into the support of some kind of sturdy timber construction. Sinjenasta jumped in after her, rocking the vessel. *Sit and strap yourself in.* She did as she was told without voicing any of the hundreds of questions running around her head. *Normally you would*

314

be given a blindfold, but Drakon has assured me it will be
too dark for you to see anything anyway.

With no warning, they started moving. Bronwyn felt the cold night air blow stray strands of hair from her face. Her nose tickled, and she felt like sneezing again. The boat entered the cave. Total blackness enveloped them. The same musty odour that filled the previous travellers' nostrils now filled Bronwyn's.

The only indication of their speed increasing was the volume of air Bronwyn's head was being pushed through. Her cheeks and nose felt cold: she covered them with warm hands. The speed increased until they were shot into the whirlpool. Without warning, Bronwyn's hands were torn from their protective place over her face. She couldn't help but let out a scream. She heard Sinjenasta's deep, smooth voice in her head, calming and soothing her, reminding her she could trust him. He would protect her. It was difficult, but she stopped screaming as they spun faster and faster, out of control.

Bronwyn's eyes were shut tight, teeth gritted in forced silence. Finally the maelstrom spat them out, and they dropped metres into the calm waters of Vellonia's underground lakes, where Bronwyn's belt unbuckled by itself.

Jump out now.

Bronwyn struggled to lift herself onto legs as slackly fluid as the water they had travelled on. The easy part was falling out of the boat. Noise from the tumult assaulted Bronwyn's ears, as it dropped cascades of water into the underground lake. She was disorientated, confused. She followed Sinjenasta, who spoke into her mind, directing her to safety. The icy river had recently come from its origins high in the mountains.

Bronwyn concentrated on swimming after the big cat and tried to ignore her chattering teeth. She was too cold to even feel happy when sounds of the large animal lifting himself out of the water reached her. By the time Bronwyn touched land, her strength was barely sufficient to lift her out of the frigid liquid. Numb fingers cried out in pain as they scraped on the rough surface of the cave floor. She sat in a shivering puddle and tried to recover.

Why don't you make use of some of your skills? The light was only slightly improved in the cave, and Bronwyn could barely see Sinjenasta's outline. It took a few moments for her to realise what he was saying. She placed icy palms on the ground and willed heat to rise. An ancient warmth filled her body. Hands and feet throbbed in excruciating pain as the blood vessels dilated to receive much-needed blood. It was like she was being stabbed by hundreds of tiny knives. Pain subsided and her clothes started to steam. She directed the heat out of her body and directly to her clothes, which dried in seconds.

You have to learn to have more control over your mind. You can't afford to stop thinking because your body is suffering. I shouldn't have to remind you to warm yourself. Follow me, and don't make a sound.

Bronwyn kept her reply to herself. The cat hadn't even bonded with her yet and he was already as bossy as her aunt. Maybe she should refuse the bonding and save herself years of torment. On the other hand, she should have thought of warming herself. Her aunt would have berated her for the same thing, saying she had learned nothing over the past eighteen years.

As they made their way through Vellonia's underbelly, Bronwyn remembered she was in the dragon city. It was exciting, but at the same time she could hardly believe they were there. She had always imagined their entry to be greeted by hundreds of welcoming dragons, not to mention how magnificent the city would have looked. At the moment she could barely see anything—not that it mattered. The only things to see here were dirt and rocks.

Bronwyn spoke to Sinjenasta, mind to mind. *Where are we going?*

Drakon's Sacred Lake. It lies beneath the city. Most of the dragons don't even know it's here.

That's pretty sacred. What's that got to do with us bonding?

Stop asking questions.

You don't know, do you?

Of course I know. It would take me too long to tell you. Just trust me.

Bronwyn had heard those words so many times before that she was heartily sick of them. One day the trust she was always told to concede would lead to disaster. She hoped today was not the day.

Sinjenasta's soft paws made barely a sound as he padded through the caves. Any sound he did make was on purpose, for he wanted to ensure Bronwyn could follow easily. The only other noise Bronwyn heard was a faint drip, drip, drip, which echoed, the plonk of each drop repeating itself once to run into the sound of the next.

Due to Bronwyn's near-blindness, progress was slow as she tentatively moved forward. She had no sense of time passing. At some point she wondered if they had been here for minutes or days. If Sinjenasta decided to leave her, she would be in trouble. Without his guidance, Bronwyn could see herself wandering around disorientated for days, until she died from lack of water and starvation. Her thoughts fueled her sense of uselessness and inferiority, and she feared she would never truly be independent. She wanted to be the one who was in charge and knew what to do for once, but how could that happen when she couldn't even find her way out of a cave?

Oppressiveness smothered her. Indecision overtook her. Bronwyn stopped walking. Sinjenasta eventually became conscious of the fact the realmist was no longer following him. By the time he found her, she was curled up like a fetus on the hard, uneven floor, hands clutched protectively around her knees. Her eyes were clenched shut, blocking out the reality of total blackness. If she kept them shut, she could imagine that when they opened she would be able to clearly see everything around her.

Sinjenasta lay next to her, leaning against her at the same time. Bronwyn felt his feline warmth radiate comfortingly through her clothes. *Bronwyn, I'm here with you. You'll have to get up and keep going. We don't have far to go now. When we rise, I want you to hold onto my tail.*

"I'm scared." Her voice sounded small in the vast, cavernous surroundings.

There's nothing to be afraid of. Vellonia's caves can induce fear or self-doubt in anyone. It's part of the city's defence system. Trust me. His last two words stabilized her. Their familiarity brought her back to a more recognizable reality. They rose, and Bronwyn grabbed his tail.

Don't let go. His soft tail was her anchor. The negative thoughts faded until her head was clear of the destructive fog.

They walked for a long while. Bronwyn's stomach reminded her it was time to eat. "I'm hungry."

Not far now.

"You said that hours ago." They had skipped breakfast and now Bronwyn estimated it must be almost lunchtime. Her belly rumbled. Slowly but surely Sinjenasta became more solid to the realmist. His outline strengthened. She started to notice the rocks around her. Stalagmites and stalactites impressed her with their beauty. "Where's the light coming from?"

Our destination. I present to you, the Sacred Lake of Drakon: Vellonia's soul.

They stopped just inside the domed grotto. The ceiling was the height of two men, one atop the other. Light permeated from the walls and reflected off thousands of gems embedded in the rock. In turn, vivid colour splashed around the cavern, turning dull brown earth into the sky's brightest rainbow. Bronwyn could not fathom from where the light was coming, and she was too in awe to ask.

The lake itself was not unlike any other lake she had seen, however when she dared approach the edge, she could see clouds and blue sky reflected on its surface. She instinctively looked up, even though she knew only rock floated overhead. When she looked down again a hawk soared past, gliding through the image as if he were really there. Bronwyn stared in wonder at the beautiful body of water. Was there a world in there, a world which existed somewhere else, or was it a small world contained within these mountains? Her mind raced in joy at the marvel that lay before her.

Sinjenasta stood quietly behind her. He had seen this sacred pool of water many times and knew some of its secrets. Whilst he loved its beauty, he also knew of the price it could exact to ensure its will was done. Sinjenasta had suffered for this lake. He was a creature of Drakon, so had no choice. He knew he would continue to suffer until the Sacred Lake let him go. He was sorry to have to ask Bronwyn to make her own sacrifices, but he knew they were necessary.

Bronwyn. She turned to face the big cat whose head reached her shoulders. *Are you ready?* She nodded. *Undress and stand at the edge of the lake.*

Her eyes widened but still she did not speak. Normally she would have been embarrassed at undressing in front of another, however, Sinjenasta was only an animal, and the atmosphere in this grotto was one of complete peace. Bronwyn had never felt closer to the gods. She hoped Avruellen would have the opportunity to see it one day.

Bronwyn placed her clothes in a neat pile next to the lake. She sat on the edge and used her hand to test the temperature. Unexpectedly, and unlike the river that had brought them here, it was warm. She looked at Sinjenasta for reassurance, turned, and slipped into the picturesque pool. Soothing warmth embraced her body. Bronwyn turned back to see if the panther was getting in, when she was jerked from underneath. She had barely enough time to take a last breath before being dragged under.

Her heart pounded and she tried to kick and thrash, to escape the murderous force, but watery hands held her tight. Her thoughts were wildly fighting the serenity imposed on them by this place. Before tipping over the precipice into panic, Bronwyn recalled Sinjenasta's earlier words. It was time to master her mind. She ignored her mortality and the thought that she couldn't breathe. She stopped fighting the invisible terror, retreating to a peaceful place to consider her options. She remembered water was really made up of air. Now she just had to think of how she could convert it to something she could breathe.

She couldn't boil it because she would cook herself. How did the fish do it? Could she alter her lungs? Avruellen had never mentioned whether or not one could alter one's body. In the distance, her lungs were crying out for oxygen, her body doing its best to grab her attention before it died. She called out to Thireos, God of beasts, to show her in detail what gills looked like. If she didn't receive an answer she would soon be dead. An image appeared in her mind. Bronwyn thanked Thireos and focused her will on the picture that was her only salvation.

She could feel her body losing consciousness. Pushing worry aside, she concentrated on her lungs. She realised the minute particles forming her lungs alternately winked in and out of sight. One instant they were there, the other they weren't. Like pieces of a puzzle she replaced the different particles as they flickered in and out. When one particle disappeared she immediately replaced it with one that would help alter the form of her lungs. Her chest was shot with excruciating pinpricks of pain every time she replaced a particle. Finally she saw in her own body, the image she held in her mind. Against instinct, but too exhausted to care, she opened her mouth and felt a solid mass of liquid rush into her chest.

She couldn't believe she had done it! It was a strange sensation to be breathing underwater. Bronwyn opened her eyes, newly oxygenated blood causing the black spots to dissipate. She had never been so close to death. Now what? She could not feel Sinjenasta's presence anywhere. Had he abandoned her? Was this all a ruse to kill her? She didn't think so. The great cat could have sliced her open with his claws any time he chose. In her recaptured state of consciousness she realised the force that had dragged her under had let go. Was this the test, to alter her body? Bronwyn decided to float back to the top.

The journey to the surface was gradual. Bronwyn enjoyed the relaxation of weightlessness. Light pierced through to where she floated; she was almost there. Her head popped through the soft barrier. Bronwyn looked up at the same blue sky and clouds she had seen earlier. This lake wasn't under Vellonia. She had no idea where she was. She couldn't breathe again. Was she on another world? Chastising herself for being stupid, she dove underneath the water and took a breath. She would have to reconvert her gills to lungs. She dreaded the pain, but felt confident she could do it.

The process took a couple of minutes. She emerged a second time to gulp in fresh air. Turning her head this way and that, revealed no sign of the creature she was to bond with. She was surprised to see her clothes lying on the lip of this other lake. It was as warm out of the water as it was in. Bronwyn let her body dry in the sun before she dressed. The land surrounding the water comprised of gently rolling hills, adorned with thick green grass, dotted with ancient trees whose canopies cast vast, cooling shadows over the countryside.

Bronwyn called out for her companion. Drakon's panther did not reply, but a young man did. He stepped out from behind an ancient trunk. Bronwyn held her breath as a tingling warmth spread through her body as she looked into his blue-green eyes. She had never seen a man so beautiful, with smooth, pale skin, straight nose, and black hair. He was dressed in earthy tones and had a bow slung over his shoulder. The arrow he held was red at the tip, indicating he had recently shot some poor animal. Even with that knowledge, she found she couldn't take her eyes off him.

His intense stare made her feel as if she were still naked. He spoke in a soft, deep voice, which held an air of quiet confidence. "How do you come to be here, Princess?"

Bronwyn had to clear her throat before she could speak.

"I jumped into the lake, and here I am."

"Well then, if you prefer not to tell me, that's okay." Maybe he didn't realise the true nature of the mass of water he lived next to.

Bronwyn knew she had to bond with Sinjenasta and wondered if maybe he had noticed a big black panther anywhere.

"Why do you seek such a dangerous creature?"

"He's my friend, and I need his help." The handsome young man hesitated an instant, guilt altering his features.

"I'm afraid I've done something you will not like." Bronwyn again noticed the red tip of the arrow.

"Where is he? What have you done?" The young man turned and walked back behind the tree. Bronwyn followed, heart sinking with each step.

Her worst fears were given life when she saw the carcass of her companion hanging upside down from a low branch, Sinjenasta's nose almost touching the ground. She ran to the body and felt his soft coat. She couldn't believe he could be killed so easily; Drakon himself had sent him to her. This couldn't be happening. Bronwyn looked into his lifeless eyes. Stunned, she stepped back and fell on her bottom. Her triumph of earth magic a moment ago had turned into tragedy. Her failure to bond with the giant cat was sure to affect what she had to do. Were they all now condemned to failure?

The young man sat on the ground opposite the young realmist. "I truly am sorry. If I had known he was yours I wouldn't have killed him."

Bronwyn looked up to yell at the man who had stolen away the future of Talia; her future. Her words stayed in her throat when she saw his tears. He was truly sorry. She could almost believe he felt her pain.

Bronwyn knew she had not known the panther very long, however he was her only link to where she had come from. The knowledge that they were to have bonded gave him a special place in her heart. It was all over now. Would The Circle be able to start again? Bronwyn called out to Drakon. "Where are you? I need you to bring Sinje back." She stood and repeated her words, screaming this time. "Damn you, Drakon. You call yourself a god? Some pathetic god: you couldn't even keep one of your own alive."

There was no answer, and the young man looked at her as if she had lost her mind.

Bronwyn turned away from the dead panther and stared into the distance. She thought aloud. "What do I do now?"

She honestly had no idea where she should go. If she went back to Vellonia, if she could get back, would she then be able to find her way to the surface.

"Stay here with me. Let me make it up to you, Princess." The young man stood in front of her and stared into her eyes once again.

They stood so close she could practically feel the warmth emanating from his body. His proximity muddled her thoughts. She put in an extra effort to make sense. "Why do you keep calling me Princess?"

"I thought I recognised you. Are you not a princess of Veresia?" She felt relief at those words. Veresia did exist here. It seemed she had just been transported to another place within Talia.

"I'm not a princess—far from it, in fact. Can you tell me where we are?"

"You don't know?"

"Well, I just asked didn't I? Which part of Talia are we in?"

"Talia?"

"Yes, Talia. The Realm in which Veresia exists." His lack of comprehension alarmed Bronwyn. Had she travelled to a realm no one knew about?

"We are in the Sacred Realm. The Realm from which all others were modelled."

His handsome face was not enough to sooth her anymore. She shouldn't be here and Sinjenasta shouldn't be dead. What had they done wrong? Maybe they should have waited longer to bond. Bronwyn decided what she had to do. Even if it meant her death as well, she had to try to get back home. She couldn't save Talia whilst she existed in this other realm.

"Could you please help me take the panther to the lake?" He could not understand why, but agreed nonetheless. Bronwyn was sickened by the rustling of the grass as they dragged the panther's corpse through it. The sound on its own was not the problem, just the knowledge of what was making it.

They were both puffing by the time they reached the lake—Sinjenasta was heavy. Bronwyn proceeded to disrobe. She felt she should do everything she had done previously or she may not reach Talia. The young man did not turn away to save her modesty. He stood transfixed, drinking in her beauty.

Bronwyn dove into the ripple-less mirror. It broke her heart in a way she didn't understand, to know she was leaving this man, a man whom she had only just met. The whole situation was surreal. Bronwyn swam to the edge of the lake and grabbed Sinjenasta's tail. She dragged the panther in with her and kept hold of his tail, as he had told her to do earlier that day. "Goodbye." She didn't know what else to say.

"Good bye, Princess."

Bronwyn relived the pain of converting her lungs to gills. She dragged the panther behind her, the resistance slowing her progress. How long should she swim down before swimming up again? Hoping she would not just return to the newly discovered realm, the realmist swam until, unexpectedly, she touched bottom. There was nowhere to go now but up. She prayed she would return to the underground cave. During the journey to the surface Sinjenasta's tail seemed to disintegrate until Bronwyn stopped to check what was happening. The panther was no longer there. Left with a few strands of fur between her fingers, Bronwyn looked around but couldn't see him anywhere. She had lost him again.

She felt like a failure, salty tears mixing with the warm, fresh water of the lake for the remainder of her ascension. This time she commenced her transformation before she reached the surface. When she broke through, her lungs gulped musty cave air. She had done something right. When she looked up, the coloured lasers of light shooting around the grotto dazzled her eyes.

Welcome back. Glad you could join me. Sinjenasta casually licked a gigantic paw.

"But, but.... You were dead. Is it really you, Sinje?"

As you can see, I'm not dead. I don't know what reality you were in, but you spoke to me where I went. I was certainly not dead.

"Is it possible we could have gone to two different places?"

Anything's possible. In any case, we're bonded. Can you feel it?

Bronwyn climbed out of the water. She stood and contemplated. She shut her eyes and spun around. Without opening her eyes she stopped, turned to her right and pointed directly at the large panther. "I can feel where you are. I can feel that you're alive." She opened her eyes and smiled at her newly-bonded companion. "I'm so glad you're alive. I thought we'd failed."

You thought you had failed?

"Yes. But it seems I didn't." Bronwyn approached Sinjenasta and embraced him in a large hug. "You're so soft."

Stop using me to dry yourself and put some clothes on. We'd better get moving. There's still something we have to do for Drakon.

Bronwyn held onto his tail to go back through the dark tunnels. This time she was in much better spirits. Her head was filled with an image of the handsome stranger in the other realm. Why did the man of her dreams have to exist somewhere else? She couldn't wait to tell her aunt about her discovery of a new realm—if indeed, that's what it was. It may have just been a trick of the lake. If everything she saw was truth, Sinjenasta would be dead. Maybe the stranger was also a figment of the lake's imagination. That would be a shame.

Bronwyn had the sudden urge to sneeze. It took all of her will to keep quiet. A second sneeze attempted to burst forth. After a while, the urge abated. Bronwyn spoke to her creatura mind to mind. *What is it we have to do for Drakon?*

I would rather not say.

Do you think I would refuse the task if I knew what it was?

You don't actually have to do anything if you don't want to. The situation will unfold as the Realms intend. Sensing she would get no more out of him, she amused herself with daydreams of the stranger whose name she had never asked.

Through the mind link she had with the panther, she was aware they were approaching the place where they had initially dragged themselves from the freezing waters. Bronwyn was slowly grasping the reality of being bonded. She could smell traces of what Sinjenasta could smell. Through his understanding, she knew what it was they smelled. "So that's what I smell like to an animal." There was another stronger smell which raised the hackles on the back of the panther's neck.

"What's that?"

Our prey.

"I didn't know we were hunting anything."

We are. He stopped. *The thing we are hunting must be killed. You will probably have a million questions when you see whom I am trying to kill, but keep silent. Either help me, or stay out of it. Drakon has ordered this creature to death, however my attempt may not succeed. If I die, you will feel it in your bones. You will feel pain for weeks, maybe months. Your whole body will ache and your mind will grieve.*

"Why didn't you tell me that before we bonded?"

That was your teacher's job. I would have thought Avruellen was a better teacher than that.

"Well, she probably mentioned something, but it didn't sound that bad."

Another thing. If we get caught, which is likely, don't say who sent us, or why. Secrecy is our biggest weapon at this point.

A shuffling noise echoed in the distance. The panther led them toward it. They walked past their arrival point and further, to where the boat would have taken them, had they followed the path of the humans before them. There was a little more light in the direction they travelled, outlines emerging around them, as they had before entering the grotto.

Sinjenasta halted behind a large rock. Bronwyn heard his voice in her mind. *You can let go of my tail. Stay here and watch. Don't make a sound.*

She obeyed. When he padded out from behind the relative safety of the rock, Bronwyn's heart skipped nervously. She dared to peek after him. He was sneaking toward the biggest creature she had ever seen. Instinctively Bronwyn knew it was a dragon. He, or she, appeared to be examining a boat. It may have been the one that had brought them here.

Was that the creature Drakon wanted dead? Bronwyn puzzled as to why he would want one of his own slaughtered. Better still, why didn't he just smite him down? He was a god, after all. The closer Sinjenasta was to the dragon, the more apparent it became that the dragon had a huge size advantage. Bronwyn thought of the panther as being a large, strong creature, but compared to the dragon he looked like a kitten. She was seized with fear for her creatura—he could not possibly defeat that monster; Bronwyn gripped the edge of the rock so hard her fingers hurt. Was it too late to make him come back? This could only end in disaster.

Sinjenasta crouched low as he skulked into the more illuminated region in which the dragon was standing, bronze lamp at his feet. His panther heart thumped loudly in his chest. He was within leaping distance. Adrenalin raced through his body as he drew back, then launched himself out of the shadows and toward the dragon's throat. Bronwyn could barely look. Would the dragon see him in time to defend itself? Apparently not. The panther landed on the creature's back, between large, leathery wings. He dug razor claws in, to keep his grip, and without hesitating, clamped his jaws on the unsuspecting animal's neck. The dragon let out a wild squeal. The noise shot through Bronwyn's ears, leaving them ringing. Surely other dragons would hear and come down to help their comrade.

Bronwyn didn't want to see such a magnificent creature die. Avruellen had always told her what a great friend they were to humans. On the other hand, she definitely didn't want to see Sinje die. The dragon was doing its best to dislodge the panther, but its short arms couldn't reach behind that far. What the cat was doing was not going to kill the dragon, although he was obviously in a lot of pain. What was Sinje trying to do, wear it down?

Bronwyn heard the dragon speak in mind voice to her creatura. *Who are you? Why are you doing this? Let go before I'm forced to kill you.* Sinje didn't answer; he just clamped his jaws down tighter. The dragon stopped dancing around and jumped in the river. He placed his back under the freezing water, totally submerging Sinje. Bronwyn couldn't see what was happening any more, and forgetting all reason, ran to where they had commenced the melee.

She looked down and saw the dragon thrashing about in an effort to keep Sinje under water. Bronwyn wasn't sure how long panthers could hold their breath, however the dragon seemed as if he could stay there all day. The dragon tilted his large, scaly head up, locking eyes with Bronwyn. Vicious black orbs threatened her. She didn't know what to do and was practically paralysed with fear. Jumping in to help didn't appear to be a sensible option; maybe she should plead with the beast. It was probably too late for that and they did, still, have to try to kill him. What was she going to say, "Please, sir dragon, leave my friend alone so we can kill you?" She didn't think so.

Time passed. Sinjenasta couldn't hold out for much longer, but if he released his grip, the dragon would turn and kill him with his giant maw. Bronwyn shut her eyes to break the chain of fear the dragon created with his stare. Realmistry was almost useless against dragons; they had practically invented it. She drew her sword and jumped in, eyes still shut. She opened them underwater. She assumed she had one attempt at putting the blade in the creature's belly. She could see a darker mass in front of her. Hoping the dragon hadn't turned Sinje toward her, she gathered force from the roiling water and used it to push her body toward the thrashing pair. Sword held out in front, she braced for the impact.

The blade, given to her by Avruellen, struck the dragon. Dense scales resisted for a moment, then gave way as Bronwyn released the rest of the water's energy. She could hear the death squeal from underwater. The sword lodged in the beast's belly. She released her hold on it and returned to the surface, frantically swimming around to find Sinje. A red hue sullied the water. She hoped none of it belonged to her creatura.

Sinjenasta, realising the dragon had ceased thrashing, even moving, unlocked his jaws. He was almost out of breath; it was all he could do to push his nose into the sweet air. He wasn't sure what had happened, but when he saw Bronwyn, he was relieved she had decided to get involved. His relief was short-lived. Standing above them, at the edge of the stained water, taking in the whole scene, were two murderous-looking dragons.

Bronwyn followed Sinje's gaze and when she saw the massive creatures she knew they were in trouble. The young realmist's heart pounded even harder at the realisation they had been caught. The brief belief they would exit the river alive disappeared, sinking heavily to rest as a great weight on the bottom of her mind.

"I am Jazmonilly Accorterroza, Queen of Vellonia, and I want to know why you have killed my nephew." Bronwyn groaned. Out of all the dragons in the world, they had to murder royalty. The fact she had murdered at all should have been a shock to her. The realmist had never killed before. She turned her head and saw the carcass floating on the water face down. What had she done? She had spilled blood, lots of it, to end another's existence. Guilt and horror forced her to see herself in a different way. By the time the dragons fished her from the river to face the wrath of the dragon queen, she didn't care what might happen.

23

Blayke sat quietly beside the neatly made bed. Agmunsten had managed to stabilise Arcon, and they had moved him to his own room. The young man sat and waited. The leader of The Circle had exhausted himself trying to save his patient. Zim had sent food in to Agmunsten after he had been shut away for more than a day and night. The servant conveying the meal had found him lying on the ground. Unable to wake him, she had called Zim, who had performed some basic healing and carried him to his room; Agmunsten would be okay, he was just exhausted. Arcon, on the other hand, remained frighteningly close to death. Agmunsten had only half-done the job.

As each minute passed with no change, Blayke worried more. Phantom had taken his place on the window-side table. The owl had not moved since Arcon's arrival. Blayke knew Phantom would almost certainly die of grief if the old realmist died, and was almost sure he would too. The man lying in the bed was practically his father; he had been the one who had comforted him when he was sad, played with him as a young child, nursed him through every illness, and he was the person he clung to at night when he had woken from every dragon-spawned nightmare. He couldn't see how he could live through the grief of losing Arcon and sobbed every time he thought about it.

Fang was a comfort. The rat stayed with him and tried to cheer him up, every now and then recounting some funny story or other about Arcon. Blayke also talked to the unmoving patient, hoping he heard. Blayke could hear muffled commotion outside the closed door. It sounded as if dragons were running past, some shouting as they went.

"Fang, could you go and see what's happening?" The rat nimbly climbed down the young man's trouser leg and squeezed under the door.

Fang stayed close to the wall to avoid being trodden on by any passing dragons. People were small enough to notice him, but he doubted dragons were. It seemed as if the procession had passed, so the small creatura continued down the hallway following the noise. He wondered if any other rats dwelled within Vellonia, caves being an ideal hiding place, although there was probably not much food. A rat would be safe here, a dragon would not waste the energy to catch one for the pathetic amount of food it provided, and Fang had never heard of dragons being afraid of rodents. Many a poor rat had been unfairly killed by a terrorized house-wife.

His search took him down two flights of stairs—hard work. Scurrying along the hallway, he passed a familiar open door: the one that gave access to the caves below. Voices filtered up the stairway, angry dragons arguing. Fang started down. At the bottom he saw light coming from down the hall. Following it, he discovered a dungeon. He could see five dragons, their bulk filling the foyer, no room for even a creature as small as he to pass.

He crept as close as he could. Looking up to see the dragons' faces so far away, yet so frighteningly large, was dizzying. Queen Jazmonilly was one of those arguing. "They should be put to death."

Then Zim. "We can't just kill them."

"They *just* killed Symbothial Accorterroza, may Drakon protect his soul."

"We don't have the full story."

"There is no full story, son. He must have discovered them trespassing. God knows how they got in in the first place. Symbothial probably confronted them and was attacked."

"Mother, I'm at least saying we should consult Agmunsten first. We don't even know who these two are. I sense she's a realmist. The panther, as we all know, is of a particular breed that has been extinct for a very long time." Zim said no more. All the dragons present knew what the panther symbolized, but none wanted to confront it. In addition, Zim recognised Bronwyn's symbol. He could not yet tell his mother, it may throw distrust over any decision Agmunsten would make, if he woke up.

A third voice dared place itself between the arguing royals. "You are upset, My Highness, and rightly so, however we must exercise patience. If we kill them without at least an explanation, we are no better than the humans think we are. As one is a human, Agmunsten must be consulted. In any case they cannot escape our cells, realmist or not. Let them stew awhile, and think about what may happen, whilst we discuss the issue." Queen Jazmonilly bared her teeth.

"I would see them put to death as soon as you have your information, Bertholimous. There can be no other way. Murder of a dragon in Vellonia itself? I need to inform my husband of the situation. Since you're so willing to keep them alive, you can stand watch." The queen pushed through the group, heading for the upper levels of Vellonia. Fang flattened himself against the wall.

Three other dragons followed her out, one almost squashing Fang with a swinging tail. Fang waited until Bertholimous made himself comfortable on a dusty bench seat; these cells had obviously lain vacant for some time. Blayke's creatura pushed through cobwebs as he made his way toward the row of cells. He found the first two stored foodstuffs, while the two opposite had closed doors.

The gap under the doors was tall enough to fit a plate underneath. Fang crawled under the first one. Sitting in the corner, barely illuminated by light filtering under the door, was a human, face resting on bent knees. Fang could barely make out the figure. The silhouette was smaller than Blayke's would have been; that was enough to tell Fang it was a woman. He couldn't believe this woman, or any woman, could kill a dragon. She must be a special person—or extremely lucky.

There was nothing else he could find out about her, so he moved on to the next cell. The cell seemed empty until a pair of yellow-green eyes opened to stare straight at Fang. The creature must be very large if its eyes were anything to go by. The rat turned around and scampering as fast as he could back under the door. He took a few deep breaths. He didn't know who they were but he was sure Blayke would be very interested to hear the news. It might even take his mind off Arcon for a few minutes.

The next few hours within Vellonia were tense. Zim contemplated how much worse things could get, and it was a depressing trail of thought. Everything had been going as smoothly as could be hoped, except for the knowledge that the Gormons had begun arriving on Talia. Within the space of a few days, two of The Circle had taken gravely ill, and a third, potential and necessary member, had been imprisoned for slaying a dragon.

Zim thought about Symbothial. They had grown up together, cousins who were as brothers. Zim found it hard to control his own grief and anger at the sight of Symbothial being dragged out of the lake with Bronwyn's sword protruding from his belly. He couldn't fathom why she had done it. Could leaving Avruellen have had such an effect on the young girl, or had the panther poisoned her mind? He had called out to Drakon but had received no answer. Even more puzzling was figuring out what the Dragon God had to do with it all.

The dragon city would have five days of mourning in which all would be called to return and none could leave. Zim dreaded the time. He knew from past experience that with every dragon venting their sorrow, he would be drained. Watching his immediate family come to grips with the death of a young dragon whom they all loved, would be difficult. Vellonia could ill-afford to lose any of her population. A female dragon had the possibility of having a total of four children in her extended lifetime. There was celebration if she managed to produce one. Zim suspected Drakon had taken a hand increasing the population in the past two-hundred years, knowing the threat they would eventually face.

Zim's ruminations were interrupted by a summons to Agmunsten's room. Zimapholous arrived to see the realmist sitting up in bed, consuming chicken soup. His voice was quieter than usual, however he was finally recovering. "Agmunsten, my dear friend, glad you decided to wake up."

"I've been catching up on all the sleep I've had to forego since this damn crusade began. How's Arcon?"

"Not great, but he's still alive."

"Well, that's something. I should be up and about tomorrow morning. I'll have to continue with him then. I'm hoping it won't be as draining as last time. I'm not as young as I used to be."

Zim stood for a while and sized up whether or not his friend was strong enough to take some more bad news. "There's been a ... development."

"I was wondering when you'd get to that. I've been hearing you dragons thunder about the city all afternoon. Are we under attack?"

"Sort of. Symbothial has been slain." Agmunsten choked on a mouthful of soup, spluttering some back into his bowl. Zim continued without waiting for any prompt. "It appears one of the slayers is Bronwyn, Avruellen's apprentice."

"But why would she?" The Head Realmist drifted into his own world for a few moments. Thinking time over, he leaned down and placed his bowl on the floor. Tired legs slowly followed, and he gingerly stood. After assuring himself he was not about to fall over, he dressed.

"So much for tomorrow morning. Take me to her now. I need to find out what's going on." Zim did as he was asked. He knew Agmunsten needed rest, however the situation required his intervention as soon as possible, as his mother was likely to lose patience and have Bronwyn put to death whilst no one was looking. The old realmist had no choice but to take his time, a shuffle the most energetic pace he could manage.

Bertholimous stood and greeted the duo. "Has the queen sent you?"

"No Bertholimous. I thought Agmunsten should question the girl. Someone should have her side of the story."

"I agree, Zimapholous. I was afraid your mother, our beloved queen, had sent you to finish them off." Agmunsten was not pleased at the assumption that Bronwyn's fate was already decided.

"Let's just see what she can tell me. Please open the door." Bertholimous lit another lamp and handed it to the realmist. Zim waited outside whilst Agmunsten performed the interrogation; as weak as he was, he was still strong enough to defend himself against an inexperienced realmist.

Bronwyn looked up as the door opened. So this was it, they were coming to execute her. She knew she deserved it. Why had she listened to Sinjenasta? Had Drakon really ordered him to kill the dragon? Probably not, or they would not be in this much trouble.

The man they had sent looked relatively old. Bronwyn could tell he was a realmist, and he seemed familiar somehow. The short white hair and long white beard accentuated a kindly face. That's who he was. She remembered Agmunsten from the meeting of The Circle that night, which seemed like a lifetime ago. "I see you know who I am, child. Please tell me what happened, Bronwyn." She couldn't lie to this man, however she had promised her creatura she would say nothing.

"I can't tell you."

"If you don't tell me, I can't help you."

Bronwyn's eyes held little hope. She kept her answer as brief as she could. "It's true, I did kill that dragon. That's all there is to tell."

"You know if I don't get a satisfactory answer there's nothing I can do to stop Queen Jazmonilly from ordering your death, and that of your accomplice."

"I know." Bronwyn shrugged as nonchalantly as she could. "Can I at least see Sinjenasta before we die?" Agmunsten's frustration at her lack of openness ceased at the mention of her companion's name.

"I'm sure we can arrange something. Well, it was nice to meet you in person, Bronwyn. We may get you out of this yet." Agmunsten turned his back on the forlorn young woman.

"It was an honour to meet you, sir. Sorry it had to be in these circumstances." She let out a hopeless breath as the door shut behind the visitor.

Agmunsten carried his lamp into the next cell. Speaking to Bronwyn had been more enlightening than he could have hoped. What the hell was Sinjenasta doing caught up in all of this? He would get to the bottom of this if it killed him. He shone the lamp toward the huge panther lying quietly against the back wall of the small room. Agmunsten didn't recognise the animal lying there. "Sinjenasta?"

The creature opened his eyes, blinking in unaccustomed illumination.

"Is it really you?"

Yes, Agmunsten. How's Bronwyn?

"She's OK, all things considered. What have you done, getting her caught up in all of this? And why is Drakon interfering?"

I can't tell you. You'll have to ask him yourself. Agmunsten twirled his beard between thumb and forefinger. This was interesting.

He had to find some way to talk the queen out of her vendetta. They needed Bronwyn, and Drakon obviously thought they needed Sinjenasta. His incarnation into a panther was also surprising. "You've left me with many questions, my friend. Be patient. I'll sort this out as best as I can."

Don't put yourself out or anything.

"That's ungrateful coming from a creature in your current position. I'm trying to be on your side, as hard as you're making it." The panther had the good sense to lower his eyes. "Give me some time. There are other things going on here that are jeopardising everything."

You haven't told her who I am, have you?

"Who, the queen? She wouldn't recognise your name. Don't worry."

Not her. Bronwyn.

"No. Your secret's safe with me, for the moment. I'll see you later."

Agmunsten locked the door. The two dragons who waited were staring at him, willing the information to come pouring out. "I wasn't able to get much out of them, except Bronwyn admitted to killing Symbothial."

"Was it in self-defence? What were they doing down there?"

"Neither of them would tell me, Zim. I do know that other forces are at work here and I need time to think about it before anyone decides to start executing. If we do the wrong thing here, Drakon himself won't be able to save us and we might as well put out the welcome mat for the Gormons tonight." Agmunsten noticed the worry on his associates' scaly faces. "I know it sounds like we've lost before we've barely started, but we're not beaten yet. Despite our problems the situation is looking more promising than I could have hoped."

"How?"

"I can't say."

"Getting anything out of you is always like pulling teeth. So what happens now?"

"I'd better check on Arcon. In the meantime, make sure your mother doesn't make any rash decisions."

Agmunsten walked with a measured pace to Arcon's room. How much more complicated could their situation get? Avruellen would not be happy when she found out who the creature was that had taken her niece away. Drakon was her least-favourite god; this wasn't going to increase her fondness for him. His creature had managed to get Bronwyn into a precarious situation. The queen could not be allowed to kill them. That was the one thing Agmunsten could decide on. How to stop that happening was altogether another matter.

He was not far from his fellow realmist's room. Blayke came rushing out and almost collided with him. "Is everything alright young man?"

"It's Arcon. I think he's waking up." Agmunsten increased his pace as much as he could. Finally, some good news for a change.

EPILOGUE

Klazich ruled the desolate Third Realm with unrelenting cruelty, a thing that suited the inhabitants. His lifelong ambition, as passed to him by one of his two fathers, was to take the Gormons out of this Realm. Their destination was Talia, a world that had callously shunted them out countless lifetimes ago. Many Gormons had been lost, the battle the most bitter in all their history. The pathetic dragons and their lapdogs, the humans, had handed Klazich's people a mortifying defeat. How they had managed to do this was a puzzle to the new leader, and he didn't intend to duplicate his forefathers' mistakes.

Klazich was charged with the job of taking his and his brothers' and sisters' unrelenting cruelty to the citizens of the ill-fated world. Revenge would be so very sweet. He salivated at the thought; tasty, tasty humans. He couldn't remember the last time he had feasted on such delicacies. His ancestors had managed to bring some humans with them when they had fled Talia, and they were housed in small cages. They weren't prolific breeders, and as such, were a great treat, only enjoyed rarely and by few. Some always had to be left alive so more could be bred.

His hideous claws scraped the floor as he paced back and forth. The latest report from one of his high priests indicated High Priest Kerchex was continuing to wreak havoc. He was satisfactorily metamorphosing the boy's body. He would not remain an infant for much longer. High Priest Zuk was taking a subtler, less enjoyable approach. He had possessed the mind of a young princess. By all accounts she was not as difficult to coax as one would imagine. She appeared to be partial to some of the Gormon's depraved tendencies. A drop of putrid saliva oozed down his leathery chin.

The process was longer than he had originally planned. Klazich's creatures were beginning to starve. No food remained within the Third Realm, and soon they would be forced to eat the remaining humans. Gormons could survive for maybe two months without food. He had thought they would all be feasting on Talia by now. Unfortunately, the corridors between Realms had been reluctant to let them pass, and many of Klazich's Gormons had perished in the attempt, their precious bodies salvaged to feed their remaining brothers. More would be sent out when what passed for evening, in this wretched twilight place, came.

He hoped when High Priest Kerchex was fully matured he would be strong enough to manipulate the corridors. They would then rush through in their thousands and take Talia for themselves. Until then, Klazich kept watch. The humans had made many mistakes. When he reached Talia, they would pay for them. Klazich showed many rows of small, pointed teeth when he smiled, scaly cheeks rustling with the effort. He called one of his servants; a hunched, leather-skinned monstrosity skittled to his feet. "Fetch me one of the humans. Tonight I will feed as I deserve."

A low cackle shredded itself as it passed through hundreds of teeth. Klazich delighted in hearing his own raspy voice. "Children of Talia, I'm coming. We will soon feast together. Won't that be fun?"

The old human woman, who up until now had been kept for breeding, was dragged into his presence. Her mother had told her stories of Talia, stories that had been passed on by countless generations of humans who had suffered before them. To know this disgusting creature was going to destroy her ancestral home extinguished her own small hopes of one day returning. Tears of loss streamed down her face. At least she wouldn't be alive to see it. Her last moments in this realm would be spent in defiance. She would not give the monster, looming over her, the pleasure. When Klazich commenced his meal by ripping off her arm with his razor sharp teeth, she bit her tongue, stifling the scream. In the instant before her death, she gurgled a prayer to the Gods instead, and asked that this disgusting creature choke to death on her bones.

Klazic finished his meal without choking. Kneeling on the bloody floor, he licked up the last of the captive's red juices. He stood and burped, patting his distended belly, and made his way to his chambers. Gormons were born of a cruel and hard world where comforts meant nothing so lying on the hard stone floor was all the rest he needed.

Klazic grinned as he drifted off, imagining what it would be like to eat one or even two humans every day. It wouldn't be long now. Soon, maybe within days, the Gormons would suffer no more; now it was Talia's turn.

ABOUT THE AUTHOR

Dionne Lister, that's me. I'm from Sydney, love animals and spend way too much time on Twitter. I've always wanted to be a writer and now, thanks to the Associate Degree of Creative Writing at Southern Cross University, I am living the dream (obviously).

Shadows of the Realm has reached #1 on two different occasions on two different Amazon lists, I've spoken on self-publishing at the Sydney Writers Festival, and I co-host the speculative fiction book club, Club Fantasci.

If you want to see more of my 'stuff' I have a website: dionnelisterwriter.wordpress.com, drop by and say hello. I'm on Twitter @DionneLister and I have a facebook page too, and don't forget, if you liked *Shadows of the Realm*, the sequel, *A Time of Darkness* is out now!

12776463R00206

Printed in Poland
by Amazon Fulfillment
Poland Sp. z o.o., Wrocław